He would be glad when he got out of this, Hearne thought. It was the highest piece of understatement he had ever committed. He tried not to look at the quicksand only ten feet away. Maybe it was only his imagination, but he really felt that the give of the sand under his feet had increased. It swallowed more than his ankles now.

Then suddenly it became firm again, and Hearne breathed more naturally. But Etienne still motioned him to keep to the right. He kept rigidly behind Etienne, almost treading on his heels.

They were almost at the promontory. Thirty feet, or less, to go. And then, from the shadows of a jutting rock, stepped Deichgräber. He had a gun in his hand, a smile on his lips.

"Up!" he said. "Up with your hands!"

Fawcett Crest Books
by Helen MacInnes:

ABOVE SUSPICION

AGENT IN PLACE

ASSIGNMENT IN BRITTANY

CLOAK OF DARKNESS

DECISION AT DELPHI

THE DOUBLE IMAGE

FRIENDS AND LOVERS

THE HIDDEN TARGET

HORIZON

I AND MY TRUE LOVE

MESSAGE FROM MALAGA

NEITHER FIVE NOR THREE

NORTH FROM ROME

PRAY FOR A BRAVE HEART

PRELUDE TO TERROR

REST AND BE THANKFUL

RIDE A PALE HORSE

THE SALZBURG CONNECTION

THE SNARE OF THE HUNTER

THE VENETIAN AFFAIR

WHILE STILL WE LIVE

HELEN MacINNES

Assignment In Brittany

FAWCETT CREST • NEW YORK

A Fawcett Crest Book

Published by Ballantine Books

Copyright © 1942, 1970 by Helen Highet
Author's Note: Copyright © 1961 by Helen Highet

ISBN 0-449-21065-0

This edition published by arrangement with
Harcourt, Brace & World, Inc.

The stanzas from *A Shropshire Lad* by A. E. Housman are reprinted by permission of Richards Press Ltd., for the Housman Estate.

Manufactured in the United States of America

First Fawcett Crest Edition: May 1969
First Ballantine Books Edition: January 1983
Second printing: May 1986

DEDICATION: FOR G.

CHAPTER 1

Leap into Darkness

It was almost daylight. Ahead of them, the cold darkness of the early morning sky waited for the first pale fingers of light.

It should be almost time, now. Hearne glanced again at the watch on his wrist, and fingered his kit. Everything was ready. Underneath his flying suit, in the inside pocket of the torn, shabby jacket, were the tattered letters and photograph and the identification papers. He felt for them once again, and caught a sympathetic smile from the gunner who had moved up close beside him. So he was to be helped safely off the premises. . . . He grinned back to the boy, and nodded reassuringly. He wouldn't need much helping, not after the last three weeks and the practising he had been through. What had worried him most had been the thought of interception by enemy aircraft, or of being spotted after he had left the plane. That wouldn't be at all pleasant, dangling between heaven and earth with some blighter grinning as he got you fair and square in his gun sight.

But the twenty-two-minute journey was almost over: only one more minute to go. The engine was suddenly silent, and the pilot waved a bulky glove.

"That is when you get ready," he had told Hearne cheerily, over their last cup of hot chocolate. "Second time I wave is good-by and good luck."

Hearne rose and stood as he had learned during the past three weeks. The boy at his elbow steadied him for a moment. Hearne cursed his own clumsiness. These fellows seemed to move about as easily as if they were in their messroom. The gunner's fingers tapped sharply on his forearm. "All set?" they spelled quickly in Morse.

Hearne nodded again. His eyes hadn't left the pilot, silhouetted black and shapeless against the lightening eastern sky. How long, Hearne was wondering, how long did it take to

7

glide from twenty thousand feet to six? He was answered by the movement of the padded arm. Good-by and good luck. Well, here it was at last. The gunner had enough sense to stand clear, thank heavens: he could choose his own split second.

"Good luck, yourselves!" Hearne called over his shoulder. He saw the gunner begin to crack that warm grin of his, and the thumb go up. And then he was diving through bleak gray air. He started to count.

"Not too soon, not too late," he reminded himself. "Take it easy and don't think about what happens if the damned thing doesn't work." But what if it didn't? His sudden fear was as cold as the air through which he hurtled. However much he practised, he never got rid of these moments of panic. He restrained himself in time from pulling the rip cord. Not yet: the longer he fell, the quicker, the safer. Perhaps. He pulled the cord. It wasn't going to work. It wasn't going to— Then the sudden jolt to his plunging body, the feeling of being pulled up backward into the sky again, the abrupt change from the hurtling drop to slow-motion floating contradicted him. He took his first breath since he had left the plane.

Drifting down to the colorless, formless land, he strained his eyes towards the sky. In the east, the heavy black curtain was slowly rising to show a steadily broadening river of light. Its edge which touched the darkness flowed grayish-green; and even as he watched, a streak of flame lined the horizon, and the earth and clouds took shape. Then, from the west, he heard the sound of the plane's motors. They must have glided round to get well over in that direction before they had started climbing again. They had given him every chance, anyway.

He looked down at the fields, swaying gently beneath him. They were no longer formless. Dimly, he could see the triangular outline of a wood on a small ridge just to the south. That was what he had hoped for, that was what they had aimed at. Cheery lot of coots, he thought gratefully, remembering the gunner's grin. Pity they couldn't be here to see how neatly they had landed him almost on the doorstep.

He pulled on the ropes, so that he would keep clear of the trees. And then the last few feet suddenly shortened, and the ground seemed to rise up to meet him. It was unexpectedly rough: from above it had looked so smooth and simple. As he landed, his right arm reached high above his head to grasp the control rope, and the clip on his belt automatically released the parachute as it pulled him forward. He was thoroughly jarred. That was all.

From above, he had thought at one moment that he was on top of the trees, but actually he had landed almost a hundred yards from them. He must have pulled on the ropes too much. Still, you couldn't expect everything to be perfect, and a hundred yards was better than being noosed up in high branches. Around him were fields which were half moorland. No house was in sight. He looked up again at the eastern sky. It was a uniform pale gray, bleaching slowly but dangerously. Now there was light enough to see: very soon there would be light enough to be seen.

Hearne rose to his feet from where he had fallen, and started to pull the parachute's folds loose from the clump of gorse bushes against which they had blown. It was slow work, and seemed all the slower because every minute was precious. He must reach the trees before the light strengthened, and he couldn't leave the parachute billowing here as a landmark. He pulled savagely, gathering the flapping silk into a rough, cumbersome bundle. Holding it in front of him, his arms filled with its softness, he half-ran, half-stumbled towards the wood. The ground was rough but not treacherous, and the gorse bushes in their sparse clumps were now useful. He ducked down behind them, gathering the parachute more tightly as its folds slipped from his arms, cursing its maliciousness. It seemed to take a pleasure in thwarting him. Its weight had doubled.

He finished the last twenty yards in a despairing spurt. . . . The trees closed in around him, and he fell grotesquely on top of his burden. He buried his face in its folds to smother the gasps which shook his body, and then, as he felt himself stifle, he rolled stiffly over onto his back. Burning liquid welled up suddenly in his dry throat. And then at last he could breath normally again, and the cold air was drying the sweat on his face. He lay, waiting for the heavy heartbeats to quieten, watching the leaves above him suddenly waken at the touch of the morning breeze. In the world outside, a lark was singing.

CHAPTER 2

Gone to Ground

Hearne waited until the pounding of his blood had stopped. Then, gathering the parachute once more in his arms, he dragged it further into the wood. He moved quietly and capably, like a man who had so often imagined this moment that his movements were almost mechanical. When the undergrowth was thick enough to please him, he halted and eyed the ground round the bush he had chosen. He went to work with his clasp knife, cutting the turf into neat squares, stacking them methodically at his side. The loam under them he scooped out with his hands. It took time, but in the end he was satisfied. He had packed the parachute into the hole he had scraped, thrusting it tightly down under the thin straggling roots of the bush. On top of the parachute lay his flying suit and helmet, and over them all were spread the thick rich soil and the sods, fitted together as neatly as the bulging earth would allow. He had worked lying uncomfortably flat on his stomach. Now he crawled out from the thickness of the bush to find some twigs and leaves and, with luck, some stones. These he scattered over the parachute's grave, covering the gaping cuts between the sods. After two such journeys, he had finished. The evidence was well-buried.

He looked at the unfamiliar watch on his wrist. Three hours ago he had joked with the redhaired pilot over a last cup of hot chocolate. Three hours ago he had stood on English earth. Three hours ago he had been Martin Hearne with twenty-seven years of his own life behind him. Now he was Bertrand Corlay, with twenty-six years of another man's life reduced to headings and subheadings in his memory. He looked down at the faded uniform which had been Corlay's, felt once more for the papers in the inside pocket.

"All set?" the gunner had asked.

Well, that would be the last time he would listen to English for some weeks. All set. . . . He patted the pocket of the tunic

10

with his earth-stained hand, and smiled grimly. From now on, he would not only have to speak, but think, in French.

He moved slowly westwards along the wood, keeping parallel to the open stretch of fields, so that he would not wander too far into the maze of trees. He still moved carefully and quietly, but he was less worried. He had plenty of time, now that he had got rid of the parachute and flying suit. Once he got far enough away from where he had buried them, he would find some place to lie hidden until night came again. Fourteen hours ahead of him for thought; for sleep, if he felt safe enough. Yes, there was plenty of time, and plenty to think about. He would review all the details he had learned by heart, all the movements and expressions he had memorized. Nothing which he had discovered in the past three weeks must be neglected.

At last he found his hiding place under a small, unimportant-looking tree, with a tangle of bramble bushes behind him and a screen of bracken in front. When he lay stretched out under the tall curling fronds of the fern, he felt safe. Barring accidents, such as a rabbit-hunting farmer and his dog, there would be little chance of anyone stumbling across him. And a farmer wouldn't be surprised to find a disheveled *poilu* waiting for the daylight to fade. There were many of them, this summer of 1940.

It was cold and damp, but the discomfort sharpened his mind. He thought of Corlay in his white hospital bed in England, and smiled wryly as he felt the heavy dew soak efficiently through his clothes, as he watched the black bugs clinging to the underleaves of the bracken. Well, if Corlay's hipbone hadn't been shattered on the way out of Dunkirk, he might have been doing this job himself. And if Matthews hadn't been examining a boatload of French and Belgian wounded after it had arrived at Folkestone; if he hadn't seen the unconscious Corlay, believed he was Hearne, and then notified Military Intelligence that one of their men had just got back in an uncomfortably original way, then this scheme would never have been born in Matthews' fertile brain. That was like Matthews. He must have mulled it all over in his mind for a couple of days, and out of his sardonic amusement had grown the germ of an idea.

"Well, I'm damned," he would say. "Well, I'm damned." And then he'd begin to think of a use for such an extraordinary likeness, especially when he learned more about the Frenchman and where he came from. That was like Matthews. He never wasted an opportunity. Two days after he had seen Corlay, he had not only the idea shaping nicely, but also the go-ahead signal from his own department.

Strange bird, Matthews, thought Hearne, and rolled over on his side to ease a hipbone. He took some deep breaths, tautened his muscles to warm himself. His clothes would dry when the sun really got into this glade. He'd be warm enough, then. Strange bird, Matthews; he sort of sensed things coming. He'd cook up some plan, keep it simmering until the right moment arrived, and then dish it up piping hot. The right moment in this case had been a week before the French-German armistice. It was then that he sent for Hearne.

"Glad you got back in time," he had begun, and smiled quietly. Hearne knew that smile. He waited, wondering what was coming this time.

"How would you like to spend a summer in France?"

That meant he was going to spend a summer in France. He allowed himself one objection—not that Matthews would show that he had ever noticed it.

"But I've just come back from there." Thirty-six hours ago, Hearne added under his breath.

"Brittany, this time." Matthews gave his imitation of a benevolent Santa Claus. "That should interest you, Hearne."

It did, in spite of the fact that for the last month he hadn't slept in a clean bed, or seen anything which might be remotely called a bathroom. Hearne saw his leave and the quiet comfort of his flat evaporating as quickly as August rain on a hot London pavement.

"When do I go?" he asked. Brittany ... well, that was something.

"In about two or three weeks. That is, if things go the way they are shaping. Looks bad, at the moment. If there's a separate armistice, then we shall use you, because every Frenchman who can get back to his home will then make a beeline for it. A lot of them won't get back; and there will be some with the guts to fight on. But you are to be one of the Frenchmen who do get back, and stay there."

"Home?" Hearne was incredulous. Home meant relatives, and complications. He had never tackled anything so domestic as that.

And then Matthews explained about Corlay.

"Here's all the official knowledge about him," he ended, pushing a folder across his desk to Hearne. "All checked and amplified by a French Intelligence chap—Fournier, he's called—who will be one of those who fight on, so there's no danger of the wrong people learning about our interest in Corlay. You'll find that Fournier has done a pretty good job. He included a detailed map and description of the district. St. Déodat is the name of the village. Know it?"

Hearne shook his head. He had no idea where it was. He searched his memory in annoyance. Hell, he thought, Brittany is supposed to be my pidgin.

"North or South Brittany?" he asked at last.

"North. Just southwest of the town of Dol. Within walking distance of the railway line from Rennes to St. Malo. Near enough Dinan to admire the canal. Close enough to the main north road from Rennes." Matthews was speaking slowly, underlining the importance of the towns with the inflection of his voice. "And also," he added, "not so very far from Mont St. Michel, and our old friends Duclos and Pléhec, if you must send us news about your health."

Hearne smothered a smile. Matthews was at his old trick again of coating the pill lavishly with sugar. He liked to make his assignments sound like a Cook's tour.

"Duclos is still there?" Hearne asked.

"Yes, and very useful he will be from now on. I am rather afraid his archeological researches are going to be disturbed. Then, for emergency use only, you will find another friend outside St. Malo. Fournier guarantees him. You'd better talk to him about this man of his before you leave."

Hearne nodded. "And I've to take moonlight strolls round the railway line and road and canal?" he asked.

There was almost a smile on Matthews' face. "You are being sent to this farm so that, within a patch of about two hundred square miles, you can find information which will fit neatly into the reports which we hope to get from all the other patches of two hundred square miles. Then, when all the pieces of the crossword puzzle are fitted together, we will have a working idea of German intentions. Now, here are the particular pieces of information which we need. First, we want to know if North Brittany is being fortified and garrisoned for defense; or is it being prepared as a base for an attack on the British Isles? If so, then just in what way are the Germans preparing to attack? If airfields are being constructed then they are aiming for our southern ports and our shipping lanes. If huge masses of troops and boats are being prepared, then our southwest flank is in danger." Matthews stabbed at the map on the desk in front of him. "The Devon Coast, the Bristol Channel, Southern Ireland. Brittany is just the right position to try for these places. So look for airfields, troop movements, types of supplies being sent by road and rail and canal, new construction works, underground dumps, gun installations. You may not see much sense in what you observe, but your report will fit neatly into the other reports we'll receive. When we fit them together, they will make a pretty pattern. So don't even let the little things escape you. Work at night. I think you'll find plenty of material for your usual precise reports. Anything you pick up will probably be useful."

There was a note in Matthews' voice which raised Hearne's eyes from the map to the older man's face. *Anything you pick up...* Was that inflection on the *you* intended? If it were, then that was high praise.

Matthews was speaking again. "I don't think you'll find this a difficult job." Again, there was that hint of emphasis on the *you.* "I think," he was saying, "I think we can depend on you only to follow your instructions, and not to suffer from any attacks of misplaced brilliance."

Hearne's elation faded, and then he saw the gleam in Matthews' eye, and the repressed smile. He breathed again. So Matthews wasn't displeased over his last attack of "misplaced brilliance," after all. Hearne suddenly thought, perhaps he's giving me this job just because I find it hard to be orthodox in my methods. Perhaps he isn't so much against them as he always pretends to be.

Matthews seemed to guess Hearne's thoughts. "Seriously," he said, "you did a good job at Bordeaux. But I'd like you to restrain yourself on this trip. No good getting lost to us." And then, as if he felt he had been too expansive, he added, "Not after all the trouble I've had in training you."

"Yes, sir," Hearne said.

Matthews' voice was matter-of-fact once more. "I suggest you memorize the contents of that folder. You'll find all the necessary data in it, including observations on Corlay by one of his officers and by a man who had known him as a student. After you've got all that information memorized, you can start on Corlay himself. You'll visit him each day in hospital, for two or three weeks. He can talk now. Find out everything you can to fill in the gaps. Study his voice, his expressions, all that sort of thing."

"What if he won't talk? The Bretons can be very reticent, you know."

"I think he will. There is a certain amount of questioning which all strangers in Britain must go through at this time. We've never had so many aliens dumped so unexpectedly on our shores, and at rather a dangerous moment for us, too. There are rumors, even among the wounded, of what's now called the Fifth Column. Fournier has seen Corlay, and dropped him that hint. He will talk, just to identify himself."

"Well, that sounds more hopeful. . . . You say he looks like me?"

"Looks? My dear Hearne, he's the dead spit of you. If he could mislead me, you can mislead anyone who knows him."

"But his mother and father?"

"Father killed in 1917. Mother bedridden. You'll find it all in that folder. I investigated that sort of thing before I called you in. Now, if there had been a wife . . . " Matthews smiled, and shook his head slowly. When he spoke again, his voice was crisp and businesslike. "I think you're in luck, this time, Hearne. You'll learn more about your Celtic peoples in a month at St. Déodat than you did that year at Rennes University." There was the sugar coating being spread on again. "What made you interested in the Bretons, anyway? Was it because you are a Cornishman, yourself?"

Hearne nodded. "That, and the fact that I like them, and that my father spent all his time in between his sermons writing about the early British saints. A lot of them ended up in Brittany, you know."

"Déodat being one? Well, that makes one of these nice coincidences."

"I can't think of any Déodat except Saint Augustine's son," Hearne said with a smile.

"Saint Augustine?" Matthews looked startled. "Didn't know he was married."

"He wasn't," Hearne said, enjoying the shocked look on Matthews' face. He added, "That was probably during Augustine's '*O God, make me pure, but not yet*' period." For a strong Scots Presbyterian, Matthews was reacting in a very High Church manner. Hearne grinned amiably.

"Well, I'll be damned," said Matthews. "Well, I'll be—"

"That's about all, then?" Hearne asked tactfully.

"Yes," said Matthews. "Yes. I'll see you again before you leave."

"How do I go?"

It was Matthews' turn to smile. "Just drop in," he said.

The sun had come out, and with it a swarm of flies, fat black flies, inquisitive, persistent. But, at least, Hearne was beginning to feel dry and warm. He took the map out of his pocket to verify his position again. It was a detailed French map of Brittany, with well-worn creases, stains and a jagged tear over the Atlantic corner for good measure. If he were questioned, he was to say that this map had been given him at Brest, after he had arrived there by fishing boat from Dunkirk. Better allow himself a slight case of shell shock to account for the period between Dunkirk and the armistice. Shell shock might be useful later: it could explain any strangeness, any lapse of memory. So, with this map, he had found his way home to the North of Brittany. The food in his pocket could be explained away, too ... friendly peasantry department. *Could be explained away.* He smiled grimly at the phrase. He would just have to take especial care tonight in his short journey to St. Déodat, and then no explanations would be necessary to any curious patrol.

He examined the map for the last time. He must be able to remember the details of the district to the north and west of this wood, to reach the toy railway which trailed the main road from Rennes to St. Malo. It would guide him part of the way. The rest would depend on his knowledge of these thin and thick red lines and winding black ones. He had looked at them so often in the past few days that they were etched on his memory as well as on this map. At last he admitted that he could do no more, that he must depend now on a combination of intelligence and intuition. There would be no moon tonight, but if the sky stayed clear the stars would be enough. Failing them, it would have to be by guess and by God.

He settled himself more comfortably in his bracken bed. The sweet smell of fern and grass, the warmth of the sun, the increasing hum of the innumerable insects, drowsed him pleasantly. He felt himself slipping into light sleep. Tomorrow, he was thinking, tomorrow Bertrand Corlay would be home.

CHAPTER 3

Night Journey

A cool breeze awakened him. The bright green of the bracken and trees was no longer bathed in sunlight. The glade had darkened, as if a shade had been pulled down over a window. The gentle hum of insects had gone, the birds had become silent. There was only the uneasy stirring of branches overhead, the anxious rustling of the leaves. Not a pleasant sound, Hearne thought, especially when a man was hungry and cold. As the dusk deepened, he made an effort to get up. He was much stiffer than he had even thought. He sat with his back against a tree, and ate half of his rations, such as they were. The other half he replaced stoically in his pocket. If he bungled tonight, there would be another day to provide for.

At last the darkness had thickened enough to let him reach the edge of the trees. He walked slowly, even painfully at first, but by the time the first stars began to show, he was ready.

He looked at the North Star, and got his bearings. The fields ahead seemed horribly naked. In a way, he thought as he left the trees, this was something like taking a dive from a plane, except that he didn't have to worry this time about the parachute opening.

The ground, becoming more tamed as it descended, sloped gently into a broad shallow valley. The clumps of gorse grew more sparsely, much to Hearne's relief. It hadn't been so easy to avoid them at first. By the time he had reached the first cultivated patch of land, he was moving more confidently. His stiffness was forgotten, and his eyes had become accustomed to the shapes and shadows within the darkness.

He passed a house, hidden unexpectedly behind some trees. A dog barked, and he saw a dull yellow light fill one of the windows as a lamp was lit. He felt an extraordinary compulsion to stay and watch. The glow from the small

square window reached out into the coldness of the night and
held him there, standing irresolute. Then the dog barked
again, and the spell was broken. He moved swiftly away.
Behind him the light still shone, but there was no sound of
men's voices or of following feet. Then other trees and a
twist in the path blocked out the house, and he was alone in
a field of straggling corn, hedged with gnarled fruit trees.

It was strange how you could be trapped by a moment like
that, when your control over your movements was suspended, when nothing seemed to matter anyway. Strange, and
dangerous. He couldn't allow himself any off-guard moments,
he reminded himself grimly. He thought again of that light.
No footsteps, no men's voices. When the dog had barked, the
light had appeared so quickly, as if someone were lying
awake, listening, waiting. A woman, perhaps, hoping against
hope. This summer, there would be plenty of women, waiting
and hoping. And he couldn't allow himself any sentiment,
either: that was another luxury he couldn't afford this trip.
He concentrated on the fields.

The faintly luminous hands on Corlay's watch told him it
was fully an hour since he had stepped out of the woods. He
was late. Either he had gone too carefully, or he had missed
his direction. The discouraging idea that he had landed in
another part of the Breton countryside, after all, began to
take root. One minute he was calling himself a damned fool;
and then the next, he was imagining what he'd use for transit
if he found himself on the steep banks of the River Rance. It
should be well behind him. If it weren't, he'd have a nice cold
swim ahead of him. He remembered Matthews' old consolation: blessed is he who expects the worst, for he shall not be
disappointed. He walked gloomily on. If he came to a village,
he could scout out its name. Of course the villages hereabouts
would all have gold-plated neon signs and—and at that
moment, he almost tripped over the miniature railway line.
Not that it was noticeable, wandering so light-heartedly
through the grass and flowers, along the hedgerows, and
across the winding country roads without so much as a
by-your-leave. He advanced cautiously along it, moving quietly through the shadows. The new moon was not yet born.
Only the stars lighted the clear sky.

He passed occasional farmhouses, darkened and asleep in
the curves of their fields. Now and again there would be a
village to avoid. Once he came to an unexpected road and a
small wooden shed which was probably a station—nameless,

in the best railway traditions. Twenty yards away was a
hidden village, a dozen little stone houses round the inevitable
church. German notices were posted here on the wall beside
which he sheltered. But no one stirred. Reassured, he crossed
the treacherous road, his eyes searching the sleeping village.
"Café de France et de Chateaubriand," he noted. That
cheered him up, somehow, in spite of a large white procla-
mation with giant black letters shouting after him *Bekannt-
machung!*

He had reached the protection of some trees. And then a
shadow moved—just there, about fifty yards ahead, in that
unfortunate patch of open ground. He drew back against a
tree. Another shadow moved, close behind the first one. His
eyes followed their careful progress as his mind raced quickly
from one plan to another. If he kept behind these two men,
they would slow up his pace. He must circle to his left (for to
the right lay the main roadway to the coast, and he had
better keep well clear of that), increasing his speed, so that he
would pass the two men and come back to the railway line
well ahead of them.

And then the noise of heavy trucks rumbled across the
quiet fields. When they were about a quarter of a mile
distant, Hearne glanced at the watch on his wrist. It pointed
to 10:58. The trucks were traveling slowly, probably half-
blacked-out. About fifteen miles an hour, he guessed. He
strained his eyes, but the trees which were spaced along the
roadway broke his line of vision. Here and there, where the
edge of the road was clear, he could see black lumbering
shapes, like a herd of elephants stringing out towards a water
hole. Yes, fifteen miles an hour was about right. He listened
patiently, his eye on his watch. When the last of the column
had reached about a quarter of a mile away, and the hum of
engines was fading towards the coast, the time on the watch
was 11:01. They had taken three minutes to pass through
half a mile, roughly, at about fifteen miles an hour. That
would give him almost a quarter of a mile of trucks. And
many of them had been carrying oil: there was no mistaking
the noise of the chains trailing on the paved roadway, clattering above the hum of the powerful engines.

Ahead of Hearne, the two men had fallen flat on the
ground. When the sound of motors had died away, they
moved quickly towards the nearest cover. They didn't want
to attract any German interest, either. But even if they
wanted to avoid the Nazis, that didn't mean he wanted to

meet them. He moved quickly to his left up the sloping hill, working round the edge of the patch of open ground in front of him. He set off impatiently: he was losing time having to make this detour to avoid these two blighters. But his temper improved with the easiness of the ground. He could no longer see the men, but he would allow himself half a mile before he turned back towards the toy railway again. He made it in good enough time, for he found plenty of cover. He blessed the Breton habit of never clearing their fields completely of trees. He had often wondered why the farmers should have taken the trouble, year after year, to plow and reap all round every small tree. Now he felt grateful to them.

The half-mile was covered. Time now, he told himself, to swerve to his right, down through that small wood. Beyond it, he would find the railway line again. It was strange, he thought, to slip so quietly and cautiously through this peaceful countryside, past the small stone houses with their black windows staring at him like sightless eyes, past the sleeping people and the brooding church towers, while down in the valley the Nazi trucks lumbered along with their death-bringing loads.

He had entered the wood, and, for the second time that night, almost fell over the narrow tracks of the railway.

"What the hell—" he thought, and then cursed silently as he realized that he must have been working his way gradually down towards the railway all the time he had thought he was keeping parallel.

And then suddenly, a weight hit his knees, two arms were tightly locked round his legs, and he pitched forward onto his face with a grunt as the wind was knocked out of him. When he got back his breath, he found he was pinned to the ground. The larger of the two men was sitting astride him with a firm grasp on the back of his neck, with a strong knee-hold on his arms.

"He's French." The boy who was squatting in front of him, watching him gravely, pronounced the verdict in a low whisper. "At least," the whispered voice went on, "he's wearing a French uniform. But he may be a Jerry. Never can tell, these days."

"You should have let me fetch him one, lad," whispered back the weight across Hearne's shoulders. The slow drawl and flat overtones were unmistakably Yorkshire.

Hearne thought quickly: maintain he was French and speak with a bogus English accent, and he'd still lose time in explanations; or he could just speak French, and they'd still argue whether he was friend or foe. He decided to risk it.

"You tackle too high," he said in English to the big Yorkshireman. The weight on his back shifted.

"Eh, what's that?"

"You tackle too high. And for Jesus' sake, don't raise that voice of yours. Do you want to bring a pack of Nazis down on us, you bloody fool?"

The Yorkshireman dropped his voice again, but there was an angry vehemence in his whisper. "I never tackled high in my whole life."

"Well, that's no reason to flatten me now, you blithering idiot."

"Sounds as if he might be English," the boy remarked. He was feeling Hearne's pockets gently. He removed the revolver and slipped it into his own pocket. "Get off, Sam," he said then.

"Not me," said Sam, and settled his weight more squarely. "I'm fine as I am."

Hearne addressed himself to the thin-faced, anxious boy. "Go on, pick up his moosket for him, Wellington. Do you want us all to be caught?"

"What's your regiment?" the boy asked suddenly.

"Liaison officer," parried Hearne. "Ninth French Army. Sedan and points west, ever since."

"Where did you get these clothes?"

"Where did you get yours?" Hearne grinned as he looked at their blue peasant blouses, ill-fitting jackets and ragged corduroy trousers. "Look here, I could talk much better with Sam off my back, and it's about time we were moving on. I'm in a hurry, if you aren't. And you might remember that I'd have used my revolver at once, if I had been a Jerry."

"One wrong move from you, me lad, and I'll flatten you proper," Sam said placidly, and rose to his feet. He thrust one large red fist under Hearne's nose for emphasis. "See?"

"I see," Hearne said with a smile. "And even if it was high, it was a damned good tackle." Sam only grunted in reply, but an answering grin spread slowly over his large face. Strange couple, thought Hearne: the serious, fair-haired boy, thin and haggard, who spoke such precise clipped English, and the plain Yorkshireman with his broad back and vowels.

"Which way are you heading?" the boy asked. He might have been twenty, but he looked more like seventeen.

"North."

"Then we can go on together." His tone was very definite.
That would have been his answer if Hearne had said
"South."

"I don't want to lose that gun," Hearne said.

The boy smiled. "I'll look after it very well." He nodded to
Sam, who took his place behind Hearne, and set off without
another word.

They covered the next three miles in Indian-file, first the
boy, then Hearne, with the Yorkshireman bringing up the
rear. The pace was surprisingly good. They only had to slow
down twice: once when they circumvented a village, once
when they struck a broad stretch of completely open ground.
Then the choice was either a wide detour up a hillside, or a
ten-minute wait for the cotton-wool clouds to spread themselves over the hard, bright stars. The boy, to Hearne's surprise, chose to wait. It amused Hearne to see how calmly
the younger man had taken the command from the start; and
he had taken it well. This was the first time that Hearne
disagreed with him. And then he remembered that compared
to these two men he was fresh and rested. He could only
make a guess at how far they had traveled and under what
conditions. Even then, like all guesses, his would be short:
guesses didn't tell the half of it. He noticed that the boy's
jacket was too thin: he was shuddering in spite of himself.
Sam had noticed that shivering, too. He looked up at the sky
and the slow clouds.

"Blast you and blast you and blast you," he muttered with
surprising venom.

Then the light dimmed at last, and they had a few minutes' grace to cross the open ground. They ran silently with a
grim desperation. Ahead of them were some trees, beautiful
trees, lovely trees, gracious trees, noble trees. Hearn sank
breathless beside Sam on the cool, shadowed ground.

"I'm a tree lover for life," he said, but the others weren't
listening to him. The boy, standing so rigid, suddenly groaned
and moved away.

"He's ill," said Hearne in alarm, although his voice was no
higher than a whisper.

"Don't let him hear you say that. He'll be all right." But
Sam was anxiously watching the trees behind which his friend
had staggered. Hearne started to move, but Sam's hand
stopped him. "He wouldn't have you near him. Sort of
worries him for anyone to hang about him. He has these

attacks regular as the clock every hour. Ate something which turns him inside out, even when he hasn't anything left inside him to turn out."

They lay and waited. "Pretty bad attack," Hearne whispered.

"Aye." Sam was more worried than he had pretended. "Plucky lad, all right. Come all the way from a prison camp across the Rhine." He was talking now for the sake of talking. Hearne welcomed that too.

"Were you with him?"

"No. Met him halfway. I was in Belgium."

"How the devil did you get as far south as this?"

"There was some of us got lost, and we thought we'd fight our way back to the French. Funny, come to think of it. We landed in a French part of the line, all right, and there we were, moving back and moving back, just moving back without ever a stand. It was right discouraging, I can tell you. Then they told us the fight was off, and there we were slap in t' middle of France. An officer said we were to get a train to where the last English were getting off in boats. But the blasted engine-driver just spat and said the war was over. Then one of the Poles—"

"Poles?"

"Aye. Poles and Belgians and some Czechs and us. A proper tower of Babel, I can tell you. Well, this Pole, he had been an engine-driver, and we threw the Parley-voo off his cab—we were all raving mad, that we were, what with fighting our way south and then being left high and dry—and we started the train." He paused and listened. "If you don't mind, I'll go and see how his nibs is, now." He slipped noiselessly into the further darkness of the trees.

Hearne grinned to himself. And what had happened to the train, he wondered. It hadn't got very far, obviously. He saw the two dim shapes returning to his tree. Sam barked his shin on a stump, and grunted.

"Black as the Earl of Hell's waistcoat," he said angrily.

"Sorry." It was the boy. He sat down weakly beside Hearne. "Sorry. Tummy all skew-wiff." He was wiping the sweat off his brow with his sleeve. Hearne nodded. Cold sweat it would be, and the twisting pains would still be clutching at his stomach and bowels. What he needed was a rest for a couple of days and a starchy diet to cement him up.

"Do you know where you are going?" Hearne asked.

The boy nodded. "Got a man's name at Dinan. He will take us in his boat down that river towards the coast."

"Down the Rance? That sounds O.K. But can you depend on him?"

"Others have, and managed it. Well, I'm all right now for a while. Let's move."

And then once more came the roar of a huge fleet of trucks. Hearne motioned silence, and kept his eyes fixed on his watch. When he had finished, he noted that the boy was looking at him curiously.

"Let's move," he said again, and his tone was friendlier. "Can you lend us a map, by any chance? I lost mine while I was having a spot of trouble with a river, and I'm doing this sort of out of my head. We are fairly near Dinan now, aren't we?"

Hearne hesitated for a moment. "I'll put you on the road for Dinan. You'll reach it by dawn," he said. "And I can give you some stodgy food." He fished in his pocket and handed over what was left of his rations. "Rest up for a couple of days when you get there," he added. "Keep warm. Don't let them feed you shellfish, or cheese, or butter, or heated wine. The Bretons believe in a wine toddy. It cures a lot of things, but not your trouble. Herbal tea is good, and plain unseasoned macaroni or potatoes. It all tastes rotten, though."

"Yes, doctor."

"And you'd better listen to me. You've a long sail ahead on you. Now, come on."

This time, Hearne led the way.

There were still more roads to cross now, little straggling roads which twisted and turned from village to village. And there was a German patrol to be avoided. They managed that by throwing themselves flat into a ditch beside the road which they had been on the point of crossing. It was unpleasant but effective. The motorcycles swept past them, and they could breathe again in spite of the mud. When they crawled out of their hiding place, Hearne looked anxiously at the boy. But the haggard young face gave an attempt at a smile.

"All right for another half hour, I think," he said. "Come on, Sam; breakfast in bed tomorrow." Sam only gave that slow grin of his. And then they were moving silently again: walking, slipping, crouching, crawling, but always moving forward.

They had passed the village Hearne had been expecting. There was no mistaking that church tower. Norman-Gothic,

English influence, interesting, the guidebooks would say. It was interesting, all right. This was where they'd branch off, and he could make up for the time he had lost. Matthews would have been apoplectic if he could have seen him in these last two hours. "Well, I'm damned," he would say. "Of all the infernal stupidity . . ."

Hearne halted. He pointed to a line of trees. "There's your road," he said. "When you reach it, turn left and that will take you west to Dinan in six miles or so. I'll leave you here, now that we are getting towards the towns. Three's a crowd in this game, too."

They saw reason in that. "By the way, what would have happened if I had put up a real fight or tried to dodge you?" he asked, as they parted.

"Our suspicions would have been aroused," the boy said. He handed over the revolver to Hearne. He was beginning to shiver again. His eyes were looking towards the line of trees.

"In plain English, I'd 've twisted your damned neck with my two bare hands," Sam said amiably, and then he noticed the shivering too. "Time to be off, lad," he added, and taking the boy's arm pulled him quickly away. Hearne watched them go—two shadows as he had first seen them, merging cautiously into the blackness of the trees.

"With my two bare hands," he repeated to himself. Then, "See, Matthews?" as if to the stars overhead.

I wonder, he was thinking, just what did happen to that train. Well, he wouldn't know now. Good chap, that Sam. Hearne remembered how carefully he had listened to his advice about the diet for the boy. Sam would see that that young man did rest up. Yes, they were a strange couple, all right, each of them thinking he was responsible for the other. That way, even with the odds against them, they might have a chance. For a minute, Hearne envied them. The worst of his job was that he was always so completely alone. But, he reminded himself, that could also be the best thing about it, too. He looked at his watch, and smiled to himself as he noted he now called it "his" quite naturally. He had about four hours left and twelve miles or so to go. If the ground was easy and patrols not too frequent, the distance could be lessened. He should manage it all right.

As he turned eastwards, he felt more confident. In these last two hours, he had felt all the old tricks and instincts coming back to him. He was covering the ground more quickly now, decisions were easier, movements were surer.

The footling pessimism and nervousness which had attacked him at the beginning of this night were gone. When dawn came, he would be home.

CHAPTER 4

The Sleeping Village

The last obstinate stars were fading in the sky when Hearne came to St. Déodat. His arrival at this hour solved some minor problems for him, for even the early rising villagers would not yet be stirring. He paused on the path which had brought him so quickly round the curves of these last gentle hills, past the endless slate-roofed farmhouses, past the orchards and well-tilled fields. And right there, just below where he stood, lay St. Déodat: fifty, or less, stone houses clustered near the church and its soaring towers. Nothing moved. There was no sound. It seemed a deserted village, asleep in its sheltered hollow.

Hearne repressed his excitement. He had better see how far wrong he had been in his idea of the place, before he started congratulating himself. He had two choices: either he could keep to this path on the hill, rising to the west of the village, until he reached the Corlay farm, or he could cut down to the road and enter the village at the north end. He chose the second course. It was safe enough with the village still asleep. Even if some early bird did see him, it would be noted that he came from the north, which fitted in very nicely with his story of walking from the coast. Also, he would feel surer of reaching the Corlay farm if he followed the road through the village, for there were many small farms all remarkably alike scattered over the hillside. It would take some explaining if he were to approach the wrong house and claim it as his. Slight shell shock would hardly be an adequate excuse. Finally—and this was the chief reason, he admitted to himself quite cheerfully—he just wanted to see St. Déodat. He had thought of it constantly in the last three weeks; he had examined drawings, memorized descriptions, made his own sketches. He knew it forwards, backwards, sideways—on paper. Now he had the chance to walk quietly, slowly, through St. Déodat, and in the graying light he would see it as it really stood.

It was a compact little village. First, there had been the church, built in the tenth or eleventh century: the two Romanesque towers bore testimony to that. Then, gradually, houses had grouped themselves round it; and a narrow road found its way up between the little hills, from the flat plains of the northeast. By the fourteenth century, St. Déodat was a flourishing community. It had a proud castle on the western hill, and feudal overlords to bring it reliques from the Holy Land. In the market place which had formed itself opposite the church, the country people from miles around came to buy and sell. That was when the Gothic part of the church had been added by the prosperous, and grateful, villagers.

Nothing changes had been the proud motto of the castle. St. Déodat kept faith with it, although the castle now lay in ruins since its last overlord had abandoned the village for the richer graces of Versailles. Hearne wondered if he had still said "Nothing changes" when he had mounted to the guillotine. If he were a true Breton, he probably did, just to spite the howling mob. Even as the blade descended, and the unchanging Comte had change thrust upon him, his village asserted itself for the last time in its history. Its people joined the desperate Vendée revolt against the Revolution, and were rewarded by the despoiling of their castle, the burning of their houses, the slaughter of their young men in the market place. Yet their church, although bruised and crippled, still stood.

The people took courage from it, and when they came back from their hiding places they rebuilt enough of the destroyed houses to suit their diminished numbers. The market place once more heard weekly gossip. But after that bloody 1793, the inhabitants of St. Déodat avoided trouble by strictly minding their own business. And they had succeeded, at the price of becoming a forgotten village.

Hearne stopped thinking of St. Déodat's past as he reached the narrow road which entered the village. Now he was concentrating on its present. He passed fourteen houses, five of them empty (not only a forgotten village, he emended then, but a dying one; and a deserted one, in years to come, unless something were to happen to rouse St. Déodat from self-destruction), and he named them as he went. He could

no longer repress his excitement. There was no doubt about
it: he could recognize this village.

That was the house of Trouin, carpenter and candlestick-
maker. And that belonged to Guézennec, the retired schoolmaster. One small school, Hearne remembered parentheti-
cally, tucked away behind the trees beyond the houses round the
market place, despised because it was the usurper of the
education which the Church should have been allowed to
continue. It hadn't been so bad when Guézennec had been
appointed, for he was one of them, and he had been half a
priest before he became schoolteacher. But now, there was a
young foreigner in the school, a man from Lorient in South
Brittany who had studied in Paris. Kerénor was his name.
He limped badly. He lived in the little hotel on the market
square.

Hearne reached the church. On the far side of the market
place facing it were grouped the grain dealer and baker,
Guérin; the butcher and veterinary surgeon (kill or cure),
Picrel; and Picrel's mother, the widow who kept the very
small, very general store. On the north side of the square was
the Town Hall. On the south was the hotel, where the new
schoolteacher, Kerénor, lodged. It really was a glorified
pub, Hearne decided, with a few rooms to let upstairs for
occasional commercial travelers and stray summer visitors. It
was called quite logically the Hotel Perro: Madame Perro
owned it. She came from somewhere in the east of France,
had married a St. Déodat man stationed in Lyons during the
last war. But her late husband and her twenty-one years'
residence in the village were extenuating circumstances. Now
she was only half a foreigner.

Beyond the church, the road passed the curé's house.
Hearne heard the sound of running water. That would be the
stream from the western hillside, flowing under this road into
the curé's garden (and there, on either side of the road
ahead of him, were the two short stretches of stone wall to
prove his guess and give the effect of a bridge). But he
wouldn't have time now to explore the meadows below the
church, with their little lake in which the stream ended. The
sky was changing to a greenish gray. He increased his pace to
pass the last row of houses. Another Trouin lived there; and
there, another Picrel; and some "negligibles." The word had
been Corlay's. Seemingly the Corlays didn't know the "negligibles." And then he was across the piece of road which

formed the bridge, and he had reached the path which led west from the road to the Corlay farm.

He paused there for a moment to look back. So that was St. Déodat, or at least the main part of it. There were also the small farms scattered around the village. He had a feeling that he would know the fields better than the village before the end of his stay. It was through them that his business lay.

The path led him up through a thin wood. And then he was walking over Pinot's land. He could see the blue, slate roof of its farmhouse glinting in the first rays of the morning sun. He hurried. He was glad of the soft white mist which was rising from the grass.

When the Pinot farm had been safely passed, he let himself admit that he hadn't been exactly enthusiastic about crossing these fields. He looked back over his shoulder. Only the last edge of the farmhouse roof was visible. And under that was Anne Pinot. . . . Anne Pinot: just another of the minor headaches on this job. "And, by heaven, I'll keep her minor," he said savagely to himself. After all, it wasn't the first time that a man had come back from a war, and had seemed changed. It would be better to seem cold rather than to assume affection that was false; it would be kinder in the long run, for when the war was over the real Corlay would return. Not that Corlay had displayed marked sentiment when he had mentioned her name. "Arranged," he had said. "Practical and suitable. The farm is next to ours. If they were joined, they would form the biggest farm in St. Déodat, and my mother and old Pinot would stop quarreling about the dovecote."

The farm is next to . . . Why, of course, he must be now on Corlay ground. To prove it, he saw the dovecote rising out of the mist on his right, a round tower of gray stone with a pointed cap of blue slate, marking the border of the two farms. He should soon see the Corlay house. He couldn't miss it, not on this path. "Stop it, you fool," he told himself. "You're too anxious again. That won't do." He could look tired, ill, unkempt—and he probably did—but not anxious. He, Bertrand Corlay, was reaching home at last, weary and bitter, impatient of foolish questions and futile answers. He only wanted to be left in peace, to brood in his room, to take solitary walks over the fields. It would be only natural if he couldn't bear the sight of a German. And all that could be convincingly managed, if he didn't start worrying; if, he grimly reminded himself, he managed to get through the next half hour. He could almost hear Matthews saying, "Worry before, and you'll be prepared. Worry afterwards, and you'll keep your feet on the ground. But don't worry during action; that's fatal." Well, he had worried plenty in the last three weeks over the smallest detail. Even Matthews would have been almost satisfied with his preparations. And he might have some memories, before he finished this job, which would worry him afterwards. But now ... well, now the Corlay farmhouse was just fifty paces away. Hearne braced himself.

There was a short path of rough stones, patched together in the rich black earth. On one side of the two-storied house were apple trees; on the other, a hayfield almost ripe for cutting. The narrow windows were tightly shut and screened. But smoke was thickening above the chimney, as if someone had just thrown more wood on the night embers. He skirted the corner of the building, following the path into the back courtyard of the farm. The door ahead of him lay open.

CHAPTER 5

The Farm

The woman, stooping in front of the enormous stone fireplace, half-turned as she heard the footsteps on the path. The man halted in the doorway and leaned against its heavy wooden post. His black hair was disheveled, falling over his high forehead to shadow the melancholy brown eyes. His high cheekbones added to the gauntness of his face, gray in the cold early morning light. A heavy growth of short black hair shaded the outline of his jaw. His blue jacket was faded and torn. His heavy boots were so encrusted with mud that his feet looked swollen.

The woman rose to her feet, clutching the black shawl more closely round her thin shoulders. Her lips remained half-open, as if she were frozen into silence. The bright color drained from her cheeks, leaving only a network of thin red veins.

She was frightened, Hearne realized. Perhaps he looked more like a ghost than he had thought. He advanced slowly into the large room, his feet suddenly dragging on the hard earth floor. She stood motionless, her eyes fixed on his face, her voice still silent. He would have to speak first, after all. He tried to smile that controlled smile which had been Corlay's.

"Well, Albertine, I've got home." His voice was the voice which had haunted him for three weeks, day and even night. The familiarity of its accent startled him. As he heard it, so strangely translated to this room, he could smell the antiseptic cleanliness of the hospital, he could see the black hair against the white pillowcase. And then Albertine moved, and as she came slowly forward she spoke.

"My God," she was saying, "my God. It's himself."

"Yes, it's me." Hearne sat down heavily on the wooden bench at the side of the long narrow table in the middle of the room. He felt suddenly tired, very tired.

Albertine was standing over him, her rough voice hurrying in its emotion, her gnarled hand smoothing the hair tightened under her starched white cap.

"I thought you were a ghost. You were just like one, standing there with the light behind your back, saying never a word."

Hearne smiled and checked his jaws from yawning. The warmth of the kitchen was having its effect. Albertine touched him suddenly, lightly, on the shoulder, as if she were reassuring herself.

"I'm alive, Albertine. I'm tired and I'm hungry, but I'm alive."

"You've been ill." Her eyes on his face embarrassed him. He leaned his elbows wearily on the table and rested his forehead on his hands so that they partly covered his face.

"Yes," he said, with the listlessness of someone who is too tired to think, far less talk. He added, "How is my mother?"

"Just so-so." Albertine's voice was normal once more. It was a plain voice, unemotional and heavy. "When she wakens, I'll tell her. Then you can go upstairs. But first I shall give you something to eat, and then you must clean yourself. Where were you?"

It was as if she were speaking to a small boy. It seemed as if she not only kept the house and the farm in order, but Madame Corlay and her son as well. There was a curious blend of familiarity and deference, a kind of proprietary

interest mixed with critical pride. Albertine had turned away
as she asked the question. She was now stirring the contents
of the large black iron pot suspended from an iron hook over
the burning end of the log. It was more a young tree than a
log; the shriveled brown leaves still clung to the end lying
over the stone hearth, waiting to be fed onto the flames in its
turn. Albertine tasted the soup, and spooned it generously
into a thick earthenware bowl.

"Where were you?" she repeated. Hearne started slightly
and brought his gaze away from the dancing flames.

"You're tired," she said. "You're half-asleep. Eat this and
then you'll feel better. But where have you been?"

"Belgium. Dunkirk," he said mechanically and warmed his
hands round the bowl of soup. "I got to Brest in a French
boat. I was ill. When I recovered there was the armistice,
and I began to walk home."

Albertine had cut him a thick slab of coarse white bread,
and watched him critically as he swallowed the soup.

"You're hungry," she said, and moved suddenly into another room, with the quick sure movement of a practical woman
who has not time to waste over decisions. She came back with
a small piece of cold pork, a still smaller piece of sausage,
and a glass of milk. It was good milk, with the yellow cream
still there.

"The Germans haven't been here," he said suddenly.

Albertine looked at him in astonishment, her almost invisible eyebrows raised. "They came and they went. Just six men
on motor bicycles. Why should they stay here? There is
nothing for them here."

Hearne smiled as he shook his head, and wiped the thick
cream off his upper lip. He remembered the truck convoys he
had seen last night.

"Have the others in the village got home?" he asked
tactfully.

"Picrel's son. The Picrels always look out for themselves,
you may be sure of that. Trouin's son was killed, and Jean-
Marie Guérin has been a prisoner for four months in
Germany." Her voice droned on monotonously. Apart from
the family tragedies in the village, all due to the war, life in
St. Déodat was very much the same as usual. There were
the weekly markets, smaller now certainly, but then most of
the young men had been away. Even with smaller markets,
there had been enough food last winter, and enough fuel, and
enough wool. Enough was all St. Déodat had ever wanted.

Monsieur le Curé had been ill with rheumatism again, and some of the children had had a fever. But that of course was what happened when children were all shut up together in a schoolhouse. That young man Kerénor had ... And then the church bells rang, and Hearne never learned what had or hadn't happened to Kerénor.

Albertine looked at him blankly. "I was forgetting," she began incredulously. Her forehead wrinkled into deep lines so that Hearne knew the colorless eyebrows must again be raised. He looked at the prominent bones of the thin face, the bald brow with the hair combed so severely under the high cap.

"But of course you must go," he said. "Don't wait at home for me." Albertine looked relieved. There might have also been surprise on her face, as she moved towards one of the three beds which lay along the wall, opposite the fireplace. From a chest of richly carved wood, arranged as a kind of step in front of the high bed, she lifted a rosary and another black shawl.

She was at the door now. "Don't waken Madame," she said briskly. "Henri is with the animals." She nodded towards the wooden wall beside the door he had entered. He remembered the outbuilding which joined this corner of the house at right angles and sheltered both the entrance and the small court-yard from the north wind. So through that wooden wall was the cow shed. That accounted for the warm, farm smell, not unpleasant, which had filled this room.

"Henri?" he remembered to say in surprise. Henri wasn't the name he had expected.

"Yes. He came to help me, but he is too old."

"And Jean?" Jean was Albertine's nephew who had lived on the farm and done the harder work.

"Missing." Her face was expressionless, a mask of tightly drawn skin over rugged, strong bones. Then she was gone, pulling the second shawl round her shoulders. Hearne listened to her sabots clattering down the flagged path.

"I'm accepted," he thought. "I've been left in possession."

Now he would have about three quarters of an hour before Albertine returned, while Henri was with the cattle and Madame Corlay slept upstairs. He finished the last crumbs of his meal and drained the drops which had gathered at the bottom of the soup bowl. He was feeling better, already.

From Corlay, he had gathered only rough details about this

house. There were three rooms downstairs: this large room, the smaller room from which Albertine had brought the food, and a front room which was a kind of entrance-hall parlor with its own front door, seldom used. The staircase to the three rooms upstairs led from that entrance-hall place. Overhead was Madame Corlay's large bedroom, stretching across the full side-length of the house, as this kitchen did. Above the entrance hall was his room, and behind it, over the room where the food seemed to be kept, was another room for storage. Definitely utilitarian architecture, he thought. And then there was that outhouse tacked onto the end of the kitchen, separated from it by a wooden partition. There had been openings along that partition at one time, like so many booking-office windows in a railway station, but now they were shuttered and blocked. Under them, there still lay a thick tree trunk, shaped into a shallow trough. Hearne had a sudden vision of five cows shoving their heads through the five openings, their jaws working steadily, their scanty eyelashes unmoved as they watched their master and his large family grouped round the table, eating their meal with similar concentration.

And there must have been a large family at one time, judging from the size of the table with its two long benches and from the three double beds arranged sideways along the wall opposite the fireplace. Each bed had its encircling drapery, suspended from the wooden ceiling above, so that the men and women and children could sleep in the same room without offending *les convenances*. There were a chair and a chest before each bed: they were so high with piled mattresses that otherwise it would be difficult to climb into them. At either end of the row of beds were two wardrobes, broad and deep. Like the chests, they were of age-stained wood, beautifully fashioned and carved. The two doors flanking them occupied the last available corners of space on that long, well-filled wall. The one beside the back-door entrance was the one which Albertine had used: downstairs storeroom it must be. He moved across to it quickly, and glanced briefly inside. A bicycle, a bowl of milk, some wine bottles, a cider keg, some twisted rope, large iron cooking utensils, a few small barrels, a few large earthenware bowls neatly covered, all standing on the stone floor. There were two windows, both of them small and high in the wall and tightly shut. 'Ellish dark and smells o' cheese, Hearne thought. Now for the upstairs part of the house.

He took one last look at the kitchen. He would have to know it backwards. The windows here were also small. Two lay at the other end of the room with a dresser and its rows of dishes between them, while two higher windows flanked the fireplace. Under one of these was another dresser, and more dishes, under the other was a small table. Between them stood the enormous stone fireplace, with proportions and simplicity worthy of a castle hall. From the dark wood rafters overhead were suspended two hams and a long shelf containing a wooden rack. In the rack were numerous thin circular disks.

"Now, what the hell—" began Hearne. Disks . . . Probably edible; they certainly weren't ornamental. He strained his eyes, and then something clicked in his memory. Rennes, and a small inn outside the city, and a cheap student meal, and pancakes. That was it. Pancakes.

Then he became aware that someone had entered the room, that someone was standing behind him. There had been no footsteps on the flagged path outside; he was sure of that. He turned, slowly, casually he hoped. A man was standing in the corner of the kitchen, against the wooden partition which was the dividing line between the animals and the family. Behind him, a narrow door was open, a door whose edges fitted so neatly into the wall that Hearne had been unaware of its existence. Blind oaf, he said to himself in annoyance. He ought to have realized an opening would be there. There were plenty of dirty wet nights in the winter, and what peasant was going to leave the warmth of his kitchen to visit his animals by way of a cold dark farmyard? Certainly not a peasant who had arranged his eating and sleeping so practically.

The man stood silently, impassively, a small thin figure in a faded blue blouse hanging loosely over worn corduroy trousers. Behind him, there was only a black smudge, and silence. The animals must have already been turned out into the fields. There was no mistaking the warm smell of straw and cows which filled the kitchen. Cosy little joint, thought Hearne; for those who liked it that way, he added hastily, as the smell strengthened. Well, now, what should he say or shouldn't he say to Grandpa? He watched three white hens negotiate the old man's wooden shoes, and jerk their way hesitatingly into the kitchen, picking spasmodically at nonexistent crumbs with a kind of I-really-don't-have-to-do-this air. But he still hadn't thought of anything to say. It was the old

man who spoke first, as he closed the door carefully behind
him and came slowly past the end of the trough into the
kitchen.

"She's gone?" His French was heavy and slow, as if it
were almost a foreign language.

Hearne nodded, and said "Yes." That seemed to be all that
was expected of him.

The old man moved more quickly. He picked up a bowl
from the small table beside the fireplace and helped himself
to some soup. He seated himself at the large table and began
eating. He had seemingly identified Hearne in his mind, and,
having accepted him, was now concentrating on his breakfast. Hearne stood, feeling rather futile, and watched the
soup disappear. The old boy had quite a capacity, considering
his dimensions. Then Hearne suddenly realized that he was
the master of this house. He'd better stop acting like an
unwanted week-end guest. He turned abruptly towards the
doorway which he had not yet explored. Henri stopped chew-
ing and watched him.

"I'm going to sleep. I'm tired," Hearne said.

"Aye, it'll be wet tomorrow," Henri replied slowly and
amiably. His face was as weathered and as wrinkled as a
dried russet apple. He nodded sagely as he spoke. His smile
showed no teeth, but the eyes were as blue as his smock.
They looked up at Hearne with their strange mixture of
ingenuousness and shrewdness. Hearne smiled in turn, and
nodded vigorously. As he was shutting the door, he looked
back towards the table. Henri was scouring round the emptied bowl with his last crust of bread. Under the table, at his
feet, the three white hens had abandoned their condescension
and were competing openly for the few crumbs which had
escaped.

It was just as well that he was not really a hero returning
from the wars, Hearne thought, or he'd be feeling as flat as a
punctured tire after that welcome.

It was cold in this entrance hall, as well as dark, for it lay
in the southwest corner of the house. It would be a cheerless
place even when the sun did get round to it: no one used this
room. It was just a square-shaped box with more heavy
carved furniture, a flagged stone floor, a wooden staircase
hidden in the shadows of the central wall, and a front door
which was as obviously unused as it was imposing.

He mounted the staircase warily. It was really only a
glorified ladder. He could see the stone floor beneath him,

between the treads. He began to guess why Madame Corlay kept to her room. This was hardly the kind of staircase for arthritic joints. The landing at the top of the stairs was scarcely bigger than a cupboard. There were two doors. That one on his left would be the large bedroom above the kitchen, so this one must be his. He touched the latch gently and pushed the door slowly open. Inside it was dark, save for a faint blot of light where the window lay on the west wall. There was the same damp smell which he had noticed in the hall downstairs. He walked cautiously across the uneven wooden floor. His feet were beginning to feel the weight of his muddy boots. He pulled back the curtains clumsily and opened the window. There were the clean smell of trees and the nervous twitterings of wakening birds. He leaned heavily on the broad sill, formed by the thickness of the house walls. The fresh air should make him feel less tired. He stretched up his arm to touch the steep, fluting roof which flared out just above his head. Below him was the orchard, with Henri's pigs already rooting in the grass. Beyond the apple trees was a small field of grain, and then other small fields, all banked on the gentle slope of the hill. Then the fields ended, and there was a line of trees overtopped by the proud square tower of what had once been the castle of St. Déodat. So this is my home, he thought, and somehow the idea no longer felt strange.

He turned away from the window. Albertine would soon be back, and he ought to finish his inspection. There was still the third room on this floor. The door beside the carved wooden bed must lead to it. He started wearily towards the door. He ought to finish his inspection. He ought to ... and then, somehow, it didn't seem so important. Three mattresses, he counted slowly. Three. Somehow, it didn't seem so important.

He stepped heavily onto the chest lying at the side of the bed, and slumped onto the sheet which had protected the mattresses from dust. He just had time to think, as his filthy boots on the white sheet faded from his view, Albertine will give me hell for this, I bet; and then he was suddenly, beautifully, wonderfully asleep.

CHAPTER 6

Anne

When he awakened, the sun had crossed over to the western side of the house. He lay looking at the warm pool of light on the white scrubbed floor, letting himself drift slowly and pleasantly into consciousness. He could feel he had slept his fill: his eyes had lost that glued-up feeling which came with exhaustion. His mind, too, seemed to be wide-open. He felt warm and clean and comfortable. Clean? He looked at his hands in amazement. Yes, he had been scrubbed clean. And he was no longer lying on top of a dust sheet. He was between coarse linen sheets, with a broad pillow propping up his shoulders. A quilted mat, its blue pattern bleached with many washings, covered him. He was wearing a loose white shirt, and the filthy rags which had been his clothes had disappeared. He raised himself quickly on one elbow, but the contents of his pockets had been laid neatly on the small writing table near the window. Papers, clasp knife, gun. Yes, they were there all right. He relaxed back on his pillow and looked at his clean hands. Albertine had certainly been busy. He found himself grinning in embarrassment. Well, what of it? She had been midwife to Madame Corlay. It wasn't the first time she had washed young Bertrand. But it was lucky about that birthmark. He had thought Matthews was being just a touch too realistic there, when he got that chemist fellow to imitate the red splotch on Corlay's back. Strange that it should have been the first of his faked credentials to stand a real test.

It was warm in the room. Albertine had closed the windows again. He sat up in bed, swinging his legs onto the chest. He rubbed the back of his head, stretched himself and gave a long satisfied yawn. And then he smothered a laugh. Not one of his better moments, he decided, looking at the dangling legs under the short shirt. He crossed to a mirror, framed in carved wood, which hung against the white wall.

The view there pleased him just as little. The tired lines under his eyes had faded but not departed, and he had never admired Corlay's haircut anyway. Still, he did look less like himself and more like the Frenchman. He gave a wide grin to himself and saw the gap at the side of his teeth. Another of Matthews' bright ideas. "If," he had said, "if you were to smile broadly or to laugh, the gap would be seen. You must have a gap." So he now had a gap. He felt the still tender gum with his tongue. Yes, he had a gap, all right. But what Matthews expected him to laugh at on this trip was beyond him.

He opened the window. Now the fields and trees were bathed in the amber light of early evening. All the smells of grass and leaves and hay and clover and ripening wheat, distilled by the day's warmth into one sweetness, hung in the air around him. Time seemed suspended in the silence of these fields. "Why should they stay here?" Albertine had asked in answer to his question about any visiting Germans. Living here, one could become as simple as that: one could believe the delusion that peace was self-perpetuating.

There were footsteps in the room below. They were climbing the staircase, slowly and heavily. He closed the window quickly, and moved silently back to the bed. He was seemingly asleep, when the door opened and Albertine entered. There were footsteps following her: heavy decided footsteps. Hearne stiffened.

"He has been like that since yesterday morning," Albertine was saying. Not this morning then; yesterday morning.

The man grunted in reply, and Hearne heard something being set down heavily on the wooden chest beside him. For a moment he felt danger. Albertine had seen through the deception. He was caught not only helpless in bed, but ludicrous in a nightshirt. If he could get the man off-guard, if he could reach the gun on the table ... and then four cold fingers were laid gently on his wrist and stopped the wild plans. Albertine had only brought a doctor. He wondered where she had found him, for there was no doctor in St. Déodat. Doctors practised by districts, not by villages, in this part of the world. It would be just as well to stop feigning sleep. Doctors were doctors. He groaned slightly and twisted his body as his eyes opened. The doctor was shaking his white head and saying, "Very fast." Considering the emotions he had caused, it would have been difficult to have found a normal pulse, Hearne thought.

"He is awake," Albertine said, announcing the obvious.

The doctor grunted again. "How do you feel?"

"Tired." Hearne's voice was low.

"He's been ill," Albertine said.

"Wounded?" The doctor was looking at him fixedly.

"I forget things sometimes . . . It was the guns . . . "

The old man nodded his head sagely. "Ah!" he said. "Shell shock. And do you remember things now?"

"Sometimes. And sometimes I forget." He let his voice trail away in dejection.

"He needs rest, rest and quiet. No one is to worry him. If he has any more attacks, then he must rest here until he recovers. Just rest and quiet." The doctor was examining his chest, feeling his brow, looking at his tongue. Hearne wondered what all this had to do with loss of memory, and then he noticed Albertine. She was watching every movement intently. She seemed satisfied when the doctor had gone through all the motions: without them, she would have felt cheated, and the old man had known that. For good measure, he produced a box of pills. Albertine nodded sagely as he gave her full directions.

His last words were, "Don't worry if you find it sometimes hard to remember. Don't worry, and you'll be completely cured. Just rest and quiet." He shook his head sadly, lifted the heavy bag from the chest, and followed Albertine out of the room. He was still talking of rest and quiet as they went slowly downstairs.

When she returned, Albertine found him staring at the window.

"I'd like it open," he said.

"But you will catch a cold."

"I'd like it open. I am far too warm. I haven't slept indoors for almost two months."

Albertine stared unbelievingly, and then the doctor's advice must have prompted her. The advice had cost money: it must be good. *Humor him when he seems strange. Rest and quiet.* Her thin lips closed disapprovingly, she shrugged her shoulders impatiently, but she crossed the room and opened the window.

"Where are my clothes, Albertine?"

"You are to stay in bed." She might give in to this madness of opening a window, but as for clothes— Her lips formed a straight line. Her voice was harsh as if she were tired of all this nonsense. And then she was probably angry because he was ill. He didn't blame her; she had work enough to do without a sick man to add to it.

"But I am not ill, Albertine." He was reasoning gently as with a child. "My body is well. It is only my mind that is sick. I have slept enough. I need to stretch my legs before I can sleep again."

Albertine seemed incapable of grasping the fact that the sickness of body and mind could be different. They were all one to her.

"You are to stay in bed." She was quite decided. Her tone nettled him, unexpectedly. So he was to stay in bed in a short nightshirt, day after day, with a bowl of soup grudgingly but loyally brought upstairs to him. Perhaps you don't know it, he thought as he stared back at her, but I've work to do, and a hell of a lot of it too, my sweet Albertine.

He sat up in bed and swung his bare legs over its tall side. Most women would have retreated, but Albertine stood her ground.

"You'll catch cold," she said, with her masterly grasp of the obvious. Hearne looked at her incredulously and then he began to laugh, softly at first and then gradually more loudly until he was rocking on the edge of the bed. He suddenly remembered the gap in his teeth, and checked himself in the middle of a laugh. Blast Matthews: that man was always right.

Albertine's eyes were round circles. "He's mad," she said, backing to the door. "He's mad."

"I'm not mad." His voice rose. He got off the bed and advanced towards her. "I only want my trousers. Steal a man's trousers, would you?"

Then the door opened. A white-haired woman stood there, watching him silently.

"He's mad, Madame. He's mad."

"She's taken my trousers," Hearne said angrily. He was suddenly aware that his voice was loud, too loud. "She's taken my clothes. I'm not a child," he ended lamely.

Madame Corlay, leaning on her stick, looked at him dispassionately. "So you're back," she said coldly. And then to Albertine, "Give him his clothes." And then she was gone, leaving them staring at each other. So that was his mother, Hearne was thinking. Well, it certainly had been the strangest of meetings; hardly what he had been steeling himself against. Once more he had the feeling of anti-climax. That coldness, that hardly concealed look of bitterness ... What kind of mother was this, anyway? What kind of son was he supposed to be? *So you're back.* Not, *so you're home.* So you're back, with the implication that because there had been a scene, then he must be back. Yes, there was a lot to that little word *so.* . . . Corlay had talked willingly, almost diffusely, about his everyday life: about his education, about the farm, about the village and the people who lived and worked there. It seemed as if he were eager to identify himself. He had said, "So you want to know about me? Why? Do you think I am *not* Bertrand Corlay of St. Déodat?" They had both laughed at that, and certainly Corlay had proved his identity by the completeness of his descriptions. But about his personal life and emotions he had been vague, even bored. He had given a very good impression of a life which was so simple that it was dull and uninteresting. Corlay had been far from cheery: he had been unhappy and moody. But Hearne had thought that could be attributed to the obvious boredom of his past life, to the constant depression about the future of his country. It was enough to depress any man. Staring at the door which Madame Corlay had closed so definitely behind her, Hearne felt the first twinges of a new worry.

Albertine was watching him. He suddenly realized that it wasn't the fact that his voice had been raised in anger which had seemed so strange to her. It was the fact that he wanted open windows, that he wanted to dress when he should stay in bed. It wasn't the loud voice which had been mad: the loud voice was something which she thought normal. He sat down on the bed again, but his emotions were less calm than his words.

"Albertine, you know what the doctor said. You know what my mother said. All I want is to be left in peace, and to have my clothes. There is nothing mad about that. You needn't worry—I'm not going away. I'm going to stay here. Now, where are my trousers?"

"They are washed."

"Well, what about other ones?"

"I've got them all packed away with your things." She looked towards the door which he had meant to investigate, before the three mattresses had seduced him.

"Good. Shall I get them, or will you?"

She moved so quickly towards the storeroom that he was surprised. Her polite grumbling echoed back into his room.

". . . you'll just make a mess of everything," she was saying.

He waited patiently, reflecting on the charms of home life,

as Albertine made her silent journeys between the two rooms bringing with her each time a newspaper bundle smelling of some strange herb. She had obviously decided to be the complete martyr and unpack everything at once. It was just as well, Hearne thought. That made it easier for him to find his way about another man's strange wardrobe. He snapped the thin string on the parcels of yellowed paper, and began to shake out the clothes, and then paused as his eyes read the heavy black print. The clothes must have been packed away in September. *French successfully attack Siegfried Line. English allies arrive with full equipment. Miracle of the Machine in Modern Warfare.* His eyes traveled down the columns of close print. There was a glowing report on the miracle of the Maginot Line, on the modern conveniences which made life so much more pleasant for the troops. As a sour joke, someone had printed a photograph in the very next column showing the English digging in. Or perhaps he never realized it would be sour, or a joke. Only our very best crack troops, thought Hearne, standing waist-deep in mud, digging and draining a French field into a prepared line. No, it was much more pleasant to read of electric light and red wine, of underground movies and chapels, of hot and cold water and heating systems. So much more pleasant, more comfortable—so impregnable.

Albertine had finished and was standing silently watching him. He kicked the papers aside, and turned to the clothes which were laid on the bed. They weren't country clothes. They had been bought in some town. Perhaps in Rennes ... yes, that was what the labels said. Corlay must have had quite a taste for suits—not that it had been particularly good taste. But there were certainly more clothes than Hearne had expected. The chief thing was that they looked as if they might fit him. He groaned at the thought of having to put on such underwear. Yards and yards of the stuff, he thought despairingly. But if he didn't wear any of it, then Albertine would really think he was mad, and he couldn't afford to have her become permanently worried about him. The doctor had prepared her for a certain mild strangeness, but there must be nothing beyond that really to alarm her.

She was down on her knees, now, smoothing out the newspapers, folding them neatly. She wound up each little piece of string separately and slipped the knotted rolls into her pocket, one by one. Nothing escaped her careful, thrifty fingers. And then she solved the problem of what clothes he would wear. She left them on the bed, while she hung up the others inside the wardrobe or folded them neatly into the chest in front of the bed. But it was the inside of the wardrobe which interested Hearne. More than half of it was filled with books and papers. He stopped Albertine as she lifted the first armload of these, with the same look of resignation on her face which had haunted it for the last fifteen minutes.

"Don't worry about that stuff, Albertine," he said. "I can arrange it myself, later. You know you've plenty to do, as it is."

She softened unexpectedly, but her eyes also held surprise. It was the same look which he had noticed, this—no, yesterday morning, when he had had no objections about her going to early Mass and leaving him unattended at breakfast.

He pretended to be shaking out the trousers and pullover he was going to wear. "Tell me, Albertine, why is my mother so annoyed with me? She has seen me angry before now. What is wrong?"

It was now Albertine's turn to pretend to arrange her apron. "Your mother is upset about the war."

"Yes, I know. But she wasn't even pleased to see me home safe."

Albertine's voice was gentler. "You must remember your father died in 1917. And your grandfather died in the siege of Paris. So Madame is very upset about this war. Myself, I think we should thank the good God who has looked after us and let us keep what we have."

"So my mother is angry because we lost this time, because I am home safe?"

"She is angry with all the young men. She says that if a German comes near this farm she will kill him with our ham knife. She says—" Albertine stopped and shrugged her shoulders. "Myself, I think we should thank the good God who has left St. Déodat in peace."

"What else does my mother say?"

"She says that now the young men, who talked too much, have done too little; that they have sold France by all their politics."

"And what of the old men?"

"They will be punished by dying in unhappiness, for they will never live to see France free again. But they will soon be out of this life, while the young men will have to live in misery. They will suffer more than if they had died in war. Yes, she is very upset."

"Seemingly." Hearne was thinking quickly. There had been still more to Madame Corlay's bitterness than even that: as if there had been a deep conflict between herself and her son, as if what had happened to Madame Corlay's France was only the culmination of such a conflict.

"And what did my mother say about me?" he added.

Albertine looked restless. She was now smoothing the stiff white cap, tucking away imaginary stray wisps of hair. But when her answer did come, it was as direct as it was harsh.

"She did not want to see you again."

There was a pause. Hearne swallowed, and said, "Well, now ... " He couldn't think of anything to add. There was something too final about Madame Corlay's words. He picked up his clothes.

"I'll dress now, Albertine, or else I will catch that cold of yours. And then I'll walk in the fields for half an hour. And then I'll come in for supper. And then I'll go back to bed."

Albertine seemed to find this reasonable if unnecessary. She seemed relieved by the quietness of his voice. It seemed to restore her confidence. As she left the room, she walked over to the window and closed it.

Hearne waited until the heavy footsteps on the wooden stairs had faded into the kitchen, and then opened the window. He was thinking about that strange meeting with Madame Corlay. He saw her once more framed in the darkness of the doorway, dressed in black with the long gold chain gathered tightly into the small round brooch at her throat. The white hair was carefully combed, the white face with its faded color in the lips and cheeks was set in a proud, disdainful mold. It was the face of a woman of character, who had been continuously disappointed in life. She was not the negative personality he had expected. She was a self-effacing invalid only in the sense that she no longer interested herself in the management of the house and farm. But upstairs in her room, Madame Corlay was indeed a very definite personality.

It was good for his purpose, in one way, that she should have been so unnatural in her welcome. A gentle mother, full of sympathy and tears, would have worried him. And yet, in another way, Madame Corlay's attitude made things more strange and difficult. For there was the hint of dark currents in Bertrand Corlay's life, which weren't covered by the data he had learned by heart. He had studied Corlay, questioned him skillfully, memorized all the details which he and Matthews and that French Intelligence man, Fournier, had gathered. Not that he had expected Bertrand Corlay to be so simple as a string of dates and facts. Human beings weren't like that. He had only learned to know the skeleton, as it were. Now he must fill in the flesh. It might be a stranger job than he had imagined. This evening, after supper, he would unpack the books and papers from the wardrobe and place them back in the empty bookcase. He would find out a lot about Corlay, that way: books were half a man.

He went downstairs, passing through the kitchen where Albertine was working in front of the fire. The air was cool, the fields were empty. The cows had no doubt been safely locked in for the night by Henri. He walked slowly up the hill to the west side of the farm until he had reached the last field and the beginnings of the castle's woods. He halted and looked down towards the farm, towards the apple trees outside the window of his room.

It wasn't a big farm at all. It consisted of this large field divided into three for various crops, of scattered groupings of trees, of the orchard which stretched from the house up this western hill, of the meadow and hayfield edging the path to the Pinot farm. If only there had been a man to manage and work it, instead of poor old Albertine and one of her relatives, the farm might have produced more than mere subsistence. For it was good soil, and centuries of careful nursing had left the grass smooth, the branches heavy with ripening fruit. The wheat in one part of the field was standing strong and upright. The breeze whipped over its yellowing greenness and the whiskered heads of grain rustled gently like silk skirts in a ballroom.

Beyond the farmhouse, down through the fields to the east, lay the road which passed through the village. From here, he could see its church soaring over the tops of the trees which fringed St. Déodat. Still farther to the east lay the busy plain, with its highway and railway, its villages and towns. But here, on this gentle hill, touched with gold in the rich evening light, such things might be a hundred miles away. He could hear the stillness around him. Its peace made him a part of itself, holding him immobile, suspended in time like a figure on a painted canvas.

The bells from the church swung him out of his inertia. Below him the road would now have its black-shawled, white-capped women, walking with their heads already bent. He saw Albertine leave the kitchen door, and set off quickly down the path. Poor old Albertine, he thought again: her rewards were so few.

And then he saw a girl on the path, her hair gleaming in the low rays of the setting sun. She didn't turn towards the kitchen door as he expected. Instead, she had begun the climb up through the sloping fields towards where he stood. She had seen him. She waved, not excitedly, not full-heartedly. It was more of a gesture than a greeting. Nor did she quicken her steps, but walked towards him at the same steady pace. The silver-gold of her hair was unmistakable. This must be Anne Pinot. As she came nearer, and the white blur of her face resolved itself into a short nose and rounded chin, level eyebrows above grave eyes, he knew he had been right in his guess. She looked exactly like the expressionless photograph which Corlay had shown him. "Very fair hair," Corlay had said in a disinterested voice. "That's about all."

And that was about all, thought Hearne, until he noticed the eyes more blue than gray, and the sprinkling of freckles over the short, charming nose. She had possibilities, but she either ignored or despised them. Even the black dress with its bodice tightly buttoned up to the neck, with its long sleeves covering her wrists, seemed to have been chosen to constrict and hide her strong young body. Her stockings were black, and they weren't silk ones, either. Her shoes were of plain black leather, low-heeled. He found himself thinking again of Corlay's disinterested voice which had jarred on him at the time.

"Anne," he said, and smiled.

"I met Albertine." Her voice was clear and soft. She spoke French carefully, with no Breton accent and only the hint of an intonation. "She said you had gone up the hill. I wanted to see you." Her eyes were fixed on the ground at her feet. Hearne suddenly remembered that he had made no move to touch her. He took her hand awkwardly.

"You look just the same, Anne," he said gently. "Just what I hoped to see when I got back."

She took her hand away quickly, and raised her eyes.

"Bertrand," she said in that clear childlike voice which matched the simplicity of her face. "I want to tell you at once . . . Yesterday afternoon I learned that you had come back. I didn't sleep all last night. So I must tell you now. I—" The resolution was fading with her voice.

"Tell me what, Anne?" It was strange how gently he spoke to this girl, as if he were addressing a child. They stared at each other. "Tell me what, Anne?" Hearne smiled into the serious eyes.

"I do not want to—" She stopped once more. Whatever she was trying to say was too difficult for her.

"Anne, what's wrong?" He was thinking that she reminded him of a startled fawn. He found he was smiling naturally and easily at last.

She looked at him disbelievingly. He could hear the short sharp breath. She bit her lip. And then she turned suddenly and was running down the hill.

"Anne!" There was real concern in his voice. He started after her, and cursed silently at his stiff muscles. It was as if he were running on stilts. He forced himself to greater speed, but even at that he was gaining only slightly. Had she guessed? Had she found out? His thoughts urged him on. He drew level with her almost at the bottom of the field. He caught her arm sharply, so that she stumbled and exclaimed, but his voice mastered hers.

"Anne, what is wrong? You must tell me."

She was trembling. He let go her arm, suddenly and painfully aware of the madness of his emotions in the last two minutes. He felt strange and foolish. Chase a girl, he thought savagely, and you feel like some primeval Pan. Hell, he thought, think of Matthews and cold blue eyes and a matter-of-fact voice, think of a job to be done, a dirty rotten job which might bear some good, some good for others but nothing but hell for yourself.

She was looking at him, wide-eyed, the startled fawn again. She was nursing her arm; but she was still there, looking at him.

"Anne," he said. Nothing but Anne. He kept saying Anne. What else did you say to a girl to whom you had been conveniently betrothed?

"Anne," he said again. "I'm sorry. I didn't mean to hurt you. But tell me what is wrong, what is wrong."

He was tired, he thought, or else all movement had gone into slow motion. No one could have looked so long at him as this. And then her clear simple voice cut in on his emotions. *Frère Jacques,* he was thinking, either *Frère Jacques* or *Sur le pont d'Avignon.* It was that kind of voice, made to sing the simplest melodies.

"My father died two months ago."

"Your father died ... Oh, I am sorry. I didn't know." But still he couldn't fathom her meaning. He looked at her and waited.

"I am now my own mistress." She was becoming more confident.

"Yes, of course." Just what, he wondered, was she trying to say with so much difficulty and hedging? When it came, even he was surprised. He had imagined a number of things, but not this.

"So I shall not have to marry."

Hearne remained completely motionless. The blank expressionless look which he had often found useful when suddenly confronted with a strange twist in events slipped over his face. He said nothing. He was wondering just how Corlay would have really felt. Surprised, and hurt: incredulous, probably even angry. Most men would be at such a reception as this. He, himself, felt an immense load lifted from him: thank God, he wouldn't have to pretend a lot of nonsense, anyway. He felt like smiling when he remembered his elaborate plan to keep his betrothed at full arm's distance. Just another set of bright ideas he needn't have bothered thinking up, just another set for the wastepaper basket. If all the plans which he worked out and never had to use could be kept in files, how many sides of a room would they cover? Probably they would make too depressing a room: they were better scrapped and forgotten.

Anne was watching strangely. Let her, he thought. She ought to know Corlay's reactions better than he did. If he were to keep silent, with his brows down and his lips tightly drawn, she would probably read into his expression the emotions he ought to be feeling. She was losing her confidence again. Serve her right, Hearne thought. What a fine welcome Corlay was getting after having walked the length of Brittany to reach these people. Just the sort of welcome to cheer a chap up after his country had been slapped down. First of all he would have had all his ideas smashing round his head; and now he was having all his personal emotions added to the general rubble heap. He suddenly started to walk down the path towards the house.

Anne tried to match her pace to his. She was looking vaguely unhappy, he was glad to see. Poor old Corlay ... what a welcome.

It was she who had to speak first. "Please don't pretend, Bertrand."

"Pretend?" Hearne's tone was unexpectedly savage.

"Yes, *that* is more like you. Once your pride has recovered, you will be really very glad. You didn't love me." It wasn't a challenge; it was a quiet statement of fact.

"I agreed to marry you."

"That was before—" She stopped. "You see, Bertrand," she continued, "I knew all the time. I knew." Her tone puzzled him, but his face was cold and expressionless. "I haven't told your mother, yet," she finished lamely.

"Which means you think I shall tell her? That will be slightly difficult, considering the fact that my mother doesn't want to see me." He could imagine Madame Corlay's delight when she found that her son had failed her again. The Corlay and the Pinot farms would never be joined. The old quarrel about that dovecote on the boundary line would never be solved. "I think you had better finish what you've begun," he ended quietly.

It was with considerable relief that he saw Albertine approaching them, her black shawl tightly drawn round her thin shoulders, her precarious white cap soaring so securely from the tightly bound hair. It was strange that anything so fantastic was neither shaken nor blown from her head as she walked, that she could turn so quickly from Anne to him and then back to Anne without even seeming to be aware of balancing a starched cylinder on top of her crown. She greeted them with a sparse remark about supper. It was a command rather than a suggestion. He was glad to follow her into the kitchen, glad that Anne had refused to eat with them. It was only after he had entered the room that he wondered if he ought to have taken her back across the fields to her farm. But the strange thing had been that Anne didn't seem to expect that: she had moved so quickly away by herself. And stranger still was the fact that Albertine, who obviously still regarded them as engaged to be married, had most certainly not expected it.

Albertine served him a supper which was identical with his breakfast, except that a piece of cheese was substituted for the pork, and there was a small glass of cider. Henri was tactfully nonexistent, and he noted that Albertine had only set one place at the table. They must eat after he had gone. It was rather a formal arrangement for such an informally managed farm. For the third time that day he found himself wondering just what kind of chap this Corlay had really been. Of one thing he was certain: there was much more in Corlay than he had ever imagined. I don't believe I am going to like him at all, he thought suddenly.

He finished his supper quickly. Upstairs he imagined himself examining and arranging that stack of books and papers. He might find something there to solve these peculiar questions in his mind.

But when he went upstairs, the dusk had thickened in the room, and Albertine had conveniently forgotten to fill the lamp with oil. There were no candles in the candlestick on the small table beside the empty bookcase. In spite of his annoyance, he had to laugh. Albertine certainly had her little ways. He undressed quickly, alternately admiring the low cunning of women and wondering where he was supposed to wash. A small ugly-looking cabinet pulled open at last and showed a basin with a pail concealed underneath, and a tap which turned on water from a container hidden above. It was the sort of thing which small yachts and steamers like to produce to comfort their passengers for the lack of running water. It was no doubt one of Corlay's innovations, for he could think of no one else here who would have bothered about it. Anyway, it meant he could wash. In the growing darkness of the room, he miscalculated the swill of the water and felt it drip over the floor. Albertine, he thought, would— oh, damn Albertine. Of all the people he had met so far she was perhaps the kindest, certainly the most self-sacrificing; and yet she worried him the most. Partly because he realized that if Albertine were to become suspicious, then his difficulties would be enormous; it would be dangerous trying to explain things to her, trying to make her understand without giving too much information. And partly, he had to admit, because of the natural fear in every man that he is liable to be bossed by a woman. He opened the window defiantly before he climbed into the bed.

Tomorrow he would examine these books and that room next door, and then when darkness came he would have his first long walk through these green fields down towards the plain and the main railway line. Tomorrow and tomorrow, the nights after that, the next weeks ... In the middle of forming his plans, he halted abruptly. He suddenly knew that

long-term planning wasn't necessary on this job. If he could
manage to improvise from night to night, he would do very
nicely. Now, he would be very much wiser to get what sleep
he could. Later, he might not be so lucky.

He didn't waken until the sun had risen and the faint
sound of the five-o'clock bells swung over the fields into his
room.

CHAPTER 7

Stranger on the Hillside

But next morning, the books were not rescued from the
wardrobe and placed on their shelves. Instead, the Germans
came back to St. Déodat.

The news arrived with Henri, who suddenly and unaccount-
ably appeared at the kitchen door when Hearne was having
breakfast. He stood there, breathing heavily, and then said
simply, "The Boches are here."

Hearne, his elbows resting on the wooden table, looked up
at the thin little man in the doorway, and set down his bowl
of soup slowly. Albertine, bending over the heavy iron disk
which was hung over the fire, hesitated as she turned over the
paper-thin pancake baking there, and then moved so suddenly that the half-finished pancake was jolted into the flames.
She clutched the wooden spade which she had been using as
if it were now a weapon. There was silence in the long room,
except for the sizzling of the dough as it spread over the
glowing log. Afterwards, Hearne remembered that moment
by the smell of burning which filled the room: that and
Albertine's eyes, and the toothless grin of Henri with the
morning sun behind him.

"They are here? Outside?" Hearne asked the old man.
Henri shook his head slowly.

"No. Going into the village," he said.

There was an almost audible slackening of tension. Henri's
capacity for holding only one idea at a time had certainly
had its effect. He now slipped off his muddy sabots, and

walked slowly towards one of the beds. From the chest in front of it, he took out a knotted sock and a gun. The sock contained coins. Hearne heard them jangle as Henri stowed it away carefully inside his loose blouse. The gun was an old one, probably only good for shooting rabbits.

"That's no use," began Hearne gently. "They'd only shoot you in turn."

But Henri wasn't listening. He was absorbed as he began to take the rifle apart, slowly and yet methodically. Then he rummaged in the wooden chest once more, and taking a large piece of cloth which had served to bundle his clothes he tore it into strips and wound them carefully, almost lovingly, round the parts of his gun. When that was done, he carried them towards the door. Hearne rose quickly from the table.

"I'll help you," he said.

The old man was shoving his feet into his sabots. "Eh?"

"I said I'll help you."

They left Albertine, still holding the wooden spade raised in her hand, still standing beside the tub of dough. It looked as if the week's baking of *crêpes* was going to be a failure for the first time in Albertine's life. Hearne paused at the door and caught her eye.

"Better hide that ham knife, Albertine," he said with a grin, "or my mother will get us all strung up." Albertine looked at him in surprise, and then there was the beginning of a smile in spite of herself.

"God knows what Madame will say," she answered and looked at the black lava-like crust of dough on the log. She shook her head at the appalling waste. "These Boches," she said.

Hearne reached Henri at the seventh row of trees in the orchard. The old man was kneeling down under the third tree in that row, fumbling away at the turf. It had already been neatly cut. After that, the digging didn't take long. The linen-covered rifle and the knotted sock were laid side by side, and covered with the rich black earth. Henri, himself, replaced the jigsaw puzzle of turf. Watching the gnarled hands fitting each diamond of grass into its proper place, Hearne knew that Henri had been expecting the Germans. So had Madame Corlay. Only Albertine, the most practical and efficient of them all, had been caught surprised. The Germans were at Rennes, they were at Combourg and Dol and Dinan, they had long ago reached St. Malo and the coast, they had flooded the whole of Brittany to the very western

islands like some powerful turbulent tide pouring over broken
dikes into a flat plain-land. Nothing could stop them once the
dikes were down. Yet Albertine had had her own reasons,
her own brand of wishful thinking. In Rennes and Dol? But
of course: these were important towns. In St. Malo? Of
course: the ships were there. In the villages down on the
plain? Why, that could be understood: the farms there were
rich, and there were a lot of things to be bought. Bought?
Well, paid for anyway, even if the money was foreign-
looking. But up here in St. Déodat, the farms only kept the
people of the district. Kept them comfortably? Well, no one
starved, certainly. But then no one was idle. Everyone
worked, and worked hard for what they had, and that was
only enough for the people of St. Déodat. There was nothing left over for anyone else. They were all peaceful, hard-
working people on this hillside, owing no man anything. Why
should they be disturbed?

When Hearne got back to the kitchen, Albertine was plac-
ing the last thin disk of baked dough into a division of the
long wooden rack which had so puzzled him on the morning
of his arrival.

"I've sent Henri to the village," he said.

"He's got to dig the west fields." The way she handled the
rack told him she was annoyed. She was resentful over the
wasted pancake, and she was more scared than she would
allow by Henri's news. The rising note in her voice showed
just how she was going to get rid of her anger.

He cut her short. "Henri can dig for potatoes another day.
This morning he is in the village, and he is going to find out
for us if the Germans are going to stay there, or if they are
just passing through. If the potatoes worry you, I'll dig them
for you. And now you'd better tell my mother about everything. And tell her to keep calm: worrying won't help us at
this stage." He turned on his heel, and left the kitchen. That
certainly stopped the argument he could feel brewing. But
what on earth was she staring at?

As he walked up to the field, he was still wondering.

Henri had left the spade stuck into a ridge of earth. There
was another implement, too. Probably a hoe, or a mattock,
Hearne decided. Not that it mattered much: there was no
one here to see his raw technique. He smiled grimly. Once,
he had done this sort of thing for Saturday pennies in a
kitchen-garden behind a Cornish rectory. Now he was doing

it partly to keep Albertine quiet, partly to be out in the open with a good view of the path from the village.

He worked for three hours. Twice Albertine had come to the kitchen door and looked up the hill. He gave her a cheery wave, before he bent over a neat row of potatoes once more. The second time she gave a small wave back.

It was hot now, for the sun was directly above him. Soon it would be time for dinner, and Henri's return. The old man never missed a meal. But there was still no sign of anyone on the path. The sun's rays seemed to be concentrating on this patch of ground. The heat gathered in the earth round him and then struck backwards at him. This was the time when a farmer should have a mug of cider under the coolness of these trees over there, and let himself enjoy a satisfied conscience. He couldn't have the cider, but he stuck the spade in the earth and walked over to the green shade. It was good to lean his back against the trunk of a tree, to stretch out his legs in the soft cool grass. He yawned, and wiped the sweat from his brow. Still no sign of Henri, blast him. He should have been back an hour ago. And he ought to have told Henri to get him some cigarettes in the village—if there were any. He himself couldn't risk a visit to the village merely for a cigarette. But a smoke was what he wanted, right now. He looked at the farm and its orchard and fields, and thought, This would be a good way to live if there wasn't a war, if the Jerries weren't sitting on your front doorstep. Just to have a ten minutes' rest with a cigarette and a mug of cool cider; with this view of your land and your house looking as if it had grown from the earth, so natural was its shape and color; with Albertine cooking a thumping dinner for you in that enormous kitchen. No, someone younger and prettier and gentler than Albertine, he decided. That would be a good way to live. In the evening, you could have books, a radio, a gramophone; you could read, and listen, and think. Corlay could have had all that; and yet he hadn't known his luck. "I'm not interested in the farm," he had said. "My mother inherited it from her uncle. I only went to live there when I could find no suitable teaching job. I'm interested in writing." And again that unemotional voice, "Very fair hair. That's about all."

Hearne listened to the drone of bees and yawned once more. And then he was on his feet, his mind and body alert. Something had moved in that tangle of bushes beside the windbreak of trees. It might have been some animal. It might have been. Five steps, and he was past the bushes. Then he stood staring at the man sitting there. The man returned his stare, and then shook his head slowly as he grinned.

"I thought you had gone," he said. "I watched you working and then I must have fallen asleep. When I awoke just now, I thought you had gone." The words were fluent enough, but he wasn't a Frenchman.

"Why were you watching me?" Hearne spoke calmly, and his voice seemed to reassure the man.

He looked at Hearne for a minute, and then said, "To see what you were like. I don't go near farms, now, until I see what the people are like. It's difficult to tell nowadays who's a friend or an enemy."

"Who's your enemy?" Hearne asked.

"What do you think?"

"It's difficult to tell nowadays."

The man laughed silently. His teeth showed very white, and they were all the whiter against his skin, which had been tanned with exposure. His hair would be quite fair once the dust and grime were washed out of it. Determined jaw, noted Hearne, and eyebrows slightly drawn. He smiled a good deal as he talked, but his mouth was firm enough in repose. You would hardly notice the color of his eyes; it was as if the other features of his face overshadowed them. He was no fool, this man. He was waiting for Hearne to speak again.

"You want food?"

"Yes." He wasn't smiling any more.

Hearne looked at the man's torn tweed suit. It was filthy now, but once it had been good. No cheap tailor had made that shoulder line. His eyes traveled to the man's shoes, still holding to his feet by some miracle. Shoes were a good test. Just as in peacetime, you could generally tell the real down-and-out by the shoes. Fakers generally arranged to have their feet comfortable, at least. The man was watching his survey, but he didn't speak. He's exhausted, thought Hearne: he's so exhausted that he can't make any further effort to talk: he's holding tight onto himself at this moment.

"Wait here," Hearne said. "I'll come back."

Albertine was standing over the soup pot like a guardian angel. "Dinner's long ready," she began indignantly. "I went to the door to call you, but you had disappeared."

"I was behind the trees. There's a man there, and he's

starving. Get that soup into a bowl and tie a cloth round it, Albertine. And bread, too."

"But there's only enough for us, and scarcely that."

"Well, he can have mine." Albertine didn't move. He picked up a bowl and ladled the hot soup into it.

"Who is it?" she demanded. "Some beggar? You can't give to all of them." He took a large hunk of bread, and cut a thick slice of ham. He could hear Albertine flinch.

"Someone trying to reach the coast. He's either British or American. He's all in." Hearne pulled the small checked cloth off the end of the table, and folded it to tie round and over the bowl.

"But the Germans—"

"To hell with them." He finished the last knot carefully. "Don't worry, Albertine. I'll throw food to him behind some bushes as if he were a dog. I won't touch him, so I won't get leprosy. I won't give him a bed, or a wash, or any clothes, so that everyone in this house can go on living peacefully and happily." The savage bitterness in his voice struck Albertine like a bucket of cold water. She was still half-worried, half-angry, but for once she didn't have an answer, not even as much as a gesture, ready. He left her just standing there.

The man had been keeping watch for him. Hearne noted the expression on his face.

"Did you expect me to bring back a gun and a dog?" he asked.

The man smiled wryly. "It has happened, once or twice," he said. He seized the bowl which Hearne had unwrapped for him. "Hot!" He was incredulous. "Hot! The first hot food in days."

Hearne sat down beside the man and waited. When the food was eaten to the last crumb and the last shred of vegetable, he said, "What are you? English?"

"American."

Hearne imitated Corlay's English accent. "I speak English."

"You do?" It was an American voice all right, deep and comfortable. And the man was probably genuine, too. The more Hearne looked at those feet, the surer he was. It had taken a lot of walking to produce feet like that. And there had been a kind of heartfelt relief in the upsurge of his voice as he had said, "You do?"

"A little."

"You're the first farmer I've met who did."

"I'm not a farmer. I live here with my mother when I can't find a job as a schoolteacher."

"I thought you looked queer on that potato patch."

Hearne smiled sourly. "It's probably my job from now on."

"You speak English well."

"Thank you. I studied English once." Hearne looked sidewise at the man, and then added, "I used to see a lot of American movies. That gave me some idiotisms."

"Idioms," corrected the American. "Something quite different."

"Oh yes, idioms. That's the word," Hearne acknowledged gravely. " 'Honey,' and 'nuts,' and 'sugar,' and 'you can't do this to me.' You know the sort of idioms. At first it was very difficult."

The American was smiling. "I guess it was. *You can't do this to me.* Doesn't mean much now, does it?" He looked at his torn feet. Hearne looked at the potato patch.

"Nothing at all." Hearne paused. He had given the man enough time to become accustomed to him. Perhaps he could risk a roundabout question.

"But why do you have to hide if you are an American? Your country isn't at war."

There was a short laugh. "But I am. I'd just as soon not meet a German or start any questioning. Just as soon."

Hearne said nothing, but he looked interested. If this man felt like talking, he'd talk. If he didn't want to, then nothing that Hearne could say would change his mind. So Hearne was silent, but just kept on looking interested. If this man felt like talking, he'd begin in another minute. He did.

"Do you know Paris?"

"Once I was there," Hearne said.

"Do you know the Ritz?"

Hearne shook his head.

"Well, that's where I began all this." The American pointed to his clothes and shoes. Hearne smiled politely, incredulously.

"It's the truth. There I was in the Ritz Bar about five o'clock in the evening, and in came a friend of mine. He was an ambulance driver. I'm a newspaper man, myself. Well, in he came, and he said, 'We're leaving.' I said, 'You are?' and I finished my drink and I went round to the depot where his bus was stationed and got hold of him before he left. I wasn't going to ask him questions in front of the crowd of newspaper men at the bar. He didn't know what had happened, or if anything was going to happen, but they had been ordered to stand by. And when he left that night I jumped a ride with him. For two months I had been waiting for something to happen. Now it was happening. And I was going to find out for myself all about it. Well, I found plenty. Plenty. In fact, so much happened that we got sore. There we were with a Red Cross plastered all over us and some bandages and a stretcher and a portable typewriter. And there were the Stukas diving at us and hedge-hoppers spraying us with bullets as if we were an armored train. We covered over the Red Cross, and that way we managed to reach the front, or whatever you could call it. We loaded up with wounded, and by that time we were worse than sore. The man I was with didn't like the responsibility of carrying back wounded without a Red Cross sign, so like Goddamned fools, we uncovered it. We never got further than six kilometers. The whole bus went up in flames. It just went up like a torch as we were racing round to the door. Couldn't do a thing for them inside. So then we found a machine gun, and I played around with it. By this time, this was my war, too. The fellow with me kept worrying about his badge and some oath he had taken, but being an angel of mercy didn't make much sense at that time. I left him trying to patch up some refugees, swearing his heart out, and I never saw him again. Thought I wouldn't make his conscience feel too bad about me. I was doing all right, too, when I was taken prisoner. Then I cooled down when they were checking up on me. I remembered a lot of unfinished business left over from an Austrian incident in the summer of 1939. I had a hunch that the Nazis would be gladder to see me than I was to see them. So when it got dark, I walked out on them before they finished checking up. I just waited for my chance and then beat it. I've been beating it ever since."

"So I see," Hearne said, and looked pointedly at the American's feet.

"They were a nice pair of shoes, once." He paused and then added, "You know, it's strange. Whenever I met someone friendly, someone who gave me food or shelter, they always piled on the questions until I was as tight-lipped as any Englishman. You're the first who hasn't asked questions— only what nationality I was, and that's fair enough—and look at the last five minutes."

"I didn't ask questions because I get tired answering them, myself. I've been walking like you, but not so far. I got home this week."

There was a silence, which Hearne felt compelled to end. He went on, "You are probably wondering why we are sitting here. Actually, it is as safe as any place in the district. The Germans arrived this morning in the village. I've sent old Henri down to see what's happened, and I am waiting here until he returns."

"I see. I was wondering why you were watching that path. But why didn't you go to the village yourself? After all, there's an armistice, a big beautiful armistice."

Hearne exchanged a sour smile with the American. "If the Boches see young men without work to do, they will find work for them," he said. "If they see me digging potatoes, they may let me go on digging potatoes so that they can get them."

"There's someone on the path, now," the American interrupted.

But it was Albertine, walking quickly up the hill towards them. She stood before them, regaining her breath for a moment. The annoyed look had left her face. Her voice was almost friendly. "Your mother says that if the man is ill he is to come down to the house." She gathered up the bowl and cloth. "Now; at once," she added over her shoulder, and marched off downhill, her white cap bobbing with each decided step.

Hearne was unexpectedly moved by the look of hope in the American's eyes. "I didn't ask you before," he began awkwardly, "because my mother is—" He hesitated. "How do you say it? Difficult? She's very upset by the armistice. She thinks I didn't fight very well."

The American nodded understandingly. "It's her farm, isn't it?" he said. "But do you think we can risk it?"

"It seems quiet enough, just now, and the sooner we get your feet attended to, the better for them, I think. Anyway, orders are orders."

The American rose stumblingly. Hearne steadied him, and then, as he felt the man's weight slump so heavily on his shoulder, helped him towards the house. Their pace was surprisingly quick: the American must have been making a terrific effort.

"I am Bertrand Corlay. Corlay," said Hearne slowly, as they neared the kitchen door.

"And I'm—" The American hesitated as if for a breathing space. "My name is Myles."

"Tell my mother the story you told me. She may adopt you."

The American smiled, and stepped heavily across the doorway.

But, as it turned out, that piece of advice, unlike most pieces of advice in the world, had good results.

CHAPTER 8

Elise

Madame Corlay wished to see them. That was the command which Albertine had been instructed to give. Hearne exchanged looks with the American and shrugged his shoulders. The American who called himself Myles looked at the staircase and shook his head.

"You've got to," Hearne said in French.

Albertine nodded vigorously. Together they helped the fumbling man up the treacherous stairs.

"I'll never get down, not this trip," he said when they stuck halfway, which was something of a prophecy.

Madame Corlay was sitting with her back to a window. The door was open, and she was sitting there waiting for them to appear in the doorway, her hands resting on the stick which she held in front of her. She said nothing, but Hearne had the idea that her glance softened as the slow procession halted inside the room. She wasn't so angry with him as she had been, he realized suddenly. He must have done something to please her at last.

He was very formal, responding unconsciously to the erect figure, to the composed hands. "This is my mother, Madame Corlay. Monsieur Myles, an American who is escaping."

Madame Corlay bowed. The complete duchess, Hearne thought, and glanced casually round the room. Similar in size and shape to the kitchen downstairs: more windows, though.

Here the east wall had no cow shed behind it. It was an end wall, up here. Two beds, draped; three chests; dresser; desk; two chairs; and, strange among these heavy carved furnishings, a ramshackle upright piano. That would be a relic from Rennes, where Madame Corlay had taught elementary music to the tradespeople's children in order to give her son a good education. That was when her uncle had lived here and she had refused his charity, still bitter over his quarrel with her husband. Even after her husband had been killed in 1917 and she had been left alone in Rennes, even after the uncle had forgotten his anger, she had refused any reconciliation. And only when the old man had died did she come back to the farm where she had lived as a girl. But by that time, she was half-crippled and unable to enjoy it. By that time, the son for whom she had worked was the qualified schoolmaster she had wanted him to be, but a schoolmaster without any pupils to teach. It would have been better for them all, even for the short years of peace which had been theirs before this war began, reflected Hearne as he walked slowly over to the east window, if Madame Corlay had swallowed pride and ambition and taught her son to be a farmer.

Behind him, Madame Corlay was being dignified and polite. In front of him, the roof of the outbuilding came just below the window. Useful, he decided, really very useful. He went on admiring the view.

Madame Corlay had finished her gracious speech of welcome. The American had begun to reply. Then there was a crash, and Hearne turned quickly to see Myles sprawling across the rug at Madame Corlay's feet. What else could she expect, Hearne wondered savagely, as he bruised himself against a heavy table and almost upset a chair in his quick journey towards the American. But then Madame Corlay and Albertine had never been hounded over open country for three weeks.

"What did you propose to do?" he asked Madame Corlay after he had unloosened the American's belt, and had sent Albertine running for water.

"The man is really filthy," Madame Corlay said, shaking her head incredulously.

"What did you propose to do?"

"We must feed him, and let him rest here today. Tonight he can continue his journey to the coast." To the coast ... So Albertine must have reported the argument he had had with her in the kitchen, and something which he had said to

Albertine must have pleased Madame Corlay enough to thaw some of the icicles in her eyes.

"He couldn't go on tonight," Hearne said. "He will have to stay here."

"Stay here?"

"Stay *here?*" echoed Albertine, reappearing in the doorway. "But the Boches—"

That word was sufficient for Madame Corlay.

"He stays here," she said, rapping her stick defiantly on the ground. She was watching Hearne thoughtfully. "War seems to have improved you, Bertrand," she observed with a peculiar smile. Hearne shrugged his shoulders and went on with his job. Myles was recovering.

"He may be here for a day or two," Hearne said at last. This was, he had decided, a diversion rather than a complication. The stranger had already pushed Hearne into second place as far as the women's interest was concerned. And he was an intelligent man: if he were a newspaper man, then he was also a practised observer. It would be nice to know just what he had seen as he had traveled through that very interesting piece of countryside in the last few weeks. If he would talk, it would be useful. If he would talk.

Albertine said, "He can hide in the straw in the shed."

"That's the first place the Germans would look." Hearne had helped Myles onto the nearest chest and was now trying to ease the shoes off the American's feet. It was slow work. He added, as Albertine stood unbelieving, "Any place with livestock is a sure place for them to look."

Albertine didn't like that idea: it troubled her.

"Well, then, in the storeroom upstairs?" she suggested with an effort.

"Storerooms are equally dangerous. Food may be kept there."

"Then where?" Albertine was alarmed. Good, thought Hearne: it was only alarm which forced Albertine's type of humanity out of its neat, orderly groove. Fear ended complacency; fear spurred on the imaginatively lazy.

"Here."

"What?" Both Madame Corlay and Albertine had raised their voices in shocked protest.

Hearne pointed to the draped beds. "There's nothing wrong with the idea. It's a good old Breton custom. And this is one place where the Germans will not look unless they are really suspicious, and in that case no place would be safe for him at all. This is the bedroom of Madame Corlay, who is an invalid. That's the safest place for this man."

"He couldn't stay here *all* the time."

"No." Hearne repressed a smile. "Not all the time. He can use my room or the storeroom all day. But if anyone strange appears, or at the first sign of a German, then he'd better slip into that spare bed."

"And at night?" Madame Corlay's voice was cold.

"Here," Hearne said decidedly. It had to be here: his plans for these night journeys must not be interfered with. He looked earnestly at Madame Corlay; his voice didn't weaken. "Then we won't be caught unawares if someone awakens us in a hurry. And if the Germans seem suspicious and demand to search your room, then he can escape by that window over there. This is the safest place in the house for him." His tone was final.

The second shoe was at last removed. Myles had screwed up his face, but he wasn't letting any sound escape. Albertine was watching in dismay.

"It's all right, Albertine. They've stopped bleeding now. The floor won't be marked." And then as he saw her expression change, he added more gently, "Better get a bath ready for him." She nodded and left the room.

"He'll look much better when we clean him up," Hearne said cheerfully. "The trouble will be clothes. He's taller than I am."

Madame Corlay looked at Hearne, as if surprised. "Yes, he is tall," she said thoughtfully.

"And he's killed a lot of Germans. You must get him to tell you the story tomorrow."

"Tomorrow?" The questioning eyebrows were her last protest.

"Or the next day."

Madame Corlay was looking at him speculatively. Hearne wondered just what that look meant: it was kind enough, but he didn't like it somehow. She might be almost about to smile. Blast Corlay, he thought, for refusing at the last moment to give a letter or a message for his mother. As soon as they had told him of the proposed impersonation, he had shut up as tight as an oyster. Fortunately for their plans, they hadn't told him until the last day, and by that time all the information they needed was already gathered and tabulated. If Corlay hadn't been so unwilling at the last minute, then

Hearne wouldn't now be going through this miming act. It would have made things easier, all round. And it would have made things pleasanter, too.

Madame Corlay reached suddenly towards the table beside her. She fumbled, and then lifted a pair of spectacles. At that moment, Hearne bent over to help Myles to his feet.

"Better get that bath," he said, his face turned away from Madame Corlay. "I'll bring him back later to you. His story will interest you."

He helped Myles towards the landing, and closed the door of Madame Corlay's room in relief. That last minute had been really embarrassing. Blast Corlay, he thought again.

But two things he had found out. Madame Corlay didn't like to wear glasses: and without these glasses, Madame Corlay didn't see so well as she pretended.

That afternoon, Hearne worked in the field. The American, washed and fed, rested in the house. He had asked for paper and pencil, and had settled himself in the one comfortable chair in Hearne's room. "To get my thoughts licked into shape while the memory is still hot," he explained with a smile which had become broader and easier.

"They will make interesting reading," Hearne said politely.

"That's the idea."

"Sit near the open window. I'll give a whistle if any Nazis arrive. You know where to go?"

"If it isn't going to worry your mother."

"The war hasn't finished for her. This is one of the few ways she has of fighting on. And tell her that story of yours."

"I gather she has no love for the Nazis."

"She hates them passionately."

The two men exchanged smiles. Then Hearne had gone out to the field.

He worked where he could have a clear view of the path which led from the farm past the round-towered *pigeonnier,* past the Pinot lands, down to the belt of trees hiding St. Déodat. But no Germans appeared, and no Henri. Once he thought he saw Anne's smooth fair hair; once an old, slow-moving peasant woman crossed the fields to the east, and then disappeared in the direction of the Pinot farm. Behind him, the trees surrounding the ruined castle seemed silent and safe enough. On his first job, he used to imagine an enemy behind every bush, but now he was past that stage. There weren't enough Germans to surround and spy on every lonely little farm throughout occupied France. Danger would come only when suspicions were aroused. At present, he was just another peasant working in his field.

By five o'clock he was no longer annoyed with Henri: he was worried. He carried the spade and the two other tools carefully down to the house. Albertine was working in the small vegetable and herb garden.

"Henri?" he asked.

Albertine was worried, too. "I'll go and find him, the old fool," she said slowly.

Hearne thought about that. "No," he said, "you stay here. You've plenty to do. I'll go before it's dark, if he isn't back by that time." The Germans might be patrolling after dark: then the fields, and not the road to the village, would be the safer place. And he couldn't tell Albertine the kind of thing he wanted to know. He would have a better chance of finding out just what had happened to Henri—not that he could help the old boy if he were in trouble. That would be a dangerous complication. But he had to know what was going on in the village, and to discover, if it were possible, whether the Germans intended to stay. Perhaps they weren't even there now; perhaps Henri's report that morning had been only a temporary alarm. He had to know.

He walked quickly down to the village. It was strange to think how long the path had seemed on that morning when he arrived. Now he was rested, and no longer hungry, and the way was quite short. Almost too short if the Germans were going to leave some men in the village.

At the bridge on the road, a young man sat on the low wall, staring at the shallow water beneath. He looked up as Hearne's footsteps neared him.

"Well," he said, "so you're back." Light-haired, freckled, a nose which wasn't quite straight, high cheekbones, blue eyes, a twisted smile.

Hearne said, "Yes," and walked moodily on.

The young man slid off the wall and hurried after him. He limped badly. So this was Kerénor, Jean-Christophe Kerénor, the "foreign" schoolteacher from Lorient.

"How's the writing?" he asked with the same twisted smile.

"I'm looking for Henri," Hearne said briefly.

"He's at the hotel. He's had a busy day." There was only the inflection of a Breton accent in the man's speech, but the voice held the same mocking quality as the smile. Hearne said nothing. He turned into the market place. On his left

was the long, low hotel. And in front of it were two large
cars. He saw the Nazi flags, the soldiers on guard, and halted
involuntarily.

"We have guests," smiled Kerénor, watching Hearne
from the corner of his eyes. "Not so very many, but seemingly important." His arm swept to the large black-letter notices
pasted along the blankness of the hotel wall.

"Henri?" asked Hearne. Kerénor had said Henri was in
the hotel. And it was obvious that the hotel was the chosen
headquarters for the visiting Germans.

"He's all right. He's in the bar."

There were other people in the market place. Some
grouped under the trees and talked. Others walked slowly,
their heads bent. All looked subdued and anxious. The fact
that other men were on the street decided Hearne. He was
one of them—just another beaten Frenchman.

He started towards the hotel. Kerénor limped along
beside him. At first, Hearne wondered; for Kerénor had obviously never liked Bertrand Corlay. And then he remembered.
Kerénor lived here, lodging in the hotel which the other "foreigner," Madame Perro, owned.

The Nazis standing so proudly on guard didn't even seem
to glance at them. There were so few of them, Hearne
thought; so few, and yet so sure of their own safety. And
why not, if you knew planes were only fifteen minutes' flying
time away, planes which could level this village to a pile of
rubble in even less time than that; why not, if you knew that
the people in this village knew it too? Blackmail with planes
. . . only the Germans had thought of that and planned
accordingly. Here was a community of perhaps some four
hundred people in all, and it was occupied and controlled by
a handful of self-assured men. Four hundred would do what
twenty, or less, would tell them.

Kerénor followed him into the bar. As he limped, he put
his hand on his right thigh as if by leaning on it he could
keep up with Hearne's stride.

"Elise will be delighted," he said suddenly.

"Elise?" Hearne stared at the bitter smile. He was strangely uncomfortable at the naked look in the other man's eyes.

"Elise." Kerénor lingered over the name. He was hurting
himself purposely, thought Hearne. His eyes showed it: they
didn't smile, but the twist on his lips seemed to have frozen
there. "Yes, Elise. She's back too." And then he was gone.

Who the devil was Elise, Hearne was wondering. Better

get Henri. Better get out of this place before any other
riddles were put to him. He looked round the room with its
small stone-topped tables. In the large alcove at the curtained
window there was a group of men. Old men. They sat staring
at the glasses before them. Henri, his chin sunk in his gnarled
fists, was motionless. No one talked. No one moved, as
Hearne went over to the table.

He's drunk, solidly drunk, Hearne thought. He said quietly,
"Henri. Come."

Henri raised his eyes slowly, and looked at Hearne from
under his lowered brows.

"Ni zo Bretoned, tud kaled," he said.

"Yes," Hearne answered, remembering the little of Breton
which he had once known. "Yes. But Albertine wants you."

The old man rose slowly and left the table. None of the
others spoke. Henri didn't look at them; he was walking with
a visible effort towards the door, unnaturally erect, looking
neither to right nor to left. Hearne followed. At least, he
was congratulating himself, the old chap looked as if he
could make it under his own steam. One thing he must
remember about these Bretons: they were powerful drinkers.
In one way, it was funny to think how worried he had been
all this afternoon when Henri was missing, and all the time
Henri had been just drowning his sorrows. It was so funny
that Hearne didn't even feel angry. It was funny, and pathetic. *Ni zo Bretoned,* Henri had quoted: *We are the Bretons, a
hard race. . . .* There they were, not one of them under
seventy, just sitting and drinking and thinking of the national
songs, as if to cling onto some pride, as if to keep themselves
from drowning in a sea of Celtic despair. Hearne looked
back at the group of men. They hadn't moved. Henri had
already passed through the doorway with its tightly gathered
yellow curtains. He was literally walking straight home.

And then, as Hearne reached the yellow curtains, the door
behind him, which led from the bar into the restaurant of the
hotel, swung open. He turned at the grating noise of the
hinges. He could see a tablecloth in the background, and an
officer's cap lying on its whiteness. But his eyes came back to
the girl standing in the open doorway.

"God!" he said to himself.

And then she came forward. Only a girl with the face of
an angel could move like that. He suddenly realized that the
lips were parted in a breathless smile, that the large eyes were
fixed on his.

"Bertrand!" And then she had caught both his hands in hers. Cool hands, soft hands.

"Bertrand." The dark eyelashes flickered. She shook her head slowly, unbelievingly. "I've just come back. No one told me you were back until Kerénor came two minutes ago. . . ." Hearne felt the blood high in his face.

"Most touching," said Kerénor. He was standing at the counter of the bar, watching them with that same look in his eyes which had embarrassed Hearne before. Elise turned her face towards Kerénor.

"Go away, Jean," she said, but the laugh in her voice took the sting out of the words; the long look from her eyes softened the frown. Hearne watched her profile incredulously.

Kerénor bowed, and wheeling abruptly on his heel, he limped out of the door. Masochist, thought Hearne, and then as the girl in the clinging flowered dress turned her face once more towards him, he forgot Kerénor.

"You look as if you could scarcely believe your eyes," she teased in her low voice.

"I—I didn't know—"

"Of course not. I was in Paris after Strasbourg was evacuated. Now it is more—well, suitable"—her eyes emphasized the word—"that I should come back here."

Hearne stood without speaking. Who on earth was this girl? Corlay had told him of Anne, of Albertine, of his mother; of everything, it now seemed, except a goddess with green eyes and a warm smile, with smooth white skin and sculptured bones.

She interpreted his silence in her own way. "You were worried about me? And I was for you. I thought you were either dead or taken by the English and I wouldn't see you perhaps ever again. But now we needn't worry any more. I may be here for a month, two months." She paused. "When can we meet? Tonight? The usual place?"

Hearne was taken aback. He hesitated.

"What's wrong?" the girl asked.

"Would it be safe?" he hedged.

"Why not?" The large eyes were still larger. "I've so much to tell you. I must see you." It was a command.

"Of course," Hearne said. "Of course."

"Is that all you can say?" There was a frown shadowing the smooth brow.

"You are so beautiful."

She laughed, as if to herself. "That is better. . . . So you still love me?"

"Yes, I love you."

"More than ever?"

Then the grating of the restaurant door interrupted them. A large woman, tightly encased in black silk, her hair flagrantly dyed and tortured into rigid waves, had entered the barroom.

"Elise," she said, and motioned with her head towards the restaurant.

"Yes, Aunt Marie. Coming."

"Be quick then." The large woman nodded again. She looked at Hearne and pursed her lips; and then the door screeched once more.

Hearne stiffened. "Who are your friends in there?"

"Bertrand!" The girl was delighted. "I've told you before you mustn't be jealous. Business is merely business." She looked contemptuously round the empty room, at the desolate tables, at the small group of men sitting so silently in the window alcove. "We have still a lot of work to do," she added. "You will be needed more than ever. I'll tell you when I see you. Tonight . . . " She hesitated and glanced towards the restaurant door. "Well, perhaps tomorrow night would be better. Tomorrow night at ten o'clock?"

"Yes," said Hearne. There was nothing else he could say. "Tomorrow night at ten. At the—?"

"Yes, at the usual place." She gave him a last long look, a warm smile, a pressure of her cool slender hand. The protesting door was held open long enough for a glance over her shoulder and a last smile; for his eyes to see the tables beyond, empty except for one where three uniformed men had risen to their feet.

Hearne took a deep breath. He needed it.

He had left the Hotel Perro and the market place behind him before his thoughts began to take shape. He felt like a man who had been caught in a strong river current and had managed, somehow, to pull himself out onto the bank. He passed some men, but he kept his eyes fixed moodily on the road. Someone said in a strong Breton voice, "It's Corlay." But Hearne only raised a hand in greeting, and kept his eyes lowered. He had had just about enough for one night; just about. And then he remembered that tonight he'd have to try a first journey. He'd have to test that front door. Sometime before supper, he'd have to examine that lock, perhaps grease it. Sometime when Albertine was feeding the hens or even looking after the cows, for Henri wouldn't be much use this evening.

He quickened his pace. The fields were empty, the woods were silent. In the autumn, when the late evening sun rested on the rich brown leaves, the trees would match that girl's hair. But he wouldn't be here to see. By the beginning of September, his job would—must be finished. No, he wouldn't be here to see. "All right, then," he said to himself savagely. "You won't be here in September. You'll be lucky if you are anywhere in September."

In the farmhouse kitchen, he found Henri sitting at the smaller table, his elbows on the hard wood, his eyes firmly closed. There was the sound of a piano.

Albertine's face was like a thundercloud. "He came in without a word and sat down and went to sleep," she said. "Not a word out of his head, not a word. And after me worrying myself to death over him, and all the work left undone." She stopped abruptly. "What's wrong?" she asked, her voice unexpectedly softening.

"Nothing. Not many Germans so far. Just some flags and some large notices plastered on the walls. Where's the American?"

Albertine smiled and pointed to the ceiling above her head. Hearne listened more intently. It wasn't well played, and it was softly played, but there was no doubt about the tune. It was "I Can't Give You Anything But Love, Baby."

CHAPTER 9

Pages from the Life of Bertrand Corlay

When Hearne awoke next morning, his legs stiff, his arm cramped in the deepness of sleep into which his exhaustion had plunged him, he noticed first his muddied boots lying drunkenly on the floor, then his clothes abandoned in a heap beside them, and last of all the half-open door leading to the storeroom. A chair scraped; something moved. Hearne, suddenly very much awake, pulled on the nightshirt lying at the bottom of the bed and crossed quickly to the door.

It was the American, sitting on an uncomfortable chair in front of the open window. On his crossed legs, he balanced a book and some sheets of paper. He saluted Hearne with his pencil.

"Sorry if I woke you," he said. "But I had to get up to stretch my legs."

"Very difficult," Hearne answered, looking at the mass of objects which were hoarded in the room. "This place looks like a furniture shop. We never throw anything away."

"Some people would pay a lot of money for much of this stuff."

"But they seldom do."

The American grinned. "I guess not. We are all bargain-hunters."

"How is your writing getting on?"

"Not so hot. But I am getting the stuff onto paper: that's the main thing."

"It must be very interesting."

"It'll sell, anyway."

"Won't it be dangerous to take notes along with you?"

"I'll abandon them if need be. Meanwhile I get everything in order, and I'll remember the facts better when I see them written down. That's the way my memory works."

"Are you comfortable? Did you sleep well?" Hearne was being the polite host.

Myles laughed. "After three weeks of straw, if I was lucky?"

Hearne smiled wholeheartedly. Then Myles wouldn't have heard him last night. Not that he had made much noise: the door had worked smoothly enough after proper coaxing. He had left the house at ten when everyone seemed asleep, and he had returned before dawn. Myles hadn't made any joke, either, about the clothes on the bedroom floor. Perhaps the curtained window had blocked enough light so that the American had only noticed a crumpled heap instead of mud. And dampness couldn't be seen; it wasn't likely that anyone moving quickly through another man's bedroom was going to stop to touch things. Hearne waited for a stray allusion; if Myles had noticed anything, now would be the time for one of his cracks. But Myles was smiling placidly, trying without success to ignore Hearne's nightshirt. *Chapter nineteen,* thought Hearne: *The Bretons at Home*. He looked down at his knees, wondering how they'd appear in print.

"I'd better get dressed. I seem to have slept very late," Hearne said.

"It's almost ten o'clock. I suppose that's almost the day over in this country."

"Almost. I've been ill, so Albertine lets me sleep half the day. Now I've got some work to do. I write, too."

"What's your line?" The American was interested.

"Oh, only small things." Hearne was charmingly modest.

"I'd like to see some of them."

"Thank you. We must compare our different styles." Hearne smiled and nodded towards the pages of notes on the American's knee. "Now, if you will excuse me ... " He bowed as gallantly as he could in the short shirt.

"Of course." Myles was being equally gallant. He saluted again with the pencil. He was trying valiantly to hide a private joke. Hearne kept his face straight with difficulty. This was a moment when he would have liked to discard this French-intoned English for his own voice to say, "Go on, old man, have your laugh. It's on me." He bowed again.

"Hope I'm not disturbing you," Myles called after him. "This was Albertine's idea. She wouldn't have me downstairs in case anyone looked through a window. Which reminds me—did you see many Germans yesterday?"

Hearne came back to the door. He had pulled on his crumpled trousers and the harsh wool sweater. "Not many, so far," he said. "There were some officers in the hotel, and a handful of soldiers. But not enough to patrol the farms. Not yet, anyway. I think you'll be safe."

"As long as I keep away from the main road and that railway. That's how I found myself on your farm. Two nights ago I was down in the valley. It wasn't so healthy, so I came up onto the hillside."

"I wonder what the Boches want down there?"

"It's a main line from Northeastern France to the coast. I'm telling you I saw enough stuff being rolled over these tracks to set up whole airfields."

"But couldn't they fly planes? Why do they send them by train?"

The American was very patient. He was, decided Hearne, a decent sort of chap. And he liked to explain. "You fly planes, certainly. But then there are the spare parts, and the oil, and a hundred other things to fix up an airport."

"But we had some aerodromes near here, I think."

"If they weren't destroyed completely, they are only being fixed for decoys. The Germans are building others. And this part of the country is good. It can't be shelled from the English coast, but it'll make a good springboard against Southampton and Plymouth. These airports are springing up everywhere. I'm telling you I saw them with my two eyes. I could name ten places I've come through, all of them with new camouflaged airfields. They are so well hidden—netting and leaves over the planes, lying well-spread-out beside clumps of innocent trees, with little runways to hayfields which are the real taking-off point—that I almost got caught at one of them. I had been coming through a thicket of trees, and there was a path ahead. At one end of the path was a plane all in fancy dress; at the other end, there was a hayfield. I had been avoiding a big hangar and a fine airfield about three miles away to my left. It must have been a dummy. I guess the idea is that the British will probably find out there's an air base beside village X. They will come over and bomb X, and will naturally aim for the flying field. The Germans at point X, but just a mile or two from danger, will smile and rub their hands and go on bombing Britain."

"It would be very important then for the British to find out—" Hearne halted and shrugged his shoulders. "But it would be too difficult."

"It would be important. And not too difficult. I, myself, could tell them of several places which would interest them. And I'm willing to bet the British have ways of their own for finding out."

Hearne shrugged his shoulders again. "It seems so hopeless," he said.

The American smiled. "The British don't know what that word means. They can drive an American nuts with their slowness and self-complacency. But they never think anything's hopeless."

There was a pause.

"How are the feet?" Hearne asked politely.

Myles looked at them in their white linen wrappings. "Doing nicely, I think. This was Albertine's idea, too. She covered them with some kind of paste which her grandmother used. It certainly looked moldy enough, but it's working miracles. They don't even hurt now when I stand on them."

"Good," Hearne said, and turned towards his room. "I must work now, if you'll excuse me." He bowed gravely. The

American saluted again with the pencil; his eyes weren't at all grave.

It didn't take Hearne very long to jot down in his private shorthand all the particulars he had noted last night. He considered that journey merely as a kind of introduction to the countryside round the railway. Tomorrow, he would explore westwards and watch the roadway from Rennes to St. Malo on the coast. Once he got accustomed to short cuts and patches of good cover, he would travel more quickly. But even judging from what he had seen tonight, his job might be quite useful. That idea cheered him; he wrote quickly and continuously. When the time came to get a report sent out from Mont St. Michel he could choose the most urgent of these points. Meanwhile, like the American, he was noting everything down.

Myles's remarks had only confirmed his own observations. There was some terrific construction work going on up there to the north of St. Déodat. He remembered that the railway ran through the old town of Dol before it swerved northwest to the coast. And northwards above Dol, the land was a flat plain, miles and miles of plain, most of which had been reclaimed from the sea. The more he thought of Dol, the more interesting he found it. First, there was the railway direct from the east to Dol. Secondly, Dol was connected to Dinan by a good road, and Dinan was at the end of the canal from Rennes. Thirdly, there was a main highway from the east which ended at St. Malo on the coast, and that highway cut across the road from Dinan to Dol. So Dol could be served three ways if the traffic were heavy towards that town. And Dol, lying back from the seacoast, commanded a long stretch of plain. Yes, this job he had to do might be quite useful.

He finished his last entry, and looked round the room for some place to keep these notes safely. The empty bookshelves yawned at him from the corner. "Stop gaping at me," he told them. "I'll soon have you filled up." His words gave him the idea: the safest place for his sheet of paper, and the sheets which would be added, was the inside of a book. He looked at the rest of the furniture: this table on which he had written, with its one unlocked drawer kept obviously for writing material; the chest beside the bed; the wardrobe; the concealed washbasin affair. None of these was practicable: Albertine had access to everything. The only thing which

wouldn't interest her would be the contents of the bookcase.
He rose and walked over to the bed, pulling the cover aside.
He felt the mattresses: straw, feather, wool, in that order.
No, he decided: they'd only ooze if he slit them, and their
depths could lose anything they were hiding. It would have to
be the bookcase.

Unlike the rest of the furniture, it was a rough, amateur
piece of work. Whoever had made it had been impatient. The
shelves hadn't been sandpapered sufficiently before the first
undercoat of stain, and the varnish had been scantily applied.
The top and sides had been finished well enough; viewed that
way, it wasn't a bad job at all. But the man who had made it
hadn't bothered about the rest of it. He had probably thought
it didn't matter because the books themselves would hide his
unfinished work. At the moment, standing empty as it was,
the bookcase looked as hideous as a child with ringworm.

By dinnertime, the task of sorting the books was only
half-done. Albertine, bringing some food to the American in
the storeroom, halted in amazement at the litter surrounding
Hearne on the floor. He followed her obediently downstairs,
and ate his meal in silence. His thoughts would have increased Albertine's amazement. After some attempts to talk
about the potatoes which he had bruised yesterday in his
digging, she was left to concentrate on the fire and the soup
pot. "Back to your old ways," she had said sourly, and the
remark only added to Hearne's thoughtfulness. He finished
the food hastily, hardly concealing his impatience to be back
in his room. As he mounted the stairs, he found his excitement
growing. Albertine was calling after him something about
pictures on his wall. He paused on the top step to shout down
"Later! Later!" and then he was once more among the piles
of books.

But he wasn't alone. The American had hobbled to the
connecting door as he heard him return.

"Hello," he said in a mixture of surprise and pleasure as he
looked at the books on the floor. "Can I help?"

"No. It's all right. It will be bad for your feet; you must
rest."

"As you like," Myles said stiffly. "Thought I could lend a
hand, that's all."

Hearne relented. He lifted the small pile of fairly recent
novels which he had discarded as being of no interest to him,
and carried them into the storeroom. "Here's something to
read," he said. "You shouldn't try to walk about so much."

"To be perfectly frank, that was all I wanted ... just something to read. Thanks." He looked at the novels. "If," he added, "if my French will take me that far."

"It will be good for you to read French. You've still a journey to make."

"Yes, I wanted to ask you about that."

Hearne looked at his watch. "I'll be finished in one hour, or perhaps two hours at the most. I shall come and talk with you then. O.K.?"

Myles laughed unexpectedly. "O.K.," he echoed, and laughed again.

Hearne closed the connecting door firmly behind him. "Now," he said to himself with considerable satisfaction, and sat cross-legged on the floor.

The books were indeed a strange collection. As he had pulled them out of the wardrobe that morning, Hearne had noticed two things. One part of this small library was formed of old books, badly printed in eye-straining type. Their bindings ripped at a touch, the paper was yellowing not so much with age as with cheapness. But the other part, and by far the greater part, had been bought within the last two years. Handsome volumes they were, with binding and paper and type to shame the older books. The first thought that struck Hearne was that Corlay must have been making money then with his teaching. The older books, obviously second- or third-hand, were a monument to the days when Madame Corlay had pinched and scraped to let her son stay at the University. Then, when he had a job, he had begun to buy himself some new books. It was just after this solution that Hearne saw the signature on each flyleaf, together with the date when Corlay had added each book to his bookshelves. The solution crumbled away. Hearne examined all the new books methodically; his mind was a strange mixture of excitement, dawning suspicion and dismay.

The earliest date on any of these newer books was January 20th, 1938. By that time, Corlay had been out of his temporary teaching job for over six months. For six months he had been living on the farm, dependent on Albertine's work for his food, on his mother's generosity for his pocket money. Hearne had seen enough of the life on this farm to know that there was little pocket money for anyone. Madame Corlay's dress had been of the ageless variety, of a cut and color which a careful woman would wear for years. Her one piece of jewelry, the gold chain and brooch, had obviously

been inherited like the house and furniture. The piano was a
relic of the hard years in Rennes. There was no wireless set,
the usual consolation for an invalid.

Hearne rose on impulse, and went over to the wardrobe
again. He counted the jackets and suits thoughtfully: more
than he would expect for a man in Corlay's position. He
fingered the materials; they felt as new as they looked. Cheap
clothes, imitation smart clothes, none of them any older than
two years. Hearne was thinking, I don't like this at all.
Perhaps Corlay had saved enough money, somehow; perhaps there had been a legacy; perhaps he had won a lottery.
Perhaps any of these. Perhaps. Hearne shook his head slowly, and walked back to the books.

The second thing which had startled Hearne that morning
was that Corlay had rarely finished reading a book. Or else
the man was a genius and could read through uncut pages. In
the whole collection, there were only about ten books with
the pages entirely cut. The rest had pages cut for the first
chapters, and occasionally some pages cut at the end. But not
one of these books had been read right through.

Hearne found himself looking at the bookcase. I bet he
made that, he thought; made it, and then lost interest in it
before he had it properly finished. The wood was sound, and
the design was an attempt at a piece of modern furniture.
Corlay must have seen some pictures of Swedish modern.
That was what he had copied. Grand ideas he liked. Grand
ideas ... The phrase haunted Hearne. He shook himself free
of speculation and went back once more to the books. The
beginning of the riddle would be solved with them, he felt.

He would begin with the earliest volumes, and here Corlay's passion for inscribing his name and the date would
prove invaluable. Hearne laid the books in rough groupings,
according to the dates on their flyleaves. Each heap of books
on the floor represented a year of Corlay's intellectual life.

The first book belonged to 1928: a school prize for ancient
history. Next came 1930: a school prize for medieval history, and three textbooks on French history, with the sections
on Brittany closely underlined and annotated. By 1932, Corlay was at the University of Rennes; and for the next four
years, the books were texts on either French literature or
history, or potted biographies of famous Bretons such as
Jacques Cartier, Surcouf, Mahé de La Bourdonnais, or
abridged cheap editions of Chateaubriand, Lamennais, Briz-

eux, Renan, Villiers de l'Isle Adam, Abélard. And these were all Bretons, too, reflected Hearne.

It was just at this point that Albertine had appeared with food for the American, and had reminded him sharply that dinner had been ready for half an hour. If only, he had thought, as he followed Albertine downstairs, if only people would stop being well-meaning, if only they'd leave him alone.

But now, at last, both Albertine and the American had been settled.

"Now," he said to the books with considerable satisfaction. "Now ... "

CHAPTER 10

Poems for E.

Hearne adjusted himself comfortably on crossed legs, and reached for the 1937 pile of books. There were magazines, too, in this lot, but the subject was uniform. It was politics.

Corlay had definitely been interested in Breton nationalism. That was hardly surprising after his earlier choice in history and literature. But he had also now branched into Royalist ideas. Perhaps he had thought that Brittany's cause could be best served by a restoration of a King in France. And then, in the summer of 1937, he had ended his subscriptions to Royalist publications as if he had had a sudden revulsion. After that summer, there were no books or magazines on the Royalist side. In fact, from the summer of 1937 until January 20th, 1938, there were no books bought at all. That was when he was unemployed. Then, in January of 1938, began the new series of books—first editions, modern, well-bound, well-printed. But, Hearne reminded himself, Corlay was then still unemployed. He sat and looked at these recent additions to the library, the witnesses of Corlay's unexpected prosperity. As a last excuse, he thought that a friend might have sent them to Corlay. A friend ... but a peculiar kind of friend. For these books dealt with the decadence of democracy, the future for men of action, the new order in economy and politics.

"Well," said Hearne, "well, now."

He felt he could do with a cigarette, or a drink. He rose and went to the window. The air was heavy with the smell of the fruit trees after rain. But at least it was clean. He looked at the pile of Fascist literature on the floor: at least the air was clean.

There still remained one heap of books to be examined. They looked like copybooks. Hearne picked them up one by one, glancing quickly but methodically through their pages. Corlay's writing was flamboyant, but in spite of the excesses of sweeps and curls the pen-marked pages were easy to read. Most of the notebooks belonged to his university days. At first, he had been a prolific note taker and underliner, but the lecture notes tailed off as his classes progressed. By the end of a year, they were short and uninterested, and the margins were filled with the variations of the Bertrand Corlay signature.

But two notebooks really attracted Hearne. The first was a desultory diary, or, rather, a series of condensed complaints. Corlay had been an unhappy young man: little, if anything, had pleased him. He hadn't liked his schoolteaching job—the pupils were uniformly stupid, his fellow teachers were nincompoops. But when he lost that job, then his scorn switched to the unfairness of a government which preferred a Paris to a Rennes degree. There was a hint of "victimization," of persecution for his nationalist beliefs. And yet, when he came back to live on this Breton farm, it was strange that he seemed still unhappier. This time he railed at the stupidities of the Breton peasant, the banalities of country life with its mixture of coarseness and superstition. Occasionally there would be a page concentrated on the Corlay family. He went to some length to identify his ancestors: all of them seemed either very noble or very brave or very artistic, or all three. His last entry, dated January 7th, 1938, stated flatly: "It is intolerable that we should have been forced to live like animals. Once our name was famous, but now we must be content to eat and sleep our way to death. I will not be content." That was the end of the diary.

It was nice that he could eat, anyway, Hearne thought grimly. That was more than some families were able to do.

He carried the second notebook over to the window. He

felt he needed some more fresh air to help him finish this job. So Corlay would not be content. . . .

The second book contained Corlay's own writings. They amounted to exactly eleven pages—the sum total of his work from August 1937, when he had come to live on his mother's farm, until January 1938. January 1938. The date haunted Hearne. Something pretty powerful had struck Corlay's life in that month. January 1938. Hearne roused himself to look at the eleven pages of poems and epigrams. It was just as he feared: Corlay would probably have made a good farmer. His curse was his desire to live in the Ritz, to be a Breton without living in Brittany, to be the best poet explorer cinema-star orator artist statesman tennis-champion scientist of his time. He was mentally aged fourteen, except that that slandered most fourteen-year-olds.

The joke is on me, Hearne thought savagely, and went back to the books. Corlay's possibilities were more than either he or Matthews had bargained for. He began to jam the books into the bookcase. Automatically he chose the heaviest volumes for the two lowest shelves, but the books he had tried to thrust into the second bottom shelf wouldn't fit. They overlapped the edge by two inches. Hearne struck at them impatiently with his fist. *The Myth of the Twentieth Century . . . The Myth of the . . .* "Damn you all to hell," he said, and gave a blow with the side of his wrist to their bold titles. His wrist hurt, but the books didn't move. They couldn't, for the shelf was not wide enough for their breadth: the shelf could only hold the smaller octave-size books. Whoever heard of anyone making a bookcase with the small books on the second bottom shelf? And Corlay had taken some trouble about that. The back of that second bottom shelf had been blocked in to hold the smaller volumes securely. Blocked in . . . Hearne's fingers lightly tapped the back of the shelf. It was of lighter wood, possibly a thin plywood. Between it and the real back of solid wood there must be a space. But how to get into that space was another question. Corlay must have been a cleverer carpenter than Hearne had imagined.

But he needn't have credited Corlay with too much skill. As he pushed and shoved and pressed the false back with the palm of his hand, it suddenly slid along grooves in the two shelves which it had separated. The end of the plywood panel came out of the side of the bookcase and stuck there incongruously, quivering with the force of Hearne's effort. It was as easy as that. He pushed the panel back into position, and looked at the side of the bookcase. Simple, but neat enough, he decided. An imitation join going up the whole length of the bookcase, like the stripe on a Guardsman's trouser leg, had disguised Corlay's subterfuge.

"Cunning chap I'm supposed to be," Hearne said. Cunning: still another aspect of the simple Corlay, the misunderstood genius. Hearne grinned. "I really begin to think I'm a bit of a stinker," he added. He pushed the panel sideways once more, slowly, carefully this time, so that the plywood board wouldn't crack up. This secret compartment might have its uses. It had, as he found out when the panel was slipped aside to its full length. There, in front of his hand, lay two notebooks and some sheets of paper fastened together with an elastic band. As he removed his discovery, he replaced his own notes in the neat recess. And before he closed the false shelfback once more, he retrieved his revolver and map from the unlocked table drawer. They would be safer inside that bookcase, if any stray Germans had the inspiration to search for weapons. Then he stacked about twenty of the narrower volumes along that shelf. They would be a safeguard if the American got tired of vicarious passion in high places, and abandoned the overcomplicated emotions of the novels for a walk, perhaps a talk, in this room. Hearne filled the other shelves, too, for good measure. The room looked neat once more; that should keep Albertine happy.

He carried the treasure-trove over to the table. Now he might find something really solid. He might as well admit his excitement.

First, he examined the papers. Two sheets were joined together with a rusted clip: one, a map of Northern Brittany with neat, red-ink numbers over certain villages and towns; the other, a typed list of names and street addresses, with red-ink numbers in the margin opposite each name. He would study this combination later; perhaps, and this was the likeliest guess, these were the names and districts of trusted Breton nationalists. Strange that Corlay should have taken so much trouble to hide them, for Breton nationalists hadn't been proscribed, even if they weren't exactly loved, by the French government. Perhaps Corlay had been hiding the list from his mother: she certainly didn't agree with any separatist ideas. She believed that the Bretons were the flower of the French Republic, and flowers wither when they are cut from their stalks.

Next came three sheets of paper, this time pinned together, listing dates and names of cafés. The dates ranged on a monthly average from January 1938, until the end of August 1939. These sheets were all typewritten, too, which meant that this stuff had been given to Corlay, for Corlay had no typewriter. Meeting places and meeting times: that was the best guess Hearne could make, but the information on these sheets would need more careful examination when he was less pressed for time. He slipped the rubber band round the papers, and placed them between the double sheet of worn blotting paper which lay inside the table drawer. He closed the drawer thoughtfully, and abstractedly picked up the two notebooks.

They were of a nobler brand than the copybooks which he had found in the wardrobe along with the books. They even had mock-leather covers. He had the sudden premonition that they belonged to Corlay's period of unexpected prosperity. When he opened them, he saw he was right. One was a diary; its first entry was under the heading January 18th, 1938. The other contained Corlay's poems, each neatly dated at the foot of its page. The first of these poems had been written on January 25th, 1938.

January 1938 . . . January 1938 . . .

"Well," said Hearne, "what a peculiar thing." His sarcasm left a smile on his lips until he began to read the poems. They were highly emotional, increasingly passionate, but obviously sincere. Poor devil, he thought, she twisted him around all right, whoever she was. And then he came to twenty lines of verse written in October. They described Corlay's love with great detail. I don't know about the hips and breasts, but there's no mistaking the eyes and hair, Hearne thought. He re-read the description of the hair—autumn leaves caught in the warmth of the late evening sun. He remembered his walk yesterday, on his way home from the village. "Damn," he said aloud, "damn it all." He was suddenly annoyed, almost angry. And then he laughed. "Fool!" he said to himself. Matthews, no doubt, would have put it more strongly. It only proved, anyway, that Corlay wasn't a good poet.

Towards the end of the poems—there were fourteen in all—it was obvious that Corlay had achieved quite a lot. The last effusions were almost hysterical with joy. It embarrassed Hearne to read them. "All right," he said irritably, "I get the idea. All right." And then one line held his attention. *In the shadows of the dovecote, fortress of our love and of our*

secrets . . . Dovecote. Could that be the place which Elise
had meant when she had asked him to meet her? If so,
then he hadn't the excuse that he didn't know what she was
talking about. And he had been hanging onto that excuse. It
had been going to preserve his detachment tonight when ten
o'clock came, and he was securely and respectably in bed.
But now, it was entirely his own choice whether he met Elise
at the dovecote or not. The choice was his own, and he didn't
want to make it. The girl was dangerous; and it wasn't the
belief that she was a Breton nationalist which made her seem
dangerous, either. He wouldn't go, he decided; he'd read that
diary in bed.

And yet, the line of poetry haunted him . . . *fortress of our
love and of our secrets.* . . . What secrets? Secrets of love,
secrets of Breton autonomy, what secrets? He paced the
room, his head bent as if his eyes could read the riddle in the
unevenness of the floor. Business before pleasure was one of
Matthews' original remarks. No, he wouldn't go, he repeated,
and thought of Matthews' cold blue eyes. Business before
pleasure. And then the idea came to him that he was thinking
of Elise solely in terms of pleasure. Could it be possible that
she might be part of his business, too?

It was almost time for supper. He placed the two notebooks inside the table drawer and resumed his restless walking round the room, his hands in his pockets, his eyes still
fixed on the lines of the scrubbed white floor. He was wasting
time, he thought in sudden depression: he should be concentrating on railways and canals and roads. And yet, as long as
he didn't understand Corlay he would feel in danger, and
therefore be in danger. For there was something which worried him about Corlay, something indefinite as yet, something
increased by today's discoveries. He had thought the examination of these books and papers would have settled his
mind. But it hadn't. January 1938, he thought again . . . *of
our love and of our secrets.* Secrets. Probably the word
meant little: just a poet's addition to perfect a meter or
complete a line.

He halted at the window. He could always read some of
the diary before ten o'clock. Then, he could decide whether
he was imagining possibilities, or whether he was just trying
to find any old excuse to see her again. He turned from the
window as he heard Myles's footsteps crossing the storeroom.
It would depend on the diary, then, he determined, and faced
the opening door.

"Pardon me. Am I disturbing you? I thought I heard voices, and that you had finished your work."

"Voices? Oh, that was me. I've a bad habit of talking aloud."

"You do?" The American looked both amused and relieved. "I knew a man from Texas once, who used to talk to himself. He used to be alone out on the range for long stretches at a time. That's how he started the habit."

Hearne said quickly, "How's the reading?"

"Not too good. I slept some of the time, I must say. My French can't be as good as my French friends pretended. By the way, do you understand everything I say?"

"Enough."

"You speak quite good English. Your accent is your own, but you have the grammar all right."

Hearne tried to smile calmly. "Oh, I had plenty of grammar at school. I even took a degree in English at Rennes University."

Myles looked as if he believed that. There was no reason why he shouldn't.

"And I had some English friends at the University," Hearne went on glibly. "One in particular used to talk a lot to me in English. That was after I got to know him of course."

"Of course." There was a reminiscent look in Myles's eyes. "Last summer—" But Albertine entered, and the story of last summer ended before it was begun.

"Food!" said the American, and this time the look in his eyes was much more understandable. Albertine was actually smiling. Her nod was approving as she looked round the room and saw the neatly arranged books.

And then downstairs, someone knocked.

"The front door," said Albertine needlessly. The three of them looked at each other. "It must be Monsieur le Curé; he always uses the front door."

Again there was that knocking. "Very powerful man, Monsieur le Curé," Hearne observed, and saw a sudden fear on Albertine's face.

"It doesn't sound like him," she said slowly, her cheeks paling.

Hearne took command. "Go downstairs slowly, call you are coming, and don't be afraid. Give me that food." To Myles he said, "Into bed with you."

As he opened Madame Corlay's door, he saw Albertine

was indeed going slowly. He planked the food down on the
table beside Madame Corlay, covering the eyeglasses heavily
with the bowl of soup. There was a snap as the bowl tilted
over its victim.

Madame Corlay's amazement at their sudden entry gave
way to partial understanding as Hearne put his finger to his
lips, pointed downstairs, and sat down in a chair at some
distance. She tightened her lips as she heard Albertine's
voice, and then a man's voice, firm and assured. He was
speaking careful French, loudly, coldly, with that unmistakable authority. The white draperies were pulled roughly back
into place, swayed, and then hung rigid in their heavy folds.
Madame Corlay looked as if she were about to explode.

"The Boches," she said.

"Gently, gently," warned Hearne. He was listening to the
footsteps on the stairs.

Albertine had come up with more speed than she had gone
down. "They've come. To see if we have room. For soldiers."

"I'll see them," said Hearne, and rose quickly.

But there was no need. A German officer stood in the
doorway. Behind him was a soldier.

CHAPTER 11

Visit of Inspection

"You are the owner of this property?"

The German's voice was as coldly assured as his face.
Under the exaggerated peak of his cap, the straight features
pointed expressionlessly towards Hearne. His eyes and skin
and hair were colorless: it was as if the uniform blotted them
out. All you noticed was the regularity of the outlines of his
face, the assertive confidence of his body.

Hearne shook his head wearily, and gestured towards
Madame Corlay.

"You are the owner of this property?"

Madame Corlay, her eyes still dilated from the effect of the German's salute, nodded abruptly.

"How many rooms do you have in this house?"

There was a silence.

"Six," Albertine said.

"How many rooms?" the German repeated, his eyes fixed on Madame Corlay. She sat quite still, her hands clasped tightly on her stick. Her knuckles were white.

"How many?"

"My servant has told you." Madame Corlay's voice had tightened, but it was still under control. Hearne watched her not without admiration.

"Is this the only servant?" The German pointed towards Albertine.

"There is Henri, who works on the farm."

"And this man?" The German indicated Hearne, slouching on his chair.

"My—" there was the slightest hesitation, perhaps a catch in Madame Corlay's breath—"son." Her eyes met Hearne's. He had stiffened involuntarily. She smiled gently, and he relaxed. She knew, he was thinking, she knew; or did she? If she had known, what had prevented her from saying "A man who pretends to be my son"?

The officer crossed over to the fireplace, and examined the view from the windows on that side of the room. "Quite good," he said, as if to himself. Then he walked quickly over to the window which overlooked the farmyard, passing the bed with the white draperies gathered round it so innocently. Madame Corlay, Albertine, Hearne, were as motionless as the soldier at the door. The officer opened the window, and they could hear German voices in the yard. The voices suddenly were silenced, as the men saw the captain at the window. He beckoned once, sharply, silently, and turned back into the room. Behind him, the breeze from the opened window fluttered the white curtains and the draperies on the bed.

Albertine hastened to close the window. "Madame is ill," she said reprovingly. "She will catch pneumonia."

But the German wasn't listening to her. He was standing impatiently at one of the tables, his fingers tracing the carving round its edge, his eyes on the doorway where the soldier still held his pose. They heard quiet, quick footsteps on the stairs, and then a little man slipped into the room. A thin little man with spectacles and opened notebook and poised pencil. Apart from the uniform weighing so incongruously upon him, there was little about him which seemed military. An auctioneer's clerk, thought Hearne; that was what he was, an auctioneer's clerk dressed up as an officer.

"Captain Deichgräber?" His voice was as quick and light as his step.

The tall officer left the table. He spoke rapidly in German. "This isn't bad. It is the best I've seen. It will have to do. The colonel will be furious, but you will have to explain to him that the only castle is in ruins, that this is the best house we can find near the village. You can make it comfortable for him. Have a look at the other rooms on this floor."

"Very good, Captain Deichgräber." The quick footsteps pattered into Hearne's room. When he at last came back, the notebook was closed. The reedy voice went on, "Two other rooms, Captain Deichgräber. Four officers could sleep there once we cleared all the rubbish out."

"Good."

"Then, Captain Deichgräber, there's the hall downstairs for a dining room, and also downstairs there is accommodation for four soldiers."

"Good." The officer called Deichgräber felt in his pocket for a cigarette case. "You can tell them of the arrangements," he added, and motioned with his cigarette to the owner of the house as he sauntered to the door.

"You will be requested to leave here by tomorrow. These rooms are urgently required." The little man's French was excellent.

"Tomorrow?" Hearne spoke for the women. Albertine looked as if she had turned into a pillar of salt. Madame Corlay's nostrils showed a strange rim of white, as if they had been molded from wax.

"I said tomorrow. No doubt you will be able to stay with friends until you come back here. It will only be a matter of weeks, September at latest, before you return. You will be recompensed for any damage, of course. And one more thing; leave such things as these"—he swept his arm towards the china and crystal displayed on the dresser—"and your linen and blankets. We can make the decision what we need of them. You will be adequately recompensed for any damage, you may be sure. I shall be back here tomorrow morning before you leave." The tone was so polite, so correct, so insufferable.

I'd like to kick those shiny teeth down your scrawny throat, thought Hearne. He said, "But my mother is an invalid."

There was a blank stare.

Captain Deichgräber had turned at the door. He hadn't liked Hearne's interruption. "Your mother can stay with friends. If necessary, she may have a permit to travel to a relative." Hearne thought, now isn't that generous of him? But he kept silent. Seemingly Captain Deichgräber hadn't liked Hearn's restraint, either.

"You, yourself, need employment," the German went on. "We don't tolerate unemployment. There will be a job for you."

"I am a farmer," Hearne said quietly. "I don't need a job."

"You will not be needed on this farm for the next few weeks." Both the officers were smiling now, but there was no hint of amiability in these smiles. "All the harvesting necessary can be done very quickly when it is efficiently done. We shall see to that. You will be back in time to dig for next year's crops."

"And this year's?" It was Albertine now. "We live on that: that's all we've got."

"You will be paid for anything we need."

Hearne looked at the two men. Using just what for money? he thought savagely.

Perhaps Deichgräber hadn't liked the look in his eyes. Perhaps Deichgräber didn't like him at all. Anyway, his voice had hardened, his careful accent lost its Frenchness.

"Your name?"

"Bertrand Corlay."

"Tomorrow you report for work at the Hotel Perro in St. Déodat. Tomorrow. You understand?" He turned to his auctioneer's clerk. "Make a note of his name, Traube."

Traube was looking suddenly thoughtful. "Bertrand Corlay," he said slowly. "One moment, please, Captain Deichgräber." He reached into his breast pocket and produced another notebook, a small insignificant one. But what his quick fingers found on the second page did not seem at all insignificant. He glanced sidelong at Hearne, and then back to the book again. "Bertrand Corlay," he said softly. Hearne stood looking at the little man, hoping he didn't seem as alarmed as he felt. What had they against Bertrand Corlay? Perhaps he wouldn't even be given that twenty-four hours' grace until tomorrow, to make his escape. Perhaps, within the next ten minutes he would be marched right into the village, between that deaf-mute soldier and his comrades downstairs.

Deichgräber had noticed the change in Traube's expression. He threw his cigarette on the floor. Together they walked towards the window beside the fireplace and stood there, with their backs to the room. Traube was talking quickly. Deichgräber was holding the small notebook. When they at last turned round to face Hearne, the German's expression was masked, but it was a thin mask hardly covering his anger.

"There has been a mistake. This house will be hardly suitable for us." He looked at Hearne. "Corlay, you have wasted my valuable time. Why did you not tell me your name?"

Hearne reddened. He avoided the look which Madame Corlay was giving him. Even Albertine was watching him curiously. "I'm sorry," he said stiffly. "I gave it to you as soon as you asked me." No, Deichgräber didn't like him, quite decidedly no. I must, thought Hearne, have an unfortunate way of answering him, or perhaps he feels he has lost face.

It was Traube who broke the tension in the room. He moved quickly to the door and waited there for Deichgräber. The two officers were once more correct, even to the precision of their parting salute. But as they reached the bottom of the stairs, Deichgräber's anger broke loose. Traube, it would seem, was trying to restrain him. Hearne tried to catch the words, but the voices were pitched too low. All he could learn from some of the German words which floated upstairs was that Deichgräber was furious at having been made to look a fool, while Traube was being philosophic about it all. He had obviously been more accustomed to rebuffs in his past life than the very assured Deichgräber.

The front door had closed noisily. There came an angry command, heavy footsteps running round the house to the front entrance, the shuffling of boots, the clank of gun butts on the paved pathway, the steady rhythm of precision marching. Hearne moved over to the window and cautiously looked out. Only four soldiers and two officers. He watched them march away until they reached the Pinot land. After that, the path to the village was hidden by trees.

"Such a beautiful right wheel," he said, as he turned back into the room. "They came more quietly than they left, didn't they?" He picked up the burning cigarette. The two women didn't answer. They watched him in silence. "Albertine," he said, "go all through the house and see if we are really alone. Ask Henri how many soldiers there were down in the back yard." Albertine was still watching him; her mind was fumbling for an answer to all this. She took the cigarette end which he presented her with a slight bow and stood there, holding it.

"Go, Albertine," Madame Corlay said. Albertine came back to earth. She looked at the offending cigarette, picked up the bowl of cold soup, and moved slowly to the door.

"Tell us quickly, Albertine," Hearne said urgently, and the tone of his voice arrested her attention. He pointed towards the bed which had concealed the American. Albertine's eyes widened, a hand went up towards her opened mouth, and she scurried from the room.

"I believe she forgot all about him for a moment," Hearne said smilingly, but Madame Corlay wasn't thinking of Albertine, or of Myles.

She was picking up the pieces of glass from her broken spectacles on the table. She shook her head sadly. "You did not need to do that," she said. She raised her eyes to his. So she had guessed.

When she spoke again, her voice had hardened, and her lips were twisted bitterly. "Bertrand seems to have had powerful friends," she began, and then she was weeping quietly. All the pride had left her face. She was an old woman mourning her son.

Hearne walked over to the window. It would be easier for her if she would really let herself cry, he thought. Behind him there was only silence. He looked down on the fields, but all he could see was the slow tears falling so quietly over the bloodless cheeks.

Albertine had returned. "All gone," she announced triumphantly from the doorway. "Tell the young American I've brought him some hot soup." She carried the steaming bowl into Hearne's room.

"All clear," said Hearne and walked towards the bed. "All clear," he repeated, and pulled the white folds aside.

The American stepped out slowly. "Just wanted to make perfectly sure," he grinned. "Got rid of them all right?"

"I hope so."

"Smooth bit of work." Myles was looking at him curiously. You're not the only one who's puzzled, not by a long chalk,

thought Hearne. Only Madame Corlay in that room had
seemed to understand just what had happened. Only Madame
Corlay and the peering Traube. Even that other officer,
called the Ditch-digger, had been out of his depths.

Hearne steered Myles towards the door. "Supper," he said,
"is served."

"You think it's wise? Not that I'm an anxious man, but I
don't trust those bastards a square inch."

"It's safe enough at the moment. But we may have to
hurry you away from here. I'll talk to you about that later.
Now you must eat, and I have things to discuss here." He
nodded over his shoulder to Madame Corlay. Then to Albertine, waiting outside on the small landing, he said, "Lock all
the doors, and bar them. If we have any more visitors, they'll
come announced. See that Monsieur Myles has enough to
eat. And you can open that last bottle of wine. If we don't
drink it, others may." He smiled pleasantly as he re-entered
Madame Corlay's room. One thing, anyway, he was thinking—
Albertine has had enough shocks today to complete her
education.

He said to Madame Corlay, "I'd like to talk a little with
you, if I may." He drew a chair towards the old woman,
again sitting erectly with her hands clasped on the walking
stick. The knuckles no longer showed white.

"Yes?"

"First of all, when did you guess?" That could apply to
either Corlay's "powerful friends" or to himself. If she really
knew about him, that was . . . He might have jumped too
quickly to conclusions in this last half hour. He would soon
learn, anyway.

She returned his look calmly. Her voice was gentle.
"About you?"

He now knew, anyway. He smiled halfheartedly. Damn, he
was thinking, you couldn't have been so good after all.

"I wish you hadn't broken my glasses," Madame Corlay
said with some asperity, and narrowed her eyes as she looked
at his face. "Yes, as far as I can see, the likeness is remark-
able. Are you Breton, too?"

"I am a Celt," admitted Hearne truthfully.

"Yes, you look like Bertrand: you even talk and move like
him. At first, I thought you were my son. And then the little
things were different."

"What?"

"Albertine talks with me a good deal. You see, we've been

a long time together. She came to this farm when she was a girl, and she has stayed here ever since, except for two visits to Rennes when I needed her. One was when Bertrand was born: the other was when I was very ill. She was waiting here to welcome me when I came back after my uncle's death. So, you see, we talk a good deal."

Hearne smothered his impatience. "Yes?"

"Although I sit up here, I know what's going on downstairs. When Albertine told me how much easier it was to live with you nowadays, I thought that perhaps war had made you gentler, more sympathetic. Suffering can do that to men. You didn't grumble about the food, you didn't grumble about Albertine going to Mass, you didn't grumble at having to eat in the kitchen. Apart from the time when you lost your temper with Albertine in your bedroom—when I first saw you—you did seem changed by the war. I was beginning to hope that perhaps some good comes of war even in little things, that perhaps you had stopped being so self-centered and opinionated. Then you offered to work in the fields, you helped the American and even admitted, at that time, that clothes for him would be a difficult problem as he was so tall. Taller than you. Bertrand would never have admitted that. Then you went down to the village to find Henri. And today, Bertrand would have gone down to welcome the Germans himself. He might even have offered them wine. He would certainly have not risked hiding the American."

"That's incredible," burst out Hearne, and then lowered his voice. "Why?"

"I don't know why. All I know is that he would have. He never thought of anyone except himself since he was a small boy. You see, that's how I guessed. You had the one quality which Bertrand lacked. Even Anne, when she came to see me that evening you went to find Henri, even she thought the war had changed and improved you. I found in you, and Anne did too, just what I always had looked for in my son."

Hearne's eyes were fixed on his hands. He cleared his throat, but he didn't speak. Whatever was coming was going to embarrass him. He knew that from Madame Corlay's voice.

"And that was," continued Madame Corlay, "just ordinary human kindness. That was something Bertrand couldn't even understand."

There was a pause.

"You called the Germans his friends," began Hearne, and

then stopped. This was far from pleasant. He felt he was probing an open wound.

But Madame Corlay's strength of character was equal to the strain. She didn't try to dodge the unspoken question. Her voice was hard, as if she was determined to force herself to speak. "I don't know exactly," she was saying. "I don't *know*. ... He had strange friends, strange ideas, and he had some strange money too, in recent years. I made that remark about his 'friends,' because I was so angry at having the Boches give favors to my son."

"Yes, it looked like a favor. On the other hand, it may be their way of winning over Breton nationalists. Your son was a nationalist, wasn't he?"

"Certainly. That I do know. But then he has also been a Royalist, and at one time he was a Communist. That was after his revulsion from the Church."

"He had many enthusiasms."

"But only one at a time." Madame Corlay paused. "You may think I have driven him to these—enthusiasms. I assure you, I made excuses for him every time, until last year when this terrible war began. You may think I am a bitter old woman, but my bitterness only began then."

Too late, thought Hearne pityingly: too late. If less excuses had been made ten years, even five years, ago for Bertrand Corlay, there might have been no bitterness today. There were some types of men whose willfulness thrived on the excuses that were made for them. And they were the kind of people who never knew when they had gone far enough in their selfishness, who never knew when to stop. The more allowances that were made for them, the more they presumed.

"Perhaps we are doing your son an injustice," he said out of his pity for the tortured old woman. "Perhaps he is a true Breton loyalist."

Madame Corlay said wearily, "The true Bretons are not paid."

"He showed you money?"

"No. But he didn't bother to hide the fact from me that he could buy clothes, and books, and drinks at the hotel. Once, I asked him. He said his writing was successful."

"Perhaps it was."

Madame Corlay smiled sadly. "You are too kind."

"No, I'm not. Both of us have definite suspicions, and I

won't deny that they are strong ones. And yet, the only
conclusive proof would be if we could really know where
that money came from. It might, as I said, have come from
newspaper articles, or reviews, or short stories." Certainly
not from poems, Hearne added to himself. "Now, one last
thing. Was there anything else which you noticed about me?
You see, I wouldn't like the Boches, or any friends of theirs,
to get suspicious."

"You need not worry. Any people like that would not
notice the quality which my son lacked. It is only someone
like Anne, or myself, who wanted to love him, only someone
who wanted more kindness in his heart, who would . . . "
She halted. And then, wearily, she added, "No, you have
nothing to fear."

"Your son is now in good hands, Madame Corlay. He was
wounded, but he is recovering. And he may be thinking over
things. Many men do when they are ill, when they have
ceased to be the very self-efficient creatures they thought
they were. Perhaps when he comes back, you will find the
war *has* changed him. Mental and physical suffering are good
purges, you know."

There was a silence, and then Madame Corlay spoke
again. "Perhaps. Now, I have answered your questions. In
return, I shall ask you only one. Why are you here?"

"Because I am an enemy of the Germans. For me, the war
has not yet ended. That is why I was sent here."

Madame Corlay sat more upright. Her voice was clearer.
"That is enough for me."

She was about to say more, when Albertine entered. "I've
opened the wine, Madame. But the American won't take any
until you have had the first glass."

Madame Corlay was smiling. Watching the pleasure in her
eyes, Hearne wondered how he could have been so mistaken
when he had first seen her. An honest laugh, a kind word, a
friendly idea: they didn't cost much. The more he thought of
it all, the more Corlay seemed just a bloated fool.

"Ask Monsieur Myles if he will be so good as to join us,"
Madame Corlay said. "And over in that dresser, you will find
four glasses."

"Your best crystal?" Albertine was shocked.

"Four glasses, Albertine."

When Myles came, there was an uncertainty in the way he
halted at the threshold of the room, there was a hesitation in

his usually cheery smile. He thinks we are going to turn him out right away, guessed Hearne, and gave him a reassuring grin. But Hearne's guess was only half the explanation, as he knew when he caught the American's wary eyes fixed on him. Myles was doing a little thinking about the Germans' hasty departure.

Albertine had filled the four crystal glasses. In her nervousness, the bottle neck struck lightly against the rim of one of them, and a thin clear note shimmered through the still room. The light was fading. The massive furniture stood like black shadows against the white walls.

Here we are, thought Hearne: two old Breton women, an American who'll probably go through worse before he's better, and an Englishman who spends his nights hiding in ditches. What would they drink to?

It was Madame Corlay who gave the toast, leaning on her cane as she rose slowly and painfully to her feet.

"To our war," she said; and no one smiled.

CHAPTER 12

Rendezvous

The Corlay farm was asleep. The only light left burning was in Hearne's room. He sat at the table, his watch in front of him, the diary propped against some books. He had opened it in excitement, but long since the excitement had given way to disappointment, and then the disappointment had given way to exasperation. He turned over another page. Just the same old thing, he thought, just the same old thing.

May 15. Met E.
May 20. Met E.
May 21. Talked with H.
May 25. Met E. Visit to Paris planned.
May 29. Talked with H. Meeting at Rennes.
June 12. Met E.
Met. . . . Met E. . . . Met E . . . .

All the consciously fine writing of the earlier diary had disappeared. Since January 1938 everything had become concise, objective. E. was obviously the beautiful Elise. H. . . . that was something which Hearne could not yet understand. And nothing which he read helped to explain H. Perhaps, thought Hearne flippantly, H. was a brunette, just to complete the circle: Corlay had a redhead in Elise, a blonde in Anne.

Only once did anything longer than these brief memoranda appear. That was in December 1938, when Corlay had made his first speech. Then he had written: "The audience was small, necessarily, but appreciative. It was a terrific experience to feel them respond. When I admired, they admired. When I hated, they hated. Today, they could be counted in tens, but tomorrow they may number hundreds, even thousands." There had been some other speeches recorded after that, but Corlay had managed to curb his self-approbation. It must have been quite a strain. Once he had noted that he was tired and depressed, but that E. was encouraging. It was shortly afterwards that the trip to Paris had taken place. E. had been there too. There were no more entries about tiredness or depression after that visit to Paris.

But not all the notes were devoted to meetings with E. or H. Occasionally there would be only a number within a neat circle. Hearne remembered the loose sheets of paper held together with the elastic band, and the numbered map. Something made hard sense somewhere. Even this diary might become interesting if he only knew exactly what Corlay had been doing. His guesses weren't enough: he had to know. He had to know what Corlay's game had been. Then either he could stuff the diary and papers back into their hiding place and forget about them, or—and Hearne drew a deep breath— they might prove to be something much more than interesting.

Anyway, he consoled himself, he had spent just as useful a day as he would have done lying on his bed or digging in a field. For one thing, he couldn't have handled that conversation with Madame Corlay if he hadn't found out more about her son than he had memorized in an English hospital. So nuts and double nuts to Matthews. The trouble with people with cold blue eyes was that they kept floating in front of you with a reprimanding look.

He strapped the watch onto his wrist thoughtfully. Twenty minutes to ten. Nuts again to Matthews. He wasn't going to

leave this self-imposed job half-finished. He had to find out
Corlay's game, and Elise was his last chance for that. With a
suspicion of a smile, he lifted his pencil and copied Corlay's
writing as carefully as he could. "*July 9, 1940*. Met E." He
closed the diary and placed it in the drawer.

And then he unlaced his boots.

Outside, the stars were dimmed by broken clouds. The young
moon was shrouded. There was a smell of rain in the air.
Hearne knelt under an apple tree, and pulled on his boots.

He approached the dovecote with a care which would have
seemed exaggerated to most people. But Hearne had learned
that no care was ever exaggerated: not in this kind of work.
When he was satisfied that the surrounding fields were really
as deserted as they looked, he advanced through blocks of
shadows to the dovecote walls. There he paused, leaning
against the curved side of the tower. He regained his breath,
his eyes and ears alert. No windows. No sound of any
movement. He edged carefully towards the door. It lay open,
a black gaping hole in the rough wall. There was still no
sound. Either she was late, or he had credited that line of
poetry with too much sense. The half-light of the moon faded
behind the thickness of a cloud. He moved quickly into the
darkness of the tower.

The door hadn't been opened: it lay, torn off its hinges and
abandoned, in the middle of the uneven earth floor. He
tripped over it in the darkness, as his eyes looked up to the
broken roof with its slits of night sky. He regained his
balance, and cursed under his breath. And then something
moved behind him.

He turned quickly, and instinctively reached for the shadow which had separated from the blackness of the wall.
Then, as his mind caught up with his instinct, he softened his
grip. What would have been a stranglehold became an em-
brace. He heard her gasp, and then there was a low laugh,
and her arms were round his neck. Her cheeks were soft and
warm. She was wearing the perfume he had noticed yesterday.

"Bertrand," she said when she paused for breath.

"Elise," he said for lack of anything better to say. From
now on, he remembered to think, it was a case of follow-my-
leader. He waited for her next move, his face pressed against
the fine silk of her hair. He was thankful for the darkness.

Even as his eyes became accustomed to its depths, he could only distinguish outlines. That made him feel safer, more assured.

The tenseness of her body suddenly relaxed. She drew away from him. "Come," she said, "we have little time. You were late."

"It was difficult, tonight. My mother was ill and restless. We had visitors this afternoon and they upset her."

"Visitors?"

"Two officers. They wanted to commandeer our house for some colonel."

Elise had moved towards a mound of earth banked against the wall; she still held his hand. "How ridiculous. ... Where is your coat? Don't tell me you've forgotten it." Her voice was half-laughing, but only half. The iron hand in the velvet glove, thought Hearne. What was he supposed to have a coat for, anyway?

"They packed away all my clothes," he answered. "I've had the devil of a time finding things since I got back." Then, as he saw her hesitating before the mound, he guessed her thoughts.

"Here's my jacket. That will do." He spread it on the earth at her feet.

"Yes, that will do." She caught his hand again, and pulled him down beside her. She was wearing a thin silk dress and little else under her opened coat. Poor Anne, Hearne suddenly thought: she never had had a chance with Corlay, not one solitary chance against this. "I shall keep you warm," Elise said. Her voice had lost its edge and was once more good-humored.

Warm was an understatement, Hearne thought. He said, "You're still as beautiful."

She laughed that slow breath-caught laugh of hers. "But tonight we have little time for your poetry, Bertrand. When I come back from Paris, you can tell me how much you love me. But tonight it is business."

"Paris?" Hearne hoped his voice was sufficiently dismayed.

"Yes, tomorrow. That was why I had to see you tonight. That was why I was annoyed when you were late. I must be back at the hotel by eleven. A lot is happening, Bertrand." There was an excitement breaking through her voice.

Hearne waited for her to speak again. She rested her head against his shoulder, and looked up towards the patches of

cloud and stars above them. He was conscious of the coldness
of the night, the warmth of her body, the line of her throat
as she watched the night sky through the gaping roof, the
perfume in her hair, the emotion in her voice. His mind was
as alert as his senses. He waited.

"Yes, a lot is happening. And you managed to get back at
the right time. Oh Bertrand, how could you have been so
stupid as to get into real fighting?"

He gave a short laugh. "I couldn't very well avoid it, could
I?"

"Well, why didn't you get captured, right at the beginning?"

"That doesn't always work: there's often a chap on the
other side who shoots first and then questions afterwards."

That made her laugh again. "You must tell me what
happened. After I get back from Paris. Now—" Her voice
was serious, assured, almost commanding. She gives the orders, Hearne judged, and the curve of her waist inside his
arm didn't soften the thought. "Now, listen. They are moving
into St. Déodat. The hotel is already taken over." She
paused for dramatic emphasis.

"So I noticed yesterday. But what trouble do they expect
here? The place has been half-dead for years."

The interruption annoyed her. "There will be no trouble
here, silly. That is why they've chosen here. Think of St.
Déodat's position. It's central. It's a control point for the
whole district. And it's safe. It's as safe as—as—"

"The Bank of France."

"This isn't the time for jokes, Bertrand, not even bad
ones."

Hearne listened to the sharp edge in her voice, and decided
it certainly wasn't the time. And yet it was difficult to restrain
his own particular brand of humor when a young woman
took herself so seriously; still more difficult, when the young
woman was so beautiful as this one. He mumbled what might
have been an apology or an endearment, and kissed her hair.

"From St. Déodat," Elise went on, "the hundreds of
surrounding farms and all the villages scattered over this area
can be controlled, just as they were by the Church centuries
ago."

Hardly for the same ends, Hearne thought, as he answered, "But St. Déodat may have been central once: now
it's isolated."

"Not with a well-made road, and that will be easy for

them. It will only be a short detour, really, from the main road in the valley."

She was excited: she was making it all sound so very important. Granted St. Déodat's one-time dominance over the district, he could still think of other places which the Nazis would be more likely to pick. Then he realized what she had meant by saying it was safe. St. Déodat *was* safe; for he wouldn't be the only one to believe it was negligible. That was its safety.

"The valley?" he echoed, picking up the emphasis she had used on that word.

"Yes." The excitement in her voice increased. "The valley— or Dol, to be precise. You don't believe me? Well, wait until you see the airfields that are being built now all round there. Wait until you see what happens in August, what the results will be by September!"

"By September?" He kept his voice casual.

"Yes!" The nonchalance in Hearne's voice sharpened her tone. "Yes, Bertrand. By August 15th the Germans will be leaving us here. Britain will be under attack. By the middle of September, Great Britain will be finished."

Hearne kept silent.

"What are you thinking?" she asked impatiently.

Hearne said, "I'm thinking that the time is short. I haven't seen many Germans about St. Déodat, so far."

"I don't think you need worry about their efficiency. The plans are all ready, the preparations have begun. In fact—" Elise's voice was a mixture of amusement and sarcasm—"in fact, Monsieur Corlay, the army is arriving the day after tomorrow."

The army ... the army ... And she didn't mean masses of soldiers by that, either. She meant the army as opposed to the other branches of the invasion horde. The military element was still to come: the day after tomorrow, she had said. The hotel was already taken over, by a handful of soldiers and some officers responsible for the billeting of the troops who were still to come. He suddenly wondered if there were any other types of Nazi at the hotel: Gestapo or Military Intelligence, for instance.

"Just who are in the hotel now?" he asked casually, and the answer this time stiffened him.

"We are." She could no longer hide her sense of triumph. "We are." She tightened her hands on his wrists until they were numbed. She raised her head from his shoulder and tried to see his expression through the darkness. "What's wrong?" she asked suddenly. He kissed her, and his thoughts were cold and bitter and completely realistic at last. Corlay was no Breton nationalist, or if he had been one, he had been sidetracked by a very beautiful body. He wondered what the correct answer should be. What would Corlay have said? The kiss ended.

"What about me?" he asked.

She regained her breath and her hands went up to her hair to arrange it.

"That was what I am coming to. . . . At present, you are to ignore the hotel. You've got to concentrate on your meetings: we are in no danger now, of course, but for the sake of results it will be wise to keep them secret from the Bretons. I'll send you a list of future dates and places, where you can discuss your progress with the men from the other districts. Then, you will also have nationalist meetings, which you are to pretend to keep secret from the Germans. In that way, you'll get more response from the Bretons. The idea is that Brittany will be separated from France, and we've got to get the people to accept it. That is why you must keep our real meetings secret, so that our connection with Germany won't be recognized, and then the nationalist meetings, which we shall encourage, will have some chance of success. If we work it properly, we'll have them accepting this Breton National State as the thing they have always wanted. There will be a German Governor, of course. I hear that Weyer will probably be chosen. And there will also be a Breton National Committee. And you, of course, will be the delegate from this district."

She laughed, and struggled free from his grip. "I thought you'd be pleased. Don't hold me so tightly, Bertrand, you'll bruise me. I'll be able to tell you more when I get back from Paris."

"Wish I were going with you again," Hearne said, and mentally thanked the diary.

"Not this time, my love. Later, perhaps. We'll see. And now I must get back to the hotel. Hans is arriving tonight."

"Hans?"

"Now, don't start all that silly jealousy again. Hans has been a good friend—to both of us. Who do you think was responsible for getting you into this new National Committee?"

"How long is he staying here?"

"The hotel is his headquarters for the next few weeks, until we get everything nicely organized and co-operative. He's got to go to Paris too, of course." Her voice was too casual, but the kiss she gave him was meant to soothe any doubts. "And one more thing, my sweet, have you still got those lists?"

Hearne remembered the map, and the list of names and addresses, and the connecting numbers. He said, "They are safe."

"Good. I'll leave a note for you at the hotel tomorrow with my aunt. I'll give you the corrections to that list. Most of our men are still intact, but one or two of them were stupid enough to get killed."

"Perhaps they surrendered to men who shot first, and asked questions afterwards."

She laughed and lifted his wrist to see the illuminated face of his watch.

"You know," she said, "I do believe carrying a gun has made your hands bigger."

"All the better to hold you with." Hearne hoped the strain in his voice would pass for emotion.

"Five minutes more," she announced. "Bertrand, do you love me as much as ever?" Her emotions were like a bathroom fixture: hot, cold, to be turned on at will.

"As much as ever I did."

"Am I still as beautiful? You haven't forgotten all your pretty speeches, have you?"

"You are the most beautiful woman I have ever seen." That at any rate was true. There was a pause. She was waiting. "Your eyes," he began, "are like the crystal depths of a sunlit pool. Your hair ... " He remembered enough of the verses he had read in Corlay's notebook: that helped him to improvise for the rest of her anatomy. One hour ago, he would scarcely have imagined such cold objectivity possible. He felt a sudden relief as he realized he was safe from Elise; and it was she, herself, who had saved him. The iron hand in the velvet glove, he thought again. She could flutter those black eyelashes, turn that profile, lift those breasts: it would all be an interesting and aesthetically satisfying performance. But the hand was iron, and the velvet glove was wearing thin. Her mind was carefully calculating. Her heart was self-possessed. She might have just as well admitted that she was an incurable leper, with festering flesh concealed under the skillful drapery of her silk dress.

He looked at the shadow of upturned face. "You beautiful bitch," he said to himself, and helped her to rise to her feet. The stipulated five minutes of love was over.

They halted at the doorway. The arc of moon was fitful, but the light was stronger than it had been inside the dovecote. Once again, Hearne was glad that the inside of the tower had been so dark.

"Don't come over the fields with me," she said. "It will be better for our plans if you seem to have no contact at all with anyone living at the hotel. It is only for a week or two. This Breton National Council and separation from France will probably be an historical fact by the end of July. That's our aim." She added a smile to sweeten her command.

Hearne looked disappointed. "But there's no one to see."

"You know this place. It's all eyes and tongues. Guess who followed me part of the way here? Kerénor."

"Kerénor?" Hearne remembered the limping man's animosity. A lot of things were being explained away tonight.

"Yes, the stupid fool that he is. We have nothing to fear from him now. We can deal with him, if he doesn't behave." She paused, and then mimicked Kerénor's voice: " 'What are we fighting for? Comrades, do not be deluded by an imperialist war.' Yes, his days of usefulness are over. Either he now co-operates, or—" She changed her voice again. "Good night, darling. It has been lovely to see you again." Hadn't it just, he thought. He let go both of her hands slowly.

"I'll think of you all the time you are away. Let me know at once when you get back."

"Don't forget the note which I shall leave at the hotel."

"I won't forget," he said, and watched her. She had drawn her coat more tightly round her. Her hair suddenly gleamed into life as the moon freed itself from a cloud. The green of her eyes had darkened. She turned her profile to look up at the sky. Hearne wondered who had first told her how lovely she looked that way. Once more he was thankful that it had been so dark and cold inside the tower. If he had been able to see that profile as clearly as this, it would have been more difficult to judge Elise correctly, before she had condemned herself with her own words. He might have been too late for his realism: he might have been caught off guard. But now, he didn't envy Corlay any more. He pitied him. How long would she consider him "useful"? And then, like Kerénor, he could be "dealt with."

"You'd better start working on your speeches, Bertrand. They are going to be important. I'll be back here in ten days' time, and we can have our first meeting with our group then. That will give us time to have some progress to report on our work with the Bretons. Use any means in dealing with them. Hans said you could have a very free hand, but try persuasion first. Co-operation makes things much easier for us than suspicion and hate, so have patience at first. You know the line: the British are treacherous cowards, the Americans are selfish cowards, the rest of France are bloodsuckers as well as cowards. A separate Brittany, friendly to Germany, can be secure and happy. You know the sort of stuff. Pile it on, but keep dangling autonomy like a big juicy carrot in front of their noses. God knows they've wanted a separate Brittany for years, but trust a Breton to stop wanting it once he gets it. At the meeting on my return, we can discuss how well we have succeeded in our various districts. These are the orders."

She gave him a last kiss, and then, freeing herself from his arms with that smile which promised so much and meant so little, she turned towards the path. She didn't look back. She wasn't the kind who did.

He stood in the cold blackness of the doorway until she had disappeared into the half-shadows of the night. Far below him, the church tower was outlined above the trees which hid the houses of St. Déodat. He suddenly remembered his emotion when he had first seen the village. Peace, he had thought, lived here. Peace? He smiled sardonically: romanticism always ended in such bathos. Life liked its little jokes: and the more bitter they were, the funnier. He must remember to laugh, some day.

A fine rain drizzled over the fields. He turned up the collar of his jacket and abandoned the idea of bed. Day after tomorrow, she had said. In that case, Myles must be on his way by tomorrow night. And that meant the job which he had set for himself tomorrow night must be done now.

He began his steady pace up the hill towards the ruins of the castle. Once over the crest of that wooded hill and he would reach the road from Rennes to St. Malo. It was strange to think that what he had learned in this last hour might be as important, in its own way, as anything he could discover in the next few weeks. He hoped, as he felt the rain settling on his shoulders and his feet settling into the soft earth, that the St. Malo road would be as interesting as the railway line he had watched last night.

It was.

CHAPTER 13

Warning for St. Deodat

There was no time for sleep. Hearne looked at his gray face in the gray light of the mirror, and shook his head wearily. He yawned, and felt his chin with his hand. No time for shaving, either: his fingers were too cold to make a quick job with Corlay's cutthroat razor. He splashed his face with the three inches of water, and combed his hair. At least, he had done a good night's work. Behind him on the table lay two pages of compact notes. On the floor were his soaked clothes. He would feel warmer once he had some hot soup inside him. There might be even some of that wine left: yesterday Albertine had carefully corked the bottle after their toast. Corked wine was better than none when you felt as cold as this.

The papers were at last hidden, the bed was appropriately rumpled, the sogging clothes and filthy boots were picked up from the floor. He stood at the door, and gave a last careful look. The room looked innocent enough to please him. As he went downstairs, he looked at the boots: they'd have to be scraped and dried as much as possible. He grinned as he remembered Elise and her half-joke about his hands being bigger. It was lucky she hadn't remembered the size of Corlay's feet: none of the shoes in Corlay's wardrobe would fit him.

Albertine had heard him coming, and had already served his breakfast. She wasn't talking, this morning. In fact, she seemed to be ignoring him. So she had been thinking about the Germans' visit, yesterday. Hearne smiled to himself as he swallowed the hot soup hungrily. Even Albertine who only wanted to be left in peace didn't like the taste that German favors left in her mouth.

At first, she paid no attention to the clothes which he had thrown on the stone hearth, but her curiosity at last prompted her to pick them up. She said something to herself, and then waited for him to explain. Hearne finished his bowl of soup, and then helped himself to some more. Albertine, standing with the wet clothes held far out from her white apron, was still waiting.

It was she who, after all, had to speak first.

"Where have you been?"

"Couldn't sleep much. Went out for a walk."

"In that rain?"

"Dry these boots, will you, Albertine? I've got to go to the village this afternoon."

"Where are your other pairs of shoes?" She was looking disapprovingly at his stockinged feet.

"Upstairs. But I don't like them: they are not strong enough for this weather."

"I told you that when you bought them." The hint of self-satisfaction in her voice was a good sign. The storm was dispersing.

"You were right and I was wrong, Albertine." He rose and clapped her shoulder. "You are always right, Albertine."

As he left the kitchen, she was already scraping the thick yellow mud off the boots and laying them down on their sides not too near the fire.

Upstairs, the American had already been installed in the storeroom. He was less talkative, today. His "Good morning" had been no more than polite. Hearne leaned his shoulder against the doorpost and watched him as he pretended to go back to his writing.

"Busy?" Hearne asked.

"Fairly."

"Too busy?"

Myles looked up from the pad of paper balanced on his knee. He kept rolling his pencil between his thumb and finger.

"Sorry," continued Hearne, "but there are some things we must discuss."

"Yes?"

Hearne looked at the American. His jaw was noticeably

stubborn; there was a wary look in his eyes. All the friend-liness had gone from them. So he, too, hadn't liked German favors in retrospect.

"I think," said Hearne, "that this is hardly the moment for you to begin distrusting me."

"Well—" said the American, and then stopped.

"Well?"

"Well, I am thinking that I'm more trouble to you than you bargained for."

It was at that moment that Hearne noticed Myles was wearing boots.

"Your feet are better?"

Myles face was expressionless. "Yes."

"Where on earth did you get those boots?" Hearne kept his voice friendly, even amused.

"Your mother gave them to me. They belonged to her uncle. I'm to get some of his clothes, too."

Hearne's voice was less amused. "And you were just wait-ing for them to arrive before you slipped away, preferably when I wasn't about the house to see where you had gone?"

Myles stiffened at the barely concealed anger in Hearne's tone. "Here," he said, "that's a bit harsh. After all, I'm only a nuisance here. I don't like putting anyone in danger the way I've been putting you all."

"And you'd have ruined everything, including your own chances to escape." Hearne's voice was calm once more. That was the trouble with a sleepless night: it made you bad-tempered whenever you felt yourself thwarted next day.

"I'll look after my own escape." It was the American who was angry now.

"Don't be such a damned fool. If you do arrive at the coast, what will you do then? Go round asking fishermen if they'll take you across the Channel? You may ask the wrong fisherman, you know."

"I'll manage," Myles said stubbornly. "I've managed be-fore."

"You'd manage much better if you would listen to me. Tonight you'll leave here. There is a man in a small fishing village on the river, just before you reach St. Malo. He will take you across the Channel. And he doesn't do it for money, either. Every able-bodied man he saves is another for the Boches to face later."

Myles said nothing at first. He was staring at Hearne, as if he were trying to read his thoughts. At last he said slowly, "I don't follow this. I'm willing to bet that you aren't doing this for the sake of my bright blue eyes."

"You'd win that bet."

That startled even Myles. He smiled in spite of himself.

"Well, why then?" He wasn't angry now, but he was still watchful.

"In the last three weeks, you've stored a lot of details inside that brain of yours. As a newspaper man, you are a trained observer. The things you would automatically notice during your journey here would be interesting and perhaps useful to the right people."

There was a pause, and then Myles answered, "I guess they would. But who are your 'right people'?"

"The ones who'll meet the fishing boat when it crosses the Channel."

The American's eyes were examining the toes of his boots.

"So you've taken all this trouble with me so that I can spill what I know to the 'right people.' ... Why bother? I know what to do with the information I've gathered."

"But you might not be able to do it quickly enough. You might take two or three weeks to reach England. *If* you go my way, you'll be in England by the fifteenth of July at the latest."

"*If* ..." Myles repeated Hearne's emphasis on the word. "Then the choice is up to me? This isn't an ultimatum?"

"The choice is yours."

The American relaxed slightly. "You are the funniest farmer I've ever met," he said, and his voice was almost friendly once more.

"I *am* the funniest farmer."

Myles shot a sudden glance at Hearne's face. It was grimly serious.

"It doesn't make sense," Myles said, and then shut his lips into that tight line.

"What doesn't?"

"Your touching farewell with these Jerries yesterday evening, and the way you've taken so much trouble to hide me here. Why didn't you give me up, then and there? You seemed to be a friend of theirs."

"Shall we say, they *think* I am a friend of theirs?" Hearne's quiet voice had no hint of mockery. He returned the American's direct look with equal steadiness.

Myles said, "You are taking a big chance on me. What if I didn't turn my information over to the proper quarters? What if I never went near your man outside St. Malo?"

"I shall see you do. I shan't leave you until you are on that boat, and then I'll get a message over to the other side to expect you and your information. They'll meet you all right."

"Well," said Myles, and gave a short laugh. "You've got it all arranged pat, I must say. You weren't a newspaper man, yourself, at one time? No? I didn't expect any company on this journey to the coast. I won't weary, anyway, I can see."

"No. I don't think either of us will weary."

The American's interest quickened. "Will it be tough going?"

"Possibly. But we'll manage. And we'll only manage if we trust each other. I am trusting you, even if your name isn't Myles."

The American was silent; his face seemed unchanged, but he had stopped playing with the pencil.

"I get it," he said at last.

"Fine. Now, today, go on remembering every detail you've seen, shaping them into order. Eat plenty, and get some sleep. You can use my bed."

"There's only one answer I'd like to know," the American said.

Hearne turned at the door. "And what's that?"

"I'll ask you when you get me onto that boat. We'll skip it now."

"O.K."

The American laughed. Hearne looked puzzled. "Kind of cute how all foreigners think they have to say 'O.K.' to an American," Myles explained.

"Or perhaps it is the way we say it?" Hearne suggested. With the smile still on his lips, he said, "And you should also rest your feet today. Better take the boots off now."

Myles tightened his lips, but he did bend down to unlace the boots.

"Yes," he said, "that will rest my feet. It will also prevent me from running away without you. Here, take the damned things." He threw them, each in turn, over to Hearne, with the beginning of a grin. "What was that about trusting me?"

"It still holds," Hearne said. "I do trust you, but I've also heard that Americans are very independent people, and like their own way best. Perhaps you might begin to think once more that you could manage better by yourself."

"Perhaps I could."

"Perhaps. But it would be better to avoid all risks. You are much too important at the moment."

"I don't think I like being important," Myles said, but he was not displeased.

"It has its disadvantages," Hearne agreed, and gave his customary bow. That always amused Myles. At least, Hearne thought, the temperature had risen again. Tonight's journey would not be such an unpleasant task after all.

"When do we start?" the American asked.

"At sunset. Meanwhile I'll see my mother and work over some maps."

"And I'll rest my feet, I suppose?"

"That's the idea," Hearne said. He paused with his hand on the door. "And I really do advise you not to leave the house until we both go. It will be dangerous not only for yourself, but for all of us here. There are Germans in the village. The soldiers are coming here in some numbers tomorrow, but there are others already in the hotel. They probably call themselves a Commission for Economic and Educational Understanding. I think Gestapo is simpler to pronounce, don't you?"

Myles gave a short laugh. "So *they*'re here," he said as if to himself. "I might have known it."

"Well, I'll see you later," Hearne said, and moved into his own room. He closed the door behind him. Already, he could feel the numbered lists, which Corlay had hidden so securely, being turned over in his hands. If they were half as good as he hoped, they would still be dynamite.

They were. He spent the next two hours happily copying the names of these men on the German payroll, noting their districts and headquarters and meeting places, memorizing as he read and solved and wrote. This, he thought, as he finished his last entry, would be a nice little surprise packet for Matthews: a sort of bonus on the side. It would be useful for the agents whom Matthews had sent into Northern Brittany to know just what peaceful citizen was a dangerous enemy. And it would be particularly useful for the French who were fighting on. They would have a special interest, a special bill to settle. What was more, if the key map and its accompanying lists had been drawn up so methodically for Northern Brittany, it also existed for the other districts of France. Hearne imagined perhaps twenty of these map sections, fitting neatly together into one large expanse of intrigue and infiltration. Now that they could be considered an actuality, the search could start for the others. Most things could be discovered, provided you knew that they did exist. That was the snag in this kind of work: there were so many possibilities that you wasted ingenuity and effort, time and trouble, just looking for something you hoped would be there. But once you had a reality to deal with, that was quite a different cup of tea. Then you could stop worrying about fifty problematical ways to be explored; then you could start working, with the added zest of knowing that you were on the right road.

Hearne folded the sheets of paper neatly. Later he would add the information which Elise had left for him at the Hotel Perro, along with a coded summary of his own observations. Together, they would all sail for England.

He was debating in his own mind whether he should make the coded summary now, or visit Madame Corlay to break his news of Myles's departure to her, or slip down to the village for Elise's instructions, when voices from the stairway decided him. Women's voices. He listened to Albertine's solid footsteps followed by lighter movements. There was a rustling outside his door, but the room they entered was Madame Corlay's. He stood with his hand on the door latch. And then, as he heard Albertine come out of Madame Corlay's room, he opened the door, quickly and silently.

Albertine had started back at his sudden appearance.

"Who?" he whispered, pointing towards the closed door of Madame Corlay's room.

Albertine was shaking her head unbelievingly. "They've turned her out of her farm."

Turned out . . . turned whom out? . . . Hearne said, "Anne?"

"Yes." Albertine was still shaking her head as she started downstairs. Only God could know where people could sleep or eat; it was beyond any human being to imagine. . . . Hearne watched her go. He thought grimly, she doesn't know the half of it; in another six months, or in a year, she may begin to understand. And there would be so many Albertines, so many simple hearts and simple minds whose orderly unimaginative lives had left them ill-equipped to grasp what was happening to the world. There was the tragedy of it: if only they could have realized the danger while there was still time, while they were still free to carry a gun and still free to make guns for themselves. Instead, they would now find that it costs three times as much to retrieve a position as it takes to hold it. And the reckoning had not yet begun. In another year, or more, the full cost would begin to be realized. Hearne suddenly hoped he wouldn't be in France at that time. He had always liked France too well to watch it weigh the load of chains it had helped to fasten on its own neck.

"Chuck it, you damned fool," he told himself. "You aren't here to worry about people who just wouldn't believe that such things could ever possibly happen to them. The first job is to worry about those who are still holding on. You're here to find out what you can to help them, and to keep your skin whole. Fat lot of use you'd be to them, if you didn't."

His face was quite expressionless as he knocked on Madame Corlay's door. "Bertrand," he called, and then entered.

Madame Corlay sat bolt upright in her chair. She was angry. If I were a German, Hearne thought, she would have struck me with that stick.

"Albertine told me," he said, and looked at Anne. Her face was quite white, and it seemed thinner, but there were no tears.

"It had to be someone," she said. Her voice was low, but Hearne felt it was being tightly controlled. "It would be much worse if I were a man with a wife and children. There are some in the village for whom it is much worse."

"But your family have lived and worked on that farm for two hundred and forty years," Madame Corlay exploded. She was taking it much less philosophically than Anne. Hearne suddenly remembered that Madame Corlay had planned that the two farms should be joined: in that sense, she no doubt felt that the Germans had taken possession of something connected with her. "Can't you *do* something?" she went on indignantly. "Can't you say Anne is betrothed to you? Can't you—" She halted. Possibly the words had sounded more distasteful than the impulsive thought. When wild ideas surged through your mind, you couldn't often tell how cheap they were until you put them into a sentence. Anne was looking at her in bewilderment.

"Why," she asked, "should the Germans pay any attention to that? They think we are lucky to be left alive at all."

Madame Corlay's face had reddened. Hearne noted the shining eyes, the trembling lip. She's going to burst into tears, he thought, and the idea so startled him that he walked over to Anne and took her hands.

"You can live here with us," he said.

"You've no reason to be so kind," Anne replied stiffly. "Not after what I said to you last time we met. And if I say I am sorry, you will think it is only because I need you now."

"No, I shan't. I believe you were sorry in the ten minutes after you left me."

Anne looked at him for a long moment. She was even smiling now. "But, Bertrand, I was."

Hearne became very aware of her hands and let them go suddenly. He faced Madame Corlay. Her eyes were fixed on the floor at her feet, but her lip had stopped trembling.

"It will be all right for Anne to stay here?" he asked.

"Of course. But the American?"

"He's leaving here tonight. I was just coming to tell you about that. I think it is safer if he leaves tonight." He turned to Anne. "We've had a man staying here. He's trying to reach the coast."

"And you've been hiding him? Oh Bertrand, how wonderful." Anne's eyes were larger than ever. "But he mustn't leave because of me."

"He has to go. The Germans will be here in greater numbers, tomorrow."

"I know. The village is being made ready for them. Half of them are to be garrisoned in the empty houses or billeted with families. The rest are to be together on the meadows beside the church."

Hearne nodded. "Trees there," he said.

"Trees?" Anne looked puzzled.

Hearne smiled. Trees were natural camouflage, just as the Romanesque-Gothic church would seem so disarmingly innocent from the air.

"Who told you this?" he countered.

"Kerénor. He came to see me as soon as Marie went into the village and told them what had happened to our farm. I've brought Jean and Marie with me." Her voice was apologetic and anxious. "They are old, and they don't eat much, and they'll help Albertine. They had nowhere to go. . . . They couldn't stay on the farm. The Germans wouldn't let any French stay around it." She looked at Madame Corlay. "Jean and Marie are so old. They are so alone."

"They can stay here," Hearne said quickly. "But what part is Kerénor playing?"

Anne smiled sadly. "He has declared war."

"What? The pacifist?"

"But he has changed. Believe me, Bertrand, he has. He has been worried about his ideas for months now. He still believes that they are the right ones, but he says the time is all wrong for them. And now he is going to—" She halted.

"Tell me, Anne." Kerénor's name hadn't been on the Nazi pay list. Elise considered him a fool who had lost, who was beaten even before he ever fought. Kerénor was just the man Hearne needed.

Madame Corlay said unexpectedly, "You can tell Bertrand. I have talked with him and he has changed in many ways too. Our enemy is his enemy."

"Kerénor wouldn't talk very much. He only hinted. . . . And I said I would keep everything secret, as his friend."

"He was right to ask you not to tell," Hearne said. "And don't tell anyone else. But I've got information I want to give Kerénor. Information which may save St. Déodat from making some mistakes. But I can't give you any information for Kerénor until I am sure that he is willing to take risks against the Germans."

Anne looked at Hearne for a moment. "I see," she said. "Well, I am sure he's already taking risks. He has a wireless set, and he hid it when the Germans were inquiring about them yesterday. He listens to London. He's making a report each day, and he has already chosen the men who are going to pass the news by word of mouth. Then we'll all know the true news. He says that is important. He says all the little things are important. Little things, he says, would add up to something bigger." Anne's voice held a note of wonder which once would have made Hearne smile. But now he knew the value of little things in the smothering blanket of enemy occupation. Anne was still talking. "He heard from London that there are Frenchmen who are calling themselves Free Frenchmen. They are fighting on, and they've their own ships and their own army. And some of the colonies are going to join them."

Hearne, watching Madame Corlay's expression, had his belief in little things such as wireless sets strengthened.

"I've got to go to the village, now," Hearne said. "Will you come with me, Anne?"

"Me?" The gray-blue eyes widened. When she smiled like that the expressionless mask vanished, and her face was suddenly and charmingly alive.

"Yes, I want you to help me, Anne. I cannot be seen

talking to Kerénor for certain reasons. And yet, I want to give him a message. So, when I am in the village, will you try to see Kerénor, and tell him some things?"

The smile on Anne's face faded, but the eyes were watching him gravely and honestly. She hid her disappointment well.

"Now, listen carefully, Anne. Tell him he is right: that the little things will grow into big things. Tell him he must get the men together whom he can trust, and as long as the Germans think they are holding Breton nationalist meetings they will be able to get together quite safely. Tell him that he must be careful, for the Gestapo are watching him; and if he doesn't seem to co-operate he is in danger. And tell him that, although he has always hated me and I've never liked him until now, this is what the Nazis want. They hope we'll hate and distrust each other, so that they can rule us easily. And if they rule us easily, that helps them in their fight against the rest of the world which is still free. So Kerénor's big job is now to unite everyone in the village. All their differences and quarrels must be forgotten if they are ever to know freedom again. When he has united the village, he can start uniting people in other villages. He must choose men who can be *trusted* to help him. And the movement will spread. And the Germans won't be able to kill some of us, without reprisals being taken against them. If we are united, they have more to fear and to worry about. Can you remember that?"

Anne nodded, and repeated his words quickly in obvious willingness to help. What he had said had excited her. She added, "Perhaps I can be of help too!" Her eyes were shining at the thought.

"But always be careful, Anne. We are fighting against a stranglehold. One slip, and we shall have our necks broken. And there is one thing more which you must remember. Never forget this." He paused to let his next sentence have added emphasis. "Do not trust Elise, or any of her friends. She is in German pay."

He might have overturned the cabinet which held all Madame Corlay's treasured crystal. The effect on the two women was as spectacular.

"Elise. . . . " Anne's soft childlike face had frozen; her nostrils dilated. And it wasn't only the fact that Elise was a traitor which had transformed her. It was the fact that he should have mentioned the hated name, mentioned it so coldly and so damningly.

"We must leave now for the village," Hearne said. "Might the American come in here to talk to you? Keep him with you until I get back. It would be dangerous for us all if he were to go out for a stroll. And don't tell him that I've gone to the village. He might get worried and come after me. He is getting restless, now that his feet are better."

Madame Corlay could only nod her answer. The name of Elise still held her silent. In condemning Elise, Hearne had condemned Bertrand Corlay. Now she knew everything. Anyway, thought Hearne, even if something goes wrong tonight and I don't get back to St. Déodat, I have warned them of their greatest danger there.

He looked at the faces of the two women. He knew that he had given his warning to the right people. They would not disbelieve it. They would not forget it.

CHAPTER 14

Collaboration

It was a strange walk to the village. When the stone bridge was crossed, Hearne breathed a sigh of relief. He felt he had performed just as neat a piece of imaginative realism as ever in his life. For Anne had asked about Dunkirk, and as they crossed the calm fields he had answered with a description of the Bordeaux evacuation (which he *did* know, at least), and multiplied its horror by ten to achieve the chaos of Dunkirk. Judging from the look in Anne's eyes, and the tightening of her lips, he had succeeded well enough. After that, they finished their journey in silence. Hearne found himself admiring a girl who had the sensibility neither to exclaim nor to commiserate.

They halted awkwardly at the corner of the market square. Anne seemed to realize that this was where he intended to leave her. She smoothed her hair nervously with her hand, half-smiled, took a hesitating step away from him. Hearne felt he was being inadequate. He reached out and touched her arm lightly. "I must try to get some brandy for my mother," he said, "before it all disappears. I'll see you later, Anne." He was relieved, and yet somehow dismayed, to see her smile become wholehearted.

"Yes," she said. "Later."

And then he noticed the appearance of a frown between the level eyebrows, and his eyes followed the sudden shift in her glance. Outside the Hotel Perro, a small thin man was standing. He was soberly dressed in black. But neither by his clothes nor by his sharp features could Hearne identify him. Perhaps he was one of Corlay's so-called "negligibles" in the village. Whoever he was, he had noticed them too. He spat out the cigarette stub from between his lips, stepped on it deliberately, and then with his hands still in his pockets and his eyes on Hearne, he sauntered into the hotel. Hearne was left with the feeling that the man had known him. He kept his worry out of his eyes, looked questioningly at Anne.

She shrugged her shoulders. "He doesn't look like a Boche," she said, "but who can tell what kind of visitors we have nowadays?"

So the man was a stranger to St. Déodat. Hearne's worry increased, but he shrugged his shoulders too and said, "Well, I'll see you later. Take care."

She laughed suddenly at the seriousness of his face, and then became dutifully grave. "You must take care, yourself," she answered, and for a moment Hearne's breath stopped. "We all must take care near this place," she added, nodding over her shoulder at the hotel. "Why don't you send Henri for the brandy? He's too old to be recruited for a labor squad."

Hearne smiled and said, "Last time he came down here, he got drunk." She laughed at that, and then she was walking quickly across the square towards the Widow Picrel's shop.

Hearne's pace was slower. There was danger in the hotel, more danger than Anne had even thought. But once he faced the yellow-screened door, he pushed it quickly open, as if by hurry he might get Elise's message and leave before he met that man again.

The bar was empty. As Hearne's footsteps sounded on the bare floor, a door behind the counter opened and Madame Perro appeared. She was as completely waved and corseted as the last time he had seen her. She concealed her welcome as efficiently as her surprise. She reached into the pocket of her apron and produced an envelope. As she handed it over the counter, she unbent enough to incline her head towards the restaurant.

"He's in there," she said, and then turned back to the doorway through which she had entered. It closed decisively behind her spacious hips. She thinks that Corlay is too insignificant for her Elise, Hearne guessed: she sees bigger fish floating round the hotel, now. He looked down at the envelope. In the same square, back-sloping, thick down-stroked letters which spelled Corlay's name was an urgent command across the top of the paper. *Open at once!* It was the Elise touch, all right.

Hearne obeyed. Inside the envelope were the new names he had been promised, along with the numbers which represented their districts on Corlay's map. But what held his attention was the hastily written postscript. *Number 8 is here unexpectedly. See him before he leaves.*

Well, thought Hearne, well. . . . He wished to heaven he were now walking across the stone bridge. If only he could have sent someone else down to the hotel for this envelope, if only— But what was the good of thinking all this? It only wasted time, and he knew it was short now. *"He's in there." See him.* He half-closed his eyes to recall the list of numbered fifth-columnists which he had found in Corlay's bookcase. Number 8. That was Dol. The name was . . . and then his memory, perhaps because he was urging it so strongly, went blank on the name. It stayed tantalizingly on the tip of his tongue. It began with B. B . . . Dol was Number 8, Number 8 was B. . . .

And then he heard the parrot-like screech of the restaurant door. He thrust the letter into his pocket, and turned round.

The small man in the black suit was standing there. He still had his hands in his pockets. A fresh cigarette drooped from the corner of the thin lips which stretched tightly between the long jaw and the pointed nose. His head motioned back over his shoulder. Hearne nodded, and came forward. The man let the door, held open by his elbow, creak into place as he turned back into the restaurant. Hearne dodged the swing of the door in time, and pushed it open for himself. Charming fellow, he was thinking as he reached the table, and sat down to face the long jaw over the checked cloth. The man had chosen a table set in the corner of the wall, where no one looking through the door or the window

would see them. But that wasn't the only good thing about
the table's position, Hearne thought. In his corner, none of
the direct light from the windows would reach him. He sat
with his arms folded so that the size of his hands was hidden.
He kept his feet well under the table and pretended to study
the salt shaker and the advertising ash tray. The man's eyes
were so deep a brown in color that some of the pigment
from the iris seemed to have spilled over and turned the
white into yellow. Above the eyes, the forehead was high and
slanting, the hair was dark and receding. The sallow face was
watching Hearne with distrust. There was no doubt of that.
Hearne restrained himself, and went on looking at the ash
tray impassively.

"Well," the man said at last. "Surprised?" The voice was
high-pitched, almost fretful.

"Yes," admitted Hearne with considerable truth. He was
fascinated by the cigarette, still held in place by the colorless
lips even as they moved.

"So now we are having our first meeting under the new
régime. It is certainly safer, anyway."

"Yes," Hearne agreed, "but is it wise to have one here at
this time? I thought we were to avoid being seen with anyone
at the hotel, meanwhile. We aren't to come out into the
open, yet. Later, but not yet."

"Wise? Sitting in this dump in this God-forgotten hole? No
one comes in here any more. They are even avoiding this side
of the square. And why do you think I didn't talk to you
when you were out there with that girl? Who was she,
anyway?"

"Anne Pinot."

"Oh." The truculence in the man's voice gave way to
interest. He had obviously known something of Corlay's private affairs. How much? And was that a sign of real friendship with Corlay, or did the man's knowledge come from
gossip? His next words with their undisguised sneer gave
Hearne a clue. "Oh, your fiancée?" The man was obviously
no real friend.

Hearne remained silent, his brow in the frown which
Corlay had adopted whenever he was reluctant to talk.

"Still unwilling to take a joke?" The man laughed mali-
ciously, showing an uneven row of fine pointed teeth, complete with handsome gold patchwork. The cigarette clung to
the moist lip. "Clever chap, aren't you, Corlay? We always
used to laugh at the way you played up to the women. But

you got results." He looked round the empty restaurant with undisguised scorn. "You got *this* made the headquarters!"

So that was what was annoying this man. He had, no doubt, thought that his own district would have made handsomer headquarters. Instead, he now felt subsidiary to Corlay, and he didn't like it.

Hearne watched the spreading brown stain on the chewed end of the cigarette. "There are more important reasons than that," he said coldly, "or this place would not have been made the headquarters. Why did you come here?"

The man accepted the change of subject quite as unsuspectingly as Hearne had hoped he would. A change of subject was only natural after the implied snub which had just been administered.

"I came to verify the points in a letter which I received yesterday."

The bitter voice told Hearne as much about the letter as he needed to know. The points in the letter had so confounded this man that he had come here at once to make quite sure there had been no mistake. He couldn't quite believe that the headquarters of the organization, which Hans and Elise had been so skillfully nursing, should really be established here.

Hearne said, "I hope the trip has been worth your while. What instructions did you get?"

"Plenty." The man jabbed the sodden cigarette end into the ash tray, and lit another cigarette. He didn't offer one to Hearne. "Plenty. Including the instructions to wait for you here until you came down this afternoon so that we could compare notes. What are your plans?"

"Just what I've been told. I'm working towards results by stimulating a series of Breton nationalist meetings, and by accenting the importance of co-operation for the achievement of our ideals."

"That would carry you through here, all right," the man assented gloomily. "But down in the towns, it is going to be more difficult. Here, the people are half-asleep. Here, the Germans haven't interfered much with the life of the district so far. But in Dol, it is different. They have been there for some weeks now. They are using many of its people in construction work, and the women don't like it any more than the men. And then I'm told to gather them all together under the banner of co-operation! I tell you, that can't be done unless the Germans don't interfere with the people's existence; and they cannot but interfere in important centers, where large-scale preparations have got to have extra labor. We'll have to use other methods in those towns, I tell you."

Hearne checked his first impulse to soothe the man. Why should he? It would be the best thing he could do if he could encourage a feeling of injustice and jealousy among Hans's chosen band. He smiled condescendingly, tilted his chair back against the wall, and watched the man through half-closed eyes. His obvious enjoyment of the man's predicament infuriated the thin nostrils.

"You think it's easy?" the man demanded.

"If you don't, someone else will."

The man stared. "So," he said softly, "if I don't find it easy, someone else will?"

"No doubt," Hearne said placidly, and yawned.

"Do you realize how important my district is? Do you realize how I have worked there for nearly two years? No one else knows all the difficulties, the peculiarities, as I do."

"Really?"

"Yes, my fine friend, really. You sit up here with your head in the clouds, thinking out grand phrases for your next speech. But it is I who work."

"And just what gives you the impression that you work more than I do? Just what makes you think Dol should be so much more important than other districts?"

"You must come and visit me some day. We shall make a little tour of the new airfields, of the new underground stores, of the new roads, of the— But what's the use? Nothing I have ever said ever convinced you."

"On the contrary. I am delighted to hear your news, for it shows our strength. As you know, I have just managed to get back to St. Déodat, and until this talk with you I wasn't sure of the progress that has been made during the last month. I used to think that Brittany would only be of political value to our friends. Now, I see that we have still a greater role to play."

"Yes, and more difficult."

"Then all the greater credit will be ours."

"Yes." The man's tone was not wholly confident. "If the right people get the credit," he added spitefully.

"That's to be seen, of course," Hearne said callously, and watched the man's reaction with a good deal of pleasure. "But why worry if *you* don't get the credit, provided the cause is victorious?"

That silenced the thin face opposite him. It was Hearne who had to speak first, after that. He said casually, "I suppose all this preparation is for attack?"

The man looked quickly up at him. "Why do you ask?" he said sharply.

"Because I prefer to be on the attacking side in this war. Defense is unpleasant since the perfection of the bombing plane."

"Oh, you can sleep in your comfortable bed without fear of bombs. We are on the attack."

"Good. The sooner the better."

"It will be quite soon. In six weeks' time. That is definite. England is beaten already. In six weeks' time, the army of occupation will be over in Britain. That will make things easier for us, then."

"You feel there will be nothing to fear here, once the Germans are occupied elsewhere?"

"Nothing to worry about, nothing that can't be taken care of by the Gestapo and a handful of planes. Some will be relieved to find they are on the winning side, although they hadn't the courage to fight for it like you and me. The others, they'll have all the heart taken out of them. This is why Britain must fall. She's the rallying ground of those who want to fight. Once she's gone, they'll be left hopeless, and when they are hopeless, they can be persuaded."

"And that's our job," Hearne said. "How are the rest of our organization? Are we meeting soon?"

"I shall call a meeting for five of them this week, and tell them what I have learned today. Then they will each hold their own meetings, and pass on my report and recommendations. In that way, we will co-ordinate our campaign, although we shall have to use our individual judgment in dealing with the particular problems of our districts. We don't all live in pleasant villages, and plan speeches, you know."

Hearne hesitated, as if he were weighing something carefully in his mind, and then he said quietly, "Are they all to be trusted?"

The man paused in lighting another cigarette. The flame from the small wax match reached his bitten thumbnail, and he dropped the smoking stub with an oath.

"Why shouldn't they be?" he said slowly. "They've all risked death for the rewards they will now get. Rewards never dulled loyalty."

"That's the point. Rewards. There may be a division of opinion about these. After all, you and I understand each other. You have a difficult, and an important, district to organize successfully. I have to make important speeches. We aren't competing. We are each sure of the rewards for our loyalty." Hearne watched the man's eyes and was content with the uncertainty which he saw there. Hearne continued calmly, "But the others may not be so sure of the results for themselves. They may be impatient. Be very careful with them. They may interpret our efforts in a wrong light, even carry tales to our German friends in order to discredit us."

The man said nothing, but there was a look of speculation in his eyes as they stared at the wall above Hearne's head. The idea which Hearne had sown was firmly planted. It would bear sour fruit.

Hearne became businesslike. He talked of the next meeting, of the problems which must be covered before it would take place. The man from Dol listened, and made his counter-suggestions as Hearne had guessed he would. That type always had a counter-suggestion ready. Then counter-suggestion gave way to detailed instructions, which were obviously pulled out of his memory. He repeated them too glibly not to have heard them only some hours before. Some of the phrases he used might have come straight from Elise's mouth.

"Good," Hearne said at last, "now, what about a date for the next meeting?" As the man searched through a small diary of closely written pages and licked the point of a pencil, Hearne was thinking of Kerénor, of Kerénor and the use to which he might put the nationalist meetings which the Nazis were going to encourage. Kerénor, if he could get his warnings to the various districts about the true meaning of these meetings, if he and other true Bretons could use these gatherings for their own purposes, could start the beginning of a powerful movement against the Germans. The Nazis would regret some day that they had encouraged the Bretons to get together. And the Bretons would play their own secret game very well. Hearne smiled to himself as he thought of the enjoyment they would get out of duping the Germans.

"What about the twentieth of this month?" the man asked. Hearne made a great pretense of concentrating.

"Good," he agreed at last. "Now where? In Dol? Café de la Grande-Rue, as usual?"

The man was pleased at the choice of locality. He nodded almost amiably, and marked a neat cross in his diary. "I'll inform the others," he said decisively.

I bet you will, thought Hearne. He said, "Any other particular news? You must have been busy in the last month?"

The man nodded, holding his head to one side so that the curling cigarette smoke would avoid his eyes. Then suddenly, he began to talk. The temptation to show the speechmaking Corlay just how little he knew about what was going on couldn't be resisted. He plunged into long details mixed with complaints and boasts. Hearne listened, his face set in an expressionless mask. Whenever the man slackened in his descriptions, Hearne would look only half-convinced, even skeptical. That was enough to start the flow again. But at the end, he gave the man the satisfaction of seeing a Corlay who was visibly impressed by the importance of the small town of Dol and its surroundings.

At last Hearne rose. "Mustn't stay too long in the hotel, meanwhile," he explained.

The man nodded. "It is sort of funny too, to see you again. We all thought you were missing for good. Marbeuf said the last he saw of you was someone dying on a wharf at Dunkirk with a couple of English soldiers lying beside him."

"Marbeuf? And how did he get away?" Good old Marbeuf, Hearne thought, whoever Marbeuf was. But he obviously wasn't someone who had stopped to see how he could help Corlay.

"A French boat took him off. How did you get away?"

"On the next French boat. I wasn't so good at using my elbows as Marbeuf. And tell him I wasn't dying. A shell exploded too near me, but I was lucky and the most I got was a bad shock. Sorry to disappoint you all."

"Same old Corlay, aren't you?"

"Only more so." Hearne stared fixedly at the small thin man.

"All right, all right," he said hastily. "Believe me, I am delighted to find that Marbeuf was wrong."

"You aren't half as delighted as I am."

"All right, all—" And then the restaurant door was opened, and two German officers marched in. They halted their stride as they saw the two men at the table. The smaller officer was Traube, the auctioneer's clerk who had surveyed the Corlay farm. He was peering uncertainly through his glasses, and then nodded as he recognized Hearne.

"Good afternoon, Lieutenant Traube," Hearne said confidently. "I hope you are well, and Captain Deichgräber, too."

"Yes, yes. Captain Deichgräber is away at present, but he will be back shortly. I see you and Vuillemin have been taking the opportunity to have a little talk."

"Quite right, Lieutenant Traube." Vuillemin, Vuillemin. . . . Something was wrong somewhere.

The other officer didn't trouble to conceal his impatience. He said quickly to the strangely silent Frenchman beside Hearne, "You are leaving now? Good. It would be better not to come to St. Déodat again until you receive definite instructions to do so." He nodded abruptly, and continued his way to another table. He slapped its top with his gloves. "Service!" he called loudly as he sat down, seemingly quite unaware now of the two Frenchmen. Traube nodded in turn, looked embarrassed, and joined the other officer.

Hearne noted that all the confidence had left his companion. As he rose to leave the restaurant and the loud foreign voices, he was still silent. Hearne glanced at his face, and felt satisfied. The small thin man had not failed to mark the Germans' contempt for an ally. He returned Hearne's look, and that seemed to depress him even more, as if Hearne's set expression only verified his own fears.

"So then, until the twentieth!" Hearne said at the door.

The man nodded. He looked smaller, thinner. He wasn't paying any attention to Hearne. His eyes were fixed on the restaurant door which he had closed behind him.

By the time Hearne had reached the end of the hotel street, the Frenchman had disappeared. Hearne paused. And then, quickly, he turned and retraced his steps.

In the restaurant, the two German officers halted their conversation only as he reached their table. Hearne stood beside them and waited for them to finish their phrases. Traube cocked his head inquiringly.

"Herr Lieutenant Traube . . ." Hearne began in a low voice.

"Yes?"

The other officer wasn't even looking at Hearne.

"That man from Dol . . ."

"Yes?" Traube blinked his eyes anxiously.

"He's behaving strangely. Doesn't like taking orders."

"So." Traube glanced nervously at his companion, as if asking for help.

The other German poured himself some more wine. "I had noticed that," he said in his precise voice. "I had noticed that. Pity he should be at Dol, of all places. How long can you control him?"

"How long do you want him to be controlled?" Hearne's voice was that of a dutiful, eager and ambitious man. But he still kept his words low. Hurry, he was saying to himself; hurry, or that little shrimp from Dol will be in here on top of you.

It was Traube who said quickly, "Until the fifteenth of August. There must be no trouble before then. After the fifteenth we shall have more time to deal with him, if he doesn't behave more rationally."

"The fifteenth," Hearne said thoughtfully. "The fifteenth ... it isn't so long until then."

"It isn't so long," Traube's companion said. His lips were actually smiling. Then he was serious again. "But if you have definite suspicions about that man, then remove him at once. We can't risk any treachery."

"I've no proof. I only had a feeling today that he was a waverer. With the proper supervision, he should be safe."

"Well, give him that supervision." The German's voice was irritable once more. "See that he's satisfied." He turned to Traube. "Would it be difficult to replace him now?"

Traube said, "Well, he knows a lot. He's been trained under us for two years. And he has done some good work in the past."

"In that case, keep him working with us. Promise him anything. Later, when we are less occupied with important plans ..." The officer removed a thread from his sleeve.

Hearne knew he was dismissed. "Very good." He clicked his heels as he took one step back. "Then you suggest I should pay an unexpected visit to our little friend at Dol? I shall make a report on that visit."

The captain nodded. Traube, watching him anxiously, said, "Yes, yes. You will be held responsible if you cannot control him. And when you visit Dol, see Major Kalb of the Schutzstaffel. He is in charge of the organization of that town."

Hearne raised his arm in the approved salute, barked the magic words, wheeled neatly towards the door.

The captain's voice, speaking in German now, carried farther than he had intended. Or perhaps he thought that this man Corlay wouldn't know much German, anyway. "... set a Frenchman to catch a Frenchman," he was saying. "But I advise you to set one of Ehrlich's men, too, Traube. And advise Deichgräber on his return, of course." Traube was mumbling a reply. "Deichgräber . . . Ehrlich . . ." was all that Hearne could catch, as he stepped out into the deserted street.

Hearne walked quickly back to the farm, arranging in his mind the information he had learned in the last hour, so that the facts which he had sifted would go neatly and easily down onto paper. It was at the dovecote that he halted, as he suddenly remembered. His subconscious had at last yielded up the name which had been haunting him. "Vuillemin," he repeated. It wasn't Vuillemin. The man was Number 8 from Dol, and the name was Bruneau. Bruneau, not Vuillemin. Vuillemin was Number 9. Now the reason for the man's worry became quite clear. The German ally had not only shown his contempt: he had even not considered it necessary to learn the right name. And the fear which Hearne had sown in the man's mind would be strengthened. What chance was there for proper rewards and recognition for Bruneau, when he was just as easily called Vuillemin?

But Hearne hadn't time to be amused. He was too busy thanking his stars that his caution with names had prevented him from imitating the German. "So then, Vuillemin, until the twentieth." That would have sounded well enough at the time. But it would have been an unsatisfactory way to end one's career.

He was concentrating on the facts he had learned from Bruneau as he climbed towards the Corlay farm. That was one way to stop thinking about the thinness of the ice over which he had performed such an elaborate outside edge. And then he realized that it wasn't his stars he should thank: it was Matthews.

CHAPTER 15

The Golden Star

As the crow flew, it was fourteen miles to St. Servan, sixteen
to St. Malo. But it took Myles and Hearne from sunset in St.
Déodat to the cold gray sky of the heartless hour before
dawn to reach the outskirts of St. Servan. They had avoided
the villages and the roads, had skirted farms and isolated
houses.

It had been a strange journey, with the tall American,
dressed in the corduroy trousers and blue smock and round
black felt hat of Madame Corlay's uncle, plodding determinedly beside an equally silent Hearne. When they had to
speak, they spoke softly, abruptly and in French. That had
been Hearne's advice. He had also stipulated that, if by some
stroke of bad luck or piece of carelessness they were inter-
cepted, the American must then forget he had ever seen the
Corlay farm. He would have to produce his own story.
Hearne, in his turn, would have to admit that he had never
seen the American before: that they had met only by the
sheerest accident in that field or that wood over there. With
Bertrand Corlay's name attached to him, they would eventu-
ally believe him; and the excuse to Elise for this night
journey would have to be tied up with the name of one of
the men on Corlay's list. He was to have a free hand in his
decisions, she had said. He was to keep his business meetings
secret from the Bretons. Elise would believe him, too.

But he felt a wave of relief when he saw the spreading
estuary of the River Rance flowing towards the Channel
coast. Ahead of them should be the straggling outskirts of St.
Servan, forming a kind of suburb to the old walled town of
St. Malo. Here, where the two men had halted, the dismal
string of small houses and small shops and flagrant billboards
had not yet begun. Here, the fields and trees still met the
steep banks of the river. Here, where the tides had swirled
out a muddy inlet, there were still small groupings of simple

houses, with their inevitable jetties and anchored boats and drying fishing nets. They could be called fishermen's villages, if barely a dozen cottages could be said to form a village. Hearne and Myles had passed two such communities, scarcely a mile apart.

"We should be almost there," Hearne said, more to reassure himself than to encourage Myles. "There are only seven houses and a pub. It's called the Golden Star. The pub, that is. We *must* be almost there." We've got to be, he added to himself, as he looked at the sky.

"Perhaps we are." Myles pointed to the fishing nets stretched between the tall poles just ahead of them. Down on the river, two black shapes of boats with furled sails pulled against their moorings. Three other smaller boats lay drunkenly on the smooth mud, where the tide had abandoned them. And then they saw the row of houses, built at the very edge of the riverbank. Some of them had ends which overshot the bank and were supported by props driven into the shore itself. At high tide, the water would lap under these gable ends themselves. Now, they looked as hunched and precarious as a man slumping over his crutches.

Myles and Hearne strained their eyes.

"Can't be sure, in this light," admitted Hearne at last. "You stay here, well in the shadow of this tree. I'll have a look."

"Sure." Myles sat down thankfully. His voice was cheery enough, but there was a drawn look in his face.

"Feet?"

"Blast them."

"Wait here."

"Sure."

The houses hugged each other tightly as if to give themselves courage. Even so, the only word to describe them was "dejected." They needed plaster and paint: that was obvious even in this half-light. In their sleep, they looked as sluttish as a sagging woman with twisted rags in her hair. Hearne counted them carefully. They looked like eight altogether, if they began and ended where he thought they did. That was the difficulty with a row of houses: it would have been simple if they had been clearly separate. One was a pub. That at least was definite. Despite its lack of paint, the lettering was still visible: faint but visible. "Etoi . . . 'Or." That must be it. Etoile d'Or. That must be it, although the three middle letters had given up all hope, and faded away entirely. Like the other houses, the Golden Star was dark and silent. It stood at the end of the row of buildings, and in its dark side wall was an insignificant door. Hearne took a deep breath. He had found the name *and* the side door. This was the place. It had to be.

He tried the handle. It turned easily. So far, so good. Inside, another door faced him. That was correct, too. He let the outside door swing behind him and stood in the dark coffin of space between the double entrance. This time he knocked: three short raps, two long. Pause. Again three short, two long. It was so dark that he couldn't even see his hand. All he was aware of was the smell of fish and decaying seaweed which still persisted here, and mingled in its own peculiar way with the stale odor of fried oil and damp walls. He knocked again in the same way. Wish to God that Basdevant would come, he thought desperately. Apart from the nausea which gripped him, he was haunted by the thought of the steadily approaching dawn, spreading inexorably from the east. As for the possibility that Basdevant might no longer be functioning here—well, that was something he couldn't even start worrying about. Without this Basdevant, there was only a long dangerous walk ahead of them towards Mont St. Michel and the archeologist Duclos. He waited, rehearsing the phrases which that worried French Intelligence man in London had taught him. Basdevant would be six feet and broad-shouldered. He would have black hair, black-brown eyes, an aquiline nose, a red complexion, strongly marked eyebrows and a bottle scar on his left temple. What the hell was keeping Basdevant?

And then the door opened suddenly and a lamp was held in front of his face so that it blinded him. He stood there, with his eyes screwed up tightly, his hands half-raised to shield them from the glare. He cursed his over-caution in not carrying his revolver: he had thought that his name of Corlay would be better protection than bullets as long as Elise and her Hans could vouch for him.

A deep voice said truculently, "What do you want?"

"This is an inn, isn't it?"

"Yes. But it's closed."

"Well, it's open now. I've money to pay for what we eat." Or rather, Myles had. The few francs which Madame Corlay had given him might be needed for the return journey.

"We?" The man's voice was friendlier. He shifted the weight of the lamp, and Hearne had a chance to see him.

"Two of us." Hearne could make out the man's face. Yes, this must be Basdevant. Fournier had indeed given an accurate description. At this moment, the man's black hair was ruffled, his feet were bare, his clothing consisted of a shirt.

"It's cold here," Hearne said suddenly, remembering Fournier's careful coaching. He spoke slowly. "We could talk better in front of your fire, if the wood is still burning."

"The wood is still burning." Basdevant stepped aside to let him enter.

Hearne hesitated a moment. Perhaps the man was getting careless, or perhaps the identification formula had to be shortened to suit the memories of his new clients. They wouldn't be only Deuxième Bureau, now: probably most of them, if not all, were fugitives.

"I'll get my friend," Hearne said and turned towards the door at his back. The man hurriedly blew out the light. There was darkness behind Hearne as he descended the three stone steps into the road, and Basdevant's voice, low, urgent.

"Hurry," he said, "hurry. Daylight is breaking."

The American was still sitting as Hearne had left him. He rose stiffly, clumsily, to his feet. He was trying to stop himself shivering in the raw morning air.

"All clear. We'll get something to eat and drink," Hearne said, and helped the limping Myles to hurry his steps. He, too, felt suddenly pretty low in the water. He blamed it on lack of sleep. Lack of sleep, he thought. Two nights over hills and fields, two nights scrabbling under hedges, two nights floundering through muddy paths. Two cold dawns with needle rain which stung your skin and froze your blood. Two waking nightmares, he thought.

"We'll get something to eat and drink," he repeated. And then as they were almost at the door, he remembered to add, "Don't say what you want to eat or drink. I'll do the ordering."

Myles nodded. His face was colorless and lined with fatigue.

"Cheer up," Hearne said, "you won't have to walk over the Channel." If Myles could have given a smile, Hearne would have had one.

The outside door opened easily and again Hearne noted that the hinges had been well-oiled. But this time, the inner door was open too. They closed it behind them, and stood

together in the darkness. Hearne unconsciously kept hold of
the American's elbow.

Basdevant's deep voice said, "Is that door closed properly?"

"Yes."

A match grated and flared. The lamp was lit once more.
Basdevant smiled amiably and spoke again. "This way, gentlemen. Had to make sure about the door. The night air is
treacherous." He was standing at the other end of the short
corridor; behind him was the entrance to a room. He had
added a pair of faded red sailcloth trousers to his shirt. He
jerked a large thumb over his shoulder. "There's a fire in
here," he said, and led the way into the room.

The ceiling was low, so low that the Breton only had to
sling the handle of the lamp over a hook on one of the
wooden beams just above his head, and the room was lighted. And there was a fire, with flames leaping comfortably on
the wide stone hearth. Myles sat down heavily on the wooden
bench at one side of the fireplace. Hearne stood in front of
the blaze and held his numbed fingers out towards the heat of
the newly added log. He heard the sound of a bottle knocking against a glass. He took the thick tumbler which Basdevant held out to him. The raw brandy stung his throat, but it
was what he needed. Myles had emptied his glass too; perhaps it was the warmth of the fire, or the fact that his weight
was off his feet, or that he was becoming accustomed to the
strange smell of the house, but he suddenly seemed cheerier.
Or, thought Hearne, perhaps he just needed that brandy as
much as I did.

Basdevant was moving skillfully about among the disorder
of the room. He noticed Hearne's expression. "This is my
own corner," he said with a broad smile. "It's warmer here
than in the front room. You see I like to live comfortably."
He swept his powerful arm round the unbelievable chaos.
"Now, what would you like to eat?"

Myles looked at Hearne, and then bent down to unlace his
boots. Hearne said slowly and distinctly, "Cold mutton and
some goat cheese."

"And to drink?" A still broader smile was spreading over
the Breton's face.

"Water."

Myles paused in the unlacing of his boots and looked sadly
at Hearne. The Englishman looked as if he meant what he

said, but he was thinking how very unpleasant it would be if Basdevant were to take him at his word.

"Dry your clothes on that line," Basdevant said as he picked up a smoke-blackened pan from the table and set its chain handle on a hook over the glowing log. He was pointing to a dirty piece of rope which was stretched across the front of the stone mantelpiece. Like all of Basdevant's arrangements, it was practical even if it wasn't beautiful. It looked worse when their bedraggled clothes were strung over the sagging piece of rope. Hearne had hung his jacket carefully, so that the two neat packages in his inside jacket pocket wouldn't be dislodged. He resisted the impulse to take them out and hold them in his hand: better, he decided quickly, to leave them where they were, to let the others think there was nothing of value in his pocket. He ostentatiously removed his penknife, his few francs, and the map. He opened it up to dry it, so that Basdevant could see what it was. But he remained standing at the side of the fireplace, watching the oil crackle in the heated pan. Even when the Frenchman handed him a red-checked tablecloth with which to rub himself down, he didn't move away from the fire and the drying clothes. Nor did he step aside when Basdevant tossed some fish carelessly into the pan. This time, the odor which filled the room was not unpleasant.

"Sorry," Hearne said, as Basdevant bumped against him. "This fire is too good to leave." As he finished drying himself with the tablecloth, he was looking round the room. The door by which they had entered was on the same side as the fireplace. Opposite them was a crumpled bed. In the wall which probably overhung the river was one small window, heavily curtained, and a flight of stairs leading to the rooms overhead. Opposite that was a wall filled with wardrobes and chairs, and in that wall was a second door. Hearne guessed that it might lead into the front room: bar was probably its real function.

Basdevant was watching him. "Cosy here, isn't it?" he asked. "How do you like the decorations?"

There was something in the big man's voice which impelled him to look at the calendars and advertisements hung on the walls. Cinzano ... Byrrh ... Quinquina ... Berger. ... From this distance they all looked equally gaudy, equally innocuous.

"Very pretty," Hearne murmured. Basdevant was still

looking at him. Hearne's eyes flickered again over the dim
walls to see what he had missed. Two small pieces of paper
were pinned up over the bed. The Breton had left the
fireplace and was now clearing a place for their meal at the
table by raking his forearm across one of its corners. Hearne
crossed the room towards the bed. Two pieces of paper: two
certificates. One was birth, the other first communion. Both
belonged to Louis Basdevant.

Hearne came back to the fireplace. "Cold away from the
fire," he said. The Breton had found the plates he was
looking for. As he came over to the cooking fish, he smiled
at Hearne and nodded as if to say, "You see. I'm your man
all right." Hearne smiled back. He was as amazed as he always was whenever he saw someone so big and powerful as
this being so incredibly naïve. It amazed and pleased him. But
that was the natural reaction, he reflected, of someone who
only measured five feet ten.

"Now we can eat," Basdevant said. "And drink. And then
we can talk, if you're still awake."

"Which reminds me," Hearne said, "have you a room we
can rent?"

"And have you some clothes?" It was Myles who spoke,
rising slowly from the wooden bench. He said in English to
Hearne, "It's no fun being a nudist. I just about left half of
my skin on that chair."

"What did he say?" Basdevant was looking with interest at
Myles. Hearne translated freely. The Breton threw back his
head and laughed. With a pair of gold earrings skewered
through his ears, he would have made a fine corsair.

"Of course," he said. "I forgot." Now, did you really,
thought Hearne and looked at Basdevant's broad back reflectively as he carried the fish to the table. "Take a blanket
from the bed. Hurry, or the fish will be spoiled," the Breton
called over his shoulder.

"And so," he continued, as they held a dark gray blanket
round them with one hand and ate the fish with the other,
"and so, you are English?"

"American," Myles said quickly.

"We haven't sailed anyone as far as that yet." Basdevant
laughed again. There was a gold tooth in the back of his
mouth. That was what had started thoughts of earrings,
Hearne realized. He saw one of Myles's eyebrows raised. This
unexpected mention of sailing had probably interested him. It

certainly interested Hearne: everything was being made very
easy for them. It must be pleasant working in the Deuxième
Bureau.

Basdevant was talking volubly, with smiles and quick gestures and a general air of comradeship. They might have
known him for years. Myles and Hearne found themselves
smiling and nodding at the right places as they listened. "It's
strange," Basdevant was saying, "very strange. Once we used
to fish over towards the English coast. But did the fishermen
in Cornwall welcome us? Not they. You'd have thought we
had been fishing right within their waters! Well, that didn't
worry us. Who's to say where one bit of sea ends and the
other begins? It all flows together, doesn't it? So, when we
were right close to the shore, we'd pay a little visit to these
Cornishmen. Just to show there were no hard feelings on our
part. And we'd get some food, or a sail patched up, or a net
mended when we were there. I remember a place called St.
Ives. . . . Ever been there?" Myles and Hearne shook their
heads. But for Hearne there was a tingle of pleasure as he
heard the name, even pronounced as it was. "Well, in St. Ives
there was an inn just down by the harbor where they used to
sell their catches of fish. We used to go there for a drink,
perhaps two, perhaps three. And as we were very sorry for
those poor fishermen in Cornwall, we'd tell them how to
catch fish. Well, then there might be a fight. These Englishmen used to lose their tempers very quickly. But they didn't
fight as well as we did. They used their fists, or perhaps,
when they got very angry, a bottle. But that's no way to
fight."

"Knives?" suggested Hearne with a suspicion of a smile.
He remembered some of the scenes in St. Ives when the
foreign poachers (every Cornish fisherman swore they
poached) started drinking in the local pubs. First, wary
silence; then boasts; then arguments and loud oaths; then
blows, and knives, and broken bottles. It was always the
same pattern. It ended with the Bretons slashing their way to
their boats, cursing the English vividly as they ran; with the
Cornishmen shaking bruised knuckles after their visitors, yell-
ing to them to bloody well stick to their own bloody side of
the bloody fishing grounds. And then three weeks later, the
Bretons would be back, smiling their way towards a bar,
talking loudly of the good catches they had had, in their
perfectly understandable form of English. The strangest thing
of all to Hearne was to know that the Bretons were more

closely related to the Cornishmen than they were to other Frenchmen, or than the Cornishmen were related to other Englishmen.

"Why didn't the Englishmen stave in your boats?" asked the practical Myles. Hearne watched Basdevant's face in amusement.

"Stave in our boats?" he shouted incredulously. It was obvious that the idea had never occurred to him. Fishermen didn't take away each other's life, that way. Poach? Yes ... but not destroy.

"You were saying something was very strange," suggested Myles.

"Ah, yes." Basdevant relaxed again. He would be an ugly customer in a fight. Whoever had given him that bottle scar was a brave man, if he still lived.

"Yes, it's strange. For now, when we go, we are given a fine welcome fit for a prince. You should see the way they welcome the lobsters we bring over, now." He paused, as if to let his words sink into his guests' minds. "When do you want to sail?" he asked suddenly.

"Tonight," Myles said.

Basdevant thought for some moments. His heavy eyebrows were bushed over his brown eyes. He said at last, "The tide will be difficult. What about tomorrow night?" He didn't wait for a reply. "Fine," he said. "Tomorrow night."

Myles looked quickly at Hearne, but he was picking the last bones carefully out of his piece of fish.

It was excellent fish.

CHAPTER 16

Trial for a Traitor

It was cold in the room upstairs in the Golden Star and it seemed all the colder because of the bareness of the place. Three narrow beds, a mattress on the floor, a rain-spotted window overlooking the river, a chair. That was all.

"Why did you bring the clothes up here?" asked Myles.

"They were dry." They damned well weren't dry, thought Myles, and Hearne knew it as well as he did. He spread his trousers and shirt flat on the wooden floor, thoughtfully.

"We'll sleep well," Hearne said very clearly in French, and sat down heavily on the nearest bed. It creaked satisfactorily. "There are enough blankets, anyway. We have thirty-six hours for sleep. That should be enough." He yawned loudly.

Myles finished arranging his clothes and his boots. He looked towards the door and pointed silently. One eyebrow was up.

Hearne nodded. The American sat noisily down on the bed next Hearne's and yawned in turn. The two men rolled the blankets tightly round themselves and then lay still. The rain had stopped. There was morning sunshine outside the window, and a smooth stretch of blue sky.

When they at last heard the sound of Basdevant's large feet moving about in the room below, Hearne raised himself on an elbow. He whispered, "We'll sleep in relays."

"You can begin. I got some shut-eye yesterday. It is only my feet which worry me. What's wrong, anyway?"

Hearne considered for a moment. He owed the American a warning. He couldn't expect any intelligent co-operation if he kept Myles completely in the dark.

"What do you think of all this?" he asked Myles.

"I liked the fire and the food."

"And Basdevant?"

"He's a big fellow, very big."

"That's just about what I thought."

The two men looked at each other and grinned.

Hearne said, "To be quite frank, I don't like it."

"Strong smell of fish," agreed Myles. And then, he was suddenly serious. "Isn't that buzzard all right? You should know."

"I thought I did. He's certainly the man I was looking for. I got his name from someone reliable." Or was Fournier reliable? God, nowadays you had even doubts of your own grandmother, Hearne thought. Or was he being too jittery, worrying over trifles, finding suspicions where there should be none? Lack of sleep, probably: perhaps if he got some sleep he would stop seeing mysteries.

The sky outside the window was a pale, ruthless blue.

"Well?" the American asked. "I'm old enough to know."

The footsteps still moved about downstairs.

Hearne spoke quickly. "This is the place, and that is the

man. He's probably just careless, or simple, or good-natured. I'm probably dizzy with sleep and cursed with a doubting mind. But, first of all, he let us into the house without proper identification. He seemed eager to get us inside. He was eager to identify himself. He was eager to get down to business. He made all the moves. And then he didn't like our idea of bringing our clothes up here. It was he who suggested we should dry them at the fire, but he didn't rush to offer us any others, although he was a good host in every other way. Last of all, he said the tide wouldn't be right: that was an excuse for a couple of landlubbers. We seemed that, all right, by suggesting something about a hole being knocked in some-one's boat."

"That explains a lot," Myles said. "Now, I'll add my nickel's worth. He lives too damned well. Did you notice the oil he wasted when he fried that fish? I'm telling you there hasn't been a farmhouse in my travels which slopped the oil about that way. And there was butter, even if it did taste like a goat. And cheese, a big one at that. And brandy, and red wine, and good coffee, and cigarettes. It's what I would call pre-armistice standard. Look, you've a farm and the Ger-mans have only started to penetrate your district, but you live more carefully than he does. He's slap bang beside St. Malo, and the Germans have settled nicely into the place by this time: I bet every inch of bread, every spoonful of oil in the district is noted down in their little black notebooks."

"We are making a nice case out of very little," Hearne said. "He may smuggle a lot of things in here, by his boat. He seems to enjoy poaching. He may even——" He paused. The room below was silent. There might have been a move-ment at the foot of the stairs.

Myles had noted it, too. "Sleep," he whispered.

Hearne added a few snores to that advice. He felt warm and comfortable. The food and wine and brandy were doing their work. Another five minutes of pretending, and he would act himself into sleep. He heard the door open slightly. Myles stirred, turning in the way which light sleepers do at the suspicion of a noise. Then the door was closed again, careful footsteps descended the steep wooden stairs.

"You sleep," Myles whispered again. "I'll keep watch."

"Half an hour. Wake me then. We may have to be ready to move on."

Myles nodded his agreement.

The blue of the sky was bolder.

* * *

Myles was wakening him, shaking him lightly but determinedly.

"Sorry," the American was saying, "but I thought I'd better let you in on this. I can't get the hang of the accent."

Hearne sat up in bed, shaking his head to waken himself fully. The room was now warm with the sunlight which streamed through the window. Later than I meant to be, he thought. The clothes stretched out on the floor were crumpled but dry enough.

He looked at Myles and grinned. "That's better," he said. "I feel much better."

"I thought you needed more than a half hour. You'll be able to run all the faster, if we have to. But look!" He pointed to the half-open door. Standing in the shadows was a thin boy in Breton fishing clothes. "I've been struggling with his language for five minutes. He's nearly bawling because he can't understand me."

The boy spoke, his dark, anxious face looking at Hearne expectantly.

"The gentleman speaks French?" His accent was pure Breton.

"Yes. What is it?"

"My sister sent me."

"Well?"

"She says you are to hurry."

"Where?"

"You must go away."

"Now?"

The boy nodded.

"Why?"

The boy looked anxiously over his shoulder.

"Please," he said.

"Where's your sister?"

"Downstairs in the bar."

"Where's Basdevant?"

"Big Louis has gone to St. Malo. He will be back in an hour, perhaps more, perhaps less. My sister is in the bar."

A sudden light dawned on Hearne. "You mean she's in charge?"

"Yes."

"Who else is there?"

"The others."

"What others?"

"The men who live here: all except big Louis and Corbeau."

"Who's Corbeau?"

"Big Louis takes him on his boat now. He's his cousin."

"And your sister sent you up here. . . . Did the others know she sent you up?"

"Yes."

Hearne bit his lip. Myles, watching the boy's face intently, said in English, "He's scared stiff at what he's doing."

Hearne suddenly got out of bed. "We'll dress and go down and see this sister. Better hurry. How are the feet?"

"Could be worse."

They dressed quickly and silently. The boy's face relaxed. His brown eyes were smiling now.

He led the way down the rickety stairs. In Basdevant's living room, he halted and pointed to the door by which they had entered this dawn.

"No thank you," Hearne said, "we want to see your sister, first." He moved towards the door which lay opposite the window in the room. His guess last night had been that it led to the bar. He had probably been right: even now, with his hand on its latch, he could hear voices arguing.

The boy tried to catch his arm. "Not that way. This way." He pointed again.

"It's all right, sonny. We're friends," Myles was saying. "We only want to thank your sister." As the boy turned his head to answer the American, Hearne opened the door.

The noise inside the little room with its four marble-topped tables, its dark wood counter, its brightly colored calendars and paper flowers on the walls, ceased abruptly. Five men, their faces bronzed and lined from sea and wind; three boys, large-eyed and alert; a dark-haired woman leaning over the counter. That was all. They seemed to be one person as they turned and looked at Hearne and Myles. However divided had been the opinions which had caused their violent discussion, they were now united in thought and reaction as they faced the strangers.

"Pierre," the woman said angrily, "I told you—"

"We insisted on coming to thank you," Hearne cut in. "This isn't Pierre's fault."

Someone cleared his throat, feet shuffled, but no one spoke.

At last the woman said, "You've thanked me. Now go as you came."

"In this daylight?"

"It is safer now than at night."

"But we have a bill to pay," the American said.

"We don't want your money."

"Big Louis will."

The woman shrugged her shoulders. "Go now," she insisted. Myles exchanged a look with Hearne. "You handle this," he said in English. "The smell of fish is stronger."

Hearne nodded. He put his elbows on the counter of the bar, and leaned forward so that his face was no more than a foot across from the woman's. She wasn't so old as he had thought. Her resemblance to the boy Pierre was extraordinary: there was that same thin, high-cheeked shape of face, the same broad brow and deep-set brown eyes. The fine black hair was smoothed into a knot at the nape of her neck. There was color in her cheeks, and her skin was tanned as deeply as the men's. She wasn't so old after all; probably not even thirty. The lines and little wrinkles on her face came from strong sun and sea wind, not from age. The large eyes, fixed on him so intently, were young, and so were her strong arms and hands. It was the severity of her hair, the seriousness of her face, the fine lines on her skin which had made her seem more like Pierre's mother than his sister. He kept his eyes on hers, and a smile on his lips, as he fumbled in his mind for a beginning. A dull red flush mounted over the color in her cheeks and surged down into her neck. She moved a step backwards from the counter, and stood under the vase of paper flowers which had been hooked to the wall. But her eyes were still fixed on his.

"Please go," she said. Her voice was quieter, now.

"Yes, we are going. And we thank you for warning us. But we must find out why you warned us, so that in turn we can warn any others who might come here, as we did."

"You could stop them from coming?" The woman's face was suddenly animated with relief.

"We could stop many."

She turned to the boy quickly. "Pierre, go down and wait at the jetty. When you see him coming, let us know." Pierre left the room obediently. Myles and Hearne exchanged glances. So it was big Louis, all right.

"We'll have a drink," Hearne said. "We'll all have a drink." The silent men behind him were beginning to worry him. "What about a drink?" he said to them. Two of them came forward, the others hesitated and then followed.

The woman uncorked a bottle of a white colorless liquid. She shook her head as she said, "You are in danger by staying."

"We'll be all right. We wakened and came down for a drink. If he comes, then we pretend nothing has happened, that you didn't warn us. And we'll leave at the first chance we get." That seemed partly to satisfy her: she was pouring the drinks carefully into the small thick tumblers.

"Tell us one thing," Hearne said. "Would it be impossible to sail from here tonight?"

The men were amused: he must have said something highly funny.

"Is the tide unfavorable?"

The men were trying to hide their laughs. One of them failed. It was the seaman's prerogative over the stupid land-lubber.

"Stop that," the woman said sharply to them. She turned towards Hearne and Myles politely. "The tides never prevent us from sailing on this part of the river at any time. There's a deep channel in the middle."

"Big Louis said the tide was wrong tonight. That was why we must wait until tomorrow."

The men were amused no longer. The mention of big Louis had frozen them into silent watchfulness. Again Hearne had the feeling that he was facing an individual, and not five men and one woman. Myles was pretending to concentrate on his drink, but his eyes were missing nothing.

Hearne went on calmly, "Are there any German-lovers here?"

The effect was electric. The woman's eyes dilated and then narrowed. Two of the men slipped their hands into their pockets. Myles reached for the bottle casually as if to pour himself another drink, but he paused with his fingers round its neck. One of the younger men suddenly cursed, spat into his drink and pushed it away from him so violently that the glass upset.

"I knew you weren't," Hearne said in the same unhurried tone, "but I had to make sure. You do not look like the type of men who would lick the soles of the Germans' feet. Some do; and some even like the taste of it."

"So what?" the young man asked, his cold blue eyes hard with anger. He looked as if Hearne's words had soured the saliva on his tongue.

"What will the other fishermen on this river begin to say

about you when they learn that big Louis sells their allies to
their enemies? And they will learn some day. You can't hide
such things: they come out."

"That is our business." It was the oldest fisherman who
spoke. The others nodded. Only the woman and the man with
the angry eyes looked as if they didn't agree with that, but
they said nothing. Those Celts, thought Hearne irritably:
clannish was another word for them. He was the stranger
sticking his nose into their business. They could say what they
liked to each other about Basdevant, but they would have no
foreigner criticizing him for them. And a foreigner was
anyone who had not been born and brought up in this little
village of eight houses.

"That is your business," Hearne agreed. "You must deal
with him yourselves. But what if other men come here for
help? Will you stand aside and let the Boches catch them?
And what is going to happen to you if Basdevant quarrels
with any of you and informs the Germans that you helped
men to escape from him?"

"He wouldn't do that," the old man said, but his tone
lacked conviction.

It was the woman who spoke next. "I'm sick and tired to
death of hearing you men talk. Shall we do this, shall we do
that? You argue yourselves into your graves. First, let Jules
tell what he knows, what we all know. Then these two men
will go away, and we alone shall deal with big Louis and that
Corbeau he brought here to help him. This man is right: big
Louis is on trial. I didn't lose two brothers and my father in
this war for other men to grow fat on the leavings of their
murderers. Jules, tell what you know."

The young man with the angry blue eyes said, "At first,
everything was as it should be. When I got back from the
war, I helped with the others. We'd sail out to fish, and we'd
take any man who had come to big Louis, and we'd meet the
English boats, and sometimes we'd land them in England
ourselves. We know places on that coast like the back of our
hand. We didn't ask for money. If they had any, they gave us
it. If they didn't, well that didn't matter. We helped nine men
to escape. Some were French, some were English, one was a
Pole. Five days ago, we no longer had to sail so far. Big
Louis said he and the Corbeau could do it by themselves. It
was safer that way, he said. And then he seemed to have
money, and food. He gave us good reasons. We could say
nothing."

There was a general murmur from the men, and a shuffling of feet.

"But two days ago I was in St. Malo, and there I saw something." Jules paused. He looked gravely from Myles to Hearne as if to warn them to listen well. "Three days ago, two Englishmen were brought here by a man from Dinan. Big Louis sailed with them that night. There was also Corbeau, and young Yves from the next village."

The woman explained, "Young Yves is the son, the only son left, of Yves who is the head of that village." She smiled as if to excuse this interruption. Anyway, thought Hearne, she is really anxious we shouldn't miss a trick. He smiled back and nodded. The only son left ... something important was behind that.

"But why did young Yves come here to sail for England? Couldn't one of the men from his own village have taken him across the Channel?"

"Old Yves had forbidden it. This was his only son, now that the other two had been torpedoed in the war."

"And young Yves was determined to join the Frenchmen in Britain, even against his father's will?"

"Yes, and he had come to Basdevant for help."

Hearne and Myles exchanged quick glances. If Basdevant had betrayed young Yves, then here was the makings of a blood feud between the two communities; if the boy's father ever learned of the betrayal, that was. And the woman realized this. Hearne could see that in her eyes.

"Go on, Jules," she said impatiently.

"Well, two days ago I was in St. Malo. Some prisoners were being marched through the street. We stood in silence and watched them go. There weren't very many, and all were wearing civilian clothes. Among them I saw the two Englishmen: the young one, and the big one with red hair. And I saw young Yves."

No one moved. The dark, silent faces of the fishermen stared into emptiness. The woman's eyes were fixed, unseeing, on the pool of alcohol from Jules's overturned glass.

At last Hearne said, "Yes, you must deal with him yourselves. And if any others come here asking for Basdevant, will you help them?"

Jules nodded slowly. "If we see them arriving. We would not have known that you were here if you hadn't been late this morning, and I saw you by the gray light. We help anyone who hates our enemies."

Hearne thought, now there's the explanation for Basdevant's haste to get us indoors. He said, "And you hate anyone who helps your enemies?"

The men were still silent. At last, the oldest one said, "He is a good fisherman, the best on the river. We'll never find another like him."

"He is brave," agreed another, "and he is clever."

"He was a good man before the Germans came," the oldest man went on, "and perhaps—" He stopped and looked at the others.

"Another drink?" asked the American suddenly. "Open another bottle." Out of the side of his mouth he said to Hearne, "These damned appeasers."

Hearne was thinking, it's no good: the older ones will remember big Louis as he was to them; they'll remember his good points, his leadership, his comradeship. They'll begin to believe that he might be the same again, if only no more refugees come to tempt him. They may even end by blaming it all on the fugitives, and they'll turn their anger against Jules for disturbing their peace of mind.

"Yes," Hearne said, "I could do with another drink myself."

The woman was listening to the reminiscences of the other men. She looked at Hearne and shook her head sadly. "You see?" she seemed to be saying. She began to wipe the counter where Jules's glass had been upset, and then she paused suddenly, her brown eyes looking at Hearne and Myles in dismay.

"Do you hear that?" she began. "It's Pierre. He's running. I told you you would be too late. Get back to your room, quick. I'll think of something else to help you. Quick."

Pierre burst into the room, incoherent in his excitement. They understood the reason for it when they at last could make sense of his news. It wasn't Basdevant or Corbeau who had arrived. It was old Yves, and young Yves, and all the men from their village. They had sailed down as far as the little bay above the jetty; they must have left their boats there, for they had suddenly appeared on the river path. And they were walking towards the Golden Star.

Even as Pierre finished that last detail, the sound of men's feet could be heard on the roadway outside.

"If they want a fight, they can get it," said the old man, and drew a knife from his pocket. The blade snapped back in readiness. Other knives were coming out.

Hearne cursed this misplaced bravery under his breath. That old fool appeased when he should fight, and fought when he should reason and explain. "Gentlemen," Hearne said. "I think this solves your problem. It is Yves and his friends who will take action against big Louis. Obviously, he has escaped and his village knows all about Basdevant. If you defend him, the whole river will judge you were guilty along with him. Your names will stink worse than the mudflats at low tide." It was his last desperate effort to cut through the dangers with which they were binding themselves.

And then the door of the bar was flung wide open, and there seemed to be a mass of brown faces and red sailcloth trousers wedging the narrow space. A tall, broad-shouldered man with red hair slipped through the sullen group of fishermen. A thin young man followed him.

Hearne put his glass slowly down on the counter, and stared.

"What's wrong?" asked Myles. The spoken English reached the ears of the thin young man. He turned his head sharply and stared at Myles and Hearne, and then at Hearne.

"Well," he said. "Well. Look, Sam, who's here!" He came forward with a smile on his haggard white face, brushing a lock of hair impatiently back from his forehead. "I must say we *do* meet in the oddest places, don't we?"

Sam came forward unbelievingly. "Can you beat that? It's his nibs, himself," he said, and his slow Yorkshire voice filled the room.

It had a remarkably comforting sound.

CHAPTER 17

First Blood

Hearne looked at Myles, and then grinned. If he had seemed a funny kind of farmer before, God knew what the American was thinking now behind those alert eyes. Alert, but tactful. He was pretending to be interested in the newcomers, and only a shadow of a smile twisted the corner of his mouth.

Hearne turned quickly to the two Englishmen and spoke in his own voice: there was no need now for his Corlay imitation.

"Better get between them, tactfully. There's no good in a fight starting now. They'd only knife each other instead of big Louis."

"You know him?"

"We all know him," Myles said.

The three Englishmen and the American grouped themselves not too noticeably across the middle of the room. This separated the two parties of Frenchmen. There had been enough interest and surprise over the foreigners who knew each other to ease the initial tension just a fraction. That, and the fact that big Louis was not here, explained the feeling of indecision in the air.

Hearne seized his advantage. "Jules," he said, "tell them how you have judged big Louis." There was a stirring at the mention of the name.

"Yes, Jules, go on," the woman said quickly. She was standing beside the young fisherman. Her hand touched his arm for a moment.

Jules looked at the men in the doorway. "We have learned what big Louis has done. We shall deal with him. It is our business." The men around him echoed his words: "... our business."

"It is also ours." This time it was the black-bearded man standing in the doorway who had spoken. That must be old Yves. At his shoulder, there was a young man with the same high aquiline nose, and the same black hair and eyes. Young Yves, obviously.

There was a silence except for the marked breathing of the men.

"We shall deal with him," Jules said with finality.

Again that ominous silence.

Hearne spoke, wondering if he'd get a knife in his back for his trouble. "Jules, why not invite them to wait to see how you deal with big Louis?"

"They are already invited," Jules said, with unconscious dignity.

"And we accept the invitation." The black-bearded man nodded to the men behind him. They entered the room singly. But the knives were no longer visible.

"Order another bottle, for God's sake," Myles said to

Hearne. "At this rate, I'll have no money left to take me to England."

"Don't worry about that." It was the thin Englishman who spoke. "Old Yves is going to take us, and he will take you too. We sort of helped his son to escape. He says he would take us to South America for that."

"England will do, this time," the American said with a smile.

"It bloody well will," said Sam.

"Looks as if they'll be ready for a fight by the time big Louis arrives," Myles suggested.

"Yes," Hearne agreed, and looked round the room, too. The two groups of men had sat at the farthest separated tables. They sat in silence, their thin cigarettes drooping from their lips, one hand round their glass of crude spirits, the other hidden by the table. The woman served them, quietly, watchfully. It was only when her eyes would turn towards the door and she would listen that Hearne could see how nervous she really was.

Myles and the three Englishmen moved back to the counter of the bar. They could relax for a moment. The young officer was looking at Hearne once more. He was the first to speak.

"Well," he said again, "you do get about, don't you? By the way, you proved to be a very good doctor. Thanks for that. I'm almost cured." But Hearne noticed that he didn't touch the drink in his glass.

Hearne said quietly, "Why did you come back here after you escaped?"

"Safest place, at present. The Jerries would think we'd make a beeline for the coast. And then, Yves had a score to settle, and we felt like that, too. That blighter Louis, or whatever he's called, can't be left to run this show. By the way, my name is Townshend, and this is Walls."

Sam grinned, and said in a mock-Oxford accent, "Pleased tomeetyou, I'm sure."

"I am Myles, and this"—the American nodded towards Hearne—"is—" Hearne's glass unexpectedly emptied itself over Townshend's leg.

"Sorry," Hearne murmured. "Messy creature." Myles smiled gently and changed the subject.

"I've been wondering who is going to take big Louis on," he said. "Or is it a mass affair?"

Sam Walls looked at him with amazement spread thick over his good-natured face. "Who's takin' him on? Who d'you think?" He held out a large doubled fist, and a slow grin widened his mouth still more. Take a couple of pounds of good red meat; shape it roughly over broad round bones; stick a round lump in the middle for the nose; cut two creases for the eyes, and a wide slit for the mouth; add two twists of flesh for the ears, bending them forward slightly; fringe with thick red hair; forget about the eyebrows; and there you would have made Sam Walls. Not a work of art, thought Hearne, looking at the honest face in front of him: just the salt of the earth, that was all.

"It won't be so easy, Sam," Hearne said. "There's also a matter of Celtic pride and Celtic blood."

"What's that?" Sam asked bluntly, with fine Yorkshire contempt.

"These men," Hearne nodded to Jules and his comrades, sitting so silently and bitterly at their table, "these men feel it's a family affair. They want to deal with it in their own way, without any foreigner butting in. Even these men," he looked towards Yves and his friends, "are counted foreigners, although they've lived only two or three miles away from here all their lives. Do you see?"

"Can't say I do, lad."

"If you interfere first, they may gang up on you, on the four of us. Not because they hate us, although they don't like any foreigner very much, but just to teach us to keep our noses out of their business."

"They would, now?"

"Yes, they would."

Sam brooded over that. "Well, I've my own pride, too," he said at last. "I don't give a booger for this foreigner stuff. I'm after that Louis. There isn't a lad here big enough to deal with him."

"They are wiry and quick; they can use a knife as well as anyone."

"That's a bloody awful way to fight."

"Very bloody," agreed Hearne with a suspicion of a smile. "But don't start the fight, Sam. You'll never get to England without friends."

"I'll get there if I have to swim for it," Sam said.

"I think I heard aeroplanes," Townshend interrupted tactfully. "Hear them?"

"Third lot in the last two hours," Myles said.

"Plenty of them about. Boats too, and barges. You should have seen them in the water round St. Malo."

Hearne said quietly, "When you arrive in England, there will be someone to meet you. Remember everything for him."

"How will they know we're coming?"

"They will. Get Yves to sail his boat towards Penzance. An aeroplane will be scouting for you, and a launch will come to meet you."

"Reception committee?" Myles suggested.

Hearne nodded. "And I'll give you a package. All of you are responsible for its delivery. You're to give it over to a man called Matthews: white hair, red cheeks, blue eyes, large straight nose, natty navy suiting sort of person. Scotsman. Matthews. Matthews. Got that?"

The three men beside him looked suitably impressed. They nodded their agreement.

"What about you? Aren't you coming, too?" Townshend's thin face was politely curious.

Hearne shook his head. "Damn those planes," he said. They all listened. Even the silent Bretons had emerged from their Celtic gloom. One of them said something. Another added to that. A third contradicted. The tension had broken. All of them were talking, it seemed, as if to make up for lost time; talking quickly, loudly, with much expression and many oaths and even an occasional laugh.

The four men standing at the bar looked at each other in a mixture of incredulity and relief. The younger Yves had left his table and sauntered over towards them. Jules, not to be outdone in politeness, had come forward too. Hearne talked to Yves, while Myles and Townshend listened intently. His father would know Cornwall? Penzance? Good. Could they sail tonight? Still better. Then they could use the darkness to run clear of the French coast, do some fishing, and get near the Cornish coast by tomorrow's sunset, when an English boat would meet them? And then his father could make a neat exit into the darkness and be fishing off the French coast by next day? Yves nodded his head gravely. Yes, that could be managed. It would be arranged that way. He had his father's permission to go now: he had to go, now that the Germans were searching for him. They hadn't found out his right name, or where he lived. But there was always the possibility of being identified by some quick Boche eye: his father had understood that danger, and so he could go to England after all.

"Excellent," said Hearne with so much warmth that Yves's serious face was suddenly wreathed in smiles.

Myles was less enthusiastic. Either his feet were starting to trouble him again, or the waiting was getting on his nerves. "Fine and dandy," he said. "Now, all we've got to do is to get out of this country. That's all."

"And settle with Louis," added Townshend.

"Aye," Sam said. They could see a thought forming in his mind. He stood in front of the two young Bretons. "Looey!" he said loudly. "Looey!" He held up his clenched hand. Some of the other Bretons had looked towards him. "Looey!" Sam repeated to all the room, jabbed the air viciously with his fist, and pointed vehemently to himself. "Savvy?" he added.

The Bretons looked at him with polite interest and amusement. One of them shook his head sadly, drew his forefinger along his throat, and clicked his tongue. There was a little wave of laughter.

Sam stood with his big hands on his hips and glared at them. "Look here, lads," he said, "you don't know my lingo. I don't know yours. But get this straight. I'm going to twist Looey's neck until it breaks." He acted his words with a good deal of feeling. The Bretons were watching without any laughter now. The words were unintelligible to them, but the realness of Sam's emotions had got through to them. The silence was broken by renewed arguments.

"What d'they say?" Sam asked Hearne anxiously.

"They see your point, and they are interested in it. But it's no good, Sam: their minds are made up already. Still, they enjoy discussing your point of view."

"Where's this Louis, anyway?" demanded Myles. He was beginning to show a surprisingly strong temper.

"I *wish* I had my gun," Townshend murmured unhappily.

Hearne thought, we are all getting a bad attack of jitters just because none of us want to see a man knifed to death. Sam wants to use his fist, Myles is feeling truculent, Townshend wishes he had a gun, and I only wish that the whole thing could have happened in hot blood instead of us all waiting here so coldly for the kill.

He said, "Sam, what happened to that train?"

"Eh, lad?"

"You remember. . . . The train the Pole was going to drive?"

A slow grin replaced Sam's glumness. "Oh, that! Well, it was this way. The Pole got the engine movin' after fiddlin' with all t'nobs and buttons, and away we went like the hammers o'hell, and we skidded round t'bends, and we blew through t'stations like a nor'easter. Then train took notion to slow down, just gradual like, all by herself. There wasn't nothing we could do about her. We tried, but she was stuck fair and proper, bung in middle of bridge. We—" Sam halted, and listened, his head to one side. A car was passing through the village. It was slowing down. It braked suddenly outside the Golden Star.

They all looked at each other. They shared one thought: Basdevant would return by boat. Who was this? The windows were too high for the men to see what was happening in the street. Jules and two others moved quickly over to the door. They had just reached the three stone steps which led up to it. The door opened. They were pushed aside by the men who had entered with so much assurance. At least, two of the men were assured; perhaps their field-gray uniforms helped their confidence. But the third man's swagger was only bravado. Hearne watched the set smile on his face and thought, you didn't want it this way: you wanted to sail back quietly in your boat and pretend you were going to help us; you wanted to hand us over to the Nazis in the darkness far away from here, so your friends wouldn't see your way of making a living; you wanted it that way, but the Nazis didn't, and they are more interested in the catch than in playing the fish; they insisted on coming back with you quickly, by car; and here you are, Louis, with a bigger crowd to damn your treachery than you had expected; you hoped there would only be the woman, and a boy or two, at this time of day; how do you like being a Quisling, Louis?—go on, look round, look at the faces, Louis; how do you like it?

Basdevant's smile had stiffened as his eyes rested on Sam, and then Townshend, and then young Yves. He had seen old Yves and the men grouped round him too; you could tell that by the way he wouldn't look at them. He descended the three steps slowly. The Germans, a non-commissioned officer and a private, had drawn their revolvers. It was obvious that they, too, had not expected to encounter so many men.

"Where are they?" It was the sergeant, speaking painfully accurate French.

Big Louis scarcely hesitated. There was a kind of fatalism about the very movement of his arm as he pointed towards

Myles and Hearne, and then to Townshend and Walls.

"You said two," the German said angrily. "You didn't tell us there were four of them."

"And what about me?" Young Yves voice was as contemptuous as his face.

Basdevant's eyes flickered towards old Yves, sitting so grimly among his men.

"What about me, Judas?" Young Yves spat out the words.

The sergeant was angry. "Why didn't you tell me there were more than two?" He was not only angry, he was worried. So, thought Hearne, there were only the sergeant and the uncertain-looking soldier, fingering his revolver unnecessarily. He had lost his assurance: he obviously couldn't understand much French, and these silent, dark faces smoldering round him had their effect. He kept his face rigid, but his eyes shifted round the room with the same nervousness which his fingers on the revolver betrayed. Even the thickest German hide must have felt the hate which poured towards the two uniforms.

Hearne suddenly relaxed. This was all going to take care of itself. He needn't worry any more. He caught Jules's eye for a moment: Jules and his friend standing strangely motionless and silent behind the two soldiers.

"What about me, Louis the Great?" Yves was challenging Basdevant boldly.

"Is he another?" the sergeant demanded. "Is he?"

Basdevant's smile had evaporated. He looked again towards old Yves, still motionless, still watching. The silence in the room was like the deep vacuum before a typhoon.

"Yes, I am," young Yves answered. "He would have told you if I hadn't brought my friends along with me."

Basdevant took the sneer with the same fatalism he had already shown. His authority had gone, and he knew it. But he still felt he held the ace of spades: he still was on the winning side.

It was at this moment that Hearne chose to pour himself a drink.

"Put that bottle down," commanded the German who was doing the talking. Hearne put the bottle down just beside Myles's hand, lying so negligently on the bar.

"Put down that glass!" The German was losing all patience.

"Why?" Hearne wasn't even looking at the sergeant.

"At once! Outside! You and these four men. Outside. With your hands raised. Hands raised!"

Hearne took a step forward. Seven feet away, he calculated. "Let's go," he said. He threw the glass of spirits at the sergeant's eyes, and dropped to the floor. Jules and his friend had moved even as he threw. The Nazis' necks were drawn back in a throttling elbow grip. The two shots echoed through the room. Townshend clutched his shoulder and swore earnestly in his light thin voice. A Breton had fallen face forward on a table. Two shots; that had been all. The revolvers clattered jarringly on the wooden floor. The two uniforms, once the Bretons' arms had released them, folded heavily forward like two sacks of flour. Jules wiped his knife on his trousers and exchanged a small thin smile with the man beside him who was cleaning his knife too.

But Sam wasn't watching Jules and his friend or the dead Germans in front of them. His eyes were on big Louis.

Myles had caught up the bottle by its neck; one smash against the counter's edge, and it became a jagged threat. Hearne picked up a chair as he rose to his feet. They, too, were watching Basdevant.

The Breton saw his only chance: it was speed. His only hope was to escape, to inform. Whirling on his heel, even as the Germans dropped, he had knifed the man who was still exchanging a smile with Jules. And as quick as Jules was, big Louis was still quicker. He knocked Jules sideways and slashed him as he went down. He had reached the foot of the stone steps.

"Throw a knife someone!" yelled the American, and flung the broken bottle at Basdevant; it struck the back of his shoulder, but the gash didn't stop him.

Then Sam moved. The shouts of the Bretons were cut off short as they saw the redhaired man launch himself head first through the air. His outstretched arms encircled Basdevant's legs, and the weight behind his dive knocked the Breton off his feet. He fell forward heavily, his head striking against the top stone step. Young Yves's foot was grinding the wrist which held the knife. The shouts broke out once more as the mass of dark-haired men surged forward.

Hearne had headed that rush. It was Sam he wanted. Myles, hobbling over to the milling group, cursing his feet, cursing everything and everyone and his lack of a weapon, saw the two men suddenly being ejected out of the crowd

like a football out of a scrum. He steadied them as they
slipped on the blood on the floor, and pulled them back
towards the safety of the counter where the woman, large-
eyed and tight-lipped, was standing. She was watching the
men round the door. The glass, which she had been wiping
on her apron as the Germans and Basdevant had entered the
room, was still in her hand.

"You were damned lucky to get out of that, if you ask
me," Myles began, and then a smile broke over his face as he
looked at Sam. "That was a lulu. Boy, that was a lulu."

"You blasted fool, hanging on like that," said Hearne,
regaining his breath.

"I was winded," Sam said. All the sulkiness and anger had
gone, now. He was smiling to himself. "All of eight feet that
was, lad. A beezer."

Hearne relented. "More like ten feet. It was a beezer, all
right. A bobby-dazzler and all, Sam."

"The best yet, Sam." It was Townshend, looking whiter
and younger than ever. His right hand held his left shoulder;
the fingers were red.

Sam's pleasure was gone. "Hurt bad?"

"I was lucky." Townshend nodded to the table over which
the Breton fisherman had sprawled. The man lay as he had
fallen. Townshend looked round the room and shook his head
incredulously. "It was less than five minutes ago that the car
arrived," he said.

The car, thought Hearne. He looked quickly at his watch.
There was much to be done in the next five minutes, too. The
bodies, the cleaning up of this room, the car ... yes, there
was much to be done.

"Dead as mutton," the American said suddenly. Like the
woman, he had been watching the group round the door.
"And some of the others seem to have been getting in the
way."

The woman's face relaxed. Hearne followed her glance
towards the men who were now coming towards the bar.
Jules was among them. His arm showed a long red cut where
he had warded off Basdevant's lunge. But he was safe. The
woman finished wiping the glass which she held in her hand,
and set it down slowly on the shelf behind her. When she
turned round again, she could smile back to Jules. It was a
pity, thought Hearne, that he would have to interfere at this
moment, but someone had to take charge. Old Yves and his

men had kicked Basdevant's body away from the door; some of them were already moving out into the street.

Young Yves walked over quickly to Townshend. "Come now, we are going."

"At once?" the American said blankly.

"At once." The boy pointed towards his father waiting at the door.

"Better take this chance," advised Hearne. "They'll get you safely to their village, and it's better for us all to leave here as quickly as possible. I'm leaving too."

"It's sort of sudden," the American said awkwardly. Hearne handed him an envelope for an answer.

"Heavy," Myles observed in surprise.

"All ready to sink, if need be. Take care of it. Remember everything I've told you?"

"Yes." The American placed the envelope carefully into a deep pocket. "I'll keep one hand on it until I hand it over to Matthews. That right?"

Hearne nodded. "For heaven's sake, see you get it across." He looked at Townshend and Sam.

"We'll get there," said Townshend, and started to move towards the door. Old Yves watched them impassively.

The American hesitated. "Perhaps I'll be seeing you some day," he said, "so you may as well know my name. It isn't Myles: that was just my subconscious coming out. I'll explain it to you some day. I'm van Cortlandt, Henry van Cortlandt. We'll get together sometime and you can tell me how this ends for you, and I can tell you how it all began for me last summer. Right?"

Hearne nodded. Van Cortlandt stepped carefully over the bodies. "What about these buzzards?" he said. "What about the car?"

"We'll take care of that."

"I hate to go while the job's half-finished," the American grumbled. Hearne gave him a grin and a wave of the hand. "Hurry, you idiots," he told the three loiterers. "What do you think you're doing? Sightseeing?"

"Well, good-by and good luck," Townshend said abruptly, making the decision for the other two.

They followed the Bretons into the street. Sam's face turned to give a last enormous grin. He jerked his thumb up, and held it that way for a moment. And then they were gone.

Hearne wished he could have gone too, could have seen

them safely onto that boat tonight along with his precious envelope. But events had moved too quickly, and that always meant plans had to be scrapped and reshaped.

He turned to Jules. "First, we must get rid of these bodies. You can put them where they won't be found?"

"When they are found, they will not be recognizable." Jules's voice was as businesslike as Hearne's.

"This place will have to be scoured: all traces of the fight must be removed. And no one must keep any of the Germans' equipment. That might mean death for the village."

The woman, standing now beside Jules, nodded. "I shall see to all that," she said determinedly. "We've had fights here before. I know what to do."

"Then there is the man Corbeau."

"He was probably left to sail back the boat safely from St. Malo. He will be late, he will be drinking. We know him."

"You will take care of him, when he returns?"

Jules nodded. "He isn't one of us," he said.

"I shall take the car and abandon it as far from here as possible. That will keep the village safe. You must look after the rest; you know what to do. And if the police come asking questions, then you will say that big Louis left to buy provisions this morning at St. Malo, that he hasn't returned. That's all you know." He looked round the set faces. "Is that clear?" They nodded. Hearne realized that what he asked of them was something they considered not so very strange, something they could do much more efficiently than he could plan. There had been no fear in their eyes when he had spoken of police: they would take a pleasure in outwitting any policeman, and there would be all the more pleasure if he were German.

"You must act quickly," Hearne said, looking at the bodies.

"Some will clean this room. I shall go with Philippe, Jean-Marie, Henri, to set some nets." As he mentioned their names, the men came forward. Jules nodded his head towards the bodies, and the men moved over to them.

Jules went to the table where the Breton had been killed by the wild bullet.

"It is sad about Robert," he said, his tone altered. "Robert was always friendly to big Louis."

Hearne looked again, and saw that Robert had been the man who had tried so hard for appeasement. "Too bad,"

Hearne said sadly, and shook his head slowly. The woman lowered her eyes so that he wouldn't surprise the smile in them. The men went gravely on with their job.

Hearne paused to pick up one of the revolvers. "I'll leave this with the car," he said to the woman. "But don't let anyone here keep any souvenir."

"I understand," she said, and turned to take the pail of water which one of the young boys had carried in.

"Good-by," Hearne said, and the Bretons nodded politely. It seemed as if they had forgotten he was even there. He moved towards the door. It was just as mad as that, he thought. You left a woman scrubbing blood from the floor, men moving four corpses into the back room, and you stepped into the street, and got into the car. You drove it straight ahead, so that the wheel tracks would look as if they had passed right through the village. You saw two middle-aged, tight-lipped women at the door of a cottage; and they didn't seem to notice you, just as they hadn't seemed to notice the uproar in the pub, this morning. Behind you was the Etoile d'Or, and floors being cleaned, and bodies being weighted for their last dive. It was all as mad and as simple as that, he thought.

He swung the car into a small road leading away from the river. Behind him, Yves and his men would have almost reached their village. Tonight, a few fishing boats would set sail and creep silently out into the estuary to reach the Channel. It would be pleasant to be in one of these boats: however great the danger, it would be pleasant. He discarded the thought of the English Channel abruptly. He'd come to that in good time, unless he ended up against a stone wall. But there was no use in thinking about that either. The job, now, was to get to Mont St. Michel, to his friends Pléhec and Duclos with his nice little wireless transmitter.

Strange how seeing men die so suddenly made you start thinking of death. Not the best frame of mind for the work on hand, he decided, and increased the speed of the car. A few more miles on these side roads were all he could risk: as it was, he had already come farther than he had intended, but the farther he went the safer were Jules and his people. Van Cortlandt and he owed a lot to the woman's courage and to Jules's frankness. As the car swayed on the road's hard stone surface, he suddenly remembered Sam's engine and the Pole who had driven it so dangerously. Perhaps it was the memory of Sam's solid voice and equally solid face,

or it might have been his idea of the Pole's vocabulary when
the engine halted so determinedly, but Hearne's spirits rose.
He would hear the end of that story yet, even if he had to
scour all Yorkshire to get it. He stepped on the accelerator to
pass a detachment of German soldiers, and flipped his hand
codfish-wise as he had seen it done from a high flag-covered
platform in Nürnberg. The junior officer saluted back. Either the car had passed too quickly, or it, itself, was a
guarantee of authenticity, for neither these soldiers nor any
of the other detachments had challenged him. But of course
all the French walked or bicycled these days, unless they
were in the proud position of being trusted by the Germans.
He had been taken for one of these, and he was allowed to
pass with the usual German contempt for an ally. An ally
won sneers just as an enemy won relentless hate. The Germans alone were beyond sneers, and worthy of love. Hurrah
for the master race, goose-stepping so neatly to the fulfill-
ment of their conquering destiny. He pressed the horn
viciously and watched a small column of soldiers scatter
obediently to the side of the road.

He curbed his enthusiasm for this kind of sport: he had
had just about enough good luck for one day. He knew when
to stop. But it was with regret that he abandoned the car, in
the ditch running along a lonely stretch of winding road. It
had been a pleasant journey after all.

There were no houses, no civilians, no soldiers in sight.
Even the sky was clear of planes. This was the moment. He
pulled the German's revolver from his pocket and aimed for
the petrol tank carefully. Quickly he felt for his matchbox.
Four matches inside. Enough. He lit one carefully and held it
to the stalks of the others. As they sizzled like a firecracker
and then flared into life, he threw them at the growing pool
of petrol and ran as if the whole German army were at his
heels. He had reached the small road at the edge of the
wood. Beyond it were fields and more twisting roads and a
ditch whose long weeds hid the gun. Any curious people
within these two square miles wouldn't be interested in him:
the car which had become a flaming torch would seem much
more important. His run slackened to a walk. He was near
the coast, now. Ten more miles, perhaps even less and he
would be at the island of Mont St. Michel.

He was still thinking of the last half hour: it had been a
pleasant journey after all.

CHAPTER 18

St. Michael's Mountain

The road to Mont St. Michel was simple, for it stretched in a series of straight lines over the flatness of the reclaimed sea land. But it was just this simplicity which added to the danger of the journey, which forced Hearne to follow the road itself and not trust himself to the emptiness of the miles of open grass and vegetable fields. Flat as a pancake, he said to himself in disgust, and there was just about as much cover as a fly would find in a stroll over a pancake. One thing he could be thankful for: he wasn't the only person on this road. Here and there was a lonely figure trudging patiently along with a heavy basket for company, or a small family group of fishers and oyster gatherers.

In front of him, a woman thickly bundled in black petticoats had halted to rest. The little boy in his faded and patched blue dress waited patiently beside her. As Hearne drew level with them, the woman lifted the basket slowly onto her back.

Hearne slowed his pace. "You've a heavy load, there," he said.

The woman gave a final heave to the basket, settling it as comfortably as it was possible between her shoulders. The black blouse was threadbare and sewn into a patchwork of mends. She was eyeing his dusty crumpled clothes, probably trying to place him within her limited knowledge of people. But at least he couldn't have seemed dangerous, even if he was filthy, for she at last gave him an answer.

"Yes," she said, and plodded on with the child half-walking, half-running at her side. He was a thin little thing, probably no more than five years old although he had the face of a child of ten. His closely cropped hair, as if shaved for scarlet fever, bristled thinly over the egg-shaped head and made his large, dark eyes larger, darker.

161

"I'll take the basket," Hearne said, "and you can take the child. He looks tired."

The woman didn't answer, but she had heard him for she gave him a long sideways look and tightened her hold on the basket.

"I said I'd carry the basket for you," he tried again, and again there was silence. He was only frightening the woman into tight-lipped distrust.

Hearne smiled. "Well, I'll carry the boy," he said. The child would be lighter than the basket, but if the woman was afraid to trust him with the oysters, then that was her lookout.

The child's body stiffened as Hearne picked him up. And then, as he felt himself quite safe on this strange man's back, with his two thin hands tightly clasped under the funny man's chin, with his bony little shanks held firmly by the big man's arms, the rigor of his body disappeared. He was speaking in his thin hoarse voice after they had gone only twenty steps: he was saying, "I've got a horse! Look, *maman*, I've a horse!"

The mother didn't speak. Her mouth had tightened as if to say, "Suchlike nonsense: teaching the boy bad habits, that's what you are." But their pace had noticeably quickened, and she was pleased in spite of the will to be displeased.

She asked at last, "Where are you from?"

"St. Malo. And you?"

"This side of Le Vivier." The admission was made grudgingly, but after all she had started the questioning. And an answer deserves an answer.

"Where are you going?" she said after a pause.

"Beyond the Mont. Where are you?"

"The Mont."

Hearne's technique had the desired result. There were no more questions. What's your business, were you fighting, are you married, what was your father, where were you born, how old are you, why are you going beyond the Mont—all these and more were stillborn on the woman's tongue.

"It's a long way for the boy to walk," Hearne said at last, looking at the island of Mont St. Michel still three miles distant.

"He is used to it." The woman wasn't being callous: it was the calm statement of an economic fact. She had to make this journey to sell the oysters; and either there was no one with whom to leave the boy, or she preferred to have him beside her.

"We come twice a week," the hoarse little voice announced from behind Hearne's ear.

"You're a clever boy," Hearne said.

"I can walk more than that."

"Then you're a very clever boy. What's your name?"

"Michel."

"That's a good name." Hearne turned to the woman, who was now listening with a half-smile. "How is the price of oysters today?"

"Bad. But it keeps us alive." And then, as if to explain why she had to provide for herself and the boy, she added quickly, "My husband is in a prison camp. It will be easier when he comes home. He was coming home, and they caught him. My brother was with him, but he got away then." She was silent for a moment. "Do you think they'll let them come home, soon?"

"I hope so." Hearne tried to make his voice confident.

"The war's over," the woman said, as if that were reason enough. "The war's over."

"So they say," Hearne said bitterly.

She halted and put down the basket to rest. Michel slipped unwillingly from Hearne's back. "So they say," she echoed dully, and looked across the flat fields on their right. Hearne followed the direction of her eyes.

"Big guns," Michel said. "Big guns. They will go boom, boom. My uncle works there."

The woman hushed the boy sharply, and then, as if afraid that this stranger would think she was related to a German, said quickly, "That's my brother. He had no job, and they took him away to work for them. Him and the others who had just got back from the war. First, they took away his boat. Then they said he had no job. Then they took him to work for them."

"And he's there, digging?"

The woman didn't answer, as if she was afraid of her information. She spoke angrily to the child. "Stop kicking up that dust, Michel. Stop it at once, do you hear?"

Michel heard.

"I suppose we are to be blind to what is going on around us," Hearne said. At regular intervals along the flat fields, about a mile or so from this shore road, were clumps of what

seemed bushes or thick trees. He tried out his idea. "What
do they take us for, anyway? As if we didn't know
camouflage when we saw it!"

The woman nodded, but said nothing, and bent to pick up
the basket again.

"I can take it this time," Hearne said. "Just for the last
mile. I won't bruise the oysters."

His attempt at a joke was rewarded with a smile, and
Michel laughed so much at the silly man that he forgot his
disappointment at losing his horse, until it was too late to
complain. His mother and the man had already walked on.

Hearne looked again towards the concealed gun emplacements. The row of scattered shrubbery stretched back for
miles. "Can't see any men working," he remarked.

"They are there, all right. They are all screened from the
road. Can you think of it? Such madness."

Skillful madness, thought Hearne, and thanked heaven that
he had had sense enough to stick to the road. Cross-country
would be impossible in this district. But in one way the
woman was right: it was incredible to what lengths of ingenuity the Germans would go. Like that batch of specially
circumcised, long-nosed Nazis which had been dumped across
the Dutch borders as pitiful refugees, in the days before their
comrades came over with flame-throwers and parachuting
nuns. The gift to see ourselves as others see us was definitely
one which God had not included in the make-up of Nordic
Aryans.

They had passed other Bretons, walking on this road which
skirted the bay of Mont St. Michel. But now they heard, and
then saw a long column of motorcyclists. They stood in the
ditch until the speeding unit had swept contemptuously by.
And then came half-a-dozen lorries, each filled with soldiers
sitting proudly erect. Or perhaps they enjoyed that attitude,
as they pretended not to notice the French who plodded on
foot or were driven into the ditches, who were smothered by
the clouds of white dust which rose from the conquering
chariot-wheels.

The woman's face was tight-lipped. Hearne spat the dust
out of his mouth; and her eyes, as she watched the expression
on his face, were suddenly friendly. They went on in silence.
There was no need of words. The heart should have no
witness but itself.

The road, as it neared the island in the bay, swerved
farther inland. They left it, as it curved round to the right,

and cut across the salt meadows instead, following a well-worn track which was obviously used by the fisherpeople or those who looked after the sheep which scattered over these strange fields along the shore. The feeling of unreality grew as they neared the Mont St. Michel. There it was, rising, like a mystic mountain of medieval fantasy and delicacy, from the strength of the granite rocks which held it secure in the surrounding miles of golden quicksand. Now the tide was out, and the long narrow causeway, which was the only connecting link between the continent of Europe and this island of tiered turrets and pinnacles, looked forlorn and purposeless. Hearne looked over his shoulder to reassure himself: he always felt the beauty of the island had to be diluted, to be swallowed with any conviction. Behind him lay the seemingly unending road, with the flat grasslands mixed with bog; and the hum of bees; and the scattered sheep; and the occasional *estaminet* advising the passer-by, with a rain-swept girl's smile on its gable-end, to drink more Cinzano; and the few indigent houses huddling together in stray groups. This part of the land was "new," and there were none of the solid, and yet romantic, old villages which covered the rest of the Breton coast. Here, it was as if the shrinking houses knew how fragile their foundations were. For to the north of the road lay the sea and the flat shore of long green-gray grass, its color sapped by the seeping of the tide as it surged hungrily towards the stolen land. Without the gray Germans, and their hidden guns and serf-labor toiling behind camouflaged screens, this would seem a fantastic place enough. With them, it was incredible.

The track through the salt meadows turned away from the shore line now, in its turn; but it was only to pass over a canal and through a small collection of houses commanding a long straight avenue of trees which led directly onto the long straight causeway. The woman halted, expecting Hearne to put down the basket.

"This is my way and that is yours," she said.

Hearne hadn't paused. He turned to the left into the straight avenue of trees, keeping to the left of the tramway lines which had appeared with the canal. The woman and the child followed.

"I can carry it more quickly," he said. "Are you walking back home this afternoon?"

The woman nodded. "It will be easy with the basket empty."

"Don't you find a better market in St. Malo?"

She shot a quick glance at him. "You know the reason," she said. "You know what happened to the fish market there."

"Yes," said Hearne, and wished he did. Too many Germans, probably, with the usual story of forced sales at their price, and payment in occupation marks.

"Aren't there Germans here?" he asked, remembering the three soldiers in the village square which they had just left.

"They have a garrison. And there are tourists. I sell these oysters to a restaurant: the owner's wife is the cousin of my godson's uncle."

Hearne tried to calculate, but gave it up. "And they pay you a good price?" he asked sympathetically.

"Fair."

"They must make a lot of money from the tourists."

The woman gave a short laugh. "Bad money. Tell me, how is it going to end? They pay money, these Germans: they don't steal. But the money will mean nothing when they are gone. Why don't they steal? It would be just the same."

"But then they couldn't say they were being 'correct.' " The Teutonic genius for self-justification was obviously unappreciated by this woman's simple, direct mind.

"It would be just the same," she repeated, stubbornly.

And then, as they stepped onto the causeway, Michel pointed to the sand stretching on either side of them.

"My uncle got drowned there," he said proudly.

"Quicksand?" said Hearne. Even men who knew their way about these sands made grim mistakes.

"Tide," the woman answered placidly. "It's coming in now. Do you hear?"

Hearne listened. His eyes followed her arm. He had seen the phenomenon before, but it still made him hold his breath. From the distance came a low continuous rumble, at first scarcely noticeable, and then surprisingly clear. The rumble became a growl, growing in intensity as the sea moved in over the flat six miles of empty sand. The growl became a tattoo of drums, a fanfare of trumpets, and then the moving mass of water at last swept into sight. Its long line rushed smoothly towards the island ahead of them. It formed one stretch of wave, always about to break, and then rolling over to let another powerful sweep of water take its place, so that the line never seemed to halt.

"There are two men on the sand now!" Hearne exclaimed.

"German soldiers," the woman said calmly, shading her eyes. "Tourists. They see the priests and the fisherwomen on the sands, and they will have their try, too."

"I wonder if they'll make it?"

"Some don't," the woman said, almost hopefully. "The path from the causeway to the front gate will be covered. We must hurry too." They quickened their pace.

The two men were running hard, but the tide was moving still more quickly. Hearne watched the greedy surge of rapidly moving water gaining so inexorably, so triumphantly.

"They are too near the walls. They'll escape," said the woman. She didn't sound as if she were rejoicing. "Unless they walk on the quicksand," she added. "Their boots are heavy for quicksand." Both she and Michel were staring at the running figures. Hearne averted his eyes: he looked at the maze of towers and turrets in front of them. From the highest spire soaring on the pinnacle of the rock which formed this island, the lacework of chapels and abbeys swirled down to the pointed roof-tops of the crowding houses, to the thick turreted wall, which encircled them all. There were soldiers on the wall, all looking towards the running men. Otherwise, it seemed an uninhabited medieval fortress.

"When I am here, I may as well visit my mother's late cousin's husband," Hearne said. "We haven't heard from him for the last two months."

The woman was scarcely listening. Her eyes were still on the two running men, as she pulled Michel quickly along the paved causeway. "They will reach the wall. A boat will be sent round to get them off the rocks," she said resignedly. And then, unexpectedly, "What's his name?"

"Pléhec."

"He keeps the restaurant next to my godson's uncle's cousin's husband. It is a small restaurant." Her pride in even remote family connections asserted itself.

"Yes, I know. He is a poor businessman."

"But it is good enough for him now. He doesn't have so many of the Germans as customers. They like the bigger places."

They had reached the rampart and followed a wooden footpath branching off the causeway. It led to a first gate, and then to a second. The two sentries stationed in the small courtyard between the two gates let them enter with no more than a cursory glance. That wasn't so surprising, thought

Hearne. With his face streaked with sweat and dust, his clothes muddied and crumpled and torn, he would have passed for an oyster gatherer. And the guards must know the woman and child by sight. It wasn't so surprising—but even at this stage in his experience, it amazed him to find how unexpectedly simple it could all be. And the simplest things were often the most successful. He never could stop being amazed at that. It was too impudent, somehow.

He bent his back lower as he climbed the steep cobbled street. It was only broad enough for four men to walk abreast. The shops and overhanging houses closed in on either side. Curios for sale, mementos of St. Michel, outmoded intimations of good things to eat, postcards, painted shells, religious relics, good-luck charms—all pathetic reminders of the Mont's one-time summer trade. Behind him, the tide had reached the walls, and the sea had become a caldron of boiling water.

The child trotted ahead. Perhaps he knew he would get some scraps to eat in that genealogical restaurant. Hearne was content to follow. Up the street they went, then suddenly they turned to the left, along a twisting alley which led them to the back courtyard.

Hearne let the basket slide off his shoulders and straightened himself, painfully. Houses all around them, two- and three-storied houses, so that they seemed to be in a maze of man-built canyons. He hesitated. Which side was Pléhec's back entrance? Last time, he could walk in at the front, but that had been almost two years ago. An army of doors and windows faced him. He wondered again just how many people could be crowded into this half of the small island. Certainly the inhabitants of Mont St. Michel had tried their best.

"They seem empty," he said, pointing to the windows.

"Many people have gone. Only a few remain."

"To feed and entertain the Germans?"

"Yes, these were allowed to stay. Pléhec is there." She pointed to a narrow door in a corner of the alley.

"Thank you."

"It is I who should thank you."

"It was nothing."

She bowed and smiled gravely, with that dignity of the Celt which is so unexpected and yet so natural that you are surprised at your own surprise. She pulled the basket over the worn threshold, and smiled good-by as she pulled. Michel was already inside.

Hearne turned towards Pléhec's doorway. He entered quickly. Behind him, the alley and the street outside were silent. The turbulent waves and jostling currents beyond the ramparts had suddenly eased into smooth noiselessness.

A man was sleeping beside the open hearth in the kitchen. At each side of the fireplace, there was a stone oven with a heavy iron door. From either oven-wall an iron rack stretched over the flames. Two brown earthenware pots had been placed in its center to catch what heat there was in the low fire. Hearne advanced quietly over the stone-flagged floor, and passed the large white-scrubbed table with its few bowls of half-prepared vegetables. From here, he could see through the half-open doorway into the front room. Checked tablecloths on small round tables, spindle-legged cane chairs. This was the place, all right. He didn't need to see the screened shop window with PLÉHEC crudely spaced on the glass. This was the same place.

The small round man in the high-backed wooden chair stirred; and said, without opening his eyes, "Closed until six o'clock."

Hearne suddenly realized by his relief that he had been more worried than he had been willing to admit. He still felt sick, though, but that was probably hunger after all. He wondered if Pléhec's skill with omelettes was still as unchanged as his slight lisp, and those two deep furrows between his heavy eyebrows. There was gray beginning to show now in the thick black hair growing in the peculiarly straight edge round the sallow face. Hearne remembered he used to wonder if Pléhec shaved that hairline. Then he noticed that the man's right hand was resting inside his loose shirt. Hearne said quickly and softly in English, "Even for friends?"

Pléhec raised one eyelid slowly. The eye, small in the heavy folds of his face, seemed reassured, for his right arm relaxed and the other eye flickered open too. Hearne waited patiently while Pléhec identified him. Each minute was sixty hours. Either lack of food, or too little sleep, or the fact that he had been living in tension ever since he had left St. Déodat, was beginning to tell. I can't have changed as much as all this, he thought dully, and pulled a wooden chair in front of him. He sat down heavily, straddling it, with his arms and chin resting on the high back.

"It just needed that," Pléhec said as if to himself in his thin light voice. When he was excited the lisp was more noticeable as he hurried his words. "It just needed that . . . the archeologist who told stories."

"Not archeologist," Hearne found himself saying. "Ethnologist." But what the hell did that matter now? Stories . . . had he ever told stories? They seemed as dim a memory as the ethnologist.

Pléhec nodded his head with surprising energy. "Yes, you always made this distinction. July, wasn't it?"

Hearne repressed a smile. The Frenchman knew quite well when he had visited Mont St. Michel.

"October," Hearne said gently. "October 1938."

"And are you to be with us for another week, this time?"

"I leave tonight."

"So?"

"So."

"No archeology this time?"

"In a way. . . . How is Duclos?"

The Frenchman looked at the large nickel watch tucked into a pocket at the waist of his tight black trousers. He had lost weight already, Hearne noticed: he could slip the watch out easily now. Once Hearne had been amazed that anyone so solidly constructed round the waistline should choose to keep a watch just there. Pléhec was speaking. "It is now almost five o'clock. He will be sitting at the table in the corner, as usual, in just one hour and twenty minutes."

"I must see him. You are sure he will be here?"

"Unless he has been arrested. And, then, it wouldn't do you any good to see him." Pléhec was laughing. He noticed the look on Hearne's face and he became serious. "Yes, I know; it's a bad joke. But we must laugh at something, these days."

"What I really need is something to eat," Hearne said. "That always improves my sense of humor."

"Of course. Of course. You must forgive my thoughtlessness."

Pléhec rose, a short round figure in tight black trousers and an open-necked white shirt. He picked up an apron from the chair, on which his black jacket and ready-made bow tie were neatly lying. "Once," he said, "I should have thought it impossible to make an omelette with two eggs. Now I can even do it with one, and I can see the day coming very quickly when I won't be able to make any omelette because there will be no eggs. You would think the hens knew that there's no use in laying, for a Boche will be there to catch the egg as it falls."

"One egg will be enough for me," Hearne suggested politely; but he was relieved to see Pléhec shake his head at that, and smile.

"And I can offer you some soup: thinner, to be sure, but still soup. And a slice of bread, and some cheese which I managed to hide in time. The coffee is unspeakable. I insult the word 'coffee' by using it to describe what we now drink. Our supplies here were requisitioned, and we have been most generously allowed to buy this." He thumped the brown coffeepot so heavily down on the wooden table that Hearne thought he had smashed it. *"Filtré,"* Pléhec added bitterly, and gave that short laugh of his. He suddenly halted, one hand holding the long twist of bread against his chest, the other's thumb ready to drive the sharply pointed knife into the loaf. "How," he said, suddenly halting and looking up at Hearne, "how did you get here?"

"Walked in."

Pléhec sawed a slice off the loaf of bread and handed it over to Hearne on the point of the knife. "Begin with that," he said. "Now, when did you so calmly walk in?" There was a mixture of amusement and irony in his voice.

"About half-past four. When the two Jerries had to run from the tide."

"Then the others would be crowding onto the wall at that side of the Mont, in order to see them. But the guards? They didn't stop you?"

"I was carrying oysters. For a woman. She went next door, by the way."

"Mathilde?"

"I don't know. Her little boy was called Michel."

"That was Mathilde." Pléhec paused, and traced an imaginary line with the knife on the table. He suddenly went to a small door in a corner of the kitchen, and called abruptly, "Etienne!"

A boy's voice answered him; there was the sound of a creaking bed and then slow footsteps.

"Is it six, already?" the boy asked as he came into the room. He smoothed back his dark hair and yawned audibly. He scarcely paused to look at Hearne. "Another?" he said.

But Pléhec had his own question to ask. "Mathilde usually leaves after five o'clock?"

"Mathilde? Oh, they try to get her away before supper begins."

"See her. ... Say I want to know if she can bring some extra oysters when she comes next week."

The boy nodded, and slipped out of the room as quietly as he had entered it. He had an infinite capacity for not being surprised, it seemed.

Pléhec was still silent as he handed Hearne a bowl of soup. Hearne took his cue, and didn't speak. But now he was worried about Mathilde, too: he must have endangered her; there must be some regulations about which he knew nothing. He had finished the soup, and the omelette was rising on the flat brown earthenware dish when he heard the footsteps on the stone-paved yard. Pléhec folded the omelette quickly and slipped it hurriedly onto a plate. He was still holding the brown cooking dish and the fork in his hands as he reached the door. He moved with surprising lightness and speed.

"Mathilde," he greeted the woman standing outside, "can you bring a few extra oysters for me when you come next time? What is the price, now?"

Mathilde talked volubly and practically. The boy who was called Etienne had come back into the kitchen. He nodded to Hearne pleasantly, took an apron from a hook in the wall and tied it round his waist. He picked up a bowl of green peas from a side table and began shelling them. Hearne began the omelette: Pléhec would never forgive him if he let the two eggs spoil.

There was only a murmur of voices now from the doorway. Then, suddenly, Pléhec's voice was normal once more as he stipulated the price. The door closed. Mathilde's footsteps faded.

"Well, how did you like it?" Pléhec asked. He was smiling again as he looked at Hearne's empty plate. "Once I should have thought it impossible to cook an omelette without one of my copper pans." He pointed to the row of empty hooks above the fireplace. "But of course, you saw that?"

Hearne nodded. He hadn't, but he now remembered that the omelette had looked strange cooking slowly in the earthenware dish, and that its texture had been drier and spongier. "It was excellent," he said, and he meant it.

Pléhec said, "I'm afraid you must lose your jacket. Would you take it off?" He handed it to Etienne. "Wear this, and go 'with Mathilde as far as La Caserne. There you will go on towards Pontorson, while she will take her usual path home. Get rid of the jacket when it's safe, and come back here. We'll need you later."

Etienne grinned and took off his apron. The jacket fitted him loosely, but convincingly enough.

"Mathilde?" Hearne asked quickly.

Pléhec spoke without turning from the small curtained window looking out into the courtyard. It was so high that he was standing on tiptoe to bring his eyes above the level of the sill. "She realizes that the son of my late wife's cousin wants to stay longer with me, that it would be dangerous for him to stay without permission—and so Etienne will wear his jacket and carry the basket, and the guards will notice that a man who came in has gone out again. That's all we have to worry about."

"And little Michel?"

"He doesn't know Etienne. He will remember the strange jacket as much as the face." Pléhec was suddenly silent. His eyes were on the courtyard. Hearne thought he heard voices, and then footsteps.

Pléhec turned back into the room. "Front door, Etienne. She's just gone. Quick."

Etienne moved quickly and silently. They didn't even hear the door close.

"Well, that's that. He'll catch up with her on the Grande-Rue, and if Madame of the long tongue from next door was watching to see anything she could see—for her eyes are as sharp as her tongue is long—she will be disappointed." Pléhec rubbed his hands with the pleasure of frustrating Madame, the cousin of Mathilde's godson's uncle. "Well, that's that," he said again, and picked up the apron which Etienne had thrown on the table. He handed it and the bowl of peas to Hearne. "Something useful for you to do. Very useful, if anyone should come in."

Hearne smiled and rolled up his sleeves: first oyster gatherer, now pea sheller and potato peeler. It was all in the day's work.

Pléhec carried two pails over to a small side table. "You'll find it easy enough," he said consolingly. "Our catering has become very simple. Just so many customers, just so much to eat for each customer, just so little to cook." He picked up a fish out of one of the pails, and slapped it onto the small table. Slitting it carefully up its belly, he raked out.

its insides. There was a grim smile on his face. "Do you know
who I like to think this is?" he asked suddenly, one hand
ripping out the last piece of gut.

Hearne nodded. "I can guess."

"And there were those among us who would say 'What are
we fighting for?' The rich said 'War means revolution: we
will lose our possessions!' The worker said 'Patriotism is for
the rich: war means we will lose our new privileges!' Well,
they know now: they got their peace, and they've lost everything. 'What are we fighting for?' Bah!" He chose another
fish, and beheaded it neatly with one blow of the knife.
"That," he said, "for all traitors who think of their own
private interests first. And this"—he selected another fish
"—this for the politicians who play with their country's
enemies for the sake of power; and—" He halted as he saw
Hearne's expression.

"Don't worry, my friend," he said. "This is a little luxury
which I permit myself each evening. *This* is not rationed. The
choice is either thoughts such as these, or a chloroformed
sleep. I prefer to keep awake."

Hearne nodded sympathetically, and finished the shelling of
the peas. They were pitiably few.

"How many customers?" he asked.

"Exactly seven. Duclos and Gouret from the Museum;
Guehenneuc, Brault, and Boulleaux, the guides to the Abbey;
old Dr. Fuzet and Picquart the notary. Yes, exactly seven.
But it simplifies things for me. It gives me a lot of free time
for more urgent business."

"Can you trust them?"

"The customers? But of course . . ." He smiled enigmat-
ically. "They come to eat here, and talk, and get through one
more evening."

"What about meeting Duclos?"

"I shall forget to lay a glass before him, and the way to
the lavatory is through here." He pointed to the door through
which Etienne had first emerged. Hearne was satisfied, and
nodded. He mentally blessed the peculiarities of the ancient
plumbing on the Mont St. Michel.

A cool draft swept into the kitchen from the restaurant.
The front door was open. There were voices.

Pléhec hurriedly wiped his hands. "Put these in the pail:
tomorrow's lunch," he said, nodding towards the fish guts on
the table; then clipped the bow tie round his neck, before
picking up the glazed black jacket. He reached for a white

linen cap, and, with a smile, placed it on Hearne's head. He was still smiling as he closed the door leading into the restaurant behind him.

Hearne settled the cap more securely on his head. *Well*, he thought, and took a deep breath. Well, here he was, in a half-lighted eighteenth-century kitchen, clearing fish guts carefully into a pail. Here he was, with a cap a foot high on his head, waiting for a white-haired archeologist to pass through to the lavatory. In his pocket was that folded wad of paper with its neatly coded phrases. Tonight, Duclos would send them out into the air.

He wiped his hands on his apron, tilted the starched cap securely over one eye, and casually turned his back to the restaurant door as it was swung open. It was Pléhec. He bustled over with quick short steps to the soup pot hanging above the driftwood fire.

"I gave him the sign," he said in a voice so low that it was almost drowned in the ladle of soup which he held to his lips. He nodded his head as if satisfied. The lines at the side of his mouth had deepened: there was perspiration on his brow and upper lip. He worries more than I do, thought Hearne: he's worried and he's nervous. Hearne looked at the anxious brown eyes. "Two lousy Boches just arrived," Pléhec muttered; and then, as he handed the ladle to Hearne, he added, in an attempt at a normal voice, "It is as good as it ever will be. Three platefuls, Etienne. Two small ladles and no more, for each person."

The door opened again. Hearne's hand tightened on the ladle.

Pléhec spoke hurriedly. "Ah, Dr. Fuzet. I am just about to bring the soup."

An old voice said, as though from a great distance, "Good." Old feet shuffled across the stone floor behind Hearne. He measured the two small ladlefuls of soup carefully into the plate, and handed it to Pléhec. Two more plates to be filled, and then the tired feet shuffled back across the kitchen floor. Pléhec followed them into the restaurant. The door swung open once more. Hearne slipped his hands into his pockets. I am near enough to the fire to drop the wad of paper into the flames, he thought. But the footsteps were light, and the hand which touched his elbow was friendly. The white-haired man with the sallow skin scarcely flickered his drooping eyelids, as Hearne turned to face him. Like Pléhec, he had aged. Like Pléhec, the lines in his face were

more finely drawn, and the shadows under the half-veiled
eyes were deeper. As he recognized the Englishman, his
smile changed from politeness to pleasure. But he said nothing.

He pointed. Hearne followed him silently into Etienne's
room.

CHAPTER 19

Contact

It was a dark little room, lighted only by one high narrow
window.

Duclos gripped Hearne's hand.

"It's good to see you, my friend," he said simply, and then
suddenly put both arms round Hearne's shoulders; and their
cheeks touched for a moment. Hearne was silent, but he
clapped Duclos' arm. It was good to see him.

"Well," Duclos said, "we must be quick. Two Germans in
the front room. And we've been watched for the last two
days. You want me to send a message?" He was unlacing his
boot as he spoke.

"Yes," said Hearne, and handed the wad of paper to
Duclos. It was a duplicate of the paper he had given Myles—
no, van Cortlandt. His observations and notes, and the list of
names and other details of Elise's organization. The Frenchman took it silently and slid it into the sole of his sock. He
pulled on his boot again and laced it methodically.

"First of all," said Hearne, "zero date is August 15th.
August 15th. Then tell them that a fishing boat must be met
off Penzance tomorrow at sunset. Penzance. Tomorrow at
sunset. American on board has vital information. Got it?"

Duclos finished tying a loose knot. "Fishing boat. Penzance. Tomorrow at sunset. American," he repeated.

"Then, after that, send the message I've given you, if you
have time."

Duclos smiled at the last phrase. "If I am not interrupted,

you mean," he said calmly. "First, August 15th; then the fishing boat; then your information. And then?"

"You've reported about the gun emplacements along the coast?"

"I've only heard vaguely about them. We aren't allowed to move about freely, you know."

"Who's covering this territory?" Hearne was half-incredulous, half-angry.

"Dunwoodie was. Haven't heard from him for two weeks. I fear—"

"Jimmy Dunwoodie?"

Duclos nodded sympathetically. Hearne paused. Jimmy Dunwoodie. Another good man ... no time for thoughts. He shook himself free from them.

"Well then, fourthly, if you still have time: guns are being mounted along this coast, between Le Vivier and Pontorson, about two miles from the sea. Possibly to guard aerodromes, which are also under construction." Must be for the aerodromes, he thought. Large batteries would be pointless here. This part of the French coast was about a hundred and fifty miles from Southampton. Big guns, Michel had said. But all guns seemed big to a child. "Further information regarding aerodromes will follow," he ended.

Duclos repeated the sentences in his low, calm voice.

"That's all," said Hearne. He looked at the Frenchman. "*Au revoir.*" And for God's sake take care of yourself, he added in his heart.

"*Au revoir.*"

Tonight, the customary phrase had a literal meaning which lifted it out of its usual offhand triteness. They meant it, both of them.

Duclos had gone, back to the dining room and his meager supper. Hearne picked up the cook's cap which had fallen from his head, and slipped back into the kitchen. Duclos would finish his dinner unhurriedly, as if he had all the time in the world; and after making his quiet good night to the others, he would walk slowly up the hill in the gathering dusk. He would pause, perhaps for the view, and certainly for breath, on each stone platform as the street became a series of steep twisting steps; and at last he would reach his narrow little house and its quiet garden under the walls of the towering Abbey. There he would settle in the high-

ceilinged room at his book-littered desk. And there he would
work until the dusk had become night, until it was safe for
him to move quickly and silently through the garden, through
a door hidden under climbing roses, into the thickness of the
garden wall—and then into the base of the Abbey wall itself.
The medieval mind which had designed that passage had no
doubt pleasanter purposes in view: but now, six hundred
years later, medieval ingenuity and secrecy had perhaps their
greatest success.

Hearne stood watching the peas swirling in the boiling pot
on the iron rack. The acrid smell of vinegar came from the
flat dish beside it, where the fish were steaming placidly. Oil
must be scarce, he thought: too scarce for fish. He looked at
the pail of fish offal. Tomorrow's lunch . . . We'll never know
the half of it, he thought: those of us who lived through this
war in safety will never know the half of it. Even if we can
imagine all the stark bloodshed which peacetime prophets
foretold, we shall never guess about the little things, the little
things which add up to a horror of their own.

He looked impatiently at his watch. In four hours, perhaps
even three, Duclos would send that message. He remembered
his last visit here, when Duclos had led him one night into
the dark narrow passage within the walls. Then it had been a
kind of joke, a strange and rather mad kind of joke. But he
also remembered the awe which had silenced his amusement
when they at last emerged from that dark journey and found
themselves inside the Abbey. They were standing in the
shadows of a narrow, half-ruined courtyard. Above them,
soaring into the night's soft moonlight, were the delicate
spires of chapels, the crenelated edge of terraces and twisting
flights of stairs, the crowding walls of mounting churches and
Gothic towers. They seemed to stretch up the steepness of
the rock as if to reach Heaven itself. It had been a subdued
and silent Hearne who had followed Duclos into recently
restored cloisters, and from there into a decrepit passage
leading down into the depths of the Abbey's foundations.
Above their heads, men had once prayed and sung, had
feasted and fasted, had fought and lived. But down here,
where Duclos was now leading him (with a torch to light up
the blocks of stone in their way), men had welcomed death
to release them from their tortures, men had gone mad in
hidden dungeons, men had been entombed alive in oubliettes.
It was one of these, a hole in the wall where men could be

forgotten by their enemies, that Duclos had discovered in the course of his excavations.

Pléhec bustled in and out of the kitchen. There was the clatter of plates. Hearne still stood in front of the fire—as if, there in the flames, he could see Duclos making his way so carefully and quietly to the secret oubliette. There had been two iron rings in the wall, at shoulder height. Beneath them lay a small heap of dust and fragments of bone. After the flesh had rotted away, the skeleton's wrists had slipped free from the iron manacles. Death had given a double release. Hearne wondered whether Duclos had buried them when he set up the transmitter that he had smuggled there, piece by piece. Or had he left them to remind himself that others had died for their beliefs—as a savage warning against carelessness? That would be like Duclos, strange mixture of idealism and practicality.

The door of the dining room opened. The firm hard step on the stone floor gave warning. Hearne carefully stirred the soup, all his attention fixed on the hanging iron pot. Light hurried footsteps followed. Thank heaven, Pléhec was watchful.

"Where is it?" It was a voice used to command and demand.

"Through there," answered Pléhec. The confident footsteps resumed their march. A door banged. Pléhec began arranging some food on the two plates which he had placed on the table.

"Less for us all tonight," he grumbled under his breath. He was grudgingly doubling the quantities on the Germans' plates. "Same price, double helpings!" The curses which moved on his lips were as blistering as they were silent.

The door crashed once more: again the steps rang on the floor.

"Such filth," said the German, with characteristic tact. He paused in his stride. "How long must we wait for the food?"

"Coming. This instant," said Pléhec.

The footsteps passed into the restaurant. Pléhec finished arranging the fish and peas on the plates. Then he spat on the fish, and smeared them carefully with his thumb. *"Garni!"* he said, grimly, and carried the plates into the restaurant.

Hearne, concentrating on the soup as if he were preparing the most difficult soufflé, could hear only the voices of the two Germans. The Frenchmen were sitting in complete

silence. "How long must we wait for the food?" There was
something familiar in that voice. Or perhaps every German
talked French with that accent. "How long must we wait for
the food?"

Hearne took off the cook's cap and walked silently to the
screened restaurant door. By standing at the side of it and
gently moving the pleated curtain half an inch, he could see
well enough into the front room. The two Germans were at a
table near the window. One was a dark-haired young man
with a high thin nose and tight eyes. He wore a uniform, but
he wasn't a soldier. The other man had his back half-turned
to Hearne. Tall; powerfully built. An officer. For an instant,
his head turned to watch the silent Frenchmen. For an
instant, Hearne could clearly see the even features, the colorless face, the smoothly brushed fair hair. He remembered the
fluttering white curtains in Madame Corlay's room, the im-
movable soldier at the door, the young captain who hadn't
enjoyed his visit. The ditch-digger ... that was it! Deichgräber. If it wasn't Deichgräber, then uniformity was still on
the increase in Germany. Deichgräber ... what the hell was
he doing here, anyhow?

Hearne moved quickly back to the table and began shifting
some plates about. Pléhec returned, fussed about the pots
and the table, and then he was back in the restaurant once
more. So it went on for half an hour, and by that time the
seven customers had all arrived and been served. By that
time the Germans had finished their meal and left.

"They've gone next door. They'll get wine and music there.
They didn't think much of this place," Pléhec said when he
returned with the news of their departure.

Hearne sat down on the nearest chair. He was tired and
hot; his worry over Deichgräber wouldn't go away. It cut
through his head like a saw. "Any guess?" he asked Pléhec.

"—Why they were here? Oh, just the usual: they come to
look us over about once every week."

"You know them by sight?"

"No; these were new ones. Picquart says they arrived
yesterday evening. You'd enjoy Picquart, by the way. Pity
you can't meet him this time. He sits at his window next the
Hotel Poulard and watches the visitors in its garden. We have
many visitors, you understand. We are now a Boche playground. Sometimes it is interesting. When Reichsmarschall
Elephantiasis was here, for example. Unfortunately, the little
bomb was not expert enough: it didn't go off. But the

Reichsmarschall left at once, and two men who had nothing to do with it were executed. That depressed Picquart. Still— it is war." Pléhec hunched his shoulders, and cut himself a slice of bread, and poured himself the last cup in the coffeepot. "It's war. Those who can help must keep alive, even if others are killed. Only those who try to help are any good to France. The others are bilge-water, not even ballast."

"Does Picquart know the names of the visitors?"

Pléhec, his mouth full of bread and the remains of some fish, nodded.

"I'm interested in the names of these two men."

Pléhec rose and wiped his mouth on a corner of his apron. "Must see if Picquart needs some more water to drink." He disappeared through the screened doorway.

He came back soon, licking his lips like a cat. Evidently Picquart's system did work well. "The dark one is secret police. Hans Ehrlich. The other is a captain. Joachim Deichgräber. Both arrived last night by car—with a lady. A Fräulein Lange. You look surprised? I assure you that we have our feminine visitors too. That is quite usual."

Hearne wasn't listening. Hans Ehrlich . . . secret police . . . Hans Ehrlich along with Captain Deichgräber, whom he had seen only a few days ago in St. Déodat. Hans . . . Hans . . . It couldn't be. He was just at the stage of imagining things, of inventing suspicions.

"What's the woman like?" he said suddenly.

"Young and beautiful. They always are."

"Red hair? Dark red—almost brown?" Like the glint of autumn leaves in the evening sun, he thought bitterly. He was being a complete fool: the girl was haunting him.

"Is it important?" asked Pléhec.

Hearne reflected for a moment. "No," he said; and then, "Yes!"

Pléhec looked at him curiously and once more pulled himself out of his chair.

He came back into the kitchen, carrying some dirty plates. "Red hair," he said

Deichgräber—St. Déodat—Hans—Elise. Hearne's intuition had completed the circle before his mind had dared. "Fräulein Lange," he said aloud. Could that possibly be her second name? Lang-e. Two syllables. And then it dawned on him. "Mademoiselle Lange." This time he gave the French pronunciation, making it one syllable. It sounded convincing.

Pléhec finished lighting the second candle before he looked up. "What does it matter?"

"A lot. If she is the girl I think she is, then she and the dark-haired Hans are responsible for counterespionage in this district."

Pléhec had closed the shutter over the small window. "So?" he said slowly. His eyes moved quickly towards the back entrance to the kitchen. His attention was divided: he was listening.

Hearne said, "They may be here for a short holiday; or they may be here to investigate. There is plenty to investigate." He thought of Duclos and Picquart, the notary; and Pléhec himself. The Frenchman read his thoughts.

"Others too," he remarked. "Guehenneuc has a small printing press. He prints sheets, and then Boulleaux smuggles them out into the mainland. Such things as the truth about Dunkirk, and about Oran. But it would be difficult to guess they came from here. And Dr. Fuzet—"

"So all your customers are in it together?"

"They don't know that."

"But you do?" Hearne grinned at the little fat man in front of him. So here was the real center of all this resistance. Pléhec had understood him. He said simply, "They don't know that either." Again he listened, his eyes slanted towards the back door. The moisture on his pale face gleamed in the light of the candles. His face seemed whiter, his hair darker. "Etienne," he said.

It was Etienne. He locked the door carefully behind him. He no longer wore Corlay's jacket.

Pléhec spoke again. "I've kept you some food." He turned to Hearne. "And you should eat some more too. There's little to offer you but scraps. But even the best people are eating pot scrapings these days." He and Etienne sat down at the wooden table with its clutter of dirty plates and emptied pots. The two plates which the Germans had used were noticeable: they still contained food. Pléhec emptied their leavings into the fireplace. "It would poison even the pigs," he said scornfully.

In the front room, French voices were again talking with their quick staccato accents. There was silence in the courtyard outside the shuttered window. The rejected food hissed and spluttered in the dying fire.

CHAPTER 20

Quicksand

If he were to be killed, thought Hearne, then he couldn't have chosen a more beautiful place to end this life. It would be almost worth dying to draw a last breath of this silvered air; to see, as his final glimpse of this world, the fragile spires and curving walls etched against the dark blue sky. The moon was crescent; the stars shone all the brighter for its half-light. Any other visual memories would be bathos after this: this was the ultimate perfection. From behind the shower of stars there should have come the soaring of pure voices in Debussy's "Sirènes." That would have the magic of this picture. Thoughts of death and sirens and glamourie. . . . Hearne smiled to himself as he stretched his body tightly into the shadow of a house wall, and waited for Etienne's touch on his arm to move on again. Thoughts of death and sirens . . . he must be pure Celt after all. This proved it. Only the Celts had thought of this island as the Mountain of the Tomb.

But he wouldn't die tonight: not here. That, Hearne suddenly knew. If you were willing to die, then you didn't. Death liked to snatch you when a hundred reasons pressed on your mind why you must live. He glanced at the thin serious face of the boy who touched his arm so lightly, who now walked so quietly beside him, matching cautious footsteps to his. The boy felt that look, but he still said nothing. Only when assured German footsteps sounded on the stone of the street and its steps would he halt Hearne with his calm grip, guide him unhurriedly and cleverly into deeper shadows, into the labyrinth of passages and alleyways which crisscrossed the Grande-Rue.

They had already passed the parish church and the gardens of the fourteenth-century houses beyond it. Above them, to their left, towered the walls rising from the central peak of the island to guard all the spires and chapels which formed

the Abbey. Down to the right would be the ramparts along
the sea edge. They were walking northwards on the east side
of the island, moving farther and farther away from the
gateway by which Hearne had entered the Mont that afternoon. And it was the only entrance and exit. But Etienne
must know another way: he was traveling too confidently
and easily. Again they halted in the black shadows of the
high crowding houses. This would be the fifth time they had
taken cover.

Two figures stood on the terrace of the street. They were
looking down towards the ramparts and the sea on the east
side of the island. The one nearer Hearne was the dark
German who had visited Pléhec's this evening. And then the
figures moved, turned to walk down the short flight of stairs
to a new level of the street, and Hearne saw them both
clearly. They were walking towards him, a man and a woman. Hans Ehrlich and a woman with a gray cloak thrown
round her shoulders. As they crossed a band of soft moonlight, flooding a short stretch of the roadway where the house
walls were lower, the woman's hair caught the faint rays and
held them prisoner for a moment. Hearne couldn't even feel
himself breathing. His arm, resting under Etienne's gentle
grip, tightened. The boy felt, rather than saw, the direction
of his eyes, for the darkness of the empty house, against
which they sheltered, was as deep as the plunge of the Abbey
wall down into the street. Together, they watched Elise pass.
Elise, or could it have been Lisa when necessary? Elise
Lange: Lisa Lange. One soft and sibilant: the other, flat and
two-syllabled and clear. The French and the German of it, as
it were. Paris, she had said. Paris . . . so she couldn't even
trust her Corlay. She probably trusted no one except herself.
Even Hans would find he had known little of Elise when she
found a *Gauleiter* of a bigger province.

They had passed. The perfume, which Hearne had noticed
on the evening Elise had first appeared before him, still clung
to the air.

Etienne shivered, as if he were awakening from sleep.
Hearne whispered "Gestapo!" and this time it was the boy's
arm which tightened. And then they were moving along the
narrow alley which skirted the open stairs of the street,
moving towards the town ramparts where they joined the
Abbey walls.

For a moment, Hearne wondered if Etienne intended to
scale the steps to the top of the rampart and climb down its

north face. But that seemed madness, for there must be patrols on top. And then, as the boy pulled him under the shadow of the rampart's tower, he suddenly knew that the boy would never have entertained such a dangerous idea. They remained motionless there for two minutes—time enough for Hearne to feel foolish at the way he had underestimated the boy. Strange, what wild ideas came to you when you found yourself out of your own particular field, as if you instinctively feared others' judgments. Hearne stopped worrying, and decided to let Etienne do the thinking. The boy knew his way about these walls and ruins. He had played there as a child, and now he was using his play to outwit those who had invaded his home. When Etienne touched his arm again, Hearne moved quickly and obediently.

He could feel Etienne leaning his weight against a part of the wall. Hearne heard the strained breathing, saw the droop of the boy's head between his shoulders as he pushed with the side of his body. A panel of stones, narrow and low, opened as suddenly as a fissure in quake-racked earth, opened only enough to let them slide through. Again Hearne felt, rather than saw, that Etienne was leaning his thin body against the cemented rocks, and then they were shut into the darkness which lay inside the hollow of the ramparts. Etienne's torch flickered and then held its beam steadily as it swept over the wall six paces in front of them. High above their heads was the rampart walk with its guardhouses. Outside, up there, the Abbey soldiers had once patrolled; and later, tourists had walked and exclaimed; and now soldiers had come back, soldiers with green-gray coats and streamlined helmets.

Etienne's torch picked out the stones he had been seeking. They were easy to find, for they were not the depth of the rest of the wall, and they formed a deep alcove or recess in the tremendous thickness of stone which supported the rampart walk. Hearne, looking quickly over his shoulder, noticed that behind them was a similar recess through which they had entered. It seemed as if there might have been a small gateway through the ramparts at this point once; as if it had been blocked up, but not with the same thickness as the walls themselves. Etienne was advancing over the thick white dust on the ground, the round circle of light from his torch growing larger as he neared the stones on which it was aimed. He beckoned Hearne to follow closely, and placed his shoulder against the stones as he gave his first word and smile. "Swivel," he explained politely, and then the torch was

switched off and there was no smile to see, only the darkness.
And there was only a feeling of effort as the thin body
strained. There was only the dead smell of forgotten space,
and the sound of a stone as Etienne's foot slipped gratingly.
And then the narrow slab of rock moved slowly aside. The
cool clean breeze from the sea ended the feeling of suffoca-
tion. In front of them was a panel of night sky, and the
gentle movement of small trees swaying like black-shawled
women at a funeral. Etienne knocked Hearne's arm impatiently. They stepped over the rough threshold of stone onto
firm earth, where the dust had been molded by rain and wind
into something solid and clean.

Hearne took a deep breath. They were outside the ramparts. For the second time that night he was thankful for the
medieval mind and its love of mysteries. Perhaps it had been
the repression of the Middle Ages, its secret opposition to
authority, which had created these ingenuities.

Etienne led a careful way through the wooded grove,
sloping inevitably towards the sea. Judging by the stars, they
were curving round to the west as they approached the north
shore of the island. Hearne tried to recapture a visual image
of the map of Mont St. Michel. As far as he remembered,
the southern half of the island consisted of the houses and
shops and was guarded by the ramparts rising from the rocky
shore. In the center of the island were the spiraling buildings
which formed the "Abbey," enclosed by steep walls of their
own. And these walls joined the ramparts of the little town,
so that the Abbey and its walls formed its northern boundary. Beyond the Abbey, towards the north shore, were only
small trees and shrub falling away to the sea, where the
precipices and rocks of the island met the treacherous sands.
Small wonder that for seven hundred years no invaders had
ever captured this island. No invaders. . . . Hearne thought of
the silent, darkened houses behind the ramparts, of the Germans taking their evening stroll while the half-fed Frenchmen
were locked indoors. Only invaders, he qualified, who had
been handed the keys of the fortress on a silver platter. That
was why Pléhec's hate had only been equaled by his bitterness; that was why this boy of sixteen had the eyes and
mouth of a man of forty.

Etienne spoke in a whisper. "Soon we shall strike the path
of steps from the Abbey's north wall. They will lead us to St.
Aubert's spring at the edge of the shore. There is an easy

way there of getting onto the sand. The rest of the shore is too steep and dangerous." Hearne nodded, and concentrated on following. The ground was difficult, but if any sentry was looking down from the heights of the deserted Abbey the shadows of the trees and bushes would camouflage their progress. It was with considerable relief that he at last saw the stone staircase. Follow that, and they would reach the shore.

But Etienne had no intention of doing anything as simple as walking down the steps carved out of the rock. He used them only for direction, it seemed. And then Hearne had to admit to himself that the ground was easier, too, at this part. By following the staircase, Etienne was saving them a good deal of effort. That was something to be thankful for, anyway. It was then that they heard the footsteps.

Etienne grasped Hearne's arm as he halted, and pulled him under the cover of a bush. They lay still, their ears straining for every sound. Yes, it was footsteps all right, Hearne decided. Two people. Not guards or sentries: the pace was too broken, too leisurely. Two men talking. Germans, of course; and Germans with special privileges too, to be walking through the Abbey groves at this hour. For no one lived within the Abbey: it was only a museum and showpiece, closing its gates to ordinary mortals each evening. Hearne waited, wondering.

At last the two men came into view: first, their heads; and then their uniforms, as they slowly climbed the stairs back to the Abbey. Two officers, Hearne could see, but that was as far as he could identify them at this distance with the tree shadows blotting out the steps as they did.

A high-pitched voice was saying ". . . fantastic. Pity you couldn't have been here when the moon is full and the tide is phenomenal."

"I can imagine it." This voice was polite, but assured. Hearne's eyes narrowed.

"The Reichsmarschall himself would like to take the whole place and set it up on the Rhine."

"Not on his estate?" The sarcasm in the second voice ended in a laugh.

The high voice laughed too, and turned the conversation. "Interesting what you've been telling me, but I assure you this place is as dead as its buildings. Have you seen its inmates? They are part of the Museum! Your—your friends have brought you on a hopeless hunt: there's no game here for them. I've seen to that already. How long are you staying?"

"Until tomorrow. I must be back then."

The men were almost level with Hearne now. His guess about the second voice had been right. It was Deichgräber, himself. The high voice belonged to an older man, a major, Hearne noted.

He was saying, "Are the others leaving with you?"

Deichgräber was answering, "No. They will probably stay longer."

The high voice hardened. "I suppose they don't trust our efficiency in these matters. How did you get mixed up with them? And what use is a woman in such things?"

"Headquarters," Deichgräber said briefly in answer to the first question. But about Elise he made no reply.

The two men halted and turned to watch the sands once more.

"Pity you couldn't have seen high tide at nighttime," the major said. And then, unexpectedly, "You might at least tell me what brought them here."

"I assure you, Herr Major, that they only tell me as much as they've told you."

"That English agent . . . he was caught on the mainland. Why do they come here? Had he friends here?"

For a moment, Hearne's heart had stopped. He didn't hear Deichgräber's reply. And then he realized that the major had used the past tense. *Had he friends here?* He thought of Dunwoodie, whom Duclos hadn't seen for two weeks. Something which they had found when they had searched Dunwoodie or his room had directed Ehrlich to Mont St. Michel. That must be it. So Duclos had been right about Dunwoodie.

Hearne heard the major say with some bitterness, "I resent this intolerable interference." He had started to climb the steps once more.

"What is it like at high tide?" was Deichgräber's answer. The two voices faded with the footsteps. Hearne drew a deep breath as the major's explanations blurred in the distance. Etienne touched his arm. Together they slipped from the cover of the bush and began the last part of their journey to the sea. Hearne looked back over his shoulder. The two figures were still climbing the staircase, their heads bent, their hands clasped behind their backs. It was a scene of touching peacefulness, with the warlike Germans indulging in the relaxation of a moonlight stroll and a chance for the practical major to mingle a few off-the-record remarks with his eulogies on nature.

Either the major's eloquence was effective, or it was just one of those damnable pieces of luck, but Deichgräber halted suddenly and turned round for his last view. Even as Hearne caught Etienne and pulled him into the nearest shadow, the German's arm stretched quickly towards the major, and pointed. The two men seemed to hesitate, and then Deichgräber was leading the major back down the rocky staircase. They were hurrying, but they were taking no special care to walk quietly. So perhaps Deichgräber hadn't been sure that he had seen anything at all, or that there really was someone. And the major was obviously under the belief that his guest was suffering from a moonlight hallucination. Even at this distance, the note of his voice was one of amused annoyance.

Hearne's eyes looked despairingly towards St. Aubert's Well, from shadow to shadow, to see where Etienne and he might slip unobserved away from the determined Deichgräber and the reluctant major. Or could present cover be trusted? Was it better to lie quietly here, or to crawl cautiously into further shadows? And what about the matter of time: could they afford to wait, for the tide wouldn't? This was really Etienne's problem; he knew the ground they would have to cover. The boy seemed to sense Hearne's impatience. He motioned with his head and moved stealthily towards the next tree. By drawing *nearer* the steps, they could follow the almost continuous line of bushes which edged the staircase at this point. And so, mad as it seemed, they crawled through the undergrowth fringing the steps, while behind them the footsteps came nearer. Hearne judged by the desperate quickening in Etienne's pace that he was trying to reach a hiding place before the footsteps caught up with them.

They could hear the words now. "... assure you ... Captain Deichgräber. ... It would have been seen by my sentries from the Abbey walls. They are constantly on watch. And how do you suppose that anyone could get here? The ramparts on the east, and the rocks on the west are well guarded, too. Where was it you saw this shadow?"

The footsteps halted. "Just over there."

"Can't see a thing," the major grumbled. "Shadows every-where. Remember how you admired the shadows playing over the sands?"

"I saw something." Deichgräber was obdurate.

"I assure you, the sentries—"

"There should be searchlights."

"There are." The major's voice tightened. "There are, when the danger is *real,* such as at high tide when boats might slip in to help someone to escape. At present, no one would venture on these sands. All that searchlights do is to make this a perfect beacon to guide English planes." He obviously didn't like this interference, and interference by a junior officer, at that. Deichgräber's officiousness was going to be a useful ally to the man and the boy who had now reached the last of the bushes. Before them, the rocky ground dipped suddenly, and they could see the wet sand gleaming darkly. Using the outline of the bush to blot out their movements, they slipped cautiously in turn over the edge of the rock. Etienne's arm steadied Hearne and encour-aged him. This sudden dip in the ground would shield them from the men behind; unless, of course, the two Germans were to retrace their steps right down to St. Aubert's Well. The stone platform on which it stood was just below this hiding place. From the well, the Germans could look back up the hill and see them.

"I trust you are satisfied?" the major said at last, breaking the silence which had become oppressive. There was a cold sweat on Hearne's brow. His tensed muscles cramped under the strain of crouching.

Deichgräber's voice was deferential but determined. "With your permission, Major, I shall continue my walk to the Chapel."

There was a silence.

Hearne suddenly realized that if Etienne didn't know much German, then the strain must be doubled for him. He clapped the boy's shoulder gently, reassuringly. That might have been a smile in reply through the blackness of the shadow. Hearne was wondering if he dared shift his weight onto the other knee, when the major answered.

"Very well," he said stiffly. "Report to me in my quarters in half an hour." The voice was as controlled as a refrigera-tor. The reprimand was not lost on the younger man. There was a clicking of heels, and probably an efficient salute to match, as he acknowledged it. Then they heard the major's footsteps climbing away from them. Still Deichgräber hadn't moved. Hearne imagined him standing half-angry, half-worried, looking at the wooded, rocky slope around him with impatience and distaste.

It was then that Etienne's hand grasped Hearne's arm again. This time, Hearne followed unbelievingly as the boy led him forwards, and obliquely away from the steps. But there was nothing else Hearne could do except follow. The boy was far from stupid. He couldn't have thought that Deichgräber's steps synchronized with the major's. There was only one pair of footsteps climbing towards the Abbey: that was obvious to anyone who listened well. And Etienne was a good listener. Hearne had had that proved to him, tonight.

Even as Deichgräber started to descend the staircase, Etienne reached his goal. It was a deep narrow fissure, a slit through the plunging rocks of the cliff. Hearne's hands rested against the cold granite walls which rose above his head on either side of him. His feet fumbled cautiously for the roughly hewn steps. At least, there was no more crouching. Etienne's arm was the guide. He would pull Hearne's shirt gently for each step forward; for each pause, his hand would press against Hearne's chest. The seeing eye, Hearne thought grimly, and stepped and paused and stepped obediently. That blasted ditch-digger couldn't see them anyway. The only danger now was that he could hear them, and that accounted for the slowness of their descent. Cautiously they worked their way down through the cleft, originated by nature, improved by man. Deichgräber's footsteps, quieter and more cautious now that he was alone, had passed well to the left of them. He should be almost at the little stone house built over the well. Yes, he must be there: his footsteps no longer grated against the stairs.

Etienne seemed to pay little attention to the German now. Their journey through the cleft in the short cliff was almost over; the rocky walls on either side of them rose higher as they neared the shore level. Hearne found it difficult not to think what happened if a fat man had to make his escape through this narrow passage. He would probably come out corrugated, if at all. But at last, he felt softness under his feet, and Hearne knew he had reached the foot of the cliff. In front of them, and to either side of them, stretched the miles of flat sand; stretching like a sheet of watered silk under the perfect sky. Too perfect, thought Hearne. A few

nice deep banks of thick cloud would have been a help.
These little puffs of smoke up there might be highly ornamental, but they only served to float chasing shadows on the
brownish sand. Still, even a few shadows were not to be
despised. And the moon was young enough not to illuminate
the whole place in efficient floodlighting. "But just where do
we go from here?" Hearne said to himself. They must reach
solid ground again before daybreak: apart from the matter
of light, there was also the tide to guard against.

Etienne kicked off the thin leather shoes from his feet.
Their lack of heels and toe caps made them look like a sort
of slipper, but they had carried him easily and lightly over
the worst ground. It was surprising how securely they had
clung to his feet like a *torero's* shoes, stamping, running,
side-stepping on the arena. Hearne, sitting on an outcrop of
rock, resting his cramped back against a dank wall of cliff,
followed Etienne's example. He flinched as his feet sank into
the sand, for here it was thick and moist, and, without the
sun to give it surface warmth, it was as cold as . . . as cold as
. . . He finished tying his boots carefully together, and draped
them by the laces round his neck. As cold as a grave, he
decided grimly, and rolled his trousers up under his knees as
Etienne had done.

The boy stood with his back pressed against the cliff. He
nodded as Hearne finished, and pointed to the left. They
moved, keeping close to the shadow of the rocky precipice.
There was no need to worry about the sound of their steps,
here. The sand deadened all noise. Once they skirted this
northern shore and slipped round to the west side of the
island, they would be safer, for at present it would be heavily
in shadow. By the time the moon, or what there was of one,
sailed over to that side of the Mont, they should be safely on
the mainland. From where they stood now, it was about half
a mile to the causeway and entrance to Mont St. Michel.
And from there, it was just over another mile to the flat
shore of the bay. Hearne remembered the little river which
flowed into the Bay of Mont St. Michel, just to the west of
the Mont itself. Now that the tide was out, it was only a thin
line of shallow pools, a skeleton river spreading forlornly
towards the sea between banks of sand. He believed he could
now guess Etienne's plan. They were to reach this ghost river
at the northwest corner of the island, and, by following its
course to the mainland from which it flowed, they could use

its banks of sand as cover. It was shallow cover certainly, but still it was cover. The danger would now not be so much from the sentries on the ramparts as from the wet sand. That was why Etienne was going barefoot. That way, even if they stepped into a quicksand, they would have a chance. With boots, there would be no chance at all. And that, too, was why Etienne was starting their journey at once; that was why he wasn't going to wait under the northern cliffs until Deichgräber had returned to report to the major. For high tide would come again in all its terrifying speed about half-past four. These seven miles of sand which stretched out to sea would be swiftly covered by the rush of waters, and the channel of the river bed would be hidden, and the sea would sweep up the river into the mainland as far as six miles deep. Hearne looked at his watch. Yes, there was no time to waste. The distance which they had covered from Pléhec's restaurant to this point was not much over a mile, perhaps even less. They had taken one hour and three quarters to reach here. It was a record of caution. He looked at the dark, thin-faced boy beside him, so silent and calculating. It seemed incredible that anyone so young as this should have such patience and restraint. War was a hard schoolmaster.

From the rocks above them came no sound of footsteps. The German must be standing quite still beside the well, searching this side of the island with his eyes. Hearne suddenly wondered if a direct path led from the well down to the shore. If there was one, they'd have to pass its mouth, and that wouldn't be a pleasant two minutes. If there was one . . . There was.

They saw it after they had gone less than fifty paces. Etienne's speed slackened, and he stood with his head slightly tilted to one side as if to hear better that way. His eyes flickered impatiently. From where they stood in the safe shelter of the rocks at the mouth of the path, they could see along the first ten feet. The track must curve round towards the terrace on which the little stone building was built over the spring, for they couldn't see St. Aubert's Well from here. If they couldn't see, they probably couldn't be seen. The man and the boy listened. But nothing stirred. It was uncanny: they had heard no footsteps climbing back to the Abbey on the hill. But at last Etienne seemed satisfied. His hand flicked impatiently towards the other side of the path. Hurry, it seemed to say: hurry! Without further delay, or even a

glance up at the path, he had slipped across its entrance.
Hearne followed as quickly. They seemed a ghost and its
shadow.

No one had been on the path. That, Hearne had verified.
The danger point was passed. Their speed increased. Three
hundred feet ahead of them was the northwest promontory
of the island with a chapel on its rocks. Three hundred feet,
one hundred yards, and they would be on the darkened west
side of the Mont. The sand was firm enough so far, and the
walking was easy. But farther out from the rocks, the sand's
color changed in light and dark patches; and even on its
apparent flatness there must have been hollows, for the
inches of water which still lay in them spread like black
shadows. Hearne was wondering which were the danger
spots, the dry or the wet sand. . . . He thought he remembered something about wet sand, but it was only a vague
memory. If it were true, then the journey back to the
mainland under cover of the flat banks of that stream would
be no picnic. It would be a hopeless attempt without Etienne
as guide. Even as Hearne worried to himself, the sand's
consistency changed under his feet. It became a soft rubber
sponge, letting his weight sink for a good six inches into it,
oozing quickly over his instep and round his ankles. It wasn't
a quicksand: it was just a hint of what they would have to
deal with if Etienne were to lead them into one. But it wasn't
pleasant. Hearne stepped carefully, so that the half-sucking,
half-sobbing sounds, when he drew each foot out from the
semi-liquid surface, would be minimized. Again their pace
slowed. Etienne gave one of his rare smiles, and pointed to
the stretch of sands to their right. He emphasized the direction by shaking his hand warningly and then pointing it
quickly downwards. The gesture was explicit enough.

He would be glad when he got out of this, Hearne thought.
It was the highest piece of understatement which he had
ever committed. If anyone could have listened in to his
emotions at that point, they would have heard one long
despairing groan. He tried not to look at that smooth treacherous surface. Ten feet away. Much too near for his idea of
comfort. Perhaps it was only imagination on his part, but he
really felt that the give of the sand under his feet had
increased. It swallowed more than his ankles now. Then
suddenly it had become firm again, and Hearne breathed
more naturally. But Etienne still motioned towards their

right, still shook his hand, still pointed downwards. He was a
nice boy, but Hearne wished he would stop the hand effects.
After all, that idea didn't need to be driven home twice. He
kept rigidly behind Etienne, almost treading on his heels. If
the boy had been afraid that Hearne would step out to the
side to walk abreast, then he had won his point.

They were almost at the promontory. Thirty feet, or less,
still to go. Then these cliffs to their left would swing round
almost at right angles to face the west. From here, they
could already see the shallow pools which traced the course
of the stream.

And then, from the shadows of a jutting rock, stepped
Deichgräber. He had a gun in his hand, a smile on his lips.

"Up!" he said. "Up!"

They raised their hands above their heads, Etienne still
holding his shoes.

"Drop them!"

Etienne did. They landed at his feet.

Deichgräber's smile changed. He had half-recognized
Hearne. He narrowed his eyes for a moment and then he said
triumphantly, "My friend on the farm! Well, now! Corlay is
the name, I believe?"

Hearne tried to make his voice sound natural, even
amused. "Captain Deichgräber, of course. Well, now we can
take our hands down."

"Keep them where they are! I was just about to waste a
bullet on each of you, but now I think you will be more
interesting as prisoners than as corpses. Will you tell me why
you are here, or do you prefer to wait until I signal for the
guards?"

"Don't be a bloody fool, Deichgräber. Do you want Ehrlich and Lisa to laugh behind your back?" Hearne spoke as
if he had the rank of general, at least.

"What has Ehrlich to do with this?" Deichgräber was
angry, but he still kept the smile which was not a smile in
place.

"Ask him."

"I shall. Turn round, and start walking back. Any suspicious move and—"

"You will apologize handsomely for this," Hearne warned
indignantly. "Why don't you summon the guards now, so that
we can end this farce quickly? It would be simple enough. A
couple of shots—"

"If you are as innocent as you pretend, there will be no need to summon the guard. If you aren't, they'll hear the couple of shots when they strike your bodies."

Hearne shrugged his shoulders. "By this time, the men I am after will have heard us and escaped. Fool," he said venomously.

Deichgräber ignored that. He pointed to Etienne.

"And who's this supposed to be?"

"He's my informant. You could do with one yourself, couldn't you?" The savage sneer, the authoritative tone, had some effect, but not enough. "Wait until the major hears about it," Hearne went on. "The new broom sweeps clean, too clean. I hope you'll enjoy your new command after this." That was a double-edged barb. Deichgräber as visitor to Mont St. Michel had not even the privilege of being a new broom.

"We'll get back to the Abbey," he said, but the calculated smile had vanished.

Hearne stood very still. He semed to be listening intently, his eyes fixed anxiously on the stony promontory behind the German's back. "I thought I heard them," Hearne said, as if to himself. His voice was a mixture of anger and savage disappointment. "Our voices must have carried. They'll get away."

"Just where are these mysterious people?" The voice was contemptuous, but Deichgräber still watched Hearne, still pointed the revolver.

"At that small chapel on the promontory. You saw it, didn't you? But let's get back to the others. Perhaps it won't be too late even then, to catch these men. Come on, Pierre—" he spoke to the boy beside him, who was standing motionless, his eyes on the ground—"we may get some results if we hurry."

Etienne had flashed a glance at Hearne at the mention of the false name. With his hands still held high, he slipped his right foot casually into one shoe. Deichgräber hadn't noticed anything strange about that. Hearne drew a deep breath.

"We'll have to hurry," he said to the German, holding his attention by the urgency of his voice and eyes. Etienne was fumbling for the second shoe; and when his foot couldn't find it, he knelt quite naturally to pick it up, his eyes still on the German, his free hand still in the air. He straightened slowly, both hands in the air now; he looked as if he were very bored.

Etienne's leg moved so quickly that even Hearne was surprised. His right foot struck the German sharply on the wrist, with a savage side-kick which sent the arm high and the revolver flying. It fell somewhere in the rocks behind Deichgräber, as the shoe from Etienne's left hand caught him across the mouth and silenced the shout from his opened lips. Hearne closed in, and the German warded off his blow with a kick from a heavy boot. The kick was sufficient to throw Hearne sharply against a low rock, and the jagged edge caught him beneath the knees like a knife: he lost his balance, falling backwards on the hard sand with a thud which smashed all the wind out of him. He lay still for a moment, his eyes closed. The German must have thought he was knocked out, for he turned and struck at Etienne. The boy slipped from his reach, twisted and turned, and ran back towards St. Aubert's Well. He looked easy to catch. The German, not even pausing to shout, was on his heels. Etienne side-stepped, was missed by inches, started running out from the shore as if he had lost his head. The watching Hearne, picking himself up dizzily from the sand, smothered a shout in his throat into a hoarse croak of warning. Again Etienne side-stepped. But this time his arm was raised. Hearne saw the gleam of a knife as the boy's arm struck at the German's neck, saw Deichgräber plunge heavily forward. He landed on one knee, his hands on the sand before him. And then the knee and hands disappeared. Deichgräber struggled, tried to shout, but the struggles became a spasm and the shout was only a whisper. The sand sucked more deeply; the grip was firm.

Hearne sat down on the rock. "God in Heaven," he was saying to himself. "God in Heaven."

Etienne came running lightly back, Etienne whose feet hadn't paused for a moment even when he had stabbed. He was searching for his shoes, picking them up carefully. He was waiting for Hearne. "Come," he said, "we've little time, now."

Hearne hesitated and looked towards the lump in the dark sands. Only twenty feet away . . . the strangled shout had given way to a moan, and then there was nothing to hear. Etienne must have read his thoughts. He said to Hearne, "He will soon be under: he struggled too much. It was either him, or us and our friends."

"Yes," said Hearne, "it was either him or all of us." But he didn't look back, as they walked on in silence. Not even when

they had reached the promontory did he look round. He was
thinking, Deichgräber must have gone right down the stone
staircase without waiting at the spring; he must have followed the path directly onto the shore while we were still
coming down that cleft in the rock. He must have guessed
that if anyone was escaping, they would make for the sand.
And then he had explored it as far west as this promontory;
he must have been on his way back when he saw us coming.
Probably he was going to explore the east part of the north
shore then. He was thorough, all right. And he was ambitious. Too ambitious. If he hadn't thought he could torture
more information out of us as prisoners, he would have shot
us dead on sight. But that was one way of dying which they
didn't teach him in a Death-and-Glory academy.

Hearne followed Etienne automatically. Even when searchlights suddenly blazed over the north-shore sands, even
when one of them swept round to the west while they both
stretched flat on the mainland shore, Hearne was apathetic.
Emotionally, he had reached saturation point. He just lay
patiently, and waited until the beam of light was switched
away.

"They can't risk it for long," Etienne whispered consolingly.

Hearne nodded. "They are worried about him," he suggested. "He's overdue. Search parties out now, probably."

"They'll find nothing. *Les lises.* . . ." The boy shrugged his
shoulders.

Les lises. Water holes. . . . So that explained the quickness
of Deichgräber's end. Hearne remembered Pléhec's vivid
description of them one evening during his last visit to the
Mont. Water holes, they were: water holes covered with a
deceptive layer of sand. Just another of Mont St. Michel's
little surprises, Pléhec had said. *Spécialité de la maison,*
Pléhec had added, and they had all laughed.

"No," Hearne said. "They'll find nothing."

"And by the time the light is good enough to search
properly, the tide will be in." The boy's voice was unemotional. He was neither triumphant nor fearful. He noticed
Hearne's curious stare.

"My father was killed. That was in the war, and that was
what one could expect. War is war. But two weeks ago my
brother was shot. Shot for something which he didn't do,
didn't even know about. He and another, just chosen blindly,
just pushed against a wall and shot in cold blood." He

paused, his voice still unemotional. *"Merde, alors!"* he said suddenly and buried his face in his arms.

At last Hearne said, "I'm all right, again," and the boy rose silently to lead him over the salt-meadows. Clouds had blown up. A wind ruffled the trees lining the bank of the small canalized river, which Etienne now followed.

"I go this way, my friend," Hearne whispered as they halted near a road. He swept his arm to the south and the west.

Etienne smiled. "Soon the tide will come in. This river will be flooded and the boats will leave from Pontorson. Pléhec said you might as well sail."

"To where?"

"Past St. Malo. Anywhere up the River Rance towards Dinan, if that suits you."

Hearne was smiling now, too. "Can I sleep on that boat?" he asked.

Etienne was politely amused.

"Sleep, and rest these blasted legs?"

Etienne was still amused, but he nodded reassuringly. "After we get there," he added cautiously.

"We shall," Hearne said with unusual confidence.

And they did.

CHAPTER 21

The Awakening of St. Deodat

Another dawn was breaking when Hearne came back to St. Déodat. This time, he did not walk through the village. This time, he did not trouble to count the Picrels, the Gruérins, or the Trouins. In these graystone houses now slept gray-uniformed men. Yesterday had been the day of their coming. Yesterday had been the day for Nazi flags and, no doubt, a Nazi band playing in the market place. Hearne wondered if they had had the insolence to play Breton songs. Yet that had happened in other places. Anyway, the Picrels, the Guérins, the Trouins must have laid themselves down to sleeplessness

with bitter thoughts last night. Grim as were his own at this
moment, Hearne wondered just how he would feel if the
names had been Jones, Brown, Robinson. Maniacal, he decided: without either exaggeration or heroics, quite simply
maniacal. He looked down the hill at the dim shapes of the
quiet houses round the towering church, and he remembered
the third tree in the seventh row in the Corlay orchard.
There would be many third trees in these farms in this hill
and valley, and in all the other hills and valleys of Brittany.
"Ni zo Bretoned, tud kaled," Henri had said.

Hearne found himself quietly whistling the refrain of *"Bro
goz ma zadou,"* the Breton national song, as he crossed the
stone yard of the Corlay farm. The kitchen door was closed,
but unlocked. Henri was kneeling beside Albertine, helping
her place the first log of the new day on the glowing embers
in the hearth. They turned round as Hearne entered. They
waited until the last line of the song was completed, and then
they came forward together, came forward almost quickly.

"You're home," said Albertine. Her voice was roughly
kind. Old Henri grinned through the gaps in his gums. He
said nothing, but reached up with his thin, corded hand to
pat Hearne awkwardly on the shoulder.

"He's ice-cold," Albertine said. "Henri, get that fire going.
Do you want him to starve?"

Henri obeyed with unaccustomed willingness.

"What's happened to your clothes? Where did you get that
hat?" Albertine looked at it unbelievingly. "It smells of fish."

"All of me does," Hearne said. He felt pleased by their
welcome—pleased and yet worried. Had Madame Corlay
talked more than he had expected? He watched Albertine as
she bustled about the kitchen. She asked so many questions
on top of one another, not even waiting for his answers, that
he was spared the agony of conversation. Where were his
own clothes, was that nice young American safe, how were
his feet and the trousers which Albertine had sewn to fit him,
had they seen any Boches, were they caught in that rain, why
didn't he get home yesterday? That last question was the key.
They had begun to get alarmed. This sudden friendliness was
chiefly due to relief. And she still called him Bertrand quite
naturally: so if Madame Corlay had told, she still hadn't told
everything. Hearne ate and watched the simple face under its
white-starched cap, looking anxiously to see if he enjoyed the
food, if it were enough. He judged from the quantity she had
placed before him that she had included her own share, and

perhaps even Henri's. Hearne ate the amount he was usually
given, and refused the rest, saying that that was all he could
eat. By the sudden light in Henri's eye, he knew his guess
about the food had been right. He gave the old man a grin,
and Albertine a hearty clip round the waist, as he rose and
walked over to the fire.

Her severe face relaxed. "You'll spoil my apron," she said,
but color had flooded into the patch of red veins on her
cheeks. Henri and Hearne both laughed.

"God," he said, "it's good to be home," and stood with his
back to the fire.

Old Henri nodded. His fingers were tapping out the rhythm
of *"Bro goz ma zadou"* on the wooden table. The sound drew
Albertine's attention.

"Henri!" she said sharply. "Your work. Jean and Marie
will be almost finished." The old man rose and moved slowly
to the door leading into the byre. He gave Hearne a side-look
and an unmistakable wink. Hearne grinned: in every language it meant the same . . . anything for a quiet life.

"What is it?" asked Albertine, sensing the conspiracy.

"Good to be back," repeated Hearne cheerfully. He heard
light footsteps coming down the staircase into the hall. Yes, it
was good to be back.

The door opened and Anne came in. She had dressed
completely, to the last button of the tight-bodiced dress, to
the last smooth braid round her head. For a moment,
watching the simplicity of her smile, the honesty of her eyes,
Hearne wished he really were Corlay. It would be something
to have a look like that for one's own.

She said, "I knew it was you. I was listening and I heard
you whistle. I knew you had come back."

There was the same directness in her speech that had
greeted him the first time they had met. Then, she had told
him she couldn't marry him. Now, she looked as if she would
marry him tomorrow. It wasn't, he thought, as he watched
the neat weave of plaited hair, it wasn't that women were
fickle. They were completely loyal: either to themselves, like
Elise, or to others, like Anne. But when they made their
illogical leaps and still managed to balance themselves neatly
in reverse, it wasn't because they had changed. They were
still the same: it was only the outside influences which had
changed, and by some strange alchemy made them feel like
saying *Yes* when they had once said *No*. Madame Corlay had
only to say "He has changed"; he had only to prove it; and

above all he had only to show his distrust of Elise. That was all—and Anne's doubts and fears had vanished. The icicles had melted. In some curious way, which he couldn't manage to analyze, he felt pleased. But it would have made things easier if she had still distrusted him; now he would have warmth and affection to deal with. Thank heaven that Anne was Anne, that complications could be kept as simple as possible. He looked at her. She was unique, in a certain sense. She was shy without affectation or awkwardness: she was innocent without being ignorant, modest without being stupid. He almost laughed at that—modest. ... It had been a long time since he had thought of that word.

"Why are you looking at me like that?" Anne was disturbed, as if she feared she wasn't pleasing him.

"It's nice to relax," he said. It was true: for the last ten minutes, he hadn't even thought of a bloody Nazi.

Albertine said, "Get those clothes off, and I'll wash them. They are smelling up the whole kitchen," and then to Anne, who was listening with a smile, "Did you wake Madame when you rushed down here?"

Anne shook her head, and the color came into her cheeks. Not, decided Hearne, because she might have wakened Madame, but because the rushing had been so obvious. He looked down at his clothes. After the second hour on that boat he must have lost his sense of smell.

Anyway, relaxing was over for the day. Albertine was in charge.

His room had been scoured and polished; otherwise, it was untouched.

The bookcase still held its secrets. The books were in the same order, even to that upside-down volume which he had left to test any curious fingers.

It seemed strange not to have the American next door to his room. In the short time he had been there, he had become a part of this house. Strange not to hear the limping step, or the deep voice talking its own variation of French. As Hearne washed and changed the disreputable blue shirt and corduroy trousers for something cleaner but less comfortable, he wondered how van Cortlandt was liking Matthews. Van Cortlandt . . . why had he called himself Myles? Probably some psychological impulse when he was forced into the danger of giving his real name, some impulse rooted in that story he had promised to tell later.—Here I am,

Myles from home, he would think. Well, that made two
stories Hearne owed himself when he got back to Britain.
When . . . Myles's—no, van Cortlandt's; and Sam's. That
would be a fair do, that would. And they would make it a
night, lad. His attempt at Yorkshire was more than the razor
could bear. He sighed, and patiently washed the streaming
blood off his chin. By the time the flow had become an ooze,
and the last slow drop had hardened into a clot, he had next's
week's plans fixed, with the help of his map. A week was all
he could depend on now. Elise was due back from her trip
to "Paris" on the twentieth of July. Ten days, she had said.
That gave him just seven days more of this kind of thing. He
might even have to work in daylight to get all the information he wanted. For when these seven days were over, he
might find little time free for himself and his work. Then he
would simply have to seize any chance he could: for with
Elise's unexpected demands there would be an end to sys-
tematic observation.

When he went downstairs, Anne was alone in the kitchen.
"Albertine's gone to Mass," she began, and then she was
looking at his chin.
"What about you?" His voice was half-teasing.
"I wanted to see you alone. Look, I must get you something for that cut." She didn't wait for an answer, but ran
lightly into the storeroom. She brought back a bottle of
colorless liquid.
"Please don't trouble," Hearne said, but inside he felt
rather pleased at her solicitude. She dabbed the liquid lightly
over the cut. She was so absorbed in everything she did, he
thought, as he watched her eyes fixed so intently on his chin.
The cut stung into life again, and he grinned as he saw the
look of dismay on Anne's face when the blood trickled over
his chin once more.
He jammed a handkerchief hard against it, saying, "Thank
you. That will cure it, I'm sure," and wondering if Adam's
rib had been better left in place. But it was difficult to feel
irritated with Anne: not when she was still trying to look
dismayed, when she trying so hard to keep from laughing.
"You wanted to see me alone?" he suggested.
She nodded, and put the offending bottle down on the
table.
"Yes. I went down to the village yesterday, and—" He
touched her arm and silenced her. He pointed towards the

thin wooden partition which separated the outbuildings from the kitchen. She lowered her voice. "Only old Jean and Henri are there," she said in surprise. "Marie has gone with Albertine."

"They'll soon be in here for breakfast. I'd like to walk in the high field. Would it be too cold for you?"

She shook her head and lifted a black shawl from the back of a chair. In silence, she walked up the hill beside him, her arms crossed under her breast to hold the shawl tightly in place, her smooth head slightly bowed, her full skirts billowing out like a black umbrella in the morning wind.

When they reached the high field, and walked on open ground with no bushes or trees near them, Anne halted.

With a smile, she said, "May I talk now?"

Hearne laughed, and nodded. "Let's keep near the cabbage patch," he answered. "We ought to have a good excuse to be up here, even at this hour."

"Excuses for everything," Anne said with surprising bitterness. "Excuses for just being on our own land, or for standing in our own market place, or—"

Hearne interrupted. "It isn't ours at the moment, Anne. They are the men in possession, whether they call it protection, occupation, or conquest. All we can do is wait, and live our own secret lives and make our own plans. They haven't possessed our minds; and they won't, unless we let ourselves be deluded. How is it in the village?"

"As you would expect. You remember I went down with you to the village on the afternoon before you left with Monsieur Myles? I didn't want to make people think I was looking for Kerénor. I walked about and visited different friends. I couldn't find him. I went to see Monsieur le Curé, but I couldn't find him either. Then when I came home, you were upstairs in your room with Monsieur Myles, and Albertine said you were both too busy. I waited, but you didn't come down; and then I had to go upstairs to read to Madame Corlay before bedtime. And then we went to bed, and I never saw you before you left. It really was such a disappointing day: nothing had come right, and I was very angry with myself."

Hearne nodded. "Too bad it happened on your first try, but don't blame yourself. It's often like that."

"But I went down to the village yesterday afternoon." Anne was smiling now, so the disappointment couldn't have been repeated. "And this time, I did see Kerénor. He was sitting on the stone bridge, alone with old Monsieur Guézennec and young Picrel. He said 'What are you doing here? Don't you know the Boches are arriving, and no one is going to be in the streets to welcome them? I'm taking you straight home.' You see, he and the others were turning back anyone from entering the village at that end. And he had men at the other end of the road to stop people coming from the farms on that side. And there *was* no one in the streets, not a soul to be seen. Even the older children had been taken care of. You know how children run out to see motorcars and soldiers? Well, Monsieur le Curé had taken them all for a picnic to the ruined castle, and he wasn't going to bring them back until the early evening; and then he was going to march them straight home—no playing on the pavement or in the market place. That's why I couldn't find Monsieur le Curé or Kerénor the day before: they were arranging all this."

Anne was excited over her story. She paused to see its effect on Hearne. But he was chiefly interested in the last sentence. "Monsieur le Curé and Kerénor—were they always friendly?"

"No, not at all."

"What is Monsieur le Curé like?"

"He's not very big. He's sort of fat. He has a deep laugh. And he's kind. Everyone likes him. Even Kerénor used to say that, as a man, he wasn't bad."

Hearne, rather impatiently, said, "Yes. But what does he feel about the Boches?"

Anne looked at him in surprise. "Why, he feels as we do."

Hearne was thoughtful. The Breton priests had the reputation of being brave men. Few of them were given to equivocation and appeasement. They belonged with the people; but he wanted to be quite sure. He asked, "What did he say in his last sermon, for instance? Were you there?"

"Oh yes, everyone was there. Even Kerénor. Strangely enough, Monsieur le Curé said something very like what you told me."

"I told you? When?"

"Just five minutes ago ... you know, about not letting them conquer our minds. He said we must help each other to keep our minds free from lies against ourselves and our true friends: that as long as our minds were free and we had courage and faith, there was hope. *He that leadeth into captivity shall go into captivity: he that killeth with the*

sword must be killed with the sword. And then we sang our
hymn—the one you were whistling as you crossed the courtyard this morning. When we got to the refrain, many men
couldn't sing any more, and the women were crying quietly."
Anne's voice trembled, and she turned to look at the trees
which sheltered the back of the village.

Hearne kept silent. *As long as the sea is its rampart, may
my country hold its head high in freedom,* he remembered.
Now the sea was no longer the rampart of Brittany's freedom; now it was the only road to freedom.

At last he said, "What about Kerénor?"

Anne was looking at the ground, digging the toe of her
black leather shoe gently into the rich earth, watching it fall
in thick moist lumps from the leather as she tilted her foot.

Hearne tried again. "What did Kerénor say about my
message?"

She faced him so suddenly that he knew she had been
trying to find courage to tell him. "He wouldn't believe me."

"Wouldn't believe you?"

"No. He said you were a Fascist; that you would do as the
Germans told you, and enjoy it."

Hearne said to himself, "The damned fool, the bloody
idiot." And then he remembered that, if he had really been
Corlay, Kerénor would have been right. He met Anne's
gray-blue eyes, anxious, worried, apologetic. "I see," he said
calmly.

"Of course he doesn't *know*—" Anne began, and then
halted.

"Know what?" he asked quickly, almost sharply. Anne's
eyes flickered.

"Know that you've changed," she said in a low voice.

He looked at her searchingly. Did *she* know? Had Madame
Corlay told her everything? He could read nothing in the
calm gentle face except trust and loyalty and—he shook
himself free from these thoughts. Now *he* was being the
damned fool: what on earth had almost made him say
"admiration"? How could she find any admiration for a
Corlay who had treated her and his own country so abomina-
bly?

"So he doesn't believe me," he said and laughed bitterly.
He still couldn't conceal his disappointment. "Did you tell
him what I said about Elise?"

"Yes."

"And even that didn't convince him I might have changed

even as he has changed?" Strange how an intelligent man
could always admit his own change of faith, and feel honest
and brave about the admission, and yet could go on distrusting any change professed by another man.

Anne shook her head slowly. She seemed to be fumbling
for words. Watching her, Hearne knew that Kerénor's com-
ment had been bitter. I bet it's a corker, he thought. It was.

"He—well, he laughed. He said that was the joke of the
year. And then he said that it just needed that touch to
convince him completely that you were a—a Fascist liar."

Hearne looked so blankly at her that she rushed on, "You
see, he thinks you have always been a bad influence on Elise.
And he says that Elise is vain and weak and may be pleasant
to the Germans, because that kind of person always is. But it
is quite impossible for her to have any power, or to be
dangerous except to herself."

"I see. And I suppose I was only accusing Elise, so that by
sacrificing her I could prove how truly I have changed?"

"That was what he thought."

Hearne looked at the large serious eyes: in the early
morning light they were gray, a soft clear gray.

"And what does Anne think?" he asked gently.

Anne smiled. "I think that Kerénor is being too clever.
He always did think too much. He'd find reasons behind
reasons, and all he did was to make himself feel clever and
unhappy. He really did love Elise once; now, I think he
despises her for what he calls her 'weakness.' But he is still
infatuated. She is very beautiful, isn't she?" There was an
anxious look in her eyes as she waited for his answer.

"Yes, she's beautiful, Anne. But it's skin-deep. She'll need
something more than that when she is reaching the age of
forty."

Anne smiled again, this time a strange little smile, but
didn't reply. She was looking at the earth once more. She was
probably thinking that forty seemed much too far off to be of
any consolation to the women Elise was going to hurt before
then.

Hearne was making a pretense of studying the rows of
vegetables. What, he was asking himself, what are we to do
now? Just leave St. Déodat to its fate at the hands of the
sweet Elise and her gentle friends? Or should he make one
more try? Monsieur le Curé ... would he listen, or had he
his own distrusts of Corlay? Hearne walked among the rows
of round fat cabbages, and wondered. After all, this wasn't

his job. . . . His job was to report on the traffic on the roads
and railways and canal. His job was to get information liable
to form a patch of the crossword puzzle which Matthews and
these other blokes in their hush-hush rooms could fit together
into a pattern of German intentions. His job was to do a
microscopic piece of the groundwork for future bombing
raids, for the upsetting of carefully laid invasion plans. He
halted and looked at the sun's broadening rays flowing over
the hillsides, over the sheltered village and open farms. By
God, he thought, anything which hurts the Nazis, anything
which helps their enemies, is also part of my job. He could
always argue that with Matthews, and he knew that, if his
real mission was well done, Matthews would listen and even
agree. *If* his real mission was well done. Matthews was a
Scot.

His best plan would have to be this: to wait until the time
came for him to start his last walk to the coast. Then
Madame Corlay, after he had left, could tell Monsieur le
Curé everything, and by that time his warning would be
believed. If, he thought in sudden gloom as he looked
towards the hidden houses of St. Déodat, if it were not too
late for some of them by that time.

Anne had come up to him. Her hand lightly touched his
arm for a moment. "Marie and Albertine are home now,"
she said. "They've just entered the house. I think I must go
back."

"So she bullies you too?" Hearne said teasingly.

"Albertine? But she's so old, and she works so hard, and
she deserves some kind of—"

"Respect?"

"Well, yes. Why are you smiling? Do I seem so stupid?"

"You seem just the way I like to think of you, Anne." He
paused. "Anne—" He paused again. Hell, he kept saying
"Anne, Anne, Anne." Was it an easy name for his tongue, or
what?

"Yes?" she said, and halted with her head slightly tilted to
one side. Not coy. No, she wasn't coy. She was just Anne.

"Never mind," he said abruptly, and began walking quickly
down to the house. She was hurrying to keep up with him.

"What shall we do about Kerénor?" she asked.

"I'm still thinking about that. Don't risk anything, Anne,
and don't worry." And then, almost as much to change the
subject as to solve a problem which had suggested itself to
him, he said, "By the way, I've been calling you Anne all the

time. But you haven't mentioned my name once today. And you call me *vous,* I notice. What's wrong? Don't you trust me, either?"

"I trust you." Her voice was very low. There was a hint of a smile in her eyes, now more blue than gray. "But, you see, I don't know your name."

He checked his pace, and grasped her arm. "What?" he said.

"I don't know your name."

He glanced towards the house. They were too near it. He turned, and, still holding her arm, led her back up the hill.

"Now, what on earth do you mean by that?" he managed to say with a show of injured innocence. So Madame Corlay *had* told her. Perhaps, as a woman, she had thought it only fair to tell the girl who thought she was betrothed to this man. Women were like that. Not that Madame Corlay need have been wary of him: not much, anyway; not as long as he was worried stiff by the job he had on hand. Then, Anne was Anne. Only swine like Corlay would hurt a girl like Anne. Elise, now—well, that was another cup of tea. She would deserve anything that was coming to her. She was just one of those bitches who went about asking for it.

Anne said again, "But I don't know your name."

It was no good evading it. That would only lessen her trust in him, and that was no good either. In one way he was glad she knew. In one way he felt relief. "It still must be Bertrand," he said slowly.

There was a shadow on her face. "You, perhaps, don't trust me," she said.

"I trust you, Anne. It just isn't safe for you to know me as anyone but Bertrand Corlay."

"Oh."

"I mean that. We are all in great danger, Anne. You and Madame Corlay must never know. Then, later, if there's any questioning, you will be able to say truthfully that you did think of me as Bertrand Corlay."

"Later?"

"Yes." Quite baldly he added, "When I have left here."

"When you have left—" Anne's voice was low enough to sound like a faint echo.

"You see?"

"Yes, I see."

"So Madame Corlay told you?" He was almost speaking to himself.

"Only," said Anne, "after I had guessed. There were little

things ... things which I had missed in the real Bertrand."
She paused as if she couldn't go on. "Oh, this is all silly. And
she didn't really tell me: only hinted, so that I was sure my
feeling was right. And then this morning, you whistled '*Bro
goz ma zadou.*'"

"Didn't the real Bertrand know that song?"

"Yes. But he *couldn't whistle*. That was something he was
very touchy about. He just sort of blew." She laughed in spite
of herself. He caught her arm again and swung her round on
the path.

"Home, this time," he said. "Albertine will begin to get her
suspicions aroused, too. And two women are enough in one
secret. I must say you kept it well, yesterday, when you were
arguing with Kerénor."

Anne's answer ended his new worry. "I didn't tell him. I'll
tell him only when you think I should."

"Two women are enough," Hearne repeated. "Good girl,
Anne," he added. Something in his voice surprised himself.
Anne was smiling again. In the warm sunlight her eyes were
quite blue, her cheeks were flushed.

They walked in silence back to the house.

Seven days, Hearne was thinking, seven days—and he
might find that not only was it difficult to continue his work:
he might find it too dangerous even to continue living on this
farm. He looked at the neat fields around him, at the slate
roof gleaming blue in the sunshine. Seven days weren't
much. ...

He was right about the danger. But the time was even
shorter than he thought.

CHAPTER 22

Captain Riedel Takes Charge

On the next day, while the people of St. Déodat prepared to
go to church, Hearne paid his official visit to Dol. It would
have to take place today, he decided that morning, for he
had his own extremely unofficial business planned for the rest

of the week. He hadn't forgotten Traube's parting shot about Agent Number 8 from Dol. "You will be responsible," Traube had said. Nor had he forgotten the German words which had followed him to the restaurant door. "Set one of Ehrlich's men, too. Advise Ehrlich." No doubt the movements of Bruneau from Dol were already being noted. And if the supposed Corlay didn't appear in Dol, then that would be duly noted too.

But there was a third remark in that short interview in the restaurant of the Hotel Perro which Hearne had not forgotten. As he cycled through the small side roads, through the thick dust of their loose surface, he was repeating to himself, "Kalb, Major Kalb. Kalb of the Schutzstaffel. Kalb, organizer of Dol. *Heil Kalb! Heil Deutschlands teurem Kalb!"* For it was Kalb who had got Hearne into this Sunday suit of Corlay's with its tight waist and flaring shoulders. It was Kalb who had got Hearne onto Corlay's decrepit bicycle, patched up yesterday afternoon with old Henri's help. It was Kalb who was drawing Hearne to the small town of Dol on a hot Sunday morning. Such an opportunity as Traube had given Hearne with that brief reference to Major Kalb was not to be missed. There were plenty of risks attached, but such risks were not only to be taken: they were to be welcomed.

There were but few travelers on the narrow, twisting roads, and they were all Bretons. (The Germans would travel by the large, first-class road where there was less dust or roughness.) Some cycled like himself, their shoulders and heads bowed over the low handlebars, their feet rotating continuously. Others plodded along between the green hedges and scattered orchards, a basket or a bundled cloth over an arm, their best black clothes already coated with the fine dust. They looked as hot as Hearne felt. Even a shimmer of heat was rising from the green grass.

When he at last reached the main road, he found his map calculations had been adequate enough. The towers of Dol's cathedral welcomed him, pointing towards the blue sky and the hum of planes. It was strange, thought Hearne, how people had come to accept that mechanical drone above their heads, as if it were as natural as the wisps of white cloud. He watched the people walking in the streets under the balconies of the old houses. But no one looked upwards; no one shaded his eyes to see what planes could be seen. In the little square which led to the Grande-Rue, the sun baked the cobblestones, and the heat, thrown back in Hearne's face, stifled him. He dismounted and walked at the edge of the narrow slope of pavement, noting the uniforms. There were more uniforms than Breton costumes in the Grande-Rue. Air Force Personnel. Air Force. Transport. Air Force. Air Force Personnel. Transport. The Bretons he saw were either middle-aged men or young boys. The younger men might now be conscripts in the "labor volunteers," like Picrel's son at St. Déodat. But it wasn't only Hearne's age which made him seem conspicuous. Some of the uniformed men who brushed him aside into the flat gutter had looked pointedly at his natty gray suiting. Hearne wondered how long he would have to wheel this bicycle along the street before someone would stop him. It wouldn't be long, he guessed.

He propped the bicycle against a café wall, and entered the airless room. He brushed the flies away from a ringed table, and ordered beer. He might as well wash out the taste of dust from his mouth before he was picked up by a curious Nazi. He settled himself as comfortably as possible on the narrow chair, ignored the proprietor's curiosity, and returned the stare of the only other customer. The man went back to his newspaper.

It wouldn't be long, he had guessed. He was right. The light beer was only half-finished when the loud step of solid boots on stone broke the drowsy silence of the bar. Hearne, his back to the door, saw the tension on the proprietor's face. The man at the corner table, after one look at the doorway, was still more engrossed in his newspaper. Hearne had only time to notice that the paper wasn't held so steadily as it had been, and then a loud voice said in atrocious French, "Whose bicycle?"

Hearne swung round to face the two men. One was moon-faced, broad-shouldered; what hair was left on his head was very fair. The other, if he had had a clubfoot, might have been Goebbels' twin brother. He had the lean and hungry look, all right.

"Whose bicycle?" It was the bald-headed man.

Hearne rose. "Mine."

"Your papers," the large man demanded. Curlylocks wasn't wasting any time. Hearne searched quickly in his pocket. He brought out his identification card and Corlay's list of his fellow traitors' names. To the the top of that list, Hearne had pinned a sheet of paper. In square letters he had printed clearly: TAKE ME TO MAJOR KALB. DO NOT SPEAK MY NAME IN FRONT OF FRENCHMEN.

The bald-headed man passed over the collection of papers to the thin, dark man. Both faces were quite impassive.

It was the little Cassius who spoke next. "It is against the regulations to leave a bicycle blocking the narrow pavement. You will accompany us. There will be a fine to pay."

Hearne looked towards the corner table and the bar. The proprietor was busy with some glasses. The other man was reading as if his life depended on it. Perhaps it did.

Hearne held out his hand for the identification papers, but Cassius placed them in his own pocket. His smile was as false as his face. The risk had begun, Hearne realized. He shrugged his shoulders, and fell into step between them. The quicker he got through this episode, the sooner he would see Kalb.

The black-haired man walked with Hearne on the narrow pavement. He kept one hand on his revolver. He certainly wasn't the trusting type, Hearne thought. Curlylocks followed, officially wheeling the offending bicycle. In this way, Hearne retraced his steps on the Grande-Rue. There were fewer people on the street now. The distant sound of singing came to them as they crossed the narrow entrance to the cathedral. Noonday service, Hearne calculated. And then the voices were hidden by the cluster of old houses, and they were passing under medieval gables and balustrades into the small square. It was at one of the larger houses here that the Nazis halted him.

"Inside."

Hearne obediently entered. A broad curve of staircase faced him along with its two S.S. men standing on guard.

"Inside." It was Cassius, again. This time, Hearne was guided by the arm into a small square room at one side of the hall. It was shuttered and cool, but that was all that could be said for it. He was alone, with the small table and two chairs for company, and with the two Schutzstaffel men thumbing their belts outside. Through the shuttered windows he could see the square, and then the bright blue blouses, all the brighter in the glaring sun, of three young Breton boys. Then the splatch of color was gone; and Hearne was left wondering just how comic it would seem to his friends when they heard he had walked of his own seeking into this dark house, out of the sunshine, never to see it again. His friends would never know, in that case, he reminded himself. That would be a bitter joke for only himself to enjoy.

Ten minutes. Fifteen minutes. Hearne paced the little

room. He rehearsed his story carefully. That kept him from thinking about the chance that he might never be able to use it. Eighteen minutes. And then he heard the quick, precise footsteps of the dark-haired man.

"This way," he said. The smile was still inscrutable.

They mounted the stairs. The guards stood immobile. Hearne breathed more easily. His confidence in his plan returned. The dark-haired man pushed a door open on the first landing they reached. By its size and magnificence, Hearne guessed this must be the most important floor in the house. His confidence increased, and he entered briskly. The man closed the door behind him, and again he was alone.

But this time, the room was large. There were pictures on the walls, an abundance of delicate furniture neatly arranged over the thick carpet. Flowers to match the long yellow silk curtains were massed at one corner of the large writing desk. Elegant, Hearne thought, and moved his eyes from the desk on which lay his identification papers, thrown on top of a large glass-covered map. And businesslike, he added, noting the row of card-index boxes, the three telephones, and the large safe half-hidden behind a carelessly draped tapestry on the paneled wall. He was sure now that the waiting period in the depressing room downstairs had seen a lot of activity in this mixture of office and boudoir. The telephones, the card index. . . . A lot of activity: enough to let him stand here, anyway. Hearne smiled to himself. The papers so openly displayed on the desk, the half-disclosed door of the safe, were rather touching in this supposedly empty room. Even if they thought you were their friend, these chaps couldn't stop setting their little traps it seemed. He sat down on the nearest chair, a gilt-edged affair with spindle legs and satin seat. The soft notes of a tremulous song filled the room. "Holy Night." . . . Hearne dropped the magazine he had picked up, and looked around him in amazement. And then the delicate sound gave him a clue. He stood up, and the music ceased.

There was a laugh from behind him. Hearne turned round; the young man in officer's uniform closed a side-room door, and came forward. "Amusing, isn't it?" he said in excellent French. "But not all my visitors are obliging enough to choose that chair."

Hearne nodded. He was annoyed, and yet more relieved than annoyed, that he should have furnished the Nazi with some amusement.

The officer's face was impassive now. "You wanted to see me?"

Hearne noticed the captain's insignia on the man's uniform, and felt his irritation increase. He kept his voice smooth. "I came to see Major Kalb, on the orders of Lieutenant Traube, stationed at St. Déodat. There were instructions, I believe, which Major Kalb was to give me. I am Bertrand Corlay of St. Déodat, in charge of—"

"I know. I know." The young man silenced Hearne with his hand. "Why didn't you come direct to this house? You knew the address."

So that was something Corlay must have memorized and never entrusted to his private notes. Anything with direct reference to the Nazis had been carefully omitted from Corlay's documents. Even the man Hans Ehrlich had only been recorded as H.

Hearne said quickly, "I arrived at an awkward time of day. I thought I would make myself presentable first, for as you see I have been traveling; and I thought I would have something to eat so as not to disturb you at lunchtime. And then, there is the man Bruneau. I wanted to find out how his work was going, before I had the honor of seeing Major Kalb."

The explanation wasn't questioned. "Sit down," the German said, and took his place at the desk. "Major Kalb has been called away very suddenly. I am his deputy, Captain Riedel. What did you want to see him about?"

"I wanted to discuss the work of Bruneau with him."

"It is satisfactory. As Lieutenant Traube noted in his very full report, Bruneau has a tendency to grumble. But he can be kept in line with adequate rewards."

"That is what worries me."

"What?"

"Adequate rewards. The fact that we have achieved such results as we have, the fact that the fifteenth of August and victory are so near, is sufficient reward for anyone who is wholeheartedly with us."

The Nazi nodded. Hearne's earnest eyes waited. Black hair, he was noting; brown eyes; mole on left cheekbone; heavy eyebrows; tanned skin; long upper lip; undistinguished nose and chin. It was a pleasant enough face, except when the eyes were wary and the lips were tautened. But now the mouth had relaxed and the eyes were approving.

"Yes?" Captain Riedel said.

"On the other hand, Bruneau is a good worker. He will work very well, if only he is promised enough. And as he has been well-trained for the last two years, it would be difficult to find someone with equal knowledge of this town and its surroundings. The data he has accumulated in the last two years are particularly necessary to us at this time."

"I agree," Captain Riedel said. He had relaxed against the back of his chair. His fingers were playing with Corlay's papers. He suddenly added, "What made you think of this?" He picked up the sheet with the printed instruction TAKE ME TO MAJOR KALB.

"The chance that I would be questioned. I wanted no fuss over any arrest. The less my countrymen notice, the easier it will be for my work."

"True. Now tell me, what else did you come to see Major Kalb about?"

"So far, the only general instructions which have been given our organization are to prepare for founding a separate Breton national state. I have been told, of course, about the fifteenth of August. But it seems to me that our organization could be of some use to you about that date."

"In what way?" There was a hint of amusement in the German's voice.

"For counter-sabotage. Some soldiers must have been talking; some quick French ears must have been listening."

The implication was not lost on Riedel. The amusement left his voice. *"So."*

"So. There are rumors among the people that something very big is about to happen. The date of August 15th is beginning to be mentioned, here and there. That rumor will spread. As the movements of troops and supplies, as our preparations increase in the next few weeks, even the skeptical will believe. You know the Bretons. You know what they will do."

"Sabotage? But I assure you, Corlay, that Ehrlich's men will find out all we need to know."

"The only men under Ehrlich who will find out anything from the Bretons will be those who are Bretons themselves. You know these people. They distrust even a man from Normandy, or Bordeaux, or any other part of France."

Riedel nodded. "I see. Then you suggest that Ehrlich should use your particular organization to discover any plots which his own men may fail to detect?"

"Only if you agree with me that non-Bretons may fail to discover what is going on in the Breton mind."

Riedel was silent. His lower lip protruded and cupped the upper one. "I am inclined to agree," he said at last. And then suddenly— "Curse those Breton swine! They respond neither to smiles nor to kicks. They live within themselves, behind a prehistoric stone wall that nothing breaks down. There's only one thing they hate as much as a German, and that's a Breton traitor. Be careful, you Corlay. I shouldn't like to be in your place if they find out about you."

"They won't." Hearne's jaws hardened. "And I don't consider myself a traitor, Captain Riedel. I'm a true patriot. I *know* that the only good for Brittany is Germany's friendship and guidance." His voice rang earnestly through the high-ceilinged room.

Riedel's anger had gone. He stared morosely at the map of the Channel coast resting under the glass top of the desk. "These cursed Bretons," he said. "When will they learn?"

"With time and patience. We shall try that first. Later, when the war is over, we can try harder discipline. But now, there is first the problem of their autonomy; and secondly— and I think this more important—there is the complete success of our undertaking against the British. For without that, the war will be long. And of all the invasion coast, we are responsible for the most difficult area to control. If we fail in Brittany, if sabotage hinders any of the Führer's plans, not only will you and Major Kalb and Ehrlich be called to account, but, Captain Riedel, I and my friends will be held responsible too. For that reason, it is necessary that we know just *where* we are to guard against possible sabotage, just *where* the danger points are, just *where* materials and men are being assembled. Then I can warn the rest of my men." Hearne pointed quickly to the map. "Look, Captain Riedel. Here is Number 8 in Dol, Number 6 in St. Malo, Number 5 in Rennes, Number 9 in Combourg, Number 3 in Paimpol, Number 4 in St. Brieuc, Number 10 in Dinan. These alone could find out a great deal, if they were only told what they were to guard against. But now, all we're told is to get the Bretons to vote the right way. They may vote the way we want them to, but that won't prevent them conspiring to sabotage. They just couldn't resist the chance if they got it! And even a small piece of sabotage can dislocate a railway, a canal, a main highway, an aerodrome, just on the very eve of its usefulness."

"Why don't you tell this to Ehrlich?" There was a touch of
a sneer in the German's voice. Hearne remembered Tacitus
and his observations on the Germanic tribes. *Invidia,* spite,
was their worst fault: that, and the baseless fear of being
encircled. Tacitus, or was it Caesar? Not that it mattered.
Only the observation mattered, now.

Hearne, concentrating on *invidia,* said gloomily, "Oh, he
isn't there. Nor is Lisa Lange," and watched Riedel innocently. "Now I hear from Traube that they may not be back for
another week or so."

Riedel rose abruptly. He paced the room. "Ehrlich has
summoned Major Kalb. Dragged him away from some trouble at the coast."

"Do you know when the Major will return? If only we had
more time before the fifteenth, we could wait for his advice."

Riedel looked angrily at Hearne. "I am in Major Kalb's
place at the moment. I know what he knows, and I can make
any necessary judgments." But he still paced the room.

Hearne said slowly: "And Traube won't be any help to us.
The army has its own job. The detection of sabotage is left to
Ehrlich's department, or to your own. It is the Gestapo and
the Schutzstaffel who will be blamed by the High Command
if we overlook any dangers."

Riedel shook his head impatiently. "I know. I know," he
said irritably. But his decision was almost made.

Suddenly he halted, and then moved quickly to the desk.
He was now a man of action. "Where did you say these men
of yours were stationed?"

"Here," said Corlay, "and here, and here. ..." He pointed
to the map, town by town.

"Well, as you've already been told, the zero date is August
the fifteenth. Aerodromes are now almost complete along this
part of the coast . . ." the captain's finger swept across the
flat plains north of Dol . . . "and from them will develop
Phase Two of our attack: Bristol, Plymouth, and the southern ports will be destroyed. Phase One, the attack on the
Channel shipping and the Channel fleet, has already well
begun."

"But the British aerodromes?"

"Attended to, from further north. But here, what we have
to worry about is the maintenance of a steady flow of
material and troops to the north coast of Brittany from the
Paris-Rennes-Brest railway. Our men are already arriving,
and concentrating west of St. Brieuc. Others must be enabled

to reinforce them continuously. Barges and light craft are being assembled. Tidal seaports along these miles of sand have to be guarded with particular care. So far the enemy has concentrated his attacks on the Norman and Belgian coasts. So far, our shipping has been safe in the small harbors of Northern Brittany. Southern Brittany's better harbors are more under suspicion." Riedel jabbed at the map of the northern coast, angrily. "At *these six points,*" he said, "your men must take special precautions to maintain order. Under protection of the aerial attacks of Phase Two, our barges and ships will sail. Phase Three . . ." His finger swept up towards the Southwest of England, and into the Bristol Channel. His eyes were fixed on the South of Ireland. He flicked his fingers over Cork. "If need be," he said, and disposed of the Irish problem.

He added, "That is sufficient for your purpose, Corlay."

"Yes, Captain Riedel. I'll direct my men immediately as you suggest, and as soon as they learn of any possible sabotage, I'll inform you at once. And, of course, I'll inform Ehrlich. Then you can instruct your men to contact my informants and go to work. This plan of yours, Captain Riedel, will be a double safeguard. The army will be in your debt, more than they will ever know."

Riedel was pursing his lips at the map. "Just what are you going to tell your Breton agents?" he said suddenly.

"Only to ensure that there is no disturbance in those particular areas. I'll put the fear of death in them, without telling them the reason why. That is your suggestion?"

"That is my suggestion." Riedel folded the identification papers and pushed them across the desk.

Hearne buttoned his jacket. He was a very serious, very exalted member of the chosen band. He gave their masterful salute, and uttered their brief confession of faith.

"One more thing. How are you returning to St. Déodat?"

"The way I came. It isn't far. And a bicycle will arouse no suspicion among the Bretons."

Riedel nodded, and looked at the map. Hearne repeated the salute. Outside the door of the room, the sardonic man was waiting for him to conduct him downstairs. The bicycle was in the hall.

Outside, he paused to run two fingers round his sodden collar. For a moment, he halted and leaned on the bicycle; then he was painfully negotiating the cobbled surface of the square.

The towers of Dol's cathedral dropped behind him. Hearne, keeping his eyes fixed on the white road ahead, only saw a map under glass and the nervous forefinger which had tapped so peremptorily. Here, and here, and here ... six points to remember.

CHAPTER 23

At the Hotel Perro

In the week that followed, Hearne made good use of his time. Afterwards, he wondered just what it was that had impelled him to work so constantly and so hard, almost as if he had foreseen dimly what was going to happen. Then he would laugh at himself, for no one except the most second-sighted Celt would have foreseen that. But there was no doubt of the solid fact—he had made good use of his time.

Each morning he would drop his damp, muddy clothes on his bedroom floor, and then drop his numbed body onto the thickness of his bed. When he awoke, his clothes would be gone, and later he would find them dried and brushed, or even washed, in the kitchen downstairs. At first he thought it was Albertine who was responsible. Then one morning when sleep was difficult—the morning after his visit to the aero-dromes outside Dol, where he had almost been caught by a German patrol—he had awakened at the sound of the care-fully opened door. It was Anne who came in so quietly and gathered up the filthy clothes. He hadn't moved, pretending to be asleep. She had gone as quickly and silently as she had come.

When he rose and dressed, it seemed as if his footsteps overhead had been the signal for Anne to have hot food ready for him. He wondered just how she had silenced Albertine, who scarcely raised one of her meager eyebrows when he came down so late. Normally, there would have been a feeling of thunder in the air at such nonsensical upsetting of routine. But instead, the weather continued fair and warmer. Albertine, eternally busy, would work about the kitchen while Anne, after she had served his meal, would sit across the table from him, and talk. Never anything about themselves or the farm, never a hint of a question about the mud on his boots or the tired look on his face. She talked about the village, which she visited daily—as if she had guessed intuitively that that was what he wanted. And Albertine would join in the conversation too, telling what she had heard that morning after Mass. In this way, Hearne knew almost as much about the village as if he had been staying next door to the Hotel Perro and the Gestapo.

Kerénor had been turned out of his room at the inn. And he had gone to live with Guézennec, of all people! It was as much a symbol of the burying of old quarrels and jealousies as anything. Guézennec, the old schoolmaster, and Kerénor, his successor, were now together under the same roof; and Hearne was willing to bet their conversation wasn't entirely scholarly, either.

The Trouins had opened their kitchen as a free house: there was no room in the small bar of the Hotel Perro for any of the villagers. Instead, they brought their cider along with them to the Trouins', and sat round the large wooden table in the evenings until nine o'clock came and it was time for all Frenchmen to be off the street.

On the day of the weekly market, the Bretons were amazed at the quickness with which their produce was bought. The market was over before it was begun, and the farmers found themselves with the right number of "occupation marks" (printed, it was whispered, in a van which stood with the trucks and tents on the green meadow below the church) in their hands, but with none of their usual purchases. For there was nothing left for the Bretons to purchase or to barter with. One large farmer, Laënnec, hadn't liked the set prices: his vegetables were a bigger and better crop than those he had sold last month for more money. He insisted on an increase in price, or at least an equal barter exchange, and had gone so far as to argue. He wasn't good at keeping his temper. Before Monsieur le Curé could reach him and lead him away to discuss the new regulations, he had thrown the worthless marks in the face of the nearest German soldier. By the time Monsieur le Curé had pushed his way to the spot, all he saw was hot-headed Laënnec being marched to the small town hall at the side of the market place. From there he had been transferred to working on the roads. Quite a number had been "recruited" for that job; but it was particularly hard on the Laënnecs, for (unlike Picrel's son and the others who were now working on the road which led through St. Déodat) Laënnec himself had been sent to some foreign country. No one knew where, although the guesses were as wild as they were numerous. Not even his wife knew. Old Madame Picrel had closed up her shop—she said her son could take care of anything left to sell—and had gone up to the small Laënnec farm to help. It was difficult for Marie Laënnec, with three small children and a baby still to be born. Even old Monsieur Guézennec had left his books to go up there to help with the digging. The German Colonel-in-Command of the district announced that he had been extremely lenient.

Otherwise, as Albertine said, things were as normal as you could expect. As normal on the surface, Hearne amended to himself. The Germans were being rigorously correct. No incidents, no Frightfulness, so far. Nothing like the last German invasion. Hearne, watching Albertine's relief, didn't voice his thoughts. What was the good of saying "Just wait until they are retreating: wait then, and see how they leave you"? Instead, he listened to the description of the band which played each day at noon in the market place, of the quickness with which huts were being built to replace the tents under the trees below the church. Even when Albertine marveled at the fact that some houses in the village had been left unbilleted while German soldiers were sleeping in wooden huts, Hearne kept silent. It would only worry her to realize the true meaning of that fact. The Colonel had decided to keep a good portion of his men together, and not let them be scattered. Then he could use them for quick action if that were necessary. Careful man, the Colonel: thoroughly realistic. *Praktisch.*

But the news which seemed most extraordinary to Albertine and Anne was that the annual *Pardon,* the procession and fête in honor of Saint Déodat, had not been banned. It was to take place as usual next Sunday. This year, the village had decided not to have any festivities after the religious ceremony, when offerings were carried to the church and those taking part in the procession mounted the worn stone steps on their knees, up to the sacred shrine preserving the bones of their Saint. On Sunday, all the people from the village, from the farms on the hillsides, would be in the market place. All would be dressed in their complete national costume. All would bring what they could spare from their fields and kitchens. Everyone was pleased, Albertine had said. Except Kerénor, Anne had added—he was worried. He couldn't guess why the *Pardon* had been permitted, and that worried him. Again Hearne could have given them all an answer. The *Pardon* had been permitted because it suited Hans and Elise and their present policy: the Breton nationalists were to be "persuaded" into accepting a separate Breton state. How could any Bretons be persuaded into cooperation if religious traditions were to be banned? And why the importance of this separate Breton state to the Nazis, except that it would be the beginning of the skillful disintegration of France? Alsace; Lorraine; Brittany; the north, with its coal fields and industries; the Mediterranean south. . . . So Hearne listened, and said nothing. What was the good?

When the women's news was exhausted, he would go back to his room. There he worked on his notes, listing his findings of the previous night, copying them into his own shorthand, adding careful diagrams or neat two-inch-scale maps when it was necessary for extreme accuracy. Then the sheets of thin paper joined the others behind the false panel in the bookcase, and he would pay his short daily visit to Madame Corlay. After that, it was a matter of preparing with the map for the journey he would make next night. He had to know each mile of ground forwards, backwards, and sideways.

It was a simple enough routine, but it was producing results. The railway, the roads, the canal—all these had repaid his visits. Trucks, oil tanks, barges, concentrations of material and troops, construction work, all found their place in the notes on the square miles which formed his "district." And above all, the airfields which were being built to the north of Dol. He could feel some pleasure as he looked at the bookcase each morning. "Thank you, Captain Riedel," he would say, and he would salute it informally with one finger and a wide grin. That was how he was feeling these days. He ought to have known that the luck was too good to hold. Especially after that long night near Dol, when the patrol just missed him by so little . . . just by a bullet grazing his thigh. He ought to have known. Perhaps, deep underneath, he did.

For when the Germans came, he rose to his feet almost

calmly. No time to move, no time to get away by the back
door. There were footsteps in the yard. Anyway, he thought,
there was nothing left lying about upstairs to incriminate
him. He even gave Anne, her eyes wide with fear, a smile of
encouragement.

It was Albertine who had voiced their thoughts as the
pounding came to the front door and they heard it open.

"The Boches," she had said, and crossed herself as if the
Devil himself had arrived. Anne rose from the table where
she had been sitting as he finished his bowl of soup. She had
been laughing at something he had said. Her lips were still
parted, but the laugh had died in her throat.

He was on his feet too. And yet he was calm enough, as if
he were only reacting to something which he had been long
expecting.

He had only time to say to the two white-faced women
"Keep silent!" and then the German lieutenant walked into
the kitchen. His hand was on his revolver. Two armed
soldiers were behind him. Two more entered from the back
door.

"Corlay?" In appearance, even in voice, the man was a
duplicate of Deichgräber.

Albertine's hand had gone to her mouth as if she were
holding in a scream. Anne stood as still and white as a
statue. She hardly seemed to breathe.

"Yes. What do you want?"

The officer pointed with his revolver to the door. "At
once!" he said.

"Why?"

"At once!"

Hearne shrugged his shoulders. He left the two women
standing beside the table. Albertine was crying silently, her
hand still held to her lips. Anne was as rigid as if she were
facing a firing squad herself. He felt her eyes follow him into
the yard.

In the high field old Jean and Marie were standing, watching. Henri had gone.

Past the heap of hay on the cobbled yard, past the pool of
water which gleamed beside the well, past the empty cart
lying backwards with its shafts pointing into the air. And
then they were round the corner of the house. He looked up
involuntarily at Madame Corlay's front window. She was
there. She had left her chair; and she was trying to pull the

window open. She must have succeeded, because as they took the path to St. Déodat, he could hear her voice. Perhaps the solid Germans grouped round him didn't know Breton: for Madame Corlay's sake, he hoped not.

And then he saw Henri. Henri had reached the orchard. He was standing there, near the third tree in the seventh row. And then there were only the fields, and the dovecote, and Anne's farm, and the thin fringe of trees. . . .

Today was the nineteenth: Friday the nineteenth. Tomorrow Elise should arrive. So it couldn't be that Kerénor had told her about his warning. In any case, Kerénor was not a teller of tales. No, it couldn't have been that. Or was it that Deichgräber had been found still alive? Or that Ehrlich's mission to Mont St. Michel had resulted in the arrest of Pléhec and Duclos? Or that Captain Riedel had become suspicious? Or that Henri had got drunk and talked about the American? Or had the boat which sailed for Penzance been captured? Or what? If only he knew, then he could muster up some kind of story, perhaps even be able to deny enough to give himself a brief respite, a chance to collect his notes from the bookcase and head for the coast tonight. He cursed silently to himself as they crossed the stone bridge into the village street. Even if he could only get a chance to make for the coast, he could always leave his notes behind. He remembered enough of the main details to do without them if necessary. But the real problem was letting Duclos know in time, so that he could be picked up on the French coast as arranged. For originally, before van Cortlandt blew in on the scene to alter things, Hearne's plan had been to visit Mont St. Michel just as he was ready to leave. Then Duclos would have sent out the chief items of his information—to make sure of its arrival—and then let Matthews know from where and when he was leaving. Matthews had given him the choice of three suitable places. Well, now, it looked as if he couldn't use that choice. Now he wouldn't even be able to get word in time to Duclos by the boat which had brought him back from the Bay of Mont St. Michel. He didn't fancy spending any extra days or nights on the shores of Brittany, waiting for his message to reach Duclos and then Matthews: not with the Gestapo hot on his trail. Now he'd better just try to get *any* boat and sail across the Channel, alone if necessary.

They had left the road and turned west into the market place, following its south side and the narrow pavement leading to the Hotel Perro. This was the way he had come when he was looking for Henri, on the day the Gestapo had first appeared in St. Déodat. The Nazi flag was still there, but now there was also a detachment of soldiers in fatigue uniform with spades and picks over their shoulders. They swung through the square. They were singing, loudly, carefully, operatically. A few civilians, their eyes averted, hurried on their business, or stopped to speak quietly and briefly to one another. The German words marched in perfect unison. They flattened your feelings as if they were a steam roller, Hearne thought. Even when the hard sound of exact boots had blurred in the distance, the chorus of voices remained like a bitter echo in your heart.

They passed two men: one old and white-haired, the other short and fat with his priest's hat squarely set above a kindly face, now more stern than good-humored. The Curé and his companion looked at Hearne with only half-interest, and backed against the wall to let the officer, the four soldiers, and Hearne pass.

They mustn't get the wrong idea, Hearne decided. He wasn't coming to visit his Nazi friends with a bodyguard to protect him. He pretended to step out of line towards the priest. It worked. The soldier behind him caught his arm roughly and forced him back into his place. There could be no doubt at all of the way the soldiers had crowded more closely around him, no doubt at all of the lieutenant's animosity in the quickly barked command, the sudden movement of hand to revolver. He didn't object even to the way in which two soldiers held him with unnecessary vehemence as they urged him into the hotel. Behind him, the two men were standing motionless against the wall: but their eyes had followed him with an interest which had become real.

Now, thought Hearne savagely as he was pushed through the restaurant, Kerénor will perhaps believe my message. But at the moment that was cold comfort.

They had crossed the floor of the empty restaurant. To their right, the bar seemed empty too. It was quiet enough. The lieutenant halted at the back of the room, and knocked neatly and politely on a door.

A voice said *"Herein!"* And again two of the soldiers gripped his arms and almost ran him through the door after the officer. Just inside the room they halted, still gripping his arms.

There were people in the room. He could hear movements —a cough, two men talking quickly to the lieutenant. But he could not see any of them, for a large draft screen stood across the entrance, shutting off the room. The two soldiers holding him had halted behind it. All he could see was a side view of some heavy furniture backed against the wall at this end of the room. Not Breton furniture, either. Probably this had been Madame Perro's living room, and the furniture had been brought with her when she came to the village. He noted some cheap prints in massive frames on the plaid wallpaper: they were views of towns. By stretching his neck, he could see the three nearest—views of *one* town, he corrected himself. Views of Strasbourg. So that was where Madame Perro and her charming niece came from—Strasbourg. That was quite possible. That explained a lot of things, quite a lot.

One of the soldiers had noticed his interest in the pictures. He knocked Hearne's head to face the screen, with a side blow from his fist. Charming fellows, Hearne thought, and then the voice which had given the command *"Herein!"* spoke once more.

"Bring him forward."

Damn it all, you don't need to shove me about with so much relish, Hearne thought savagely, and checked the impulse to hit the short nose of the long-chinned private who had taken a particular pleasure in a heavy grip on his arm. The two soldiers let him go so suddenly that he almost stumbled. He caught his balance, straightened himself in time, and looked at the table in front of him.

Three men faced him across it. Only one of them was a soldier: a captain. There, but for the grace of God and a quicksand, would probably have sat Deichgräber. The other two men, watching him intently with that close-eyed tight-lipped look peculiar to their breed, didn't need their darker uniforms to identify them. So the boys themselves were here, thought Hearne: the perverts, the sodomites, the torturers. Pleasant time he was going to have. The young lieutenant saluted smartly and turned on his heel. The soldiers followed him out of the room. He could hear the sound of heavy boots diminishing through the echoing restaurant.

And then a door, which must have led from the bar itself, opened, and closed. The girl who had entered paused, with her shoulder leaning back against its panels as she looked

round the room. There was an amused smile on her lips, a
tilt to her head which showed the line of her neck, a flicker
of black eyelashes veiling the green eyes.

Hearne felt a stab of admiration. The timing, the gestures,
the entrance, were all so perfect. It was a pity that the three
men were absorbed in watching his face. He took a step
forward.

"Elise," he said, with sufficient enthusiasm and relief and
surprise.

She walked across to the armchair beside the window. She
settled herself on one of its arms, curving her legs to the side
like a ballet dancer, one arm stretched along its back. She
looked at him directly for the first time. Her eyes widened.

"Well," she said, "and how are you, Mr. Hearne?"

CHAPTER 24

One More Day

Hearne was conscious that the eyes of the three Germans
had never left his face. He forced himself to watch Elise, to
keep his look of enthusiasm and relief and surprise in place.
Now he added blank amazement as well. "Elise!" he said
again. And then, "Is this some kind of a joke? If it is, then
it's a poor one."

Elsie dropped her posing along with her pseudo-amusement.
She was sitting very erect now, looking at him quite coldly.
"Is it, Mr. Hearne?"

"Is it what? What's that you keep saying? Misterernmister-
ern." He ran the words quickly together to form a mean-
ingless jumble.

If he was really lost, really discovered, then he was taking
the risk of adding a lot of amusement to their present
pleasure. He had always promised himself that, once he was
hopelessly caught, he wouldn't give his captors the joy of
watching him invent. But now he was finding that the word
"hopeless" didn't have much authority. He was caught, yes;
but until he knew more about the evidence he wasn't going

to admit he was hopeless. It would have been just as easy for a strong swimmer to commit suicide by drowning: even as his mind was telling him to sink, his subconscious struggled to keep him afloat.

Hearne looked angrily at the men. "What is all this about, anyway?" he said.

One of the shark-jawed men spoke for the first time. His remark was not addressed to Hearne. "I told you this was the wrong treatment for this man. Now, perhaps, you will let us follow our own methods."

The German captain moved impatiently in his chair. "The colonel has ordered this examination," he stated abruptly. He narrowed his eyes at a sheet of paper in front of him.

"Your name?" he said to Hearne. There was only hard efficiency and determined routine in his voice.

The shark-faced Gestapo man caught his breath audibly. He was watching the officer now with barely concealed amusement. The captain ignored the byplay, and proceeded, with at least outward calm, through all the stereotyped questionnaire. Date of birth, place of birth, mother's name, father's name, education, religion, attendance at university, date of father's death, date of uncle's death, other relatives living, income, political activities, career in peacetime, army service. Hearne, keeping his mind alert, concentrated on the questions, on the way they were asked. He replied easily and assuredly. But he knew that, although there was an undercurrent of friction between the army officer and the Gestapo man, it did not mean the officer would be easy to deal with. He was apparently some kind of liaison or military intelligence man, who came into contact with the Gestapo side of the occupation forces in cases of common policy, or of certain aspects of army morale, or of citizen morale when it interested the army. He was probably Deichgräber's successor: that he obviously enjoyed his work less than the late unlamented ditch-digger didn't mean that he was disposed to any kindness for the prisoner under interrogation. He was only determined that the Gestapo was to be kept in its proper place, that the army's power would be unrelaxed. And so the dry impersonal voice continued with the endless questions. And so Hearne concentrated and replied with all the strength of the details he had so painfully memorized. The way in which he acquitted himself, down to a concise account of his rescue from Dunkirk by a French trawler which had brought him as a shell-shocked casualty to Brest, didn't have any effect on the hard businesslike tone of the captain. But the two other men were now watching him thoughtfully; and it gave Hearne some pleasure to see a puzzled look on the girl's face when he answered one question directly from Corlay's secret diary. She hadn't expected that.

The captain asked his last question. Hearne gave a straight answer. The German hesitated for a moment—his first sign of uncertainty—and then looked at the two others.

The shark-faced one said, "We expected something like this. We'll continue the investigation—with your permission, Captain Holz."

The third man, who had been silently examining his finger nails, looked at Elise and said, "In my opinion, all form of oral investigation is useless." His voice, like his face, was razor-edged. He was the lad who would now spend his time in thinking up variations of torture, instead of inventing filthy jokes—as he no doubt had done before he had turned political. Razorpuss was going to supply several bad quarters of an hour before he had finished. He could hardly wait to get his innings, Hearne thought; that was obvious.

Elise came forward and leaned against the end of the table. She smelled like a flower garden on a hot August morning.

"I'd like to know what all this is about," Hearne said petulantly, and looked angrily at the girl. "This is really intolerable, Elise."

She smiled with little sweetness. One eyebrow was raised, the eyelids were half-lowered. "Very pretty, so far, Mr. Hearne. But your feat of memory is unfortunately in vain. Here is something which arrived yesterday. Captain Holz— may I?"

She stretched out an arm, and Holz placed a sheet of paper silently in her hand. He looked as if he would be much happier sitting at his desk, planning the occuption of the Isle of Wight by parachute troops as an advance base against Southampton.

Elise looked at the sheet for a moment, as if to tantalize Hearne. He was keeping the same look of indignant annoy-ance on his face for the benefit of the others' watchful eyes. He took the piece of paper when it was at last handed to him with an air of unconcern. He looked at it and thought, they can see my face but thank God they can't feel my heart. He said, a treacherous tightening in his throat almost spoiling his attempt at anger, "What the devil is this?"

It was a small sheet of paper with rough scallops edging one side where it had been torn from a loose-leaf diary. It was dirty, and creased with many folds. The writing was in pencil, small, scribbled, spilling over into the margins; but it was undeniably the writing of Bertrand Corlay.

"Elise, my own," it began, "you may be in grave danger. I am here in England at the Downside Hospital near Bath. Was brought here after Dunkirk with shattered thigh, nearly dead. Only thoughts of you kept me alive. A man, looking like my image in the mirror, came to visit me constantly. I answered all his questions, told him many details of my life but nothing about us, because I knew I must prove I was Bertrand Corlay and not a German. The English are much afraid of Fifth Columnists. I haven't seen this man for a month. He *may be now* in St. Déodat, for at the last I found out that was his purpose. He looks like me, his voice grew like mine, but he is English. I asked cautiously for my friend who had visited me. Only two days ago, I asked a young doctor. That way I found his name is Hern. Yesterday, Jacques Lassarre came to see me before he sailed. He came here from Dunkirk too, but is now going back France. I have asked him to send you this note when he arrives in France. Am writing under difficulties. All letters examined, but L. will smuggle this out. I shall return soon. Still two boatloads of wounded to sail to France. Lying here tortured to death with thoughts of you."

Then followed two lines over which Hearne had shuddered when he had first seen them in Corlay's diary.

*"Tes beaux cheveux, couleur du soleil riche et sombre,
Ils seront mon abri, me pâmant dans leur ombre."*

And then the signature: "Bertrand Corlay."

Hearne looked up at the four intent faces. His eyes were incredulous. Damn that pip-squeak of a doctor, he was thinking. It must have been Paton, who had known him at Cambridge, who thought he had a nice cushy job in White-hall and used to greet him when they accidentally met by saying, "Well, how goes the rubber stamp, these days?" And Paton, out of ignorance and genial bedside manner, had answered Corlay's innocent question. Blast Paton and blast the fates that had stationed him at Downside Hospital.

Hearne looked down at the sheet of paper again, and then quickly back at Elise. "What the devil is this?" he asked.

"What do you suppose?"

"It's a letter from me to you, but I never wrote it."

"No, *you* certainly did not," the shark-faced man said and laughed at his joke.

"It's no laughing matter." Hearne was indignant and angry. He read aloud thoughtfully, "Elise, my own, you may be in grave danger. ..." He looked again at Elise. "Indeed you may, and so may I, and all those who work with us." The intensity and urgency of his voice silenced even Sharkface.

"Whoever wrote this," Hearne went on, "knows about us, and is trying to upset our plans by the only means he has: by sowing suspicion. Cleverly done, too. See, he scribbled it hurriedly, so that if he made any mistakes in copying my writing then you would only think it was due to haste."

"And just where would he learn your handwriting?" Sharkface asked caustically.

"Only one place possible. The poem proves that. I had it written down in my diary. I was working over the last couplet. He has copied it down the old way." Hearne quoted the lines:

> *"Your tresses fair, like sun's gold at setting,*
> *Bring me sweet shelter, languorous forgetting.*

"I was changing that to:

> *'Your golden hair, like the sun's rich setting,*
> *Brings me sweet peace and deep forgetting.'*

"But he couldn't guess that. ..." The injured poet threw the sheet of paper contemptuously on the table.

The Germans exchanged amused glances. Good, thought Hearne: the more of a fool they think me, the more chance I have.

"And just where would this man find this interesting diary?" Sharkface prided himself, it seemed, on heavy sarcasm.

"*I* don't know. ... The last time I saw it was before Dunkirk. I lost everything there."

"Do I understand you mean to say—" began Sharkface with bogus politeness.

"I mean what I say," cut in Hearne angrily. "Enough of this foolishness. We are obviously in danger."

Sharkface turned a dull red. He leaned forward, opening his mouth to shout—

"One moment." It was the captain. "Who is the man Lassarre?"

"There was a man of that name in my unit," Hearne guessed wildly. It did well enough to fill the gap at the moment. But only for the moment.

"We shall find that out," Captain Holz said, and settled calmly back in his chair. Sharkface made a note on the pad in front of him.

"In my opinion, all form of oral investigation is useless." It was Razorpuss again. He was a man of one idea, it seemed. Hearne could make a good guess at that idea, too, looking at the tight eyes and spade-cut mouth, the sleek hair, sloping brow and high thin nose.

"There's still one thing, gentlemen," Elise said slowly—but her voice had lost something of its confidence. Gentlemen. . . . Hearne smothered his smile before it reached his lips. He looked reproachfully at Elise, in as good an imitation of a hurt dog as he could manage. She moved quickly over to the door which led into the bar.

"Hans!" she called, and there was the sound of footsteps. Several footsteps. So that was it, so that was it. Hearne felt a surge of excitement as his fears over this last test gave way to relief. So that was it! The real Corlay knew Hans, the false Corlay didn't. At least, that was what Elise believed.

Three men followed each other through the narrow door, and stood there in a group. All wore ordinary lounge suits. All looked at Hearne with the same blank look. He let recognition come into his eyes as they fell on the dark young man who had been Deichgräber's dinner companion in Pléhec's restaurant, who had walked on the ramparts of Mont St. Michel with Elise.

"Well, Hans," he said, "and so you've got back from Paris. Had a nice trip?" His voice was acid. He glanced at Elise. There was veiled jealousy in that look. And then, he turned on Hans.

"You wouldn't know, would you, my dear Hans, about a letter supposed to have been written by me?" His tone was vitriol itself.

The attack took the Nazi by surprise. Then his face reddened with anger and he came quickly forward into the room. Elise was sitting quite still on the edge of the desk.

The underlying suggestion had not been lost on Captain Holz. He rose abruptly to his feet, marked distaste in every movement. "Enough!" he said in German, and he did not add "gentlemen." "Enough! This is developing into a servants' brawl."

There was a cold silence. The others hadn't liked that: Elise least of all.

Holz spoke again. "Have your men, Captain Ehrlich, been detailed to search the farm?"

Ehrlich answered, "They have not yet returned with their report, Captain Holz."

Holz nodded thoughtfully. "We must find this Lassarre. What was that postmark?"

"Bordeaux." Elise's voice was toneless. She didn't look at Hearne. He was thinking. Bordeaux was a big place. At least, he had some kind of breathing space until Lassarre was found. Even allowing for the Gestapo's loving care, there was still that breathing space. As long as there was no wall behind your back and no firing squad facing you, there was still a chance. It wasn't hopeless, yet.

The men had risen.

"Elise," Hearne said in desperation. "Elise. What has happened to you?" But he was damned if he was going to fall on his knees and plead with her as the emotional Corlay probably would have done.

Her eyes wavered, and then she walked to the window. She had made her decision.

"Take him away now," she said. So she was clever enough to know that she had lost his loyalty. Whether he was found guilty or innocent, she couldn't command his blind obedience after this. "At once," she added over her shoulder, as if she were ordering a table to be cleared of soiled dishes. Her profile against the light from the window was as perfect as she probably hoped.

Razorpuss motioned with the fingers he had examined so thoroughly. The two men beside Ehrlich advanced, grasped Hearne by each arm, and propelled him towards the screen and the razor-face. He had drawn his revolver. They were taking no chances, it seemed. Hearne relaxed, and walked easily. He wasn't going to give them the slightest excuse.

In this way they left the hotel.

There were silent groups of people in the square. The news must have traveled fast. Under one tree, Kerénor was standing, and with him was a girl whose soft fair hair gleamed in the sunlight striking through the thin branches. They stopped talking as Hearne was marched past. He didn't look at them. But he knew they were still watching him as he

was led into the group of buildings on the opposite side of
the market place to the hotel. As he ascended the steps of the
little town hall, a Nazi flag swung confidently overhead.

Inside, there was a large desolate room with a few rows of
cane chairs facing an empty platform. The table on the
platform had been decorated. At one end there was the
tricolor, at the other the arms of Brittany—the black cross
and ermine fringe on silver—and in the middle, separating
and dominating in ironical symbolism, was a giant swastika.
There was a doorway beside the platform. This was where he
was to be taken.

The doorway led to a dark narrow corridor, and in turn
the corridor led to a flight of wooden stairs, circling down
into the basement of the building. The stairs ended in the
largest room of them all. It was the central cellar, and the
darkest. Round its flanks were small boxlike storerooms.
The only light streamed through their opened doors, from
their small windows set almost at roof level.

Hearne stumbled over a pile of papers in the darkness of
the central room, and was encouraged by a kick to keep his
footing. It seemed as if the smaller rooms had all been
cleared out. There wasn't even a stick of furniture in them
now. But the floor of the central room was littered with piles
of books and ledgers and papers. As his eyes grew accustomed to the half-shadows, he could also see the dark shape
of a table and two benches. More papers were stacked on the
table. The archives of St. Déodat were in process of examination, it would seem.

They had halted him at the entrance to one of the small
rooms. The smell of dampness and stale air hung round him.
After the warmth of the sun in the market place, the chill of
the basement struck at his bones. He shivered in spite of
himself. So this was to be his lodging. The ground certainly
looked cold enough. Two kicks confirmed his guess. He
picked himself slowly up from the middle of the floor. There
was no hurry: there were plenty more where those had come
from. He turned to face the three men standing at the
doorway of the small cellar. Behind him the small high
window half-lighted the room. Outside there was sunlight. He
heard the clear voices of children, raised in the excitement of
some game.

The man with the tight eyes and spade-cut mouth nodded.
The heavy oak door was closed. It shut with a deep thud,
almost blotting out the hard voice.

"Now," the man was saying, "now, we might get the truth."

No use of backing away, thought Hearne: it would only be worse if they were to get him up against the stone wall. He stood in the middle of the floor and watched the three men advancing.

When Hearne regained consciousness, the half-light from the small high window had faded. It was almost dark in the improvised cell. He lay for some minutes on the stone floor. When he tried to raise himself, it was too unpleasant. He gave up; and lay as he had fallen. He didn't even think. He felt better after the second spasm of vomiting.

At the end of half an hour or so he tried again. This time he managed to stagger to the wall. Why should he try to stand anyway, he suddenly thought, and let himself fall and slide to the ground. Why should he even sit? He wanted to laugh at himself for his subconscious attempt to assert the natural dignity of man. There wasn't much natural dignity left after three men had kicked the daylight out of you. He lay on the floor, watching the fading light. He felt the crusts of blood on his face with his left hand, and he thought of Anne. He remembered her dismay when the razor cut had opened afresh. ... He began a smile, but his jaw wouldn't let him finish it.

Well, his face wasn't too bad. Not too bad, considering. It wouldn't look exactly pretty, but at least it still felt recognizable in parts. His left hand went slowly over the rest of his body. Right collarbone gone. Well, he could have got that in a Rugger scrum any day. Probably something wrong with a rib too. He felt the sore spot gently ... yes, probably a rib. The rest was bruises, and probably a kidney afloat. If ever he reached middle age, he'd find out. He could feel the differences in the consistency of his flesh even under his clothes. Legs were all right, though. Bruised and scraped, but no bones broken. And they were the most important for him. Without his legs he could never reach the coast.

He lay and looked at the window. The bars were hardly needed. It was at least ten feet from the ground, built into a smooth stone wall. No footholds, no reach. And not a piece of furniture in the room to climb on. From somewhere in the large central cellar outside, he heard a movement. He felt his muscles tighten, and sickness once more strike his stomach.

But no one came in.

He relaxed again, and wiped the cold sweat from his brow. They weren't coming back yet. Not yet.

He licked his dry lips and moved his throbbing jaw onto the coldness of the floor.

The trouble with him was that he didn't enjoy triumphing over pain. The trouble with him was that he wasn't a natural hero. He hadn't given Razorpuss any satisfaction so far, in the way of information, but after the first ten minutes he had grunted and groaned enough. He grimaced as much as his face would let him, at the thought of that last yelp they had wrung out of him. Not very pretty, he decided: not the way you like to think of yourself behaving. Indian braves did it better. At the stake, they laughed and mocked. The worse the torture, the louder they laughed. But they didn't keep silent either, he added as an afterthought: no, they didn't keep silent. Well, he could try laughing, too. Perhaps if he used up all the air in his lungs that way, he wouldn't have any left to talk with.

When he was kicked awake, it was quite dark. The full moon's light shunned the cellar. But they had brought outsize electric torches as well as rubber clubs. Ehrlich was there, too, and the man with the shark's mouth. This time, Hearne didn't try to fight back. He let himself pass out as quickly as he could. As after-dinner entertainment, it must have been disappointing.

When he revived, there was light again from the window, the cold gray light of a morning still being born.

There was a lot of blood on the floor.

After lying staring at it for some minutes, he realized it must be his own blood. His right arm was more useless than ever, but his left could still move. Slowly, this time; but still move. He held it painfully up in front of his half-closed eyes, and moved its fingers one by one. And then the wrist, and then the elbow. Yes, the left arm was still all right, and so was the left shoulder. Back was bruised, thighs probably blue and purple by their feeling, leg bones still unbroken. Slowly he made his inventory, slowly took comfort. It might be worse. He didn't let himself think long that it *would* be worse. No good thinking about that. He lay and tried to will his strength back into his bones and muscles. No good, either, in just lying still. He had been wrong yesterday when

he thought he would just lie on the floor. That way, he
wouldn't ever get out of here, until he was walked to a firing
squad.

He raised himself on his left elbow, and rested. Then
slowly onto his knees, and rested. Then, by holding onto the
wall, he was on his feet. After a pause, he felt his way along
the wall. It was a slow job but, just as he had hoped, his body
obeyed his mind. He could move. He could stand upright—
almost. He would walk round the four walls of the room
before he would let himself sit down.

"You are not the only one," he said to himself. "At this
moment, in Europe, you are not the only man forcing himself to walk round a cell. Not by a long chalk. So drop all
your self-pity. You are lucky, compared to some."

As he almost reached the window, there was a slight sound
above his head. A sound almost like a crack. And there was a
small white ball on the floor behind him. He glanced up at
the window. In one of its small panes, there was the smallest
puncture. Slingshot, he judged, and turned uncertainly to
retrace his steps. This time he didn't hold onto the wall with
his arm. When at last he reached the little wad of paper
wrapped round the ball bearing, he didn't know whether he
was more pleased at feeling it hidden in his hand, or at
having walked by himself without any wall to prop him up.
He lay on the floor, his back to the door, and unwrapped the
scrap of paper.

One more day. Courage.

That was all it said. One more day. One more day.

God, he suddenly thought, at least I've got friends: at
least, I'm not alone.

He tore the paper into four small pieces. They made a
poor breakfast, but the hope they had given him helped him
to swallow them.

Footsteps outside the cellar door made him alert. But no
one came in. Changing guard, probably.

He felt the lead shot in his pocket, and it cheered him.
How had they known he was in this cellar? Had they been
watching all last night from the meadows behind the town
hall? Had they seen the dim light which the electric torches
would send into the darkness? That must be it. . . . Anyhow,
that meant he had friends, and patient friends. He felt better
every minute. Whoever had written that note was a good
psychologist, or perhaps just someone with a heart as well as
a mind. It came to the same thing.

As he was slipping into sleep, he remembered that this room, at the back of the building, faced not only meadows and trees. There was also the road to the right, the road leading north. That was where he had entered St. Déodat when he had first arrived. And the two houses nearest the market place along that stretch of road belonged to Guézennec and Trouin: Trouin, who now kept open house where the men brought their drinks to sit and talk together; Guézennec, who now gave shelter to Kerénor. These two houses were together. From their backs one could watch this cellar. Then he thought of the tree in the market place, yesterday, as he had been marched into the town hall. Kerénor had been there, and he had been with Anne. Anne, he thought: it was Anne who was at the bottom of all this. He was convinced of that in his own mind as he fell asleep. His sleep was all the deeper for that last thought.

This time he was awakened by a heavy, dull, distant noise. An explosion. It could only be an explosion. It wasn't likely that British air raids were being carried out in broad daylight: not yet, anyhow.

After that awakening, he couldn't get to sleep again. He limped once more round the room. He kept thinking about that noise. Perhaps two or three miles away. It might be on the railway, or on the main road down in the valley. His mind was racing now. The explosion might be accidental. But there was just a chance it had been carefully engineered.

If it had, and if it had been arranged by anyone in this village, then there was only one object in it. It was a diversion to keep Sharkface and his friends occupied elsewhere. *He* wouldn't seem so important to them today, with an explosion for them to investigate. He didn't let himself fully believe this wild hope. Yet, through the long day, as he was left alone, he kept finding explanations to justify such an idea. The explosion wasn't in the village itself, so that no one here would suffer direct reprisals. It was down in the valley within reach of twenty villages, so that the investigation would be more complicated, would take greater time. Whoever had engineered the explosion had wanted the Huns to be occupied today. Perhaps he only believed all this because he wanted to believe it, because the belief gave him courage for one more day; but he believed it.

In the late afternoon he thought he heard a distant sound of many footsteps, from somewhere upstairs. But, down here, no one came.

By the time the evening light waned, he was convinced that his guess must have been right about the explosion. Without that, he would have had an unpleasant day.

When Ehrlich, Sharkface, and two others entered the cellar late in the evening, he learned just how unpleasant the day might have been. But still they didn't get any information. The bad temper which they had been unable to conceal when they entered the room must have been considerably increased by the time they left. But long before then, Hearne was insensible.

He was becoming accustomed to the painful awakening from unconsciousness. His first worry was how long he could keep up this business of passing out before they twisted any information out of him. Next time, he was sure the technique would be changed to keep him from being completely knocked out. They would find a way, all right. He lay and worried in the darkness. He looked at the patch of window, at the strong silver of the moon. He didn't even bother to count his wounds this time. He was a bloody mess: that was what he was, a bloody mess.

And then, in the middle of his depression, he remembered that the day was over. *One more day.* And it was over. Painfully, agonizingly, he crawled across the dark floor. It was sticky; it smelled foully. Hunger was the least of his troubles: even this thirst and the swollen tongue were little enough. He had to get on his feet, he had to be able to move his body as if it were one piece, instead of the twenty throbbing nerve-ends it had become. He touched the wall and slowly pulled himself to a kneeling position against it. He felt a cool sweet sagging. When he became conscious, he found himself lying again on the floor. Once more he pulled himself onto his knees. This time he was at last on his feet. He clung to the wall in the darkness. It's getting late, he thought despairingly. *Courage, one more day. Courage;* but it was getting late. There was not much courage in the feeling of a stone wall in a bloodstained cell.

He must think of something to stop this attack of nerves. If he let his mind give way, then there was no hope at all for him. Despair never won any game. Defeat came quickly to those who thought of it.

He stood in the darkness, his weight sagging against the cold wall. Outside, the moonlight was fading. He thought of the curve of hills ... cloud shadows weaving over furrow-

stitched fields ... the smell of hay and clover under the sun's
warm rays ... the hum of bees and the clear note of a girl's
gentle voice laughing ... a light clear voice made to sing.
Made to sing *"Au clair de la lune."* Gray changing to blue, as
the sky changed above her. He thought of the blueness of her
eyes and it was the blueness of the sea, changing like the sea
in shade and sunshine. He could feel their soft coolness, their
warm clearness as if they were the gentle waves of the sea
itself. He clung to the wall, and thought of the sea's blue
depths.

And then he was walking round the wall, feeling his way in
the darkness, and the despair had been washed out of his
heart. If no friend came, he was thinking, then he would
have to work out his own plan of escape. He must do it at
once ... a few more days of this and he wouldn't be able to
escape at all. Now his mind was busy thinking of chances to
take, of ways to get the guard to come into this cellar.

From the darkness outside came footsteps on the village
road. There were voices, the sound of a cart. People were
moving about, out there. For a moment he wondered if he
had already begun to imagine things, and then the melancholy ringing of the bells in the church tower reminded him.
Today was the dawn of Sunday, today there was to be the
Pardon. The people were coming in from the farms and the
small hamlets round St. Déodat. He could almost see them
coming to the church, the women in their elaborate lace caps
and black velvet-trimmed dresses, with their stiff shawls and
aprons, the men walking carefully in their best clothes. They
were coming through the night to gather in the market place,
in time for the first Mass at dawn. He listened carefully, and
knew he must be right in his guess. There was the sound of
feet, slow hesitating feet, or the sound of wheels. But there
was no laughter, no talk. Even the children were silent. Only
the bell sounded its solemn note. Now, now, now, the notes
hammered into his brain.

He turned towards the door. Now.

He could hear a movement from the cellar outside. He had
reached the door and flattened himself along its left side:
that was the way it opened. That way he could perhaps
surprise the man who would come in.

He filled his lungs with air and let out a yell. His throat
didn't let him make much of a noise, but the guard would
hear it. "I'm willing to talk," he would say, and the guard
would halt in the doorway. That was all he wanted. It would

be interesting to see if one-armed jiujitsu would work. His breath gave out, and he listened. There was a movement from outside, the sound of a key in the lock.

"Keep quiet. Quick. Can you walk?" The voice was urgent, and it was Breton. A dimmed torch searched the room anxiously.

"Here," he croaked and put out an arm to the two figures in the doorway. "Here."

"Quick."

He needed no more urging. As he came out into the large cellar, lit feebly by a lamp on the table, a third man brushed past him. He was dragging the guard. The limp body was flung into Hearne's cell. Its swollen face and protruding tongue thudded on the stone floor. The third man locked the door, straightened his large back, and started after the other two who were helping Hearne to climb the stairs. As he passed a large stack of papers and books in the corner of the cellar, he stooped quickly and thrust the keys under the heap of documents. They were well lost. And then he was behind Hearne, pushing him up the stairs. Strong hands he had. Hearne thought of the German's twisted neck. Yes, strong hands.

"Quietly," whispered one of them, and they halted in the narrow passage. This was how he had been brought by Razorpuss, Hearne remembered. Ahead of them would be the large meeting hall with its flag-draped platform. There were footsteps, either in that hall or beyond it at the front door. The Bretons had heard them, too. Moving silently on their bare feet, they pulled and pushed Hearne, through the unobtrusive door in the passage wall to their left. He didn't even remember seeing it last time he had been taken through here.

Now they stood in another long passage, listening as they paused. The insignificant door was silently closed behind them, and then they were moving down the gentle slope of the floor. Hearne, concentrating painfully on each footstep, had only time to think, we've doubled on our tracks; we've traveled to the other end of the building—to the west, farther away from the road and church; the bells are just so much fainter. And then they were through another doorway, heavy, thick, resisting. They were back in a large room: a storeroom. It smelled like a grocer's shop. After the bleakness of the cellar it was warm and friendly, and yet nauseating. There were too many odors for an empty stomach to digest. Its comfortable stuffiness smothered. One of the men felt Hearne's weight sagging.

"Just twenty paces more," he urged in a whisper. Hearne nodded, and moved desperately forward with the two unseen and unknown friends on either side supporting him when his body faltered. The third man, the man with the strong hands, held the torch. Its dim light flickered their way through the islands of barrels and sacks. Once, when footsteps overhead halted them, the large man pointed upwards, caricatured a salute, and grinned. So upstairs in this part of the building, soldiers must be quartered.

They had reached the far wall of the room. Hearne, his sense of direction still alert, guessed this must be the outside wall of the building. His cell had faced north, the front entrance to the town hall had faced south. Then this wall would face west: it would be near the village school, for the school stood in the fields behind the northwest corner of the market place.

The torch picked out the broad double door in the wall. The large man was slowly lifting up the crossbar until its end was free of one half of the door. Supporting it there with one hand, he pushed the free side of the door slightly open, as the torch switched off. He stood there, waiting, listening. Hearne could see the black shadow of a tree, could feel the night air whip the gashes on his face, strike his naked shoulders. The Breton motioned quickly, and one of the men holding Hearne leaped down into the darkness. The other shoved him forward, and jumped behind him so that they fell together. They were lying in the shadows of a deep cart track, on grass edged with deep ruts. Above them, the large man edged his way out of the door, one hand still above his head holding the crossbar in place until the last minute. Then he jumped, thrusting the opened half of the door back in place as he leaped. The door stayed shut. The crossbar inside had fallen of its own weight and held it secure.

To the south of them was the square, and the movement of people grouping under its trees. Harder boots struck the pavement, round the corner from where they lay. Patrol or sentries ... Hearne didn't care. The jar of the six-foot drop had seared his bones like a flame. His body couldn't seem to obey him: it wouldn't rise at the touch of his companions' hands; all it could do was to lie and tremble, like a moth after its wings had struck a lighted candle.

"Quick!" The large man's whisper was urgent. Hearne

stifled his groans and raised himself slowly. They half-carried, half-lifted him into the darkness of trees and bushes. Ahead was a small square house, the schoolhouse, thought Hearne. But that was no good—it was one of the first places the Boches would look for a hiding man. Dismay and desperation gave him strength. The quicker they reached there, the quicker he could get away from it. For one thing seemed absolutely certain: the three men were determined to take him there.

They almost ran over the last twenty yards of grass. But it wasn't the schoolhouse to which they led him. They halted in the trees at the edge of the children's playground, moving cautiously into the three-walled shelter at its side.

From the darkness at the back of the shed, a voice vaguely familiar said "Splendid." Hearne, swaying on his feet, looked at the three dark shapes beside him. Even now he couldn't see their faces properly. The man who had spoken limped forward, and held his arm to steady him.

"Can you walk? Try, please." It was Kerénor, all right.

"Yes."

"Good." Kerénor was slipping a long loose piece of clothing over his head, pulling it down into place on his shoulders. When Hearne's face had struggled free from the folds of the material, he was alone with Kerénor.

"The others?" he whispered, as Kerénor wrapped a cloak round him.

"Gone to change their clothes for the procession. You and I will walk together." Kerénor had thrust some kind of hat on his head. As they moved out of the shed, towards the path which would lead them into the market square, Hearne saw, even as he felt the long skirts pull round his knees, that Kerénor was dressed as he was. They followed the line of trees across the school playground, back towards the market place. They were two priests coming to join in the celebration of their people.

The first bright streaks of light were breaking in the east. The bells halted, and then swung into a changed rhythm. The people, waiting in small groups in the market place, began to move towards the church. One of these groups, standing at the northwest corner of the square, moved forward as the two priests passed them. Hearne noted the three grim-faced men, the two white-capped women, as they walked slowly to join other equally straggling groups, walked silently with bowed heads towards the steps of the church. They would hide the two priests from the town hall and the sentries patrolling its front. Hearne's head bowed too: no one, not even those who were his friends, must see his face. He walked slowly and draggingly, his chin resting on the black cloth covering his chest, Kerénor's hand comfortingly at his elbow. He felt as old and as weak as he must have looked.

They had left the market place and crossed the road. The two Romanesque towers soared above them. The thickening stream of people paused, and moved, and paused, as those in front began to climb the stone steps to the vaulted doorway. Hearne felt Kerénor's guiding hand keep him to the edge of the crowd, close to the base of one of the towers. The group of three men and two women still shielded them. Now, as they started to mount the stairs, their bodies formed a screen behind which Kerénor opened the narrow little door in the wall of the tower.

"For the clergy," murmured Kerénor, and stood aside to let Hearne enter first, as was fitting for his marked age.

Inside, it was as cold and dark as the cellar in which he had lain.

Hearne took three steps after Kerénor, fumbled, and then fell. Kerénor had him on his feet again, urging him through the blackness. Hearne went forward blindly. All that mattered was to get one foot before another, one foot before another.

Then at last Kerénor said quietly, "Now you can faint as much as you want."

CHAPTER 25

Sanctuary

At first, he thought of his bedroom in Cornwall. It was his birthday, his fifth birthday, and his father had hung up a Chinese lantern in the window. The air blowing against the thin, flat pieces of glass which dangled from the lantern sent them swaying and striking their tinkling tune. He was lying in his cot, and he had wakened to hear the pretty colored thing sound its gentle song. The fragile notes would halt in the middle of their harmony as the wind drew new breath; they jangled into silence, and then began all over again. It seemed to him then that it was the loveliest kind of song, for it had no real beginning and no real end, and even the notes were as indefinite and vague as a song should be.

Hearne shook himself fully awake. The notes haunted him. He could hear them in their clear faintness. Perhaps he was really going mad. His eyes searched the dimly lit stone walls around him. The ceiling was of stone, rough and uneven. The floor on which he lay, wrapped tightly in a heavy blanket, was of stone too. It was dark, with shadows deepening in the corners: the only light came from a carefully trimmed lamp standing in a niche chipped out of a wall. No windows. No doors in the proper sense: just two arched openings in opposite stone walls. This wasn't a room in a house. Dismay seized him, and he struggled to raise himself on one elbow. It was more like a dungeon . . . a prison. . . . And then he saw that the rough blanket was an army blanket and an old British army blanket at that. His right arm was bandaged with clean linen, his face felt sticky with some grease. He wiped some gently off his sore jaw with his free left hand. Yes, it was ointment: a thick, black ointment smelling of tar and sulphur. His body felt clean. It was still sore, still heavy to move, but the blood and the dirt from the town-hall cellar floor had been washed off, and there was a clean white linen sheet wrapped round his body to keep the coarse blanket off his flesh. He relaxed again and lay back on the thin straw mattress. He wasn't in Nazi hands, that was certain. He looked at the faint yellow light burning so steadily, and listened. Gently, the dripping dropping notes sang through the rough vault above his head. It was water. That was it; water trickling, falling slowly. He smiled, and now his face didn't hurt so much.

He must have fallen asleep again, and he must have slept for a long time. He could tell that by this feeling of expansion which his body had: a nice, warm, comfortable feeling, a clean feeling. He closed his eyes and listened to the distant trickle of water, as he tried to fit this jigsaw puzzle together in his mind. This place wasn't a house. It hadn't been built by man, but rather by some long, patient process of erosion. The ceiling was too high for a mine: a cave, or a series of caves perhaps, would be nearer it. But just whereabouts was this cave? He tried to remember what had happened after he had crossed the market place and the road in front of the church. There had been people crowding slowly towards the steps. ... Kerénor had pulled him into the shadow of the tower, had opened that small door in its base. Then there had been darkness, and the sound of bells and the chanting of a choir had grown more distant. He thought he could remember another door, some steps, another door. He couldn't be sure. It had been too dark, and suddenly he had felt too tired. One step before another, stumbling, hesitating, leaning on Kerénor, reeling like a drunk on a Saturday night, one step before another. That was all he could remember. Then there was Kerénor's voice, no longer whispering, no longer strained. "Now you can faint as much as you want." And, by heaven, he had.

And now he was here, wherever that was.

He lay and listened to the trickling water. It must be falling into a pool in one of the next caves. There was a series of drops, which kept repeating the same notes like the strings of a violin being plucked. They almost formed a tune, but before they resolved themselves they halted, and the first notes sounded all over again. Like the tone signal of a radio station, like rain from the roof dripping into a barrel of water, like a Chinese lantern swinging at an opened window.

Then he heard the footsteps, at first an uncertain hint, then marked and sure. He kept his eyes closed as they entered the cave.

A light clear voice said, "He's still asleep!" A cool hand was on his brow, and the blanket was smoothed where he had disarranged it.

"He needed it." That was Kerénor's voice. "I don't think you have to change the bandages again. They look all right to me."

Hearne opened his eyes. Anne was kneeling beside him, and Kerénor was standing behind her. It pleased him somehow to see them both looking so anxious.

"Hello!" he said.

Anne smiled with her lips and her eyes and her voice. "He's awake."

Kerénor's twisted smile wasn't disagreeable. "Evidently," he said briefly. "How do you feel, now?"

"Not so bad."

"Good. You were beginning to worry us. I told you that you could faint, but I didn't expect quite all this."

"How long has it been since?"

"Since you collapsed? Two days and two nights."

"Was this where I passed out?"

"No. Further back there." Kerénor pointed to the opening through which Anne and he had entered the cave.

"Are we in a mine?"

"No." Kerénor's voice became informative: you could have guessed that he was a schoolmaster by trade. He sat down on the ground beside Hearne. "These rooms and passages are caves, discovered by the founding fathers of the church, no doubt, and used by them to escape from the pagans when they were searching for a suitable sacrifice on their stone altars. Later, the caves were useful against roving bands of northern raiders, and still later, against the English." Kerénor paused to let that sink in. He was smiling. So he knew now, too, Hearne thought. The schoolteacher was talking again. "Then, about four hundred years after the English, the caves were used during the Revolution, during La Vendée to be precise. That was the Breton counter-revolution, and there was much bloodshed here." Yes, Kerénor knew that Hearne was English: he was explaining French history politely for the benefit of a foreigner.

Kerénor was still talking in his matter-of-fact way. "Those of the inhabitants who managed to survive La Vendée did so by living down here along with the treasures from the church. After two months, they went above ground again, but they didn't put back the gold plate and silver candlesticks on the altar for almost thirty years. Cautious people. Now we may find these caves very useful again."

"Who knows about them?"

"The priests. The villagers had heard the stories about the caves, of course, but somehow they believed that they were either filled up, or destroyed, by Revolutionary soldiers. Certainly, all entrances from the fields have been completely blocked and forgotten. I myself didn't believe that the caves existed at all, until three days ago and a little conversation with Monsieur le Curé. The church remembered how well the caves had sheltered its people—and its treasures—and it kept the secret, believing that the less others knew about it, the more valuable it would be."

Hearne was about to speak, but Kerénor interrupted him quickly. "I want you to answer some of my questions later, so don't tire yourself now. I'll explain as much as I can." He moved to a more comfortable position and cleared his throat. "I've been thinking what I should like to know if I were you." He rubbed the bridge of his nose reflectively as if arranging his thoughts into the neatest order. Anne was sitting motionless on the ground, her full black skirt spreading circlewise round her. When Kerénor spoke again, he counted each point briskly on the fingers of his left hand. He was a good schoolteacher.

"First, the Curé and Guézennec saw you were under arrest. Second, Anne arrived and confirmed that rumor. She had come down into the village—the Boches sent to the farm, to question Madame Corlay and to search the rooms, didn't think she was important: she wasn't one of the family; she was just a visitor to them; and no one at the farm enlightened them—and she went at once to the Curé for help. Third, the Curé sent Guézennec to bring me to the square, and I was there talking to Anne when you passed on your way to the town hall. We were discussing, actually, how any escape could be managed. Fourth, Monsieur le Curé went up to the farm to see Madame Corlay. He sent Guézennec over to Anne and me, with the news that there *was* a place which could hide you for days or even weeks, *if* you were to escape. Fifth, we met in Guézennec's parlor that evening, and perfected our plans. It's next door to Trouin's house, where the men come to drink together, and we know all of them and they know us. Anyone who seemed most suited for what we were planning was sent in to see Guézennec by Trouin. All very quietly, all very simply. That's how we completed the plans. It gave us good practice for the future."

"What about Anne?" Hearne said. "This must be dangerous for her."

Anne smiled, rose quickly, lighted a second oil lamp, and moved into the next cave.

Kerénor waited until she had gone, and then said, "She's living here. . . ."

"What?"

"Easy, easy. Don't put your temperature up again. Someone had to be with you; and no one else could, without their absence being noted. So Anne is visiting her aunt at St. Brieuc. She left on Friday, after you had been arrested and everyone at the farm had answered the Boches' questions stupidly and satisfactorily. What else was there for a girl to do, whose fiancé had turned out to be quite another man in disguise? Very embarrassing for any girl living in a village like St. Déodat. Her decision to go didn't need any explaining, I assure you."

Hearne ignored the raillery of Kerénor's voice. He said, "What about a permit to leave?"

"She's had that for some time. She got it the day she was turned out of her farm. They told her she could go and live with her relatives, and graciously gave her a permit to do it. No extra charge. That was an easy way to lease a house, so thoughful, so generous." Kerénor's voice rose in savage imitation of a German accent. "Anne Pinot, born in Brittany, educated and living in Brittany, will be allowed by our gracious German permission to travel by foot (all trains being occupied by us, all buses being used by us, all petrol being commandeered by us) the distance of some eighty kilometers to the town of St. Brieuc, carrying one bundle of her possessions not larger than six kilos in weight, and there in St. Brieuc she will find a roof to put over her head (provided that the roof has not already been blown to bits or occupied by the soldiers assigned to that district) to replace the roof of her Breton farm exploited unjustly by her Breton family for two hundred and forty years and now in the rightful occupation of Brittany's friends and saviors for the essential defense of Brittany and the Reich." He had risen to his feet, and was now limping up and down the rough floor, pausing here and there to accent a phrase with two uplifted fists, raising his voice in the crescendo of unmistakable parody as he reached the end of the peroration. He ended abruptly on the highest falsetto screech. "Bah!" he said in his normal voice. "Carpet chewer!"

"They'll hear us," Hearne warned.

Kerénor shook his head with a mystery which he obviously was enjoying. "Do you know where you are?" he asked. It was strange to see him become so much the arch-conspirator. Queer fish, thought Hearne: he seemed to pass from sarcasm to mockery, from emotional animation to calm disinterest, as easily as clouds changed their color at sunset. You could never tell what he was going to say next, whether his face would freeze into remote coldness or liven with expression, whether he would be serious or amused. And in spite of all these variations, you knew you could trust him: you might not like him, not at first anyway, but you could trust him.

Hearne replied, "We are under the church." It was as

much the obvious answer to Kerénor's question as the answer was obviously expected.

"No." Kerénor was delighted with his secret. "No. Under the marching feet. Charmingly symbolic."

"Under the tents and huts?"

"Yes. Under the meadow lying in front of the east Gothic tower of the church. That water you hear is a small stream draining out of the pond in the meadows."

Anne was coming back, walking slowly so that the pitcher of water which she carried would not spill over. There were two pink spots in her cheeks. She had heard part of their conversation about her, no doubt. Hearne was about to say, "Anne, why didn't you tell us about the permit?" and then didn't, as he noticed the way she avoided his eyes. She was raising his shoulders so that he could drink, but she was watching the level of the water in the jug. If she hadn't told him about the permit, then she had her reasons. If she didn't want to explain them, then it was none of his business. Or, at least, he had no right to think it was. Perhaps she had preferred to stay at the Corlay farm rather than face the long journey to her aunt's house, perhaps she had felt that Madame Corlay's invitation would have been less warm if she knew about St. Brieuc as an alternative haven for Anne, perhaps it had been an oversight. And yet, he found himself entertaining the fantastic hope that none of these explanations was the right one.

He said, "Enough, Anne. Thank you." She still avoided his eyes. She lowered his head gently onto the mattress again, and pretended to smooth the blanket. The pink spots deepened in color and flowed over her cheeks. Hearne was suddenly aware that Kerénor was watching them both, with a strange un-Kerénor look on his face. There was a pause in which each could feel the words they were all avoiding.

Hearne said quickly, "Think I'll try to walk." He raised himself on his left elbow, disarranging the blanket which had just been so carefully smoothed.

Kerénor was smiling openly, now. "Better not," he said. "You've no clothes, anyway. I had to cut what was left of them off you. We'll have to find new ones. In any case, I want you to lie still today and save your strength for talking. I've some questions to ask you." He was serious again. The amused smile twisted off his face, and his eyes watched Hearne anxiously.

"I haven't finished my own," Hearne replied. "How many people know about me?"

"Madame Corlay and Anne, Monsieur le Curé and myself."

"How many know I am here?"

"The same again. We had to tell Madame Corlay. She was on the point of sending old Henri and his blunderbuss to rescue you. Much good that would have done, but both Madame Corlay and Henri were all set for action. So we had to tell her."

"What about the three men who got me out of that hell-hole?"

"Back working on their farms after attending the procession."

"And the three men with the two women?"

"They know nothing except the Germans weren't to notice you going towards the church. They are the rest of our committee."

"What committee?"

"Committee for the Preservation of Liberty, Equality, Fraternity." Kerénor was tensely serious. If Hearne had even looked about to smile, Kerénor would have struck him. But Hearne didn't smile . . . there was something pathetically courageous in the formation of a committee for the preservation of France in this remote Breton village. Yet, great oaks from tiny acorns . . .

Hearne said, "Good."

Kerénor relaxed again. "Is that all you want to know?"

"I'd like to know what happened when the guards were changed in the town-hall cellar."

"We were coming out of the church at the end of first Mass. It was almost six o'clock. Then systematized pandemonium broke loose. Squads of soldiers were summoned and herded us into the market place. We were counted and listed like sheep. Just when I thought we were all to be arrested—and that would have been an interesting experiment, but the Germans unfortunately thought better of it—we were all sent back for second Mass, and sentries were posted all round the church. When they let us out at last, they had decided on their course of action. A large reward was posted for your capture. Grim warnings were published about the fate of anyone who helped or harbored you. Houses were all searched from cellar to attic. Patrols are everywhere: there's a curfew for us all to go to bed early like the bad little boys we are. Then there is talk of hostages. But the only trouble is that, at present, they want to keep us cooperative—until the end of this month, anyway. You were right about the warnings you sent me through Anne. We are being maneuvered. I want you to give me the details about that."

"I've still a question. How did these three men get into the town hall? Its entrance was heavily guarded."

"As part of this German co-operation plan, a meeting had been planned for late that afternoon. If you hadn't been arrested, you would no doubt have had to speak at it. We were all told to attend, and in accordance with our own private plan, we all went. The place was crowded. No Boches were present. Elise was there, and she had got Picrel to speak along with her. He's trying to save the remnants of his business and to get his son out of the road gang. He didn't know what he was doing. Elise had persuaded him it was the only sane and sensible thing. The trouble with Picrel is that he has got accustomed to having more than his share of the village wealth and power; and he's hanging on to what he has. He's willing to be persuaded of anything which will let him hang on. It was a lively meeting. Then our Committee crowded round Elise and questioned her on the way out. The three men who had been chosen hung behind, and hid. Under that table on the platform covered by the draped flags. They just lay there and waited all through the night until the church bells began. That was their signal. I am sorry we had to arrange it so that it looked as if you had killed the German, but we must safeguard the village. You understand?"

"The village has done more than enough for me," Hearne said quietly. "How did they get into the cellar?"

"You want to know everything, don't you?" Kerénor looked at him warily.

"As someone who would like to perfect his own technique."

Kerénor's suspicion ended as quickly as it had begun. "It was simple. There might have been the noise of a movement from upstairs. The guard came to the foot of the staircase. Silence. He came up the staircase with a torch and the gun. Then he turned to go back downstairs. The door in the corridor, through which you escaped, opened. Our man came forward. In the old days he was the best smuggler in the district. Bare feet make no noise. Neither do large hands wrapped tightly round a German's throat."

"But what if there had been a second sentry?"

"One of the other men came into the corridor. German hat, German coat. Enough to pass in the dim cellar light (we are so backward here, no modern conveniences!), enough to pass for a moment. That was all we needed. From then on, he was to improvise, while the third man guarded the corridor with his knife. That was why we chose three men."

Hearne's look of admiration stopped Kerénor.

"That's nothing to what we *can* do," he said modestly. "After this war is over, the tales we shall have to tell will make strange listening. Nothing that art can invent is so wildly improbable as what happens in real life. Art and fiction are only imitation. Life is truth, and stranger than either of them."

Hearne nodded. "So I've found," he said. "There's one last thing. There was an explosion."

Kerénor said, "Yes, there was, wasn't there?" His eyes were mocking, and Hearne knew he would be told no more than he had guessed already. But, looking at Kerénor's triumph, he knew his guess had been near the truth.

"Here is your information," Hearne said. "I can give it to you as far as I can remember it, but the full proof is in my room in the farm. Who can go to get it?"

"Anne is out. I am out too—for I never went near the Corlay place, and if I were to go now, it would seem strange. There's only Monsieur le Curé left."

"Will he?"

"If he can act without being told the facts."

Hearne said, "My head is dull today."

"Take these caves, for instance. Monsieur le Curé told Guézennec about them. At the same time he suggests it would be a good place for anyone to be safe from the Germans. Then he says no more, except to tell me about the history of the caves, and he doesn't come to see you. Again, he doesn't notice that the clothes belonging to his young assistant—at present in hospital somewhere in Germany— were borrowed. But the vestry where they were stored was left open all yesterday afternoon. Again, in a few minutes I shall go back up into the church, and from the church I shall take the private way to his house. When I return I shall carry a basket of books, with food underneath for Anne and you. This afternoon when I see Monsieur le Curé we shall talk of other things, but not of a depleted larder."

"Here are the facts: I shall let you suggest them to Monsieur le Curé." Hearne's voice was beginning to tire.

His head was beginning to throb again. He felt hot. Quickly he told Kerénor about the bookcase in his room. Two notebooks, two sets of papers clipped together, a map, a French service revolver, a silencer, a pocketknife, an envelope. Kerénor listened intelligently. At the mention of the gun, he shook his head slowly.

"The arsenal will need some careful suggesting," he said, and rose slowly to his feet. "I think I'll see Monsieur le Curé right away. I'd like that list of names ... before I keep an appointment."

There was something in his voice which roused Hearne.

"What appointment?"

Kerénor was dusting the seat of his trousers. He seemed interested in the weave of the material. "After the meeting yesterday, Elise spoke to me. It's most unfortunate that Picrel turned out to be such a bad orator. There was only one thing Corlay and I had in common—the ability to talk."

"She asked you?"

"Sideways ... nothing definite. For the sake of Brittany and the chance of a really worth-while career. If I feel the call, I am to let her know, and we can meet. Added bait, of course ... the lovely Elise and a moonlight meeting. The first she's ever given me ... such an honor, such promises of delight. Three days ago even, I should have been struck dumb by an invitation like that." His mouth twisted bitterly as he laughed at himself. "But three days ago is three days ago." He looked at Hearne. "Damn you," he said abruptly. "Why did you have to be right?"

He limped towards the passage.

"I'll bring the food," he called back to Anne.

"And the clothes," she said quietly. She looked towards Hearne. "You want the clothes, don't you?"

He nodded. "Most of all," he said. There was something else he had meant to ask ... what was it? ... But he was too tired: he gave up the effort.

Kerénor's limping footsteps had dulled into an echo. Once he had the clothes, Hearne thought, he would make his plans and start the journey. Meanwhile it was pleasant to forget; to watch Anne's quiet movements about the room; to feel her bandage his arm and smooth the sheet over his shoulders; to close his eyes and listen to the distant water-music.

CHAPTER 26

"White in the Moon the Long Road Lies"

Perhaps Hearne had slept enough, or perhaps it was just that his mind wouldn't rest. During the night, he woke five times in all, and each time Anne came forward out of the dark corner where she rested. She was beside him again when his broken sleep ended at last. Her heavy round gold watch, which she had fastened by its brooch to the blanket when he had started worrying about the time, told him it was almost six o'clock.

"Six o'clock when?" he asked her, as she carried in a basin of water.

"Six o'clock in the morning. Kerénor should soon be here." She gave him water to drink, and bathed him gently.

"What day is today?"

"Wednesday, I think." She smiled. "I lose count too, you see." He looked at her pale cheeks and tired eyes.

"I owe you a lot," he said. "If I hadn't had someone to nurse me so carefully as you have done, I should still be only half-recovered. I feel I could get up today. And then tomorrow—"

"You mustn't hurry too much."

"Not too much, but I must hurry."

She felt his brow and his pulse. "You *are* much better." Her bright smile made him feel better still.

"How did you learn all this?" he asked, pointing to the bandage she was cutting from a piece of linen.

"Because of Kerénor. He was going to start a kind of clinic for the school children, but the people against it were too many for us. He wanted me to help him. He was teaching me astronomy, and his fee was that I should learn first-aid."

"Astronomy!" said Hearne in amazement. "In heaven's name, why?"

"I wanted to learn," Anne said simply.

Looking at her calm face, he knew she spoke the truth. There was nothing behind her words. She had just wanted to learn. "You certainly learned how to nurse."

Anne smiled. "Oh, I've nursed animals: they are much more difficult to take care of than people." She finished changing his bandages, gently wiping his face clean of its black grease. "Now you do look better," she said. "You are healing nicely."

Hearne's spirits rose. "When will the clothes come?" he said.

"Today. And your map and your papers too, I should think." She saw the relief in his eyes. She gathered up the basin and the towel and bandages quickly, and hurried towards the other room.

Now what had he done? he wondered. Then the excitement of the plans already half-forming drove all other thoughts from his mind.

It was nine o'clock, however, before they heard Kerénor's footsteps and saw the round circle of light from his torch coming towards them.

He settled the basket clumsily on the floor beside Hearne and said, with a pretense of lightheartedness, "Food, what there is of it. Clothes, rustic but useful. Map, holding miraculously together. Clasp knife. Gun, very much loaded and complete with a peculiar object. What is it, by the way?"

"Something to take the noise out of shooting. A silencer."

"Careful kind of fellow, aren't you?" And then Kerénor dropped the amused tone as he picked up a neatly folded handkerchief, and handed it in silence to Hearne. The small bundle had weight. Hearne looked at Kerénor in surprise.

"What's this?" he asked.

"From Madame Corlay," Kerénor said shortly, and bent over the basket again.

Hearne unwrapped the handkerchief. Inside its folds was a silver watch of an old design, with fine engraving on its cover. Within the tracery of the pattern were the words *To Bertrand Corlay on his twenty-first anniversary, 29th January, 1868.* Hearne opened the watch in silence. The thin Roman numerals were delicately painted on the yellow face: the slender hands still moved on their dutiful way. He closed the cover gently, placed the watch carefully under his pillow.

"Would you give Madame Corlay my—well, please tell her

that some day I shall thank her properly. Now I can only—"
He stopped short. He was thinking, that watch was one of
Madame Corlay's few treasures. He was thinking, that watch
has seen three invasions of France by the Germans. Anne
was watching him. He shook his head, as if he did not know
what to say.

Kerénor nodded. "I'll tell her you felt you couldn't find
words adequate enough to appreciate her kindness." Hearne
looked up quickly at the Breton, but he wasn't laughing. For
once he was quite simple and direct.

Anne said, "Just tell her what he did say. She'd like that
better."

Kerénor looked amused now. "I was just trying to help,"
he said. He looked at Anne teasingly. "Why do women think
all other women like what they like? Men, at least, know
better than that. Now, for the last things in this basket.
Here's an envelope, bulky; and sheets of paper with exces-
sively neat scratchings." He was watching Hearne's face.
"Will that do?"

Hearne, his hand reaching eagerly for the envelope and
sheets of paper, nodded. He looked through them quickly,
but carefully. It was all there, everything he had noted and
copied. He took a deep breath. God, he was feeling better
every minute. He looked up to see Anne watching him again,
this time with that little smile on her lips.

"All right, now?" she asked, trying to keep her voice
disinterested. "I'll give you something to eat, and then you
can try to dress."

Hearne nodded his answer, and patted the papers lying
under his hand. Then suddenly he asked Kerénor, "Where
are Corlay's original lists, and his diaries?"

Kerénor, limping back and forward restlessly across the
cave, forced a twisted smile. "Under study. I thought the
Committee should know just what they had to fight."

"You've seen them yourself?"

"Yes."

Hearne, watching the white face, the gaunt cheekbones,
said nothing. He thought: masochist is the word. He's made
himself read every word of Corlay's diary and poems, and
they are eating into him.

"Well?" demanded Kerénor truculently, as if he had
guessed Hearne's thoughts.

"Well?" said Hearne.

Kerénor halted. He controlled his voice with difficulty. "In a France ruled by Frenchmen, Elise would be given a trial and shot. It is the only France I recognize! Because of the Germans, we cannot give her the trial she would otherwise have had. But we can complete the rest." He paused. "I shall accept her invitation when it comes. I shall bring her here."

Anne's face had whitened. "Jean," she said, "remember that if she comes here, she cannot go back."

"No, she cannot go back. That will be definite, Anne. You needn't fear. For once I am not letting arguments and hair-splittings prevent me from acting in time. This time, I shan't reason away my anger. One learns."

There was a silence.

Anne hesitated. At last she said, "I don't trust her. She'll be the one who will do the shooting. You'll be in danger." She was looking at Hearne, her eyes wide; Kerénor noticed the look.

"Charming," he murmured half-seriously, half-ironically, and silenced her effectively. "Now eat," he said to Hearne. "And I'll get you into these clothes. What were your original plans to escape?" Except for the nervous tension of his constant pacing, he had buried his own emotions deeply enough. But he was scarcely listening to Hearne, and the Englishman was glad of that. For then the omissions in the plan he was sketching wouldn't be so noticeable. After his own practical experience of the Gestapo's persuasive powers, he wasn't going to burden his friends with much knowledge. He touched briefly on the boatman who had brought him back from Mont St. Michel, and who would take a message so that his friends in Britain would know he was coming. All Hearne wanted was to reach Dinan and give that message to the boatman. All his plans depended on that. Then he realized Anne's occupation with the food which she was dividing into two portions was only a pretense.

"You've kept too little for yourself," Hearne said, to interrupt her thoughts.

"I can't eat any more," she answered. "If you want to get dressed before Jean leaves, you ought to finish your breakfast quickly." He wondered whatever had given him the first impression that she was a simple creature. Perhaps it was her gentleness and her direct honesty which had made him think she was easy to estimate.

"You're a determined woman, aren't you?" he asked.

She laughed, wrinkling her nose. Anyway, she seemed to have forgotten to worry about his plans for escape.

But when Kerénor had gone, and Hearne paused to rest after his first attempt to walk around the cave, she suddenly sat down beside him, and said, "Wouldn't it be better if someone could go to Dinan in advance, and see that boatman, and give him your message to take to your friends to send to Britain?"

"You like your questions long," he said, and then as she laughed, "Why do you always wear your hair so tightly braided, Anne?"

The two pink spots were coming back into her cheeks, but she wasn't to be dissuaded.

"I mean," she said slowly, "if someone could go in advance to Dinan, while you were still getting stronger here, then the message would sail back with that boatman to the Bay of Mont St. Michel, and he could send it to your friend, and it would go to Britain, and then you could get away from here with all the preparations made, and you wouldn't have to wait at Dinan for all these things to happen before you could reach the coast."

"Breathing helps," Hearne said. Anne laughed in spite of herself.

"But wouldn't it be better?" she insisted.

"No doubt. But after Sunday's excitement, every man in this village will have to keep close to St. Déodat for a while, and appear to be leading a normal life."

Anne said slowly, "I suppose so. But it would have been such a good idea. It would have made everything quicker and safer for you. You could go straight to the coast without going near Dinan yourself."

"I'll manage well enough, once I'm feeling all right again. Come on, Anne, give me a hand round this room."

She smiled. "You looked like a newly born calf, at first."

"I'll be less like one this time. Just you see."

When he sat down to rest again, she said, "That must have been a nice old man who brought you back in his boat."

He had been thinking of something else, and looked at her blankly.

She explained, "When you came back from taking Monsieur Myles to the coast; when you wore such funny old clothes all smelling of fish."

Hearne smiled. "Yes, he was a nice old boy."

"Can he be trusted, really trusted?"

"Yes."

"Then why don't you tell us his name? When you are gone, there may be others from this village who want to get to the coast. He could help them too, couldn't he?"

"Yes, I suppose he could."

"Perhaps someone may be desperate and need help. Perhaps Kerénor or one of the others ..." Her voice trailed off.

It seemed, thought Hearne, as if he had now three different jobs to worry over. There was his real job, information. It came first: it had to. Then linked with that there was the safety of the men like Duclos and Pléhec who were working with him and the other agents. And thirdly, there was the beginning of secret resistance in the villages: he had to help St. Déodat, even apart from what he owed it himself. He thought of L'Etoile d'Or and of Jules, who would have taken the place of big Louis. Jules was to be trusted, but the Golden Star itself might be dangerous: too much had happened there. He couldn't send anyone there when he was unwilling to try it himself. The only really definite source of help was the boatman to whom Etienne had led him, the boatman who sailed from the canalized river on the Bay of Mont St. Michel along the coast and up the River Rance to Dinan. The boatman knew nothing about the activities on the Mont St. Michel: all he knew was that the boy Etienne and he were serving in the same cause. So Pléhec and Duclos and all their plans would not be in danger if he were to tell Anne the boatman's name. That was the main thing, that Pléhec and Duclos should be safe to go on with their work.

Hearne said, "I know him only by a nickname—Le Trapu. He is about fifty years old, short and broad-shouldered, with black hair and blue eyes. He has a boat and a sister called Marguerite. The boat has faded red sails with two brown patches. The sister has a *bistro* on the wharf at Dinan, just where he moors the boat, and anyone who is looking for Le Trapu can wait for him there. Tell Monsieur le Curé about this: he will know when a man really needs help, and he can send him to Le Trapu. But *you* mustn't, Anne; you must leave that to Monsieur le Curé. And tell no one else. Promise?"

Anne nodded, her eyes wide and serious, her lips grave.

"And also tell Monsieur le Curé that if any interesting information should be found in this district, then a man could be sent with it to Le Trapu. He will pass it on, and it will reach Britain. That may be important for us all. Can you remember that?"

"But of course." She sat silently, thinking over what he had said. "How do you feel now?"

"Not so bad."

"Should you sleep, perhaps?"

"I'll have another try on the old legs, first. You don't need to hold me, this time."

She nodded and watched his slow progress with anxiety. After twice round the room, he was forced to give up.

"Not so good," he said bitterly as he straightened himself on the mattress.

Anne brought him water to drink. "It will be easier when you try again tomorrow," she said. "You can't expect miracles."

"This afternoon," he corrected her. "I can't wait until tomorrow." He moved restlessly on his bed.

"When do you want to leave?" she asked. "Saturday?"

"Too late. Le Trapu doesn't sail on Sundays." It had been the twelfth, a Friday, when he sailed back from Mont St. Michel. Mondays, Wednesdays, Fridays from the Mont; Tuesdays, Thursdays, Saturdays from Dinan.

He said, "I must be in Dinan by dawn on Saturday. Better leave here no later than sunset on Friday." He swore to himself. "If only I could have left tonight, I could have reached Dinan tomorrow."

"No, you'll only add to your dangers if you aren't recovered enough. You'll manage Friday, all right," said Anne. "Then Le Trapu will deliver the message on Saturday night. And you can be at the coast by Sunday night. . . . Which part of the coast?"

He looked at her suddenly. Her wide eyes returned the look candidly: her face was eager and sympathetic. "Why do you ask, Anne?" he said slowly.

"I was wondering if it were near St. Brieuc." She bent down and picked up the blanket which he had thrown aside. He looked at her with a dawning suspicion.

"And why?"

She pretended to be folding the blanket.

At last she said, "I am traveling to St. Brieuc. Remember? I thought I might go with you, to look after you."

"You look after *me?* Out there?" He was shocked, incredulous; he stared at her. Then as he saw her face tighten and the light go out of her eyes, he reached up and caught her hand. "Anne," he said, "I'm sorry if I hurt you. You're kind and you're brave. But you don't know what you are letting yourself in for, if you were to travel with me, or even be found with me. You cannot go with me. It would be dangerous—impossible."

She stood, saying nothing, her eyes downcast, her hand lifeless in his. He saw he had really hurt her. "Anne," he said gently, "Anne. Anne, darling."

She flinched and tried to draw her hand away, but he held it tightly. His resolution melted. "Anne, you've got to get to St. Brieuc safely. You've got to stay there safely. You've got to keep safe."

She was looking at him now. "Others take risks. Why shouldn't I?"

"Because I don't want you to." He spoke sharply—but she was smiling now.

There was a silence. "Is that all?" she asked at last.

"Yes."

She drew her hand slowly out of his. "Do all Englishmen behave like you?" she said.

He took a deep breath. For their own mental happiness, he hoped they didn't.

"What are you thinking of?" she asked.

"I'm thinking of a poem I once knew."

"Tell me it."

"It's in English."

"I want to hear English."

He spoke it slowly, softly.

> *"White in the moon the long road lies,*
> *The moon stands blank above;*
> *White in the moon the long road lies*
> *That leads me from my love.*

> *"Still hangs the hedge without a gust,*
> *Still, still the shadows stay . . ."*

He closed his eyes, trying to catch the next phrase. Strange: when he was young and only imagined himself in love, how he could recite yards of such poems and bury himself in thwarted gloom. Now, when he really knew what the poem

meant, he was forgetting it—forgetting not its feeling, but
the words. He tried once more:

> ". . . Still, still the shadows stay:
>   My feet . . . my feet upon the moonlit dust
>   Pursue the ceaseless way.
>
> "The world is round, so travelers tell,
>   And straight through reach the track,
>   Trudge on, trudge on, 'twill all be well,
>   The way will guide one back.
>
> "But ere the circle homeward hies
>   Far, far must it remove:
>   White in the moon the long road lies
>   That leads me from my love."

It was Anne who spoke first. "It is a sad poem."

"How do you know?" he asked quickly.

"Because your voice was sad . . . Will you translate it for
me?"

Hearne shook his head. "Some day, Anne. Not now.
Later." He roused himself once more, and rose slowly to his
feet. "Now *you* are looking sad. Where's that smile of
yours?"

She found it with difficulty.

"What's wrong, Anne?"

"Nothing. At least not much. I'm worried, that's all. Brittany's coast is treacherous. I know it quite well, and there are
many places with bad tides, currents, rocks. You may choose
one of them." She was walking beside him, watching his steps
with a careful eye.

"So we are back there, again?"

"Yes."

"Would it make you any less worried if I were to tell you
that the place I shall go to has been chosen because it is safe?
You wouldn't know it; it's quite small, just west of Dinard,
but it is certainly safe. As safe as any place is, now."

Anne said quietly, "Is it St. Lunaire?"

He checked his pace, and looked at her with a mixture of
annoyance and amusement.

"I noticed your map," she explained quickly. "I noticed a
light pencil line. Or shouldn't I have?"

"No, you shouldn't." He was half-angry. Women always

wanted to know everything. But even if Anne had seen any of the other papers, she couldn't have understood the coded shorthand.

She had guessed part of his thoughts. "I only looked at the map. It was lying on the ground beside the mattress. I picked it up and put if safely with the rest of your things. I am sorry if I shouldn't have looked at it." Her tone was stilted, her face was flushed and her eyes were bright. She looked so much like a worried child that he relented and smiled. After all, no harm was done. And she had obviously thought there was nothing wrong in looking at a map: if she had had a guilty conscience, she would never have told him about it. His annoyance and suspicions melted, and he was left with a feeling of being mean and ungrateful.

He smiled again. "Well," he said, "does all that make you feel better?"

Anne nodded. "Much better. The coast at Dinard is dangerous, but further west there are safer places." She didn't mention St. Lunaire again. She stood smiling at him, and the smile was real at last.

Kerénor came again in the evening, bringing food and little news. Things were as they had been, he told them gloomily. In that case, Hearne thought, he ought to be more cheerful. Things might very well be worse: the Nazis might have discovered the real story of the escape from the town hall, its cellars might have new guests within their walls, and Sharkface and Razorpuss might very well be striding into the cave at this moment. Hearne watched Kerénor as he paced the floor, and wondered just what conflicts raged in the Breton's mind. Elise's influence wasn't so easily removed as Kerénor had pretended to believe, yesterday, when he had pronounced his judgment. Or perhaps, by making an open declaration to Anne and Hearne, he had hoped to keep his decision strong. He had probably feared he would hesitate, if he hadn't witnesses to challenge his pride. And now, even with witnesses, he was losing his determination. The coldness of reason was strangling the will to act. Kerénor was the kind of man who had to strike when his anger was at white heat; when it cooled, then his purpose wavered and the will to act became frustrated cynicism. He would always give Elise a last chance, not from kindness of heart but from intellectual self-hypnotism. Hearne looked dispassionately at Kerénor . . . *the native hue of resolution is sicklied o'er with*

the pale cast of thought, he repeated to himself. Yet, who
was he to criticize Kerénor? He thought of Anne. Yes,
anyone looking into his mind would think he was another
kind of fool. Plenty of people would judge him equally
harshly, either because he had smothered his own emotions
too much, or because he hadn't smothered them enough. But
what the hell could he do? This wasn't a case of doing what
he wanted to do: it was a case of what he had to do.
Personal feelings didn't enter into it at all. He recognized
that, and yet he couldn't stop himself from having them. So,
who was he to criticize Kerénor? A typical Nazi would
sneer at Hearne for his sentimental weakness: a typical
Frenchman would think he was cold and hard. That's the
trouble, he was thinking, he was neither of these. He was just
a compromising Englishman.

Kerénor noticed his silence. "You are tired. I'll come
back in the morning when you've had a good sleep. You can
tell me then about your plans for leaving. You've made
them?"

Hearne nodded, but said nothing. Yes, they were made,
and he wasn't going to let anything change them, either. On
Friday he would leave. Not tomorrow, but the next day he
would leave. He looked again at Anne. How long, he wondered, before this bloody war was over? How long before he
could come back?

Anne was restless. She was waiting impatiently for Kerénor to go, and when he did she went with him. "I'll walk to
the tower steps," she had said, and had lifted the smaller
lamp to light her way back to the cave.

Hearne watched the entrance to the cave blankly, and
listened to the limping footsteps mingling with the light
crispness of Anne's heels. Then the following echo died away
too. He stretched himself gloomily on the straw mattress. If
Anne wanted to walk and talk with Kerénor, then it was
nothing of his business. He, himself, had chosen to make it
none of his business. So why the devil was he feeling like
this? It was all the fault of lying cooped up in a stone coffin:
living in this cave made you imagine things. What on earth
had ever given him the idea that it would be any good
coming back here when the war was over? She was still
betrothed to Corlay, wasn't she? And if she weren't, then
there were others. She had been kind and gentle to him
because she was kind and gentle. What was there for her to
see in him, anyway?

When she returned, he was lying staring up at the rough ceiling of the cave. She didn't explain anything, and he wouldn't ask.

They ate the food which Kerénor had brought them, with little to say. The strangeness of the silence between them struck Hearne: he hadn't realized before just how much they usually talked when they were together. When Anne changed the bandages, she fastened them with special care, and she examined the cuts and bruises with capably cool hands and eyes. Nothing escaped her, tonight. At last, everything was done to her satisfaction. She lowered the lamp, smoothed the sheet under his chin. Standing beside his bed, she looked tall and slender. The smooth fair hair seemed almost silver.

She spoke softly, her voice clear and low. "Good night."

"Good night."

Well, he thought savagely as he heard her footsteps moving quietly in the cave next door, that was just as neat a piece of emotional bathos as he had ever had. The sooner he was out of here, the better.

CHAPTER 27

The Dark Wood

When Hearne awoke, Anne must have already risen. The blanket in her corner of the cave was folded in a neat square on the thin mattress. Then he heard a movement from the inner cave. Blast, he thought: he had wanted to go in there for a drink— He interrupted his thinking to listen to the footsteps. They were limping. Hearne, lying rigid on his mattress, said, "Hell, what's going on here, anyway?"

It was Kerénor, all right. He was standing in the entranceway now, with a lamp in his hand and a twisted smile on his face.

"You waken early," he said.

Hearne didn't answer.

"Do you want anything?"

"A drink—I'll get it later."

"Why not now?"

Hearne rose stiffly and went towards Kerénor.

"Walking more easily? Take this." He handed the lamp to Hearne.

"Yes. Thanks," Hearne said briefly and passed into the other cave. It was empty. Only the thin cascade of water, falling into the pool, made any sound. Only the little stream, flowing in its miniature canal, made any movement. He paused uncertainly.

"What's wrong?" asked Kerénor. Hearne wished he would wipe that grin off his face.

"Nothing." He drank from the pool, cupping his hands and letting the cold water splash over his face. His body was certainly better. He could even move his right arm as far as the elbow without any pain.

When he came back into the cave where he had slept, Kerénor was sitting on his bed. "I'll go and get our breakfast soon," he said. "Might even find some nice hot soup waiting in Monsieur le Curé's kitchen this morning. He thinks a man who might be recovering from Nazi treatment might need more nourishment. Funny thing: I am getting quite attached to Monsieur le Curé."

Hearne stood in front of Kerénor. He was listening, but not to the Breton.

"What's wrong?" Kerénor asked again.

"Nothing."

Kerénor was enjoying himself immensely. "Don't tell me you are missing Anne already."

Hearne felt his face flush, but he didn't speak.

"She's gone, you know."

"Gone?" Hearne echoed. But of course, he thought, she had to leave sometime. She had already delayed her journey to her aunt long enough for safety's sake. "How long will she take to get to St. Brieuc?" he asked more casually than he felt.

"She hasn't gone to St. Brieuc." Kerénor was watching him with a mixture of amusement and clinical interest.

Hearne said slowly, "You can stop playing for effects. Where the hell is she?"

"By this time she should have reached Dinan."

"Dinan?"

"I said Dinan." And then Kerénor relented. "She wouldn't tell me very much. She just said I was to tell you that she would see 'him' and give 'him' the message. That she might shelter with 'his' sister before she continued her journey. Does it make sense to you?"

"Partly." Hearne's voice was grim. "What message? Did she say?"

"Saturday at the seaside. Not very exciting. Or is it?"

"Exciting enough." Hearne began to pace about the cave. Anne must have gone last night after he had fallen asleep, so that she could be in Dinan before dawn, so that Le Trapu would have the message before he sailed this morning back to the Bay of Mont St. Michel. That meant Etienne would get the message today or tonight; and by tomorrow night, Friday night that was, Duclos would send the message out from his oubliette in the Abbey. Perhaps, if Le Trapu saw the boy Etienne in time, the message would even be sent tonight. Saturday at St. Lunaire. She had planned everything as neatly as he could have wished.

"But why didn't she tell me?" Hearne said at last.

"Because she was afraid you would have forbidden the idea. Anne is a well-brought-up girl. Her father's word was law. If you had forbidden her to go, she would have felt the compulsion of the old instincts to obey."

"I'm not like her father," Hearne said irritably.

Kerénor smiled, as if to himself. "No. But you seem to have a lot of authority over her. Now don't go asking me why. If you can't understand that for yourself, then it isn't worth explaining. Here, you'd better sit down and rest."

"I'm all right. I need to walk." Hearne's excitement was fading, and in its place was worry. He thought of Anne alone at Dinan, on the dark road to Dinan. She might never have reached there. His face was hard as he halted in front of Kerénor. "You shouldn't have let her go."

"I?" asked Kerénor, in mild surprise. He was no longer smiling as he looked at Hearne's face. His voice lost its raillery. He said gently, almost sympathetically, "I assure you I have no influence over her at all. She's my oldest friend here. She would talk with me when the others were still watching me with distrust, because I come from another part of the country—from the South of Brittany. But she talked with me, partly because she doesn't like to hurt people, partly because I could converse about the things she was interested in, partly because she liked me, partly because she pitied me. But the chief thing was that I was someone to talk to. You

see, her father had her sent to a good school at Dinan, but he
wouldn't let her go on to Rennes University as she wanted to
do. He brought her back to live on the farm, and betrothed
her to Corlay. He thought he was doing the best thing for
her. If Corlay had been a different sort of chap, no doubt
these simple-minded plans wouldn't have been so bad. Most
girls would make happier women if their personal ambitions
were sublimated. Well, anyway, we'd talk, Anne and I. I
would preach and she would listen or argue gently. But she
never took my advice unless she wanted to take it. Last night
was one of the times when she just listened to me and did the
other thing. You don't know Breton women when they have
all their plans made."

"She couldn't have had them made, if I hadn't talked so
damn much," Hearne said savagely. "She got me into the
state of thinking aloud yesterday. I never guessed . . . she
seemed so simple . . . so . . . I've been thinking of her as
a—well, look at her! She fitted into the background of St.
Déodat so well that I never guessed she would do anything
mad like this."

"She seemed to me to be very sane."

"But she doesn't know what she's up against. What the
devil was that message for me, again?"

Kerénor repeated it slowly. "She was going to see this
'him' and give 'him' the message, and perhaps shelter with
'his' sister before continuing the journey."

"Shelter with his sister . . ." Hearne exploded: he cursed
fluently and vividly until he had to pause for breath. "Shelter
with his sister!" he repeated. "I've never been there. For all I
know, the sister may run a brothel."

"You are worrying too much," advised Kerénor. "Anne is
no fool. She knows Dinan and has friends there. That is
where she went to school. And she has her permit with her.
She thought of everything, including leaving Jean's permit for
you."

"Jean?"

"Yes, the old man who worked on her farm. Both he and
Marie had permits too; but when you were arrested and
Anne came here to nurse you, Anne sent them up to the
Laënnec farm to stay out of the way for a while. They will
be useful there, too: Laënnec is dead. The news has just
come to his wife. Anne gave the old couple's permits to
Monsieur le Curé for safekeeping. Last night, she told me
that perhaps you could use Jean's permit, if we could change

the age in it from eighty-two to thirty-two. I think I can do that, all right."

Hearne sat down at last. "And I thought Anne needed protection," he said with a wry smile.

"That's one of her greatest charms, and it is completely natural, too. It appeals to our masculine vanity. Do you know Latin? Remember what the Censor Metellus said in the Senate? 'Nature has arranged that we can live neither with women nor without them. If we *could* live without them, then we should not have all this trouble.' "

"You forget to add that the Censor Metellus was happily married."

"I suppose satisfied men can afford to be critical: it adds to their feeling of superiority to know that what they criticize doesn't really apply to them." Kerénor was bitter once more. He didn't mention the name of Elise, nor did Hearne; but the name was there between them all the same.

Kerénor rose suddenly. "Must get the food before it is too late. Then after that, I'll have to leave you. I am to appear before some Nazi committee for instruction on what I may teach in the village school."

"How are things up there?"

"According to plan. Trucks have visited the farms, and the shops, and the houses even. We might have had a plague of locusts. We never knew we had so much until we saw the truckloads driving away. What is left can only be bought and sold at fixed prices, fixed for everyone except the Boches. They are scattering worthless marks about like confetti. And there are some among us—not many, but still some—who are selling to the Boches. They know the marks mean nothing, but they think Nazi good-will means a lot. We've got a little list starting. These false Bretons will get paid in full when we start marching towards Berlin. Even Picrel's son agrees that there can be no pardon for his father. He's first on the list. We are deeply ashamed of him."

"Picrel, the man who owns so much?"

"That's why, I suppose. Strange, isn't it? He's a great Christian by his way of it, and I have never professed to be one. Yet the one aim in his life is to hang onto the possessions he has got. Worldly possessions. If I remember my New Testament correctly, worldly possessions weren't held in great esteem. In fact, if a man gives up honor or humanity for the sake of what he owns, then he is betraying the principles of Christianity. When I watch the Picrels scrabbling at German feet for the sake of their property, do you know what I believe? I believe that if Christ came back today and preached to the people, the Picrels among them would have him shot against a stone wall as a revolutionary."

There was a pause, and then Hearne said, "Yes, I think you are right. And now, having disposed of Picrel, what about the others in the village?"

"Standing fast. Before, there were two types of people in the world. People from St. Déodat, and foreigners. Now there are people from St. Déodat, foreigners, and filthy Boches. You can rest about your escape, by the way. The Boches are now convinced that you called the guard in on some pretext, throttled him, and made your escape. They don't think you could go far, and they keep searching all the neighboring farms. All they've discovered so far were two escaped prisoners of war, poor devils. The Boches have offered a stupendous reward for you. They describe you as an Englishman under the assumed name of Bertrand Corlay."

Then the Germans had found Lassare at Bordeaux and questioned him, Hearne thought. He said, "What do the people of St. Déodat believe about me?"

"They still think you are Bertrand Corlay, and you have become a sort of village hero. Those who have seen you swear that you *are* Corlay, and that the Boches are lying so that someone might be tempted to betray you, for the Boches know that Bretons don't betray a Breton. Anne suggested that we should just let the people go on thinking that you are Corlay, because that would make up to Madame Corlay for what she had to suffer before. Monsieur le Curé agreed to that, and so, there we are. To St. Déodat, you are still Bertrand Corlay, the reformed. They'll probably carve a memorial to you in the church, when the peace comes. I've always wondered who chose national heroes: it's interesting to find out."

"If Corlay comes back after peace—"

"Then he will reform with great sincerity to live up to the character you have left for him, as soon as he finds it gives him enough esteem and power. That's all he wanted, anyway. He backed the wrong horse, that was all."

The idea of Corlay returning vindicated, accepted, conforming, depressed Hearne still more. Once it would have amused him as Kerénor was amused. But now he thought of Anne, of Madame Corlay and the two farms which she would like to see as one.

Hearne rose and walked round the cave. Eleven paces by thirty-six paces: eleven by thirty-six.

Kerénor paused at the entrance. "Don't walk much," he advised.

"I'm all right." And then as Kerénor still halted, watching him, "I am just getting ready. I am leaving tonight."

Kerénor said, "Anne thought you would leave tomorrow."

"I'm leaving tonight."

Kerénor was smiling again. "If you hurry, you may even catch up with Anne at Dinan."

Hearne halted. "Who said I was going to Dinan?"

"There's got to be some limit to your sense of duty. Even an Englishman must be human, sometimes." Kerénor started to limp away.

"One moment," Hearne called after him. "That's what I meant to ask you two days ago. How did you and Anne learn I was English?" He watched Kerénor's face, half-turned over his shoulder. I wish to heaven, Hearne was thinking, I didn't always seem to amuse him so much.

"You were unconscious, weren't you, for over two days?"

"I talked?"

"You did."

"In English?"

"Mostly."

"What about?"

"Partly nonsense, partly sense."

"What about?"

"Yourself. Don't look so worried, even if Anne sounds the same in both languages. She knows only schoolgirl English. She couldn't understand everything."

Kerénor enjoyed his exit. He was a last-word man.

They stepped out into the shadows of Monsieur le Curé's sheltered garden, and felt the real air with its cold sharpness encircle them again. Kerénor, who had led Hearne through the caves and passages up into the ground floor of the tower, through the silent church, out through the Curé's private door leading to the shrubbery and his house, now grasped the Englishman's arm. They halted. They listened, and when they were satisfied moved quietly on under the shadows of the trees beyond the house. Then the garden ended.

Ahead were fields. West of them, to their right, lay the road and the last houses in the village and the stone bridge and the path to the Corlay farm. On their left were the

meadows and trees under the east spire of the church, and
the rows of neat huts filled with sleeping soldiers. The last
quarter of the moon was in the sky, with clouds and the
feeling of rain to come. They saw the shape of a patrolling
sentry, and then he was hidden by the corner of a hut. High
above them was the intermittent drone of planes.

"Many of them in the last week," whispered Kerénor,
pointing upwards. "We hope they may be British, because
they fly to the northwest and don't come back."

Hearne said nothing. They weren't returning British
planes. Their engines hadn't the right sound. They were Ju
88's. He thought of the aerodrome he had found on that last
journey towards Dol. The planes were no doubt flying to its
well-camouflaged fields, while the former French airport had
its quota of dummy planes and visible hangars. He smiled in
spite of himself. This war had its childish aspects. . . . If the
results weren't so grim, you would laugh at them. He looked
at the darkened village over his right shoulder. You would
laugh, if the results weren't so grim.

He followed Kerénor, who was moving with surprising
speed and silence on the smooth grass. They had crossed the
stream flowing to the pond down in the meadows. Kerénor,
using the scattered groups of trees for cover, was circling at
some distance round the German's camp, to enter the wood
beyond the pond. From that point, he had explained with the
help of the map in the cave, he would leave Hearne to strike
northwards until it was safe to turn west for Dinan. This was
how Anne had gone last night. It had been, and ought to be,
simple.

Hearne felt in the pocket of the worn French army-jacket,
with all its markings ripped off: watch, map, matches, gun,
silencer, knife, some small money forced on him by an
embarrassed Kerénor, and the sheets of neat notes. He
pulled the old cap still further down over his eyes. He was
glad now that he had rejected the offer of Jean's permit and
the fancy dress of an old peasant. If he were caught, Jean's
permit would only lead the suspicious Boches to Anne. It was
better this way. It meant he would have to keep hidden in
the daylight, and move only during darkness. But that was
something he could do. And ahead of him were only two
night journeys. Dinan was roughly ten or twelve miles away
to the west. From there, northwards to the English Channel,
was slightly more than that distance. He could manage it. His

legs were strong again, and all that was left of the Gestapo's attentions was a stiffness in his back, a carefully bandaged right shoulder, some bruises, and a tenderness in the stretch of the skin forming over the cuts. He could manage it, not exactly comfortably, but sufficiently capably if he didn't meet downright bad luck.

"How are you feeling?" Kerénor whispered.

"Unbelievable." It was true. The strange freshness of the air made him feel as though he could walk thirty miles before sunrise.

They were at the wood. The trees were neatly spaced, and there were winding paths beneath the branches. Here and there they passed a stone bench. It was the kind of place in which lovers walked in every country, escaping from the hard eyes of their parents and the ridicule of their friends.

It was Hearne who gripped Kerénor's arm, this time. His quick ear had heard the light crack of some twigs. They halted behind the tangle of a thorn bush, with its vague sweet scent encircling them. At first Hearne thought the man on the path ahead, with his arm coupling a girl, was some young Breton who had risked the Nazis' anger to walk with her here. And then, as the two figures crossed the patch of faint moonlight on the path, he saw the man's uniform and the girl's gleaming hair. He knew by the sudden intake in Kerénor's breath that he had recognized them too. It was Elise, with the man Ehrlich. But Hearne no longer saw Elise. He was staring at Ehrlich. The expression on the German's face was very different now, very different from that he had worn in a cellar of the town hall. Hearne's hand tightened on his gun: he fitted the silencer carefully over it, his eyes still on the German's face.

And then, as they passed a stone bench, Ehrlich pulled the smiling girl down onto it. Her head was thrown back and the hair was loose and soft, its thickness catching the stray beams of light through the leaves overhead. She was laughing now.

Kerénor stiffened. His lame foot slipped and a twig snapped. Ehrlich looked quickly towards the bush behind which they were hidden. His hand left Elise and went to his holster as he rose, peering into the darkness.

Kerénor stepped silently out of cover. Perhaps he felt discovery was inevitable and had decided to give Hearne the chance to get away. He limped slowly forwards. Ehrlich's gun was out. Elise had risen, turning as she started to her feet. Hearne, still standing behind the thorn bush, saw the loose coat swing open as she turned, saw the whiteness of her body. Kerénor had seen too. He halted, and his low voice lashed her dispassionately. The German smiled, and pointed his gun; but Kerénor's savage words didn't halt.

Hearne moved slightly to one side so that his aim might be completely accurate. The pang at his shoulder as he raised his forearm was an unnecessary reminder of the cellar, of the torch which had lighted him as the three other men had held him down, of the amused face of Ehrlich behind the torch. There wouldn't be any more cellars for Mr. Ehrlich to preside over. There wouldn't be much more of anything for Mr. Ehrlich. His love-making was as practised as his torture, but there wouldn't be any more of either for him.

The German was still grinning. He motioned impatiently to Elise to stand away from him, as he raised the revolver.

His voice was as low as Kerénor's. "Trouble-seekers find trouble," he began, and the girl laughed softly, her head thrown back, the white curve of throat outlined against the loose thick hair.

There was a thick hiss, a stiffening of the German's shoulders. He was a marionette whose strings had been cut. He sagged, slipped slowly to the ground. He lay as he had fallen.

Elise's soft mocking laughter had halted. The parted lips stiffened to scream as terror gripped her throat, but the limping footsteps had already reached her, and hands stronger than terror strangled her cry. Even after the last vague attempt to free herself from the death grip, even after the frenzy of her struggles had given way to limpness, Kerénor still held her crushed in his hands. The coat slipped from her bare shoulders. He dropped her suddenly, stood motionless, looking down at the red gold spilling over his feet.

Hearne came forward from the thorn bush. He touched Kerénor's arm gently. Kerénor did not move.

"Hurry," Hearne said. But Kerénor didn't hear.

"Listen," Hearne whispered urgently. "How near are we to the north edge of the wood?"

Kerénor looked at him dully. All emotion had left his face. "Another five minutes." His voice had all feeling cut out of it.

"You get towards that side of the wood. When you hear a pistol shot, start running, keeping to the shadows, using the trees. Get back to the north end of the St. Déodat road and

innocent, that she had been misled by Corlay. Kerénor had held to his wishful thinking, until tonight. And then, there had been no doubt left.

Hearne paused as he reached the crest of the hill, and looked back at St. Déodat. It was a group of vague black shadows clustering under the proud towers of the church. This was the way it had been when he first crossed this hill four weeks ago. Then he had believed it incapable of change. It still looked the same, but the changes were there, as deep and powerful as they were invisible.

The clouds had spread into a dull gray coating over the sky, and the first fine needle-spray of rain stung his cheeks.

He left St. Déodat and crossed over the hill.

CHAPTER 28

Fishermen's Rest

The greater part of the town of Dinan stands securely within its walls, high on the edge of an escarpment above the gorge of the River Rance. But outside the walls, down at the water's level where the boats trading from the coast come to anchor at the small wharves, there are old houses beside the Gothic bridge, and expensive restaurants placed to catch the superb view. Marguerite's café did not belong to that class. It was one of the smallest and oldest houses, whose front room served as an informal club for the men who worked on the boats.

So the bargewoman had said, pointing to the quay. It wasn't far: just across the cobbled wharf. There were one or two men loitering there already, waiting either to load or to unload some boat. If he hurried now, he wouldn't be noticed in this light. The men, he saw, wore old army jackets to shield them from the rawness of the cold dawn. This added to his confidence. He chose his moment, stepped quickly onto the wet paving-stones from the barge, and moved boldly towards Marguerite's house.

The barge, too old and too decrepit to have been commandeered by the Nazis, rested quietly and innocently at its mooring place. Already it had forgotten it had carried him four miles down the River Rance to the Dinan quay. The woman who had helped him to cross the river was still standing on the deck of the barge, waiting for the restaurant keepers to come down to buy her small stock of produce. For the smart restaurants now had their clientèle of German officers, and the vegetables and butter had to be fresh every day for them. Hearne turned as he reached the narrow little house which the barge owner had pointed out, and looked back. The woman moved as if to let him know she had seen him. He pulled his cap further down on his head. But neither of them waved. He wished she had taken the few francs Kerénor had given him; heaven knew she needed it, working that old tub by herself, with her husband dead and three children to feed. Her husband had been killed, she had said simply. In the war, Hearne had guessed, for when she saw his stained tunic and battered cap, she had given him shelter at once. Another barge was slipping into its place beside the woman's. It would have helped him too, she had said, as if to explain why he mustn't pay her. The barge owners were now so accustomed to picking up stray men wandering near the locks on the canal that they kept a watch for them. It seemed as if many of the escaping men struck naturally towards the Rance, knowing that its waters would lead them to Dinan, and then from there by wooded river-banks to the coast.

Over the door of the house were slanting fading letters, but they still spelled *Marguerite*. Hearne turned down his jacket collar, wiped his face with his sleeve, and pulled the door quickly shut behind him. The square room was small and dimly lighted. It smelled of stale tobacco smoke and vinegar. Two men were sleeping slumped across one of the half-dozen small tables which had been jammed into the available floor space. A bar faced the door. Behind it were empty shelves, a fly-spotted mirror, a vase of large yellow paper daisies. On its left there was another door. On its right, a staircase.

One of the men half-raised his head from his arms, his eyes scarcely open, and then slumped back across the table. The other still choked and snored alternately.

The door beside the bar opened, and a woman stood there.

This must be rising time for her: she was still fastening her dress. Her black hair was plaited into two thin pigtails falling over each shoulder. She fastened the last button, twisted the meager plaits of hair into a knot behind her head, and jammed them into place with the large hairpins which she had been holding in her lips. That let her talk, anyhow.

"No food for an hour," she announced. "You can sleep at one of the tables." She pointed a square hand to the two men.

Hearne made his way past the crowding tables and stood in front of her. She was a short broad-shouldered woman, almost as square in shape as her brother. She had his blue eyes, too, and the black hair without any grayness showing, although she must have been fifty at least. She even had the same laugh-wrinkles round her eyes and mouth, grooved deeply into the coarse tanned skin. She waited for him to speak, her hands on the place where her hips might once have been.

"Marguerite?" Hearne asked.

She nodded, watching him closely. She couldn't quite place him, but she would certainly know him again.

"Le Trapu told me to come to his sister if I needed a place to rest."

"Where did you meet him?"

"Sailed with him two weeks ago from the Bay of Mont St. Michel."

"He's not here."

"I know. But he will be here tonight."

Her eyes flickered towards the table with the two sleeping men.

"Did you come here for breakfast?"

Hearne shook his head.

She nodded over her shoulder, and he followed her through the door into the small room, which was a mixture of kitchen, bedroom and sitting room. It was surprisingly clean and neat, but the faint smell of vinegar still persisted.

Hearne sat down on the wooden bench at the side of the fireplace. He looked at his filthy boots, the stained corduroy trousers.

"Are you waiting for him to arrive?"

Hearne shook his head again. "Not exactly. Tonight I must travel again, and I wondered if I could stay here."

"This isn't a hotel."

"Your brother said—"

"Him!" she snorted. "The trouble he gives me!" But her voice was less annoyed than her words.

"He said you could beat trouble any day," Hearne said with a smile.

"That man!" The tone was amiably contemptuous. "He's a sailor, and as stupid as they are made. He wouldn't know trouble if he was to meet it."

"He's a very good sailor."

"Him!" Her sisterly admiration was amusing enough, Hearne thought, but he hadn't come here to be amused. He said, suddenly serious, "I sent a message to Le Trapu. It should have reached him here yesterday morning before he sailed."

"You did?" The voice was noncommittal, but the clever eyes were watching him curiously.

"Yes. And I wondered if the message reached him."

"My God, how should I know? He never tells me anything." She turned abruptly and began to fuss with a coffeepot.

"Perhaps you know if the girl bringing the message arrived safely?"

"A girl? What are you worrying about that for? You look to me as if the only thing you should worry about is the Boches. You're as bad as—"

"Him," Hearne finished quickly. "But *did* this girl arrive? And has she gone?"

"You're all the same, you men. A girl's a girl. There's a dozen of them hanging round here every day. Can't get the place cleared of them. How should I know what girl?"

"She should have arrived in the early morning." Hearne's voice was worried. Anne hadn't got here; he was almost sure of that now.

"She has fair hair ... blue-gray eyes ... a short nose with freckles: seven freckles." He stopped short in embarrassment. God, he thought, such abject foolishness. What had happened to him? Blithering here like an idiot to this old pot, who wasn't even bothering to listen to him.

She finished cutting the small loaf of bread and dropped the slices into a shallow basket. "Sounds as if that might be the same girl," she said casually, but there was a gleam of laughter in her wrinkled eyes.

Hearne sat quite still. He felt hollow inside. Some day, he thought, as he looked towards the solemn Marguerite, some day someone who needs sleep and food and information is not going to appreciate your sense of humor. Some day someone will— He restrained himself, and played her game. At least, Anne was safe so far.

"Here's all the money I have," he said with excessive calm. "Will it buy me something to eat, and a place to rest until the night comes? And while I eat, would you tell me what you know?"

Marguerite looked at the money thrown on the table, and then looked at his white face. The calmness of his voice stung her into remorse.

"I don't need your money," she mumbled. "You'll need it yourself before you reach the coast." And then she grew angry. "What's her name, you who come into my house and ask me questions and try to make me tell you things I'll tell no one?"

"Anne," said Hearne, and he was smiling now. "Anne."

"And what is yours?"

"She didn't know my real name."

Marguerite had recovered her humor. "That's what she told me. Strange thing, I told her, to go gallivanting over the countryside for a man whose name she didn't even know." But her voice was kindly, and her eyes laughed at Hearne's expression. "Cheer up," she said, "I don't blame you for getting angry with me. You don't know my little ways. Take your money before I change my mind! And here's something to eat. You need it, I'm thinking."

"How did you know I was going to the coast?" Hearne rose stiffly and went over to the table.

"Well, she's gone there."

"She's *gone*?"

"Yes. Where did you think she was? Hiding under the bed?"

Hearne looked at her bleakly. "Please tell me," he said, "just what happened when she came here. Was she all right, why did she leave so quickly, where did she go? Did she see your brother?"

Marguerite relented and forgot her little ways. "I just had to know whether you were the man she told me about. I didn't want to give the right information to the wrong man. You've got to be careful these days. Now, here's what happened . . . " She cut him a thin slice of sour cheese and poured some brown liquid into his cup; then she began the story—it was long, but neatly told.

Anne had arrived, had seen Le Trapu and talked alone

with him in this room. Then she had rested and changed her clothes, for her dress was covered with mud and dirt. She had left that dress here, and Marguerite's niece had given her a blouse and skirt and wool jacket in exchange, for the dress was good rich cloth, and not the kind of material you could buy nowadays. Then, with some food wrapped inside her shawl, she had insisted on setting out again. It was all right to travel in daylight, she had said, for she had a travel permit and money enough. She had even insisted on leaving money to pay for the food she had had. She wanted to go away at once, it seemed, because otherwise she couldn't reach the coast in time.

Hearne rose, and walked across to the fireplace. "Just where, at the coast?" he asked. He thought, St. Brieuc, no doubt: where else?

"She didn't tell me that. You can talk with him about it—she discussed a lot of things with him in the hour before he sailed. He always had a soft spot for blue eyes and fair hair."

"I wonder if your brother will be here before I leave?"

"He told me to keep you here until he came. He thought you would be here."

Hearne looked up at that. "He did, did he?"

"He did." She watched him curiously. "Better come and finish your breakfast. Then you can sleep upstairs."

Hearne came back to the table. There was still one important thing to ask. "Have you had any visits from the Boches?"

Marguerite allowed herself another half-cup of the tasteless coffee. "Patrols look into the bar every now and again to check up on the men they find there, but they haven't found anyone yet who couldn't be accounted for. The Boches don't come as customers, not after the first week. Our drinks didn't agree with them. The other restaurants are bigger and smarter, and they get good food there. Here they have to eat what we've got to eat, and they don't seem to enjoy it." She suddenly laughed, and plunged into a long story of what had happened that first week when some soldiers had bought drinks at the bar. She had mixed them, herself. The soldiers gulped almost half the drink before they realized how bad it was. Then they swore she was trying to poison them.

"Me!" Marguerite said, and picked up the last crumb of a crust with her wet forefinger. "Me!" She looked so outraged, so indignant, that Hearne grinned.

"What then?" he asked.

"Things looked bad. Yes," Marguerite admitted thought-fully, "it was as dangerous as facing a herd of mad pigs in an orchard. Especially when a sergeant was called in. He took a swill, and then his face puffed up till it looked as ugly as his other end. It was hard to tell the difference: you couldn't tell whether he was coming or going." She shook her head slowly, smiling broadly as she enjoyed the memory.

"And then?" prompted Hearne again. This was one story he was going to hear the end of, anyway.

Marguerite shrugged her broad shoulders. "Well, I pick up their glasses, one by one. And I empty them slowly into three clean glasses, see? Then I hand two of them to Jacques Hémar and Yves Andhouard who are standing there at the bar watching everything. And I take the third glass myself. And I say, 'Jacques and Yves, show them how Bretons can drink!' And, before their very eyes, the three of us swallowed the stuff down to the last dreg."

"Yes?"

Marguerite looked at him quizzically. "The Boches went away."

Hearne's disappointment was her reward. She loved it. She cracked with laughter, smacking her hands in delight against her thick thighs. When she had quietened, and wiped the tears from her eyes, she said in a casual voice, "But you should have seen Hémar and Andhouard and me standing in this kitchen ten minutes later, spewing our guts out." She paused, and admired the effect on Hearne. "Sh! Not so loud," she warned. "But God knows you look as if you needed a good laugh. And sleep, too. Here, get upstairs before these men outside waken and start shouting for some-thing to eat."

Hearne followed her quietly upstairs. The small square room showed by the gray light from its narrow window a welter of acquisitiveness and thrift. He picked his way through the empty boxes, casks, bicycle parts, wine bottles, piles of newspapers, and broken ornaments; and looked care-fully out of the window. Back yard, he decided.

"If you leave by the window, there's a vine to help. But don't go upsetting my hydrangea pots on the ground," Mar-guerite said and opened a panel in the wall, to reveal a concealed bed.

"You should be as safe here as the others," she said. "Come on, get in. I've no time to waste."

Hearne looked doubtfully at the box bed, in spite of its cleanness, and climbed in obediently. He put out his left arm instinctively, as she shut the door.

"Don't worry," she said. "You can open it from the inside. You can breathe too. See?" She pointed to the decorations across the top of the panel, carefully carved to make the ventilation holes look artistic.

Her voice came through the panel. "I'll lock the room door, and I'll make a holy row on the staircase if anyone who shouldn't tries to come up here. All you've got to worry about is the fleas the last man left behind him."

But if there were any, he didn't notice them. He thought, sleep is impossible here, lying like a sardine in its tin. Yet it seemed only ten minutes later when Marguerite's large-knuckled hand was shaking him impatiently to rouse him.

"He's here," she was whispering. "He's down at the boat, waiting to sail. The weather's just right for it. Hurry." Her words awakened him as thoroughly as a bucket of cold water.

He stumbled cautiously across the room. By the light from the window, he guessed it must be almost night. Probably about nine o'clock. "What—" he began, but she silenced him with a finger at her lips.

"He'll explain when you are safely away," she said.

At the top of the narrow wooden stairs she halted him again. "I'll go down first and start serving at the bar. Then you just come down quietly and walk out. Don't stop for a minute."

Hearne listened to the loud voices coming up from the room beneath. "Won't it be dangerous for you if someone sees me?"

She shook her head impatiently. "A man coming down these stairs doesn't surprise them. They've come down themselves." She smiled and patted his shoulder. "Now get to the boat. I'll have some more stories for you next time you come back. And you can bring me some real coffee." And then she was moving silently down the staircase, her weight balancing from side to side as she placed one foot carefully in front of the other.

He waited until he heard her voice raised in a shout of laughter and the sound of glasses being clanked heavily down on the bar. A heavy blue haze of smoke filled the little room. But no one turned to watch him slip out of the door, cutting off the warm thick air and Marguerite's story-telling as he closed it behind him.

A cold wind ripped the darkness. He paused in the shadows of the overhanging eaves of the last house in that row. Across the narrow cobbled street was the wharf. From the large restaurant further along the riverbank came the ebb and flow of music. His eyes searched for the outlines of the boat. There she was, pulling gently against the mooring rope. He gauged the distance with his eye. It would take only ten seconds of quick movement. He gathered his confidence and a deep breath, and walked smartly across the quay.

There seemed to be no one on board, but a hand pulled him down behind a heap of sails and covered him loosely with their folds.

"Half an hour," Le Trapu whispered, "and it will be dark enough to sail."

Hearne pushed aside enough of the sail to breathe. He lay and listened to the rise and fall of the violins from the restaurant, the lapping of the tide's ripples against the boat's sides. Once he heard marching feet, and held himself ready to slip into the cold water. But the feet marched on, and his tense muscles relaxed again.

Before the moon had risen, the boat was moving gently into midchannel. The dark banks of the river rose steeply on either side. The wind which had cut through his jacket, as he had left Marguerite's house, now filled the sails. It was only then that Le Trapu left the other man to steer the boat and came forward to talk to him.

He gave Hearne a nod of recognition, and sat down silently beside him.

"Where are we bound?" Hearne asked.

"*You* ought to know."

Hearne looked at the square-set face with its thick growth of hair on the jaw. "Do you?"

Le Trapu raised his eyebrows and shrugged his shoulders. "The boy Etienne brought me back an answer to take you to St. Lunaire."

Hearne relaxed. *Brought me back,* Le Trapu said. That meant Anne's message had got through to Etienne. Hearne asked, "Answer to what?"

"If I should sail you there."

Hearne was silent, trying to puzzle that one out.

Le Trapu spoke again. "It was the girl's idea. She said you

were hurt, that the Boches had got you for a while. She thought you might come to Dinan, although she hadn't wanted you to come, because you'd want to make sure of that message. So I asked the boy Etienne what was I to do. And he came back with the message to take you to St. Lunaire if I found you."

"Did the girl say where she was going?"

"To the coast."

That was as much as he knew already, thought Hearne. He stared moodily at a patch on the sail. After the strain of worrying about these last miles, it was a strange feeling to sit in a boat and feel them floating past. That was like life ... you worried and you schemed, you sweated and you suffered, and then something quite different happened, and all your careful plans were just so much sawdust.

"I'm giving you a devil of a trouble," Hearne said.

"No trouble. It's quicker this way. Three hours, four hours perhaps in all. It is simple. No trouble." The Breton was equally awkward. He rose and moved to the stern, as if he were afraid of further thanks.

Hearne lay still, his eyes watching the riverbanks, his mind filled with crosscurrents of emotion. The wooded gorge gave way to sloping fields and woods, and small dark huddling villages. As they passed them stringing along the riverbanks, Hearne remembered L'Etoile d'Or. He wondered how Jules was getting on. He'd make a good boss if he married that girl behind the bar: she was the one to give him the confidence he needed. It was strange to think of big Louis' body anchored in the mud and slime at the bottom of this river. It was strange to think that they might even be sailing over what was left of it—for the estuary was now broadening, the banks were widening, and there was the hard square shape of the first big town on the right bank. Hearne, stretching his cramped legs painfully in the bottom of the boat, felt the spray sting his face, and smelled the first real saltness.

Le Trapu came forward, and pointed to the distant bank.

"St. Servan, and then St. Malo," he said. "From now on I'll be busy. Once I get her out between St. Malo and Dinard, I'll talk to you again." And then he had gone back to the tiller.

Hearne, remembering the picturesque shapes on his map of this river's estuary, felt a chill going through his body which didn't come from the wind. In this darkness, with white clouds chasing each other across the sky, with the slice of moon and scattered stars still struggling to break through the heavy drift of mist, he didn't feel like talking much. He only half-smiled at Le Trapu's canniness: no chickens being counted here before they were hatched. *Once I get her out, I'll talk to you again.* Anything they planned before this getting-out business might be just a waste of breath. It might, thought Hearne, as he felt the boat rise and fall and shiver as the strong currents tried to pull her their own way. It might, but it wasn't going to turn out like that. He concentrated on that thought, as if by keeping his mind fixed on arriving at St. Lunaire the boat would be bound to get there.

He could see the black shapes of curving rocky peninsulas, of scattered islands like so many boulders dropped into a pool of racing currents. Once the moon struggled free of its shroud long enough to throw a sickly gleam on the water. Hearne wished it hadn't, for the *Marguerite* appeared to be heading straight into a whirlpool, and between them and the cliffs of the shore were needles of rock round which the cross-currents fought and slavered. If he only knew more about sailing a boat, he thought, he wouldn't need to imagine himself as a steersman. Perhaps he could relax then, and let Le Trapu manage it all by himself. There was only one thing which gave him any pleasure: the little boat's speed had increased. At this rate they would soon be in the open Channel and then St. Lunaire was only three or four miles to the west of them. The salt spray covered him as the *Marguerite* suddenly plowed across a stretch of broken water. Hearne was relieved that the moon hadn't tactlessly emerged at that point, to show him just how broken it was. And then the boat plunged forward again: the water against its side stopped jabbing at the planks, and hissed as it streamed smoothly past.

Hearne was startled to hear a voice bellowing in his ear.

"We're out now," Le Trapu explained.

"Thank God," Hearne said, unclenching his hand from the mast and relaxing. "I'm all worn-out, steering. I'd rather meet a German patrol, any day."

That amused Le Trapu. "Each to his own job," he said politely.

"Didn't know a boat was so damned noisy," Hearne said. "All creaks and sighs and groans."

"Nice little breeze. And nice moon. It was bad for us when it came out for a few moments."

"When do we reach St. Lunaire?"

"Very soon. If the light were better, and thank God it isn't, you would be seeing the way the rocks stick out between the two bays. I'll take you to the west bay."

Hearne nodded. "That's the one further away from the town," he said. "That's the one."

"We'll run in as near the coast as we can. You can wade ashore. Good sand, big dunes, and no houses. You can lie up there quietly all tomorrow."

"Yes," said Hearne. That waiting wasn't going to be much fun. He couldn't allow himself to sleep. He'd just lie and worry about this job: worry how he could have done more, or could have done it better. Not that it mattered now at this stage, but at least it would keep him from thinking about himself. And his personal thoughts were far from pleasant at the moment. It had to be this way. The job first: it had to. Damn it all, he said to himself, why do you have to keep persuading yourself about that? You know it's first. You can't think of Anne or yourself until it's all over. When you chose this kind of work, you were choosing a moment like this, even if you didn't know it. He looked at the black streak of coastline, with the darkness hiding the arcs of sand pointed by cliffs. Perhaps Anne would follow that shore road to St. Brieuc, perhaps she might even think of him as she looked over the waters. Shut up, he told himself savagely, shut up. She had only been kind to him because she *was* kind. She couldn't help but be sweet and gentle. If she had felt the way he felt, then she would have waited at Marguerite's house in Dinan. She would at least have said good-by. Shut up, he said to himself again. He should know it was better that she didn't wait, that she didn't say good-by. Now he could stop sentimentalizing, and prepare for a cold swim. That would cool his brain for him.

"St. Lunaire. East bay," Le Trapu said, pointing. Hearne looked, but there was nothing but blackness, perhaps at the most a faint smudge of gray where the sand of the bay swept out to the sharp teeth of the rocky peninsula. There was no doubt about that spine of rock. Its cliff rose darkly up in a savage line against the sky, as if to protect the town sheltering back in the mainland.

Le Trapu's man was bringing the boat in a wide sweep round the headland now, into the second bay. Le Trapu was working swiftly and furiously with the sails. Their speed slackened. They drifted towards the long gray curve of sand, growing grayer and wider. Behind it was a stretch of soft darkness. Golf courses, Hearne remembered from his map. Miles of them. This was the place.

Their speed slackened still more, they were almost drifting in.

Le Trapu was beside him again. "Can't risk any further. Can you swim?"

"Yes."

"Good. It's very shallow. Stay in the dunes all day. Don't leave them. They're safe."

Afterwards Hearne remembered the insistence of the Breton's voice. But at the time, he only nodded, and slipped over the edge of the boat, holding his gun in his right hand. Only the left arm was good for swimming, anyhow. He hung onto the side of the boat for a moment, Le Trapu bending over to hold the left hand secure.

"Bonne chance alors. Au revoir," he said, and released his grip on Hearne's hand. Hearne drew his knees up to his chest, his feet against the side of the boat. He shoved against it, and felt himself glide out into the water free of the boat. He paddled softly with his left arm, as he felt for the sand and touched nothing. Six strokes later, he felt again and touched bottom. He waded slowly in over the long stretch of shallow water, keeping only his head and his right hand above water until he was forced to change to crawling on his knees. At the water's edge, he came in with a curling breaker, and rolled flat on the sand. The waves' last flow licked his face as he turned his head to watch the boat. He could see it only because he knew it was there. Already it was swinging out. Soon it would be just another fishing boat crossing the bay.

He gathered breath, and started the long slow crawl over the cold sand. When he got back to Britain, he could start thinking about the pain which gripped his right shoulder, about the spasm which dragged at his back muscles. He lay over on his left side and wrung the water out of his jacket pocket and slipped the gun back into it. He needed his right hand free—such as it was. Then, with his face muscles set in an ugly grin which had nothing to do with amusement, he pulled his body over the shore.

It was heavy going, for the dripping clothes and swamped boots had the weight of lead; and he was weaker than he had thought. In spite of the constant effort and movement, he was deathly cold and shivering uncontrollably by the time he reached the first curving bank of sand. He rested there. Then he pulled himself up over its soft face towards the waving spikes of grasses. Twice he slipped, and dug in with his knees and elbows to stop himself from sliding back to the shore. But at last he had his left hand round the toughness of the grasses. They cut into his flesh as they took the weight of his body, but he was over the last lip of the dune and he let himself roll gently down its grass side until he rested at the bottom of its hollow. There were bushes near. He crawled over to the largest clump. Gorse bushes. Painful, he thought, but at least safe. He groaned to himself, and looked for the easiest entrance to the sweet-scented tangle.

And then he heard a step. A careful step, as if someone had halted uncertainly.

Oh God, he thought despairingly. He forced his right hand into his pocket. He rolled over quickly on his side, aiming at the half-crouching figure. It moved forward as he steadied himself.

The whispered words were like the touch of the wind on the tall grasses round him.

"I was watching for you."

That was all; but his heart leaped, and he forgot the throbbing shoulder and the coldness and the numbing sickness.

"Anne," he whispered.

And then she had slipped, as quietly as she had come, down to where he lay. "Anne," he said, and gripped her so that he felt her bones yielding under the pressure of his arm and heard the short gasp as the breath left her body.

"Anne," he whispered again, and kissed her.

CHAPTER 29

End of a Mission

The spreading gorse bush grew at the foot of a short, steep bank, bearded with tall, waving grasses. Its heavy branches swept to the ground at its front and sides; at its back, they clutched the top of the bank and trailed beyond. They formed a perfect, but painful screen, Hearne thought, as he forced the stubborn branches apart and held them that way until Anne, her hair protected by her rough woolen jacket, could reach the free space of ground between the roots and the bank. Then he entered the thorny tangle, letting the branches fall to the earth again behind him. They had torn his hands and lashed his shoulders, but the shelter they offered was safe. Anne was lying on the sparse, stubby grass which forced its way up through the sand. He stretched himself carefully beside her. It was too dark to see her face, but the arm which he had thrown round her measured her heartbeats. His left hand pulled the jacket back from her hair. It was no longer tightly braided; its soft, loose silk covered his fingers.

"I can't even see it," he said bitterly. "And I can't see your face properly. There's only a black outline which is you. And we'll have to talk in whispers, and we dare hardly move in case we lose an eye." He looked up at the dark mass of branches sweeping arc-wise above their heads to reach the steep bank behind them. "Hell of a lover I am, bringing you into a place like this."

She laughed softly. "I like it," she said. "I feel safe here. And I feel so happy." Suddenly the laughter in her voice stifled, and he knew she was crying.

"Anne darling," he said. "Anne!"

"I'm just so happy," she repeated. "I thought Le Trapu was never coming, that he had missed you after all, that you had both been caught. And then the light was so bad, and the clouds made so many shadows on the bay that there might have been fifty fishing boats there or none at all. Then the clouds thickened and a mist moved in from the sea. Even at the very end, I wasn't sure it was you. By the time I left the dune where I was lying, and hurried along to where I thought I had seen you go, I began to imagine that I had been dreaming. And then, I found you."

Hearne, his lips touching the smooth cheek, didn't answer. He was thinking of the danger Anne had been in, of the risks she had taken. At last he said, his voice now normal, "How long did you wait?"

"I came this afternoon. There were others walking on the sands of the bay, so it was quite safe. Near the rocks beside the town there were German soldiers." A hint of laughter entered her voice. "They were trying to learn to swim. I watched them from the dunes, as some other people were doing. I just sat down there, and the tall grasses were higher than my head, and no one noticed me. After an hour, I moved further back into the grasses, and I lay there in the sunshine, waiting for the darkness."

"Any other Germans?"

"Some on leave from the town were walking along the sand. They kept looking at the sea."

"What about the golf course?"

"Some Boches were playing there. Madame Chevel said they were staying in the big hotels, and in the villas the Parisians used to own. The Casino is filled with them every night. People believe something is going to be started here very soon, because a lot of boats have been bringing loads to the small quays on the other bay. Some say it's ammunition, and some say building material. But everyone seems to think the Germans' holiday will soon be over, and that there's going to be work here for them. There are a lot of soldiers in the town, and on the beach in the other bay in front of the Casino."

"Who is Madame Chevel?"

"I stayed with her last night. When I arrived in St. Lunaire, I was hungry, so I joined a queue outside a baker's shop. There was a woman like Albertine standing beside me. That was Madame Chevel."

"You've only to smile and wrinkle this nose of yours, Anne"—he kissed it and won a little laugh—"and even the Albertines offer you shelter."

"It wasn't my smile; it was what I said to her when three soldiers marched past the length of the queue, went into the shop, and came out eating the last pies."

Hearne laughed too, and ran his hand over the soft hair lying so close to him. "And where is Madame Chevel now?"

"Asleep in her little house. And I am on my way to my aunt at St. Brieuc."

Hearne was silent. He was wondering if all women were naturally adept at this kind of game. First, there had been Elise, and now here was Anne who, for a different cause but with much the same skill, had managed to plan her way to the coast. Plan his way too: he owed much to her cleverness and foresight.

"What's wrong?" Anne was asking. She stretched her free arm across his shoulders. "Oh," she said, "you are cold, so cold. And you've let your bandage slip out of place." The concern in her voice pleased him.

"I'm warmer than I was. I'm feeling better every minute."
He tightened his grip on her waist. "Darling, why did you
come here?"

"I wanted to see you." Anne so direct, so honest. No
hedging. Just *I wanted to see you.* There was a pause, and
then the whispered voice was so low that he could hardly
hear it. "I had to see you leave safely. If I had gone to my
aunt's house, I should never have known that you had even
reached here. I should never have known what had happened
to you."

"And what happens to me . . . does it mean so much?"

Anne was silent.

"Does it mean so much?" he repeated.

"I kissed you," she said, in a very small voice.

His left arm, encircling her waist, pulled her closer. "Darling," was all he said.

And then, later, "If kisses show how much, then you know
now how much it means to me, too." He kissed her once
more. "I couldn't be sure, Anne. I'm a jealous kind of chap. I
worried about you being engaged to Corlay. You aren't the
kind of a girl to let herself get engaged to a man without
having liked him enough at one time. Then I thought you had
been kind to me because you were sorry for me, or because
you hated the Boches so much, or both. It wasn't until I saw
you out there among the dunes that I let myself think of
anything more. Even yet, I can't quite believe that you love
me; you'll have to say it, to make me believe it."

"Why do you want to believe it?" Her cheek was warm
with the hot blood under the fine, smooth skin. Her heart was
pounding again against his arm, her voice was half-laughing,
half-serious.

"Because," he said simply, "I am coming back here after
the war ends. And if I'm coming back, I want to know you'll
be here."

"Yes," she said slowly. "I'll be here. I'll stay at St. Brieuc
and watch for you coming from England. After the war . . ."
This time, the tears which came could not be controlled or
explained away. She caught him convulsively and buried her
face in his shoulder. It was his right shoulder, and it hurt like
hell, but Hearne found a fierce pleasure in the pain.

"After the war," he said firmly, "I'll be here even if I have
to swim across." His voice was calm, determined.

Anne had stopped crying. "Your arm!" she said, suddenly
remembering. "Your shoulder!" Her hands were gently feel-

ing for the bandage, gently arranging it to make his shoulder
more comfortable.

"I'd rather have your head than a bandage." he said.
"Leave it, Anne. There's still one question I'd like to know
the answer to. It keeps haunting me. Were you ever in love
with Bertrand Corlay?"

Anne's words were clear and direct. "I wanted to fall in
love with him, at one time. I thought I could. But I didn't."

"Why did you want to fall in love with him?"

She bent over suddenly to kiss his cheek. "Because I was
young, and he was so very good-looking."

"What? Corlay? He's as ugly as—well—" He halted in embarrassment.

"Then only you think so." She kissed him again. "You are
the strangest man."

"Why?"

"You keep silent when I want you to talk. And when you
do talk, you ask questions."

"Do I?"

"Yes."

"But I've so much to find out about you. There's so much I
want to know. First tell me how much you love me, then tell
me about you . . . everything you can remember, little things,
anything."

"First, you must tell me how much you love me. You will
teach me how to say it. That will give me courage."

He said seriously and gently, "Do you ever need courage,
Anne?"

"Sometimes."

He kissed her. "I don't think words are very adequate for
this moment."

"No?" She was half-laughing.

"No." He was half-serious.

Later, she said, "And I can't even say your name. You've
never told me it." It wasn't an indirect question: it was a
simple statement, tinged with surprise and melancholy.

"Martin," he answered. "Martin—" He halted. "The other
name you will know later, Anne. Later when it is safe for
you to know it. Now, I must just be Martin."

"Martin," she repeated, giving it the French pronunciation.
"Martin." Her finger traced a line across his forehead and
down the side of his cheek.

Hearne stiffened suddenly. He laid a finger across her lips.

They lay in silence, straining to catch any sound. At last Hearne relaxed. "Thought I heard feet crumpling shells on the shore," he explained. They listened again.

At last, Hearne spoke softly, "You didn't know my name, you still only know half of it; you don't know what kind of job I have, or how much money I make or don't make; you have scarcely seen me except when I was worried, or tired, or smelling of fish, or all bloodied up. And now I've chosen a gorse bush to drag you into, and my wet clothes are leaving a damp trail of sea water over you, and the sand is still sticking to a week's growth of beard, and yet you say you'll marry me. God, however did I have the luck to find you?" His eyes, now accustomed to the blackness round them, tried to see her face more clearly. His lips touched her eyes and hair.

"There are so many things to—" he began and then halted. "We've so little time left."

"At least we've until dawn, and then through the day, and then through the evening, until darkness comes again."

"No, Anne. You can't wait all that time. You must go before light breaks. You must be on the road to St. Brieuc by morning. You must."

She lay very still.

At last she said, "Can't I even wait on the dunes, just to see you leave?"

"Anne, darling, I'd only worry about you. Better reach your aunt. If I only had time I'd take you there and see you into her house."

At first she didn't speak. And then the soft voice had tightened. "How long have we together, then?"

Half an hour, or an hour at the very most, Hearne thought, with his heart as cold as the damp clothes clinging to his body. He said, "Not long enough for any more talk, my love," and kissed the smooth outlines of her face. "Not even for the reasons why I adore you." Her skin was soft as a child's. Her hair smelled of sunshine and fresh winds.

They both flinched when they heard the explosion. Anne had instinctively tightened her arms round his neck, wincing as one of them scraped against the sharp-edged spines of gorse.

"Something's gone up," Hearne said. "Something's blown sky-high. About two miles away, beyond the town. What the devil could that be?"

"The little docks on the east bay, where the river runs into the sea," Anne suggested. "Madame Chevel said that was how they were bringing the ammunition—by boat. But it's all guarded: there are soldiers there."

Hearne nodded. He was alert, listening.

"What's that?" Anne asked, flinching again.

"Rifle fire over there. Sounds like machine guns, too. What the dickens *is* this, anyhow?" He struggled to a kneeling position, his head and shoulders bent, his hands still holding Anne.

Then they heard the footsteps, running footsteps, footsteps coming near them, footsteps coming from the golf course behind them. Again there was rifle fire, but this time stray shots sounded from this side of the town in counterpoint to the continuous staccato beat from the east bay.

"Hell's broken loose," Hearne said. "I'm going out for a look-see." He started to crawl forward to the place where he had found their entrance.

"Perhaps your friends?" Anne said.

He shook his head. "They wouldn't make all this racket. They do it very differently. Sounds to me like a raiding party." He thought grimly: it would be just my luck to have chosen to leave St. Lunaire on the night after a prearranged raid.

The footsteps were further away now. As Hearne parted the branches cautiously, he heard someone fall, and then there was a torrent of descriptive adjectives.

"British," he said to Anne. And then, in alarm, "They're going away." He stooped down to help her rise. He ripped her cardigan from the thorns. To their right they saw the disappearing heads and shoulders of the two last soldiers, as they jumped down onto the shore.

"Hurry, darling, hurry," Anne said, "quick, quick." He took her hand and together they raced for the edge of the dune. From somewhere behind them, perhaps from the hotel across the golf course, came a furious burst of firing.

"Keep low!" he urged, and slid over the end of the dune, dragging Anne with him. She was talking so quickly he could hardly separate the words.

"Good-by, darling, good-by. And come back. Martin!" But even as she was speaking, he had to whistle shrilly to the running figures. Three boats near the beach. From the other side of the rocky peninsula, flames were rising, and the firing was heavier.

One of the soldiers had heard him. He stopped and half-turned. Hearne waved his left hand, and whistled again. The officer bringing up the rear also halted and looked round, and then waved in turn. Urgently. The rifle shots were coming nearer now. A machine gun crackled on this side of the town, too. The rifle shots were coming nearer.

"Go on, darling," Anne said. "I'll be waiting at St. Brieuc." The officer waved again. Hearne could hear him swearing as he waved. He crushed Anne's hands convulsively. He couldn't speak. He turned and ran towards the four soldiers who were waiting for him.

He remembered her as he ran, standing quite still, her back against the dune, her hand frozen in mid-air. She would be smiling. If he could see, she would be smiling.

Hearne turned to look towards her for the last time. She hadn't moved. Her hand was still upraised.

And then, from where he now stood, he could see the moving shadows as well as hear the sound of their rifles. They'd get her. If she stayed behind, they'd find her. The moving line spread thinly, unevenly, but still dangerously, towards the shore.

Hearne started to run back to the dunes. Behind him, he heard the officer's voice raised angrily. The bullets were finding range now. Sand spurted to the side of him. "Anne," he called. "Anne. Come. Quick." And she was running towards him. She seemed to stumble just as she reached him, but his arms were ready and caught her, and then holding her round the waist, her arm resting on his shoulder, he pulled her with him towards the four waiting soldiers.

"What the bloody hell do you think you're playing at?" said the officer. He looked at Anne. "But what's all this?" Then, looking at Anne, he was suddenly silent, and stepping to her other side crossed arms with Hearne to sweep her along between them. They were in the water now, the surf round their feet, the breaking wave catching their waists. Beyond the waves at the edge, it was shallow and smooth.

The officer was talking all the time. "Good show!" he was saying. "Not bad at all. We gave 'em a pincer movement all right. Pinced them with their panzers down!" He looked approvingly towards the red semicircle of sky beyond the rocky peninsula. "I wonder how many of the others got on that side," he went on. "We nabbed three officers from the hotel, and disposed of the rest. They are in that boat moving out there, trussed like hens. But of course that other bay's the really exciting one." He nodded casually to the east. "Casino's over there, jammed full of them. And there's the town too. Well, we'll soon know what happened." His calm voice had brought them to the boat, and the bullet splashes were now behind them.

The boat curved out into the bay to follow the others.

The roar of its engine hid the clatter of machine guns from the beach. The water shoreward was cut and furrowed.

"Jeez, throwing stick grenades and all," a soldier said. "Everything but the kitchen sink." A second voice said "No good!" with mock concern. "Wouldn't they like us to fire at them and show them what to hit? Poor old Jerry can't get on the target . . . what a blee-ding shame!" Other voices were talking too, counting wounds, remembering jokes, now that they were leaving the bay with a flaunting trail of foam behind them.

But Hearne, kneeling beside Anne, heard neither the roar of the engines, nor the broken rhythm of the machine guns on the beach, nor the jubilant voices of the men. He only heard the strangled breathing of the girl, only felt the warm trickle of blood from her mouth. He watched the face of the man who had pushed him aside, watched the skillful fingers working by the ghastly light of the flares straining their way up into the sky.

The officer returned from his tour of the crowded boat. "Worst is over now," he said as he looked down at Anne. "We got her in time, I think. By the way, do you happen to be Matthews' young man who was to be picked up on Saturday? Matthews was fuming when he found we had this operation all planned for tonight. Might have been nasty if you had crossed the Nazis' trail when they were on the warpath."

Hearne shook his head. Better that, than this. Better that than Anne lying at his feet with a bullet in her lung. He pressed her hand convulsively.

She opened her eyes, and he knew there would be a smile in them if he could see clearly.

The last flare filtered away. Above them was the drone of planes, searching in vain. The stark coast of Brittany had darkened into the night. But the coldness had left his heart. Within his grasp, Anne's hand moved gently, hopefully.

AUTHOR'S NOTE

There are three questions that anyone who reads my novels usually asks me when we meet. *What is true? How much is invented? Did you yourself experience any of those situations?*

I like these questions. An interested reader is an encouragement to a writer. Curiosity, when it deals with books and ideas, is a compliment. Besides, a reader ought to know something about a writer's methods, for he has given his time to considering the writer's words, to thinking about the writer's basic philosophy. If we demand an honest statement of the ingredients of every package of food we buy, it seems odd that we should treat our minds more carelessly than we do our stomachs. False pretenses in the world of ideas (and literature conveys ideas, or opens a new door to the view of the world outside our own lives, or discloses a different light on what we have either accepted as fact or dismissed as exaggeration) can be as deadly in their effect as the adulteration of food. The writer who alters the facts of history, or twists events into a false pattern, to suit his own ideas, is providing his readers with his own package of particular poisoning. The mind is more vulnerable than the stomach, because it can be poisoned without feeling immediate pain.

So there is a particular obligation laid upon any writer dealing with contemporary history; and even novelists who write adventure-suspense stories must be very conscious of it. Unless, of course, their themes and backgrounds are far removed from reality. Then they can be completely fanciful. Whether or not a group of champagne-drinkers in a mythical kingdom feel themselves threatened by the hop-growers in an equally mythical neighboring queendom can be as merry a romp as the witty writer—and he had better be witty—can pull out of his imaginative hat. But a writer who deals with a serious theme, however amusing he can be at times, has to face much research, much comparison of viewpoints and reports, much examination of his own mind and conscience, before he even starts setting his characters and plot into their background.

Background . . . There lies the answer to the first question. The backgrounds of my novels are as factual as I can make them. The physical backgrounds—the places I describe—are fairly simple to reconstruct. They are countries I have visited, customs and peoples I have seen. (This rule is true for all my novels except *While Still We Live*.) Occasionally, in dealing with street addresses or with a specific village, I avoided using real addresses (which might cause trouble, even danger, for people living in an occupied town) or the real place names. (For example, the village of "St. Déodat" in *Assignment in Brittany* does not actually exist, although I have known several Breton villages which it typifies.) I did this in order not to endanger anyone. You must remember that when *Above Suspicion, Assignment in Brittany,* and *Horizon* were published, the Nazis were occupying the countries I describe in these novels. If I related the beginning of an underground movement against the Nazis in a small Breton or Tyrolean village, I did not want any real name attached to the fictional place I mentioned. (You may think this was excessive caution. Yet, after the war was over, I met several veterans who—when the fighting ended in Brittany—had taken a free day to track down the places described in *Assignment in Brittany*. They were wryly amused to learn they had spent hours in searching for an entirely imaginary St. Déodat. But the Germans took things more seriously, and were very thorough in working over every scrap of fact about the resistance to their conquest: therefore I tried to give them no such scraps.) Apart from such precautionary measures, the scenes of the novels are as real as I can make them, both from my memory and from my reading.

But there is more than geography in a background. There is history, too: past history, present history, politics, and religion. That is the hard work involved in forming a true background for a novel. It means research: a good deal of collecting facts, comparing various points of view; and yet this research either does not appear in the novel at all, or is only quietly introduced through characters. A novel is not a thesis, or a sermon, or a political pamphlet.

So all this background is accurate to the best of my knowledge and observation. This is the true part of the novel. Against it, I set the imaginary characters and the imaginary plot. Characters and plot—these are invented. That is, I do not take people I meet and put them into my novels. I imagine my characters and their stories, creating people from what I have observed in life. Their actions and reactions develop the plot; and, in turn, the plot develops their characters. There is nothing mysterious or improbable about this creation of imaginary people: we all have, somewhere deep inside us, a reservoir of our unconscious observations; ever since we started being interested in people, in listening to their words and wondering not only about what they said but about why they said it, in watching their behavior and wondering not only about what they did but about why they did it, this reservoir has been gradually filling up. For centuries before Alexander Pope observed that the proper study of mankind was man, the storyteller—whether he was poet, or dramatist, or romancer—had been tapping that reservoir. Two hundred years after Pope, we have all become conscious of the subconscious, thanks to men like Freud and Jung and Adler. But creative writers did just as well, if not better, when they relied on their own observations and meditations about the human race. Actually, if they inquire too scientifically into the subconscious, they may find that their stories change into case-history notebooks, and that they are no longer novelists, but analysts. For art is selective, and instinct is often the selector.

And there is the answer, too, to the third question. The idea that a novelist must actually be writing from his own experience, and that he must experience everything in order to write, is a misconception. How could a man write of the physical pain and extraordinary emotions of a woman in childbirth, if he could not describe something that was totally impossible for him to experience? How could a writer describe death or illness when he himself was a healthy specimen? Birth and illness and death have often been part of the most moving scenes in some

303

of the finest novels. A novelist does not need to be a cripple in order to make a character who is a cripple come alive on the written page. A novelist does not need to be an extremist in politics in order to describe a Nazi or a Communist. He does not have to experience murder or treason or political violence before he can realize what these things mean. Does a surgeon have to undergo all the major operations before he can perform them? With knowledge, and thought, and deduction, and trained fingers, and—most of all, perhaps—instinct, a surgeon does his job. With instinct fully alive and responsive, he could even come close to knowing the actual pains and fears that his patient is undergoing. A novelist is like the surgeon in many ways. He does not need to experience, himself, before he can deal with a subject. He, too, does need to have thought about the subject, to have studied the available facts. But, unlike the surgeon, the novelist can allow himself to feel the pain and the fears: he can become, in imagination, the patient, and he does. In the world of his mind, he can experience anything he describes. It is painful, at times, to be a novelist.

But it has its pleasure, too: for instance, the look on a reader's face when he says (half rueful, half amused), "You know, I sat up till two o'clock last night to finish that story!"

HELEN MacINNES